I0636136

THE BANNOCKBURN SPELL

NANCY ADAMS

The Bannockburn Spell
ISBN # 978-1-78184-597-4
©Copyright Nancy Adams 2012
Cover Art by Posh Gosh ©Copyright December 2012
Interior text design by Claire Siemaszkiewicz
Total-E-Bound Publishing

THE BANNOCKBURN SPELL

Dedication

For my friend Rhonda, and my sister in-law Kate. I'm truly thankful for all your support (and wine), your friendship (and wine), you gave me while writing this book. Oh and did I mention I was thankful for the wine!

For Chelsee, future U of A Grad, babysitter extraordinaire and St Albert's best hidden secret. Thank you for giving me the gift of time and…Twilight narrations.

And for my editor, Sue. Thank you for your advice and wisdom with my 'baby'.
Not to worry, I plan to thank you the proper way…with wine of course!

Prologue

Scotland
Twenty-Five Years Ago

"You want a story, eh!" James MacKenzie rubbed his chin thoughtfully as his granddaughter curled up in the chair next to him.

"Yes, please, Granddad."

"And what kind of story would you like?" James turned to his three grandsons, who were wrestling on the floor. "Oye! Enough you three. Sit, or it's bed for the lot of yah."

When there was some semblance of order, he asked again, "What kind would you like?"

"Oh." Sarah, the only girl in the family, clapped her hands. "Something with kissing." The boys moaned in unison.

"What's wrong with kissing?"

"Tell us something with a battle," Richard, the eldest at thirteen, spoke up.

"Yeah! A battle," Gavin agreed.

"How about you, William?"

A slow grin claimed the boy's face, bringing the unusual mixture of browns in his eyes to life. "Tell us about Bannockburn."

"Oh, not again." It was Sarah's turn to huff. "We heard that last time, Will."

James sat forward in his chair and addressed the boys sitting in front of him. "You boys want to hear how Robert the Bruce, with only a handful of men, defeated that devil Edward and his hordes?"

"Yeah!" the boys called together.

"You want me to tell you how the Bruce, armed with only a battle axe, chopped Henry de Bohun's head clean off?"

"Yeah!" the boys cheered.

"You want to hear about blood and guts, and spells that bind long-lost loves together?"

The boys once again were about to call out but stopped.

"Love spells?" Rich asked.

"Oh! I want to hear that part." Sarah clapped excitedly.

"Booo! No girls' stuff," Gavin and Will called together.

"Gavin! Will!" Sarah pouted.

Jane suddenly called out from the doorway, "What is going on in here?"

James turned in his chair to face his wife when Gavin announced, "Granddad's telling us a bedtime story."

"Yes, I can hear that." She placed her hands on her hips. "And which story would that be?"

"Bannockburn," Will informed her.

Jane slowly shifted her glare from Will to him. "Is that right?"

James sighed as his wife gave him the 'We've been over this before' look. "I'll make it short tonight."

She clicked her tongue. "Mmm, I just bet."

James winked at his wife and received a snort in return. Directing his attention back to the children, he asked, "Where was I?"

"You were just about to tell us about blood, guts and people chopping off heads," Will reminded.

"And the love spells," Sarah added.

"I'll get to that, but first the battle."

James went into detail about the Battle of Bannockburn. Explaining how the great clans came together to battle the English. How King Robert used his superior military knowledge to trick the English straight into a trap.

He told the children how Scottish lairds, knights, and even ordinary men, had boldly met the English head-on. Swords clashed, men screamed. Arms, heads and other appendages were severed clean from the useless English, their blood and bodies covering the ground. He told them of great feats of heroism from the MacKenzie clan. How their Laird, Alasdair MacKenzie, single-handedly saved his friend Fergus, Laird of the Kennedy clan, from six...no, seven huge English knights, dressed from head to foot in battle gear.

He told the children of the death of Alasdair's son and the next to lead the MacKenzie clan. He too had fought hard, making his father and clansmen proud, but he had fallen when he had gone to the aid of a friend who had become pinned beneath his horse. As the young MacKenzie had helped his friend, a sneaky little English demon had stabbed him in the back.

"When are you going to get to the part about the love spell?" Sarah pouted.

"Right now." James sat back. "After the battle was won, the Bruce and his most trusted vassals sat around a fire discussing the battle. Spirits were high of course, they defeated the English, but the Bruce realised not all was well."

"It wasn't?" Rich asked. "Why?"

"Alasdair MacKenzie, his friend and greatest ally, lost his son, you see, and with the death of his son, the joining of the MacKenzie and Kennedy clans would no longer be possible."

"What does that mean?" Gavin asked.

"Alasdair's son was to marry Fergus Kennedy's daughter, for not only would it unite the two powerful clans but their children were very much in love."

Gavin dropped his head onto the pillow he was lying on. "The girl stuff."

"Shhh, Gavin!" Will hushed. "Go ahead, Granddad."

James nodded. He was more than pleased that Will found this story interesting. For the first time in a long time he was hopeful that the Contract would be fulfilled, and that two young souls, who shared a deep love, could finally be one.

"And he was killed," Sarah repeated. "That means Fergus' daughter was alone. That's so sad."

"There's hope, lass," James soothed. "As the lairds sat around the fire, a young woman was called forth to tend to the wound Alasdair had received saving Fergus. Her name was Kassandra, she was a beautiful woman with hair the colour of honey and eyes as green as Irish moss. Her family was well respected and known in both the highlands and lowlands, but they were also greatly feared."

"Why?" Sarah asked.

"Because Kassandra was from the Cochran clan, and all who knew the Cochrans knew that they had a gift for seeing the future. Just as the Sinclairs could heal the body and soul and the Mackays could speak without uttering a single spoken word."

Rich snorted. "That's not scary."

"Aye it is, if they see the death of the person wanting to seek a glimpse into their future."

"Did she see a death?" Will asked, wrapping his arms around his knees.

"No, she saw something else. While tending to the MacKenzie's wound, she overheard the lairds talking about the death of Alasdair's son and how he had loved Fergus's daughter. While the vassals sat round the fire with their King, Kassandra's small voice broke the silence."

"They still will be," The young woman said.

Alasdair slipped a finger under the young woman's chin and slowly raised it to meet his stare. "What did you say, lass?"

"Speak up, child," Fergus ordered gently.

"I said they still will be." Her eyes fell flat and all emotion wiped clean from her face.

"Who will 'still' be?" Alasdair asked.

"William and Meghan will join, but not now. I see them. William." Her glowing green eyes locked on Alasdair first. "He looks like you, with your eyes, but darker hair. He will be a warrior and he will receive payment for protecting ones with wealth and distinction."

James winked at Will when Rich nudged him. "It's your turn to be in the story." Little did Richard know that the tale James was telling them was not just a story, it was a historical fact.

Just then, Jane walked into the room and addressed Will. "Could you come and help me with Roy?"

"No, he can't, Jane, I'm telling him about…"

"I know exactly what you are telling them." Her glare warned of trouble to come. "Roy is searching around the back garden, digging holes, looking for his bone and Will is the only one he will listen to."

"Fine," James huffed. "Go on then."

"It's okay, Granddad. I heard the best part anyways." And with a shrug, Will left with his Grandma.

"Keep going, Granddad," Sarah pleaded.

James gave her a wink and continued.

Kassandra's eyes drifted to Fergus next. "Meghan will have the Kennedys' flaming hair and your sense of loyalty. It will be her stubbornness that will cause the two to remain separate." She blinked several times before her eyes came back into focus. "They will need help if they are to join."

"What are you saying, lass?" Alasdair asked. "That you see them joining?"

Fergus sat forward, fists clenched. "How can that be?"

"I do not know how it can be." She squeezed her hands together. "I just know it will be."

There was silence for a few minutes until Alasdair asked, "When will this happen?"

"I'm not sure. But I feel it to be long from now."

"Why will Meghan be stubborn towards William?" Fergus' words were edged with confusion. "All know they share a great love."

"Many years will pass. Her soul will not recognise his. She will need help remembering." Kassandra informed him quietly.

"What kind of help?"

Looking back and forth between the two Lairds, the girl explained, "They will need binding."

Alasdair gave a heavy sigh. "Explain to Fergus and me what this binding is."

"My Lairds, a binding will force them to be close to one another. When they are separate they will feel…uncomfortable."

"How so?" Alasdair asked.

"My gran, who has performed the binding the most, says that most women suffer a mild stomach ailment and the men become restless, sometimes even a little aggressive. The effects occur when they are separate, but wanes when they are together."

"Why is that the way of things?" A menacing scowl accompanied Fergus' question. "Why must they suffer these ailments?"

"The discomfort comes only when they fight it. The quicker they admit their love, the quicker the binding fades."

Alasdair watched the woman as she finished tending his wound. "What do you mean by 'the binding fades'?"

"Only when both, the man and woman, share their true feelings, will the binding fade between them, leaving their love to fill the void." The young woman looked from Fergus to Alasdair. "It is a love that only exists between two souls that were meant to be together. The binding doesn't work on those who were not meant to be one."

"So we will never truly know if this binding works because it will happen a long time from now?"

"That is what I have seen, my Laird."

For several long minutes, Alasdair and Fergus stared into the flames, while their King and friends waited. Then looking to Fergus, Alasdair asked, "What is needed for this binding?"

Fergus gave an accepting nod.

"All that is needed is the marriage agreement between your two clans."

Fergus shook his head. "We had no need of one."

"The binding," the girl began, "is woven into the words of the marriage contract. Once both have read the contract, the binding will take hold. I will need it written onto parchment in order for the binding to hold true."

"What if others read the agreement? Will they become bound instead?"

"No. This binding is for them and them alone. No other can become bound by reading the words." Kassandra gifted the men with a breathtaking smile. "They are two souls that belong together. Time and distance will not keep them apart."

"Okay, off to bed!"

"What!" Sarah gawked. "That's it? What happened to Will and Meghan? Do they find each other? Do they fall in love?"

"I don't know. But I can tell you the marriage contract has never been fulfilled."

"So they don't get together and fall in love." Sarah huffed unhappily, then mumbled before kissing him goodnight, "That was a bad story, Granddad."

"'Night, night, my darling," James called as Sarah stomped her way to bed.

"I liked the killing part, but the girly stuff was okay too," Richard informed him with a shrug.

"What did I miss?" Will asked, breathless, as he joined them then looked around. "Where's Sarah?"

"She went to bed because there was no kissing." Then Gavin mumbled, "I hope I don't have a spell put on me?"

"There are no such things as spells," Richard assured Gavin, pulling him from the room. "Granddad was just telling us a story."

Will shrugged. "'Night, Granddad." He followed his brothers.

"Will," James called.

Stopping in the doorway, Will turned to face him. Even at eleven, Will was a good-looking boy, a MacKenzie through and through. With dark brown hair and the odd mixture of browns and yellows that made up his eye colour, he was a dead ringer for his father, as well as many other MacKenzies, including

Alasdair. "I was wondering why you like hearing about the Battle of Bannockburn so much?"

"'Cause I want to be a soldier when I grow up."

James chuckled. "And so you will be. Off to bed now."

Will stepped from the room but stopped once again this time with a frown.

"What is it, boy?"

"Will you tell me how the story ends tomorrow?"

James joined his grandson by the door and placed a hand on his shoulder. "No."

"Why?"

"Because I don't know how it ends, only you do."

Chapter One

Toronto
Present Day

"I followed her to the airport. She won't make a scene here."

Narrowing his grey eyes, Rob followed as 'she' wheeled her luggage into the terminal.

Meghan. Damn, she looks good. Real good. Not that she ever looked bad. She had this unique pull over him that he still couldn't figure out. He watched her ass sway seductively as she made her way through the terminal. There was something different about her since the last time he had seen her. Her red head was held high, her shoulders were back, and her stride was determined. Confidence. It was radiating from her. He hadn't seen that side in a while, not since he had broken it.

"Are you sure you can get it, Robert?"

He cringed. Normally he loved talking to a woman who had a deep sultry voice. Add in an accent, any accent and it made her all that more appealing. Yet every time this woman spoke to him, a cold shiver ran through him causing the hair on his neck and arms to stand up.

Emily Alexsandrov. Her name conjured visions of a little girl with long blonde ringlets and big blue eyes, skipping happily along with a giant lollipop.

The vision shattered when he met her in person. A classic Eastern European beauty, she was the epitome of sex. Tall and slender, with straight brown hair and the lightest green eyes, she had a body that left most men either drooling or running for cover. Her appearance, however, was only the tip of a sharpened blade.

As well as speaking five different languages, Emily also had a degree in business, and contacts — business and personal — in almost every country in the world. And to keep that blade sharp, she was the new head of the Alexsandrov crime family. The same family his father was partners with and the same family he owed a very large sum of money to. And now that he was out on parole they wanted to collect.

"I said I could, didn't I?" he snapped into the cell, then quickly caught himself. "I told you, she carries it everywhere with her."

There was a long pause before Emily purred into the phone, "Just remember, Robert, there is more than one type of interest."

"I remember." Did he ever. Christ, he could still hear the screams. Emily had had her favourite associate Ivan show him first-hand what other methods of interest would be collected if he failed to deliver payment. "I'll call you when I have it."

He flipped his phone shut. "Bitch," he muttered, trailing behind Meghan as she approached the security gates for international flights.

International? Where the hell was she going? He had to get it now. There wouldn't be another chance once she passed through security.

"Shit!" Where were the long lines that normally snaked through the Toronto airport? He watched as she passed through the metal detector, unaware that he was so close to her.

Now! It had to be now! He moved towards the metal detector, squeezing past a few other passengers, when a very large boarding agent blocked his path. "Your boarding pass and identification, please, sir."

"I don't need one. I just need to speak with that woman." He pointed.

"I'm sorry, sir, you must have a boarding pass," the man informed him in a curt tone.

He watched as she collected her carry-on bag and began to walk away.

"Fuck!" he gritted out between clenched teeth.

"Sir!" the agent said loud enough to draw unwanted attention. "You'll have to leave this area, or I'll be forced to call airport security."

Raising his hands, he slowly backed away from the security gate. He stood staring after her, clenching his hands into tight fists.

He had spent two years of his life stealing back the money he had gambled away. Two years of finding the right women with the right bank accounts, and now he could end up with a bullet in his head all because Meghan was taking a fucking holiday.

There was a light snap as he squeezed his cell. He brought the cell up and looked at it, then without thinking, he flipped it open, and typed out a message.

Once he located her red head, he waited to see her reaction. She slowed her pace as she read the message but continued towards her gate.

Wanting to slam his fist into something, he pounded in another text and locked his eyes on her once again.

She stopped this time, staring down at her phone. Then she slowly lifted her head and studied the other passengers.

Squeezing his teeth together he typed in one last message.

'I'll B waiting 4 U Meghan.'

He watched as she disappeared from his sight. Before leaving he stopped briefly at the Departures monitor and scanned the list of flights, stopping on Edinburgh. Her parents were Scottish and he recalled her mentioning something about wanting to visit her grandfather. She had a personal connection to Edinburgh. The big question was how long would this holiday last? He didn't have a lot of time but he was confident that she wouldn't be away for long. He had witnessed the love she had for her family and friends, she had told him how she needed them in her life. No. This trip wouldn't be long.

Two weeks. He would give her two weeks and if she wasn't back by then, he would find a way to get her back.

* * * *

Edinburgh, Scotland

"I can't believe I let you talk me into this."

"Stop bitching. It's not going to hurt you to take a vacation."

"Vacation!" Meghan snorted into the phone. "You call getting chased out of my home, my work and my country a vacation?"

Ryan laughed into the phone.

She loved to hear him laugh and it wasn't because he was her little brother, but because his laugh always made her smile.

"This was the easiest way. Now I can hunt that prick down and not have to worry about you in the process. Besides location, what else is going to change? You'll be with family, Dad is just a younger version of Duncan and as long as you have your laptop you can work anywhere. On top of that, it can be a vacation."

"I'll miss shopping and my friends." She pouted. "I'll miss shopping with my friends. Who am I kidding. I'll just miss the shopping."

Ryan chuckled. "Your friends want this as much as I do and I'm sure you'll get your chance to hit the stores over there." There was a brief pause. "Duncan is excited to see you. It's been a long time since you've seen him."

"Same amount of time as you." She bumped into a man who stopped in front of her. She mouthed a 'sorry' and continued to search for her flight's luggage carousel.

"I know. But I can't get away right now. I have to reopen my case on your ex."

"I'm sorry, Ryan." She bumped someone else. This time it was a woman from her flight, the one with the little boy who had kept giggling at a movie she had put on for him. She smiled her apology and worked her way around to the far side of the carousel where only a few people stood waiting. "I never thought Rob would come out of jail ready to hunt me down."

"I know." Ryan sighed. "I didn't mean anything by it. Hey, I've got a long list of people that want you to email them once you're settled. Number one being Mum."

"I will," she promised.

"Listen, I have to catch my Captain before he leaves so I can fill him in. When I have something I'll email."

"Okay." She rubbed her temple. "God, I sound so pathetic," she mumbled into the phone. It wasn't like she wasn't going to see him again. This relocation was only temporary.

"Aww! I'll miss you too, big sis," Ryan teased.

"Shut up!" she mumbled jokingly, ending the call with Ryan laughing on the other end.

Will had three main priorities—home, shower and bed. He ran a hand through his hair and sighed. Damn, he was tired.

Offering himself up to be a chauffeur to Duncan's granddaughter hadn't seemed like a bad idea at the time. Yet after the week he'd had in Spain, entertaining a tourist for a few hours was not at the top of his list, no matter who her grandfather was. Regardless, he had agreed to pick up Meghan, and his pride would never allow him to back out of an agreement.

With his laptop case in one hand and his tote bag slung over his shoulder, he dodged the numerous travellers making their way through the customs area as he focused on the goal at hand—picking up and dropping off Duncan's granddaughter. If they timed it right they would be able to collect her bags, get through customs and get on the road in a little under an hour, assuming the lines were short and Meghan didn't hold him up.

Except Meghan was a city girl. He cringed. Maybe an hour and a half.

The baggage area was packed with people trying to retrieve their luggage. He glanced up at the Arrival screens. Her flight had arrived early. Perfect, he might able to get underway sooner than expected.

He strode into the crowd huddled around the baggage carousels and scanned the area. Red hair and green eyes. Bloody hell, this was Scotland, every third person had red hair. Fortunately, not many people on the flight from Toronto had red hair. Two so far and both women. One, talking on a cell on the other side of the carousel. The other stood just in front of him with a luggage cart full of bright pink bags and she was still scanning the carousel.

Will groaned and changed his timing to at least an hour before they started for Little Glen. Stepping up beside the redhead closest to him, he noticed her flawless make-up, and how not one strand of her hair was out of place. The words *'high maintenance'* rang out in his head. Not his type. He thanked God then cleared his throat. "Meghan Kennedy?"

After hearing her name, Meghan searched the crowd. No one was looking directly at her so she turned off her phone and jammed it into her purse. Watching the bags slide by, she heard the greetings of families picking up loved ones. All that hugging, kissing, and 'I missed you' made her want to puke, or cry, she wasn't sure. She caught a glimpse of her bag as it slid past on the carousel and she darted between two elderly ladies who she remembered from the plane. And the only reason she remembered them was because of the matching bright blue T-shirts they were wearing. She had laughed when she had first seen them boarding the plane and had read the front of their shirts. One had a picture of a giant fish with, 'I kissed the Cod' printed below it. And the other said, 'Newfie Screech Survivor'.

"Meghan Kennedy?"

Stunned by the deep voice, she tried to stop short but it was too late, she was already in motion and fell back, landing hard on the Newfie Screech Survivor's suitcase.

"Are you Meghan?" The man chuckled.

Meghan groaned, feeling heat spread over her face as she pushed her hair away. "Yup, that's me."

Amazingly, that was the first time in his life that Will had ever been surprised—she was not what he had expected. She was clumsy but stunning even with her hair in her face and her cheeks pink. She was your classic redhead with golden highlights, which shimmered when the light hit them, and her eyes were more turquoise than green. What caught his attention—apart from her glowing hair and lively eyes—were her lips. They were full and lush, and the delicate shade of pink had them crying out to be kissed.

The concerned tone from an elderly woman pulled Will from his stupor. "Are you all right, my dear?"

"I'm fine, nothing bruised but my pride."

"And your behind," the elderly woman teased.

Will held out his hand to her and pulled her upright. "Same thing, isn't it?" Meghan sighed, rubbing her backside. "I'm really sorry, I hope I didn't squish anything?"

"Don't you worry about that." The woman waved her hand as she walked away with her friend. "You just take care of that bruised pride."

"Yeah." She laughed lightly, then mumbled, "Lot easier said than done when I feel like I have a bottle of Newfie Screech up my butt."

Will chuckled, he couldn't help it. "Do I want to know what Newfie Screech is?"

"It's a strong rum from Newfoundland that could peel the paint off a wall. It's good with eggnog though." She gave him a once-over. "Who are you?"

Will cleared his throat in an attempt to hide his laugh at her blunt question. "William MacKenzie. Duncan, your grandfather, is a friend of mine. He asked me to give you a lift to Little Glen."

"That's right, my chauffeur. Thanks for the help, William," she said, extending her hand.

He took her small hand in his and shook it. A sudden familiar feeling had him glancing down. He had held this hand before, he was sure of it. He frowned. But he would remember if he had met a woman as pretty as Meghan before. "Will's fine and you're welcome." He let her hand go.

"Have you seen your bags yet?" His voice was smooth. Silky smooth.

"That's what I was making a dive for when I tripped." She rubbed her behind again.

"Right." He chuckled. "Here, I'll help get them."

"I can do it," she said lightly. "Besides, I think I need to walk off my bruised pride." She rolled her eyes. "Be right back."

After crossing to the carousel, she waited as her bags slowly snaked their way towards her. She peeked back over her shoulder. *Wow! So that's William MacKenzie.* Duncan had said he would be taking her to Little Glen. He was not what she had expected. She had assumed an older friend of Duncan's would be picking her up, not this hot hunky Scottish stud. Oh boy was he hot! A double 'very' hot! Duncan had mentioned that they were good friends. It seemed strange that a man closer to her own age would socialise with her grandfather, let alone consider him a friend. Hot or not. Friend or not, she welcomed the fact he had agreed to drive her to Duncan's.

The crowd had all but vanished, so there was no jockeying for the best position around the carousel. So she waited while her luggage slowly curved around a bend and crept its way closer.

Okay, I'm here. A gradual uneasiness inched its way into her stomach and her head started to throb. *Now what? I just wait.* She didn't like that idea any better than letting Ryan solve her problems. She sighed and gently massaged her temples.

As her bag approached, she reached forwards to grab the handle only to stop when Will plucked the bag off the carousel. Startled, she straightened and turned to find herself staring into the most mesmerising eyes. A feeling of recognition filled her. She had seen eyes like his before, a light mocha surrounded by rich chocolate brown. They had an almost hypnotic quality to them, calling to her, willing her forward. A schoolgirl flutter swirled in her stomach. Blinking, she stopped herself from closing the small gap between them and leant back.

What the hell was that? Her face began to heat up and were her palms sweating? *Eww, gross.*

She drew in a slow breath. She hadn't had this reaction to a man in a long time, not since... Oh, no way! That was not happening again.

"Is this it?" Will asked, not bothering to hide his amusement.

"No." She cleared her throat, keeping her eyes glued to the carousel. "This next one is mine too." She felt Will standing behind her, could feel him staring at her.

"Long flight?"

"Yes, very long," she answered, still focused on the carousel.

"You must be tired."

You have no idea, she thought to herself, then lied, "No, I'm okay, just a little headache."

He nodded. "Then why do you keep yawning?"

Had she been yawning? She blinked, trying to remember. Huh, maybe she was. Really, how could she not be tired? Could be the fact she hadn't seen Duncan in ten years, or maybe it had to do with her dickhead ex-boyfriend chasing her from her own country. Regardless, how was it that she hadn't noticed how her body was reacting and Will had?

Stepping back, Meghan shrugged. "Maybe a little tired," she admitted, unsure about his watchful gaze. "I'll be good as new after we hit the road."

Chapter Two

Will smirked and looked at his sleeping passenger. *As good as new, huh?* Meghan had rested her head back and sighed about an hour ago and that was it, she'd fallen asleep.

She drew in a deep breath, her dark lashes fluttering, her lips parting slightly. Will cursed himself and turned his focus back to the road.

Chauffeur, shower, sleep. Don't get distracted.

Who was he kidding? It was too bloody late for that. The moment she had got into his Land Rover, he'd been distracted, becoming too aware of her. He glanced at her again. Duncan hadn't been forthcoming when Will had asked about her. Will knew that Duncan and his late wife Ruth had only one son, Gordon. He also knew that Gordon had moved to Canada a couple of years after he had been married, and that there had been a disagreement, which sparked the move. Duncan mentioned his grandkids every now and then, and Will knew there were three, a girl and two boys, and he had recently found out that Meghan was the eldest. Yet it was obvious from his limited description of her that Duncan hadn't seen his granddaughter all that much.

Will slid his gaze back to the road when Meghan opened her eyes. Straightening, she glanced to her right. "Will?"

"I'm here." The response was automatic and came out of nowhere. He gripped the wheel, annoyed with the ease at which he had answered her. "And here I thought ye weren't tired," he added. *Shit!* He hadn't intended the words to come out that harsh, so he softened. "Have a nice nap?"

"I guess?"

He could see her eyeing him strangely.

"It took me a minute to remember where I was." She sat forward, rested her head in her hands and looked out of the front windshield. "I forgot how beautiful it was here."

"When was the last time you were here?"

"The last time?" There was the slightest hint of apprehension in her question. "About...ten years ago. My brothers and I spent two weeks with Duncan."

"You've been gone a long time. No wonder Duncan couldn't give me a clear description of you."

She blinked. "Pardon?"

"When I asked Duncan what you looked like all he could give me was red hair with green eyes."

"Okay," she drew out the word. "And what colour hair and eyes do I have?" The question dripped with sarcasm.

"I didn't mean to put you in a defensive position." He fought to hide his smile. "It's just obvious that Duncan hasn't seen you in a while if he can't describe you."

"Well, his memory can't be too bad." She grabbed a handful of hair. "Looks red to me, and I'm pretty sure my eyes are still green."

"Actually, I would say your eyes are more turquoise than green and though it's obvious you are a true ginger, I'd bet those blonde highlights are not natural."

The description was given without as much as a glance. Meghan stared at him. Of course, her highlights were fake, but her eyes, she had always thought of her eyes as being just green. To hear them described as turquoise was new, and it caused a weird fluttering in her belly.

Damn it, she hated that! And why was he so damn observant? He was a man. Men did not describe things in that much detail, unless it was in reference to chest size.

She also hated losing to a smug male. Even if he was right. She had had enough losing to pompous-I-know-everything males. This time she wanted to win, even if it meant lying. She huffed, annoyed that she had allowed this stranger to ruffle her feathers.. "Are you sure you want me to take that bet? I won't be the one to lose."

"Hmm," he purred. "Like to gamble, do you?" There was a hint of humour in his words.

"It wouldn't be the first time," she lied…again.

"I think it is the first time." He leaned towards her and rested his elbow on the centre console between their seats. His words dropped to a silky whisper, his accent becoming thick. "Better be careful or I just might take ye up on that bet."

She turned to meet his brief gaze and…forgot to breathe. Again, a sense of recognition filled her chest. She had stared into those eyes before, but when?

He looked back to the road. "I should warn ye, when I make a bet I expect the other party to hold up their end, no matter the stakes."

Crap! That damn fluttering started up again, and something else she hadn't felt in a long time, something she couldn't afford to feel while she was over there. And that was desire.

She swallowed hard. "I know." Her voice cracked and her cheeks heated. "I know what a bet is and I understand the rules."

He watched the road ahead. "I hope so."

* * * *

The sun was hidden behind the mountains by the time Will drove into Little Glen and even though the buildings were large grey shadows, Meghan found familiar memories beginning to return. There were a few new buildings, but other than that, Little Glen was exactly the same. She glanced off to the right into black shadows, to where the old ruins used to sit at the top of the hill. Ten years ago she and the boys had made it their goal to get to those ruins, only to be stopped at every turn. A decade had passed since then, yet she felt that same urge to get to the top. She wondered if they were still there.

The memory faded as Will pulled to a stop in front of Duncan's large two-storey cottage. A lump rose in her throat, but she swallowed hard and forced it back down when her door opened. Will stood close, giving her an odd frown before holding out his hand. The moment their skin connected, a tingle spread through her palm and fingers, and the heat from his touch climbed up her arm. She was so startled by the sensation that she barely noticed that he had pulled her from his truck and had let her go. She wanted to ask him if he had felt the strange tingling, but didn't for fear she was the only one.

She flexed her hand as she focused on Duncan's home. The off-white house still had dark brown trim around all the windows, as did the heavy wooden front door. The roof was the same shade as the trim and it held two stone chimneys—one at each end of the house. And besides the new wooden fence with a small front gate—it hadn't changed. It was as if time had stood still and she was back in the past. A sense of peace surrounded her and she suddenly felt at ease. Little Glen seemed untouched by the world. Too bad she wasn't.

"Duncan's waiting," Will stepped next to her, holding her bags. The nudge was gentle but she was thankful for it.

She had just opened the small gate when the front door suddenly opened. Duncan filled the doorway. He was tall, proud, and impressive as ever. His thick grey hair had only small traces of the light brown it had once been, and his intense green eyes studied every detail of her. The years had done nothing to him but had given him a more distinguished look.

"Took you long enough to bring her here, boy?"

"She had a run-in with a suitcase," Will explained.

"Oh?"

"Yah!" She shrugged. "The suitcase won."

Will watched as Duncan stared at Meghan. He hadn't seen Duncan smile like that in a long time.

"Well, are you just going to stand there, lass, and let this damp weather eat away at my old decrepit bones?" Duncan mumbled.

Even though Meghan's smile was bright, Will didn't miss how her eyes glistened. Tears? It was too late to see clearly. She walked to her grandfather and threw her arms around him. "Hi, Grandpa."

"I told you not to call me that," Duncan scolded lightly and returned the hug. "Reminds me of my grandfather. He was a grumpy old man, unlike th' charming man who stands before you."

"Charming," Will choked out.

Duncan grinned and let her go. "Come inside, Mary was kind enough to make a nice supper for your arrival. You too, Will," Duncan ordered.

Will followed them into the warm house and was instantly surrounded by the smell of fresh bread, roast of lamb and rosemary. His stomach rumbled. He hadn't planned on going in. He had to get some sleep before he started researching his next few jobs. But after smelling that lamb, he reassessed his list of priorities and put eating at the top.

"So, did Mary volunteer or was she commandeered?" Will asked, setting Meghan's bags down.

"Are you afraid she may like cooking for me, or maybe you just want to keep her talents to yourself?"

"Both." He shrugged out of his coat. "I don't want to lose her. She's a damn good cook and a great housekeeper."

Duncan ushered them into the dining room where Mary was placing the last of the dishes on the sideboard.

"Evening, Will," Mary greeted warmly.

He gave her a kiss on the cheek. "So tell me, did Duncan drag you over here, or did he ask nicely?"

"Will, no man has ever dragged me anywhere. Duncan was quite respectful when he asked me to cook supper. I think he was trying to impress his granddaughter." She peered around Will and gave Meghan a friendly nod.

Mary clicked her tongue and glared at the men. "Come in, child. It would seem these two fully grown men have forgotten their manners. I'm Mary Brooks. I live here in Little Glen and take care of young Will."

Meghan's curious gaze travelled from Mary to Will.

"Mary takes care of my house when I travel and cooks me the occasional feast."

"Oh, stop," Mary gushed, her cheeks pink. "You three sit and eat before it gets cold. I'm off home. Meghan, welcome to Little Glen. If these two get to be too much, I'm just down the road. Will, I'll see you tomorrow." Mary turned her attention to Duncan, her cheeks still pink. "Good night."

"You two sit," Duncan barked the order as he watched Mary. "I'll be a moment," he added, then rushed after the older woman.

Will and Meghan both stood, staring after Duncan, then turned to each other and laughed. Will noticed how her entire face lit up and her eyes became bright.

"So, what's this Mary like, she's not going to take advantage of Duncan, is she?"

Will chuckled, filling three glasses with wine. "Maybe. Mary can be quite persuasive when she wants to be."

Taking the seat across from Meghan, Will watched as she leant back in her chair. She wasn't as tense as before, but she wasn't relaxed either. He squeezed his fist, wondering if she had felt...

"I'm starving," Duncan announced, interrupting his thought. There was a wide grin on his face. "Let's eat this food, or Mary will have my hide. And then we will go in to th' sitting room and Meghan will tell me what trouble she has been getting into."

Will shifted his gaze when he caught her low gasp and watched how her eyes grew wide in surprise.

"Hah! I knew it." Duncan winked at Will. "Always getting into trouble, this one."

Will suppressed his laugh. For someone who professed to gamble she didn't have much of a poker face.

She narrowed her eyes at Duncan as she addressed Will, "Don't listen to him, that old noodle of his" — she swirled her finger around in circles by her temple and whistled — "isn't as good as it used to be."

Will's laugh mixed with Duncan's.

"Besides, you'd know if I had gotten into trouble," she began picking up her wine and shrugged. "It usually makes the news."

Meghan had enjoyed dinner, she couldn't remember the last time she had sat and enjoyed a meal. It had freaked her out when Duncan had wanted to know what trouble she had got into — she had actually frozen, not knowing what to say. She had no idea if Ryan had told him why she had come. God, she hoped not, because there was no way that she would go into detail about the past year in front of Will, a total stranger.

Luckily, Duncan had changed the subject and had asked about her parents, but he'd moved on from that topic just as quickly. It was no secret that Duncan had never liked the idea of her parents moving to Canada. Her father and Duncan had had quite a falling out over it before they had left. Her mother had said that their relationship had never been the same.

Sinking down into a large chair next to the fire, Meghan sighed. Now this was nice, she hadn't been this relaxed in a long time. Will sat across from her on an old worn leather sofa as Duncan brought in a tray with three small glasses of port and handed them each a glass.

"To Meghan," Duncan began. "Welcome back to Little Glen."

She smiled at the sweet gesture and glimpsed at Will.

Raising his glass, he flashed her a unreadable look. "Welcome, Meghan."

Meghan focused her attention on the glass she was holding when the euphoric sensation flooded her veins. It caused her heart to pound and her vision to blur. *Jesus, he caused that with just a look. What would it be like to kiss him?* She focused on sipping the sweet wine and listened as Duncan told Will about current events in Little Glen. But concentrating on the conversation was nearly impossible. All she remembered was the sexy lilt to his words. *'Welcome, Meghan.'*

The way he had said her name...oh man. His voice caused the warm and fuzzies in her belly, and that accent of his made her name sound so sensual that her toes curled. It was crazy to be this turned on by the way he had said her name. Yet she was.

Finding the fire a safe substitute, she gazed into the glowing flames and let what was left of the tension ease from her shoulders. She looked around the familiar room, remembering her last visit, until she found herself staring at Will again. She was able to admire him for the first time without him noticing.

There was an attractive confidence about him that she found appealing. And she'd bet her turquoise eyes and fake blonde highlights that under those clothes was a lean, well-developed, body.

She liked how his thick brown hair was kept short and neat. Sexy neat not nerdy neat. And how the day's worth of dark stubble on his face couldn't hide his strong jaw line or his full mouth – it just gave him a rugged, more dangerous appearance.

His eyes, by far, were the focal point of his face. The combination of different shades of brown was unusual, giving them a strange hypnotic effect and his dark eyebrows only intensified their appearance. To top it all off his accent was as sexy as hell and could easily push a nun into thinking dirty thoughts.

Meghan sighed dreamily. The perfect man. Just what she was hoping *not* to see. But if she was in the market for the perfect man, Will would definitely fall into that category. Too bad she wasn't looking. She sighed again but this time with disappointment. Tilting her head back, she closed her eyes.

An hour later, Duncan sat at his desk, a beaten leather case sitting before him. The time had finally come. It had taken a good many years but Meghan was back.

Meghan. She had turned into a striking woman. She had the traditional Kennedy colouring, except the eyes. Her eyes had a mixture of his green and Ruth's blue. Turning in his chair, he faced the portrait of his love. Meghan even resembled Ruth a little. He turned back to face the leather case. He placed his hands on it and expelled a long breath.

He had been surprised when she'd called last week and had said she wanted to come and stay with him.

She had told him her reason, but he knew that there was more to it. Ryan had already filled him in on the past year's events. Had told him what had been done to her and how she had changed from the hellion she had been to—as Ryan had put it—normal and boring. Two words Duncan would never have thought to describe his Meghan.

As selfish as it was, her visit was the opportunity that he had been waiting for. He had promised James MacKenzie on his deathbed that, if the opportunity presented itself, he would bring the families together. Well, now was the time, he wouldn't get another chance.

Meghan was one hitch to his plan. She was so bloody stubborn. Normally, Duncan was proud of that particular Kennedy trait, however there were times it did get in the way. Although Duncan was certain that Will could handle anything she dished out. He was smart, financially secure, worldly, seeing a lot in his thirty-four years thanks to the military, and with Will being a former soldier, there was no concern with him protecting her. It was a natural instinct for him. That was clear when he'd carried her up to bed.

'Don't wake her.' Duncan had had a hard time hiding his laughter as Will had tried to figure out a way to pick to her up. But when he finally had her in his arms and he'd turned to Duncan, there had been nothing but absolute certainty in his words. *'I won't.'*

He closed his eyes and silently prayed.

They would be a good match. He liked the idea of Meghan marrying a man like Will.

He flipped open the leather case and pulled out a single sheet of parchment.

And he had just the thing to start that particular ball rolling.

The contract.

Chapter Three

Meghan woke early and frowned while stretching lazily under the heavy down comforter. How had she got to bed last night? The last thing she'd remembered was sitting by the fire, all comfy-cosy listening to Duncan and Will discussing some local news. And now she was here in bed? She pushed herself up and looked around the room. Duncan?

No, that was crazy. He was an old man. Though he was in great shape she doubted that he'd carried her upstairs last night. Still, how did she…Will?

"Noooo!" She threw off the covers. Why would he do that? She swung her legs over the side of the bed. The image of dark intense eyes filled her head, the warmth of strong arms surrounding her, and hearing Duncan's, 'Don't wake her'.

"Holy crap!"

It had to be a dream. Her last thoughts were about how hot Will was. Her mind must have just continued with those thoughts and created the dream. *Oh, please let it have been a dream!*

She placed a hand on her chest as a nervous fluttering caught her off guard and she knew, knew with all her being that it was not a dream. "It's nothing, it didn't mean anything. Will and Duncan are friends. He was just helping Duncan. He was just being nice." She spoke the words aloud, as if doing so made them true. She walked over to the window on the opposite side of the bedroom, trying to ignore the fluttering and peered out at the grey day.

Scanning the small village she smiled. It was good to be back. Ten years was too long. A dark grey shadow loomed in the distance and she shifted to get a better view. The castle ruins. A smile tugged at her mouth. They were still there, the last remaining tower still stood out like a beacon, calling to travellers and locals alike. They called to her now, just like they had called to her ten years ago.

During that last visit, Duncan had forbidden her and Ryan and...Scott—her heart squeezed when his face flashed before her eyes—from going up there. 'It's too dangerous,' Duncan had said. 'The old castle still has stone falling from it.' Not caring, the three of them had tried several times to reach the keep, but Duncan had somehow managed to catch them every time.

A familiar feeling started to pull at her, an itch of sorts that need to be scratched. She tore off the pants and shirt she had slept in and searched through her suitcases for her running pants, a T-shirt, her hooded sweatshirt and her black baseball cap. Grabbing her purse, she then dumped out the contents, searching for something to hold her hair back, when she noticed her cell phone. Tapping in her passcode, she watched the glowing faceplate. No coverage. She didn't think that there would be but had to check. She had meant to leave it in her apartment, but force of habit had had her dumping it in her purse with the rest of her junk. Pausing, she ran her finger down the smooth edge. With all her travelling, she had almost forgotten about the text messages she'd received before leaving Toronto.

The first two had made her uneasy, not knowing who had sent them. But the third message, had actually made her heart jump.

'I'll B waiting 4 U Meghan'. Who had sent it and why wasn't the name or number of the person displayed? She frowned, turned the phone off and gently placed it on the dresser.

The house was quiet when Meghan crept out onto the front step and sat down to put on her shoes. The closer she came to starting her run, the stronger the drive grew to hit the pavement. Running had become her salvation ten years ago, after Scott had died. It was an outlet where she could physically work off frustrations, plus it gave her the private time she needed to sort out any problems in her life.

She walked to the lane outside Duncan's house, and stopping beside the small fence, she supported herself while stretching her limbs.

She still couldn't believe that she was there. She stared up at the old stones. The past year had been nothing but a long, dramatic nightmare. She really needed this, being away from her life, away from her parents and friends. Ryan was right. She made a mental note to *never* tell him that.

This forced vacation would help to clear the garbage from her head and there was lots of it, mounds of it. She needed to become the person she had been before the mess had all started, before her ex-boyfriend Rob — aka 'Dickhead' — had entered her life.

Rob entering her life had been like getting sucked into a tornado. He had left nothing but a trail of ruins. And to finish her off, she caught him cheating on her with a blonde bimbo and then he was arrested for theft. When it had all been over, she'd felt dizzy, confused and very much ashamed of herself. The peace of Little Glen would be a nice, calm change.

The small village was silent as she made her way through. Buildings she remembered from her last visit began to fly past, and by the time the library passed on her right, her feet were in sync with the music pumping in her ears. The monument that marked the centre of the village passed on her left as she continued up the long road that led to the old ruins. She reached the hill and passed a large house on her right. The hill was steep and not part of her normal routine but the loud music that vibrated through her body gave her the extra drive she needed.

Standing by the large window in his office, Will sipped his coffee as he fixed his eyes on Meghan. He had just come back in from getting his coffee when he caught sight of her. When he carried her to bed last night, he had noticed dark shadows under her eyes, just as he'd noticed her lips slightly part when he had placed her on her bed. All he had been able to think about was kissing those lips as he had driven home. He'd been so aroused by that one simple feature of hers that he did have a shower when he got home — except it was cold and a waste of time. He didn't sleep much either because of those lips.

The thumping of a large black tail interrupted his daydream. He grinned, looking down into soulful brown eyes and a large mouth filled with white sharp teeth.

"Hey yah, Lucy." He patted the window ledge, and the dog hopped up, placing her two front paws on it. An idea formed as he scratched the dog's ears.

"Want to go for a run?" A loud bark echoed through the office. "Come on then." He walked to the front door with Lucy trailing behind and paused before he opened it.

He gave his very large black dog a stern warning. "You be nice to Meghan."

He knew the dog understood when her ears flopped to the sides of her head and her tail pounded on the floor.

When he opened the door, Lucy stiffened beside him, sniffing the air, ears perked up, waiting for his command.

"Go." The dog tore out of the house, across the driveway and out onto the road. By the time he was standing by the window in his office again, Lucy was just reaching Meghan.

Meghan continued up the hill. It was steeper than it appeared. Her breathing was harder and faster than what she was used to, and her legs were screaming for her to stop, but she ignored the feeling, knowing full well what the consequences would be.

She continued, and as she adjusted her ear bud, she caught movement out of the corner of her eye. Her steps wavered when she saw a large black dog running beside her. She came to a stop. Her breathing was fast as she placed her hands on her hips, searching for the dog's owner. The panting beast sat down in front of her, its ears up, staring at her. Large white teeth instantly caught Meghan's attention. She tensed, until a long pink tongue flopped out of the side of its mouth. Meghan chuckled. If she didn't know better she could swear that the dog was smiling at her.

"Hello, dog, what's your name?"

The black beast wagged its tail.

"You shouldn't be out here by yourself. Go on home." She snapped her fingers in the direction of the village, and the dog followed the instruction and began to trot back down the road. She put her ear buds back in and continued, only to be stopped two seconds later when she noticed the dog running beside her again.

"Go home dog." She snapped her fingers towards the village for a second time. "Stubborn mutt."

The next time she didn't even get her ear buds back in before the dog reappeared at her side. Sighing, she asked, "You aren't going to let me finish my run are you?"

Big brown eyes twinkled up at her.

"Come on then, let's find your home."

As Meghan walked past the house at the bottom of the road, she noticed a large figure leaning against the stone post that held a black iron gate.

"Good morning, Meghan." Will's deep greeting triggered goose bumps to appear on her arms and chest. Stopping abruptly, she stared at him. His hair was still messy from sleep. He wore a pair of baggy old jeans, a blue sweatshirt, and a pair of flip-flops. He looked as though he'd just fallen from a magazine ad.

Smile, you idiot! her inner voice ordered. "Hi."

"How was the run?"

"It was good," She lifted the brim of her black ball cap. "Until this black beast started following me. Do you know…?" She stopped in mid-sentence when the dog trotted over to Will and sat down. "It's your dog?"

"Yes, she is. I saw you run by and thought you might want some company."

"Do you always let your dog run on a road by herself? She could've gotten hit by a car."

His eyebrows rose the slightest amount as he studied her. "Impossible, this road is a dead end. And I'm the only one who drives a motor up here."

"Hmm, of course you are."

Will fought hard to suppress a smile. She didn't believe him. He found that interesting, because he never lied. But she couldn't know that. She didn't know him. Yet.

His gaze floated over her face. Damn, she was pretty, with her cheeks all flushed, and her eyes narrowed in doubt. Feisty, very nice. Will locked eyes with hers and stepped forward, holding the bottle of water out to her. "Thirsty?"

"Thanks." She took the water, giving him a puzzled frown while opening the cap. "You took quite a chance. What if I was afraid of dogs?" She took a long swallow.

"I told Lucy to be nice."

"You told her to be nice." She studied him for a second. "Huh! You don't look like the naïve type."

Will bit the inside of his mouth to keep from laughing.

"She's a big girl. I bet she's rattled a few nerves in her time."

"Lucy." He intentionally focused on her mouth. "She's a pussycat."

She leant back when she asked, "Compared to who?"

"Me."

She snorted in disbelief. "Is that so?"

Again, Will had to fight the urge not to laugh out loud. The way she went from startled to annoyed in the blink of an eye was comical.

"Funny, I'm not scared by either one of you. Thanks for the water, Will." She gave him a wink, then turned.

Will watched as she started to walk away, he couldn't hold it back any longer and threw his head back and laughed. It wasn't the answer he had been expecting. He wanted her to blush as she had yesterday in the airport. Nevertheless, this feisty side was more to his liking, and that wink. She was playful too. Very, very nice.

"Meghan!" he called out before he could stop himself. She turned to face him, just as she had taken another swallow from her bottle. He almost groaned out loud as he watched her lick the water from her lips.

"Yes?"

"How about letting me try to rattle you tonight over drinks?"

He thought he saw doubt cross her face but she raised her chin, just a little, then nodded. "Okay. Duncan and I will meet you at The Black Ale. Around seven?"

Trying to turn him off by dragging Duncan along wouldn't work, he happened to enjoy Duncan's company, so the joke would be on her.

"Great, I'll see you both then." He grinned back at her. She gave him a confused smile, shook her head, then continued with her run.

Will stood rooted to the spot watching her. The sway of her hips held his attention until she was out of sight. He knew now how she must have come to have such a nice backside—running up hills would do it.

He was surprised that she'd tackled his road first. It wasn't an easy climb.

Before turning back to the house, he glanced at the old keep. A thick grey mist hovered along the bottom of the great wall, giving the impression the ruins were floating on a cloud.

The old castle had been in his family for over a thousand years, and they still owned it today, though now it was a pile of stones. Tourists would come every once in a while to see it but would leave shortly after, as it didn't offer much in the way of grandeur. There were other castles in Scotland that offered more, which was fine with him. He couldn't care less if the tourists came or not. He liked it just the way it was and had always felt drawn to the old keep and would usually end each of his runs up there. Meghan must've felt that same pull. Why else would she try his hill on her first day here?

A memory he never knew he had flashed before his eyes. A woman with long red hair and a long green gown was waving to him from the top of the great wall of the keep. A sudden fear pulled at his chest as he waved back, a fear that he would never see her beautiful face again.

Will blinked and the memory was gone. He walked back towards the house with Lucy at his side and stopped to look back up at the wall. Even though he couldn't see the redhead's face clearly, he knew with his entire being that it was Meghan standing on that wall waving to him.

Chapter Four

The Black Ale was a typical pub—dark wood, dartboards, with bits of the local history tacked to the walls. The bar was across from the main doors and ran almost the length of the room. Off to the left there were a few tables where locals chatted, a pool table and two dartboards. To the right there were a few more tables, booths against the front of the pub, which was lined with windows, and a larger stone fireplace with two overstuffed chairs on one side, a small matching love seat on the other, and a small table between them. The coffee house furniture was a nice touch and somewhat comforting, reminding her of the many times she would go out with her friends to sit and chat over coffee.

Meghan pointed to the two comfy chairs. "Would you like to sit by the fire?"

"No, but I will accommodate you this one time."

Meghan rolled her eyes. "Grumpy old far—"

"Watch it, young lady."

"Well, it's true." He had been since she had told him they were going out, yet had quickly changed his tune after she had mentioned that Will would be meeting them, although sometimes it was hard to tell. "Go sit down grumpy, or I'll make you get your own drink."

She followed Duncan over to the fireplace, took off her heavy sweater and threw it on the loveseat. He sat down in one of the chairs and sighed. Meghan squinted at him and teased, "You look pretty comfortable in that chair, Duncan."

"I'm only sitting here because you wanted me to," he said in his usual gruff tone.

She raised an eyebrow. "Mmm! Likely excuse. Now what would you like…?"

"Here's your Guinness, Duncan."

Meghan flinched as the words were spoken from behind her. She could hear Will's tease fill her head. *'How about letting me try to rattle you tonight over drinks?'*

She huffed silently. Was there really any trying involved? Her heart had already jumped at hearing his voice and the mere thought of him standing behind her caused her body to stiffen, and were her hands sweating again? *Ewww!* Honestly, she didn't like how he was able to 'rattle' her so easily.

Taking a silent breath, she turned and looked up into his handsome face.

"Is white wine okay?" he asked, handing Meghan a glass.

"Yes. That's…" *Careful now*, she lectured herself. *Act casual.* "Thank you…" She sighed. "Will."

Damn it!

So much for acting casual. And took a long gulp of her wine before she plunked herself down. She hadn't come all this way to fall for some hunky Scotsman. It didn't matter that he was tall, dark and super-hot. She had to snap out of it.

Will had noticed Meghan the moment she had walked into the pub. An aura of temptation surrounded her and all she was wearing was a pair of jeans, and a heavy knitted grey jumper that had large grey buttons keeping it closed and was belted at her waist. Her hair hung down her back in long soft curls. Her cheeks had a rosy glow from the cool night air and her lips were lightly glossed, making them full and enticing. The urge to go over to her and run his hands through her silky hair and taste those glossy lips made the muscles in his arms and chest flex involuntarily.

He had ordered the drinks in the hopes it would give him enough time to gain his composure before joining them. And it had worked until he had walked up behind Meghan. He tried to focus on a greeting but got distracted by the sight of her behind and how her jeans clung to the flare of her hips. He pressed his lips together, annoyed with his lack of focus. He appreciated a nice behind as much as the next man but to be so entranced by it that he lost the ability to mumble out a greeting was a first.

Joining her on the loveseat, Will breathed in her scent. It was light, fresh, and... Christ almighty, wasn't it enough that her presence alone affected him? Did she have to smell damn good too? She was making him dizzy, and it took all his concentration to focus on what Duncan was asking him.

"Well, how was your last job?" Duncan asked, frowning at him. "It was a footballer, wasn't it?"

"Mmm, plays for a team in the Premier League. It went well, not too much trouble."

Meghan gave him an odd look. "Your last job was a footballer?"

Duncan answered for him. "Will owns a personal protection business. He's protected some big important people, even a few movie stars. He's become very prosperous."

Meghan stared at Duncan, puzzled. "Okay." She turned back. "So you're a bodyguard?"

"There's a little more to it than that but it's along those lines."

"Don't you have to have some sort of special training for that line of work?"

"Will served with the Royal Marines' Special Boat Service. For what? Eight or nine years?"

"The what?"

"SBS, it's a Naval unit."

"SBS." She frowned. "Don't you mean SAS?"

Raising a single eyebrow, he turned to face her. "Excuse me?" He was insulted that she would think he had got the name of his old unit mixed up with those...paranoid, glorified, media whor...

"You mean SAS, right?" She blinked innocently at him.

He paused, studying her. *Shit!* She was serious. He laughed. He couldn't help himself and gave her a simple answer, "I served with the Navy for ten years." Then he took a drink. She really had no idea what the SBS was. He liked her even more because of that. He wouldn't be forced to ignore her questions or flat-out tell her to mind her business like he had to with others when they had asked about his time spent in the Navy.

Besides, his old life was history and he wanted to know more about Meghan. "What about you, Meghan, what did you do in Toronto?" Will watched as she started to talk but was cut off.

"After graduating top of her class from university, Meghan was hired by a small but prestigious publishing house," Duncan answered with a hint of pride.

"Duncan, I can speak." She glared at her grandfather again.

Will instantly recognised what the older man was doing. Duncan was matchmaking. He wasn't subtle either. And by the flash of annoyance Meghan gave her grandfather, she just thought that he was sharing personal information.

"I'm a copy editor. I deal mostly with children's books," she explained. "And the firm is smaller, but we have a great reputation with our clients."

"You sound like you really enjoy it."

"I do." Her smile was wide and genuine.

God, he had missed that smile. It had been so long since he had seen it.

Will blinked, startled by the sudden thought. How could he have missed it, if this was the first time he saw it? Where had that thought come from? He had to focus hard on Meghan as she continued.

"It's a great place to work and I've met some really talented and amazing people."

"Now she's going to try to write her own book. That's why she came to Scotland, she needed inspiration."

"No, I'm not, Duncan!" Meghan snapped. Colour flooded her cheeks.

"That's what you said on the phone."

"I was being sarcastic." She gave Duncan a hard glare.

If he wasn't already intrigued with her, he would be now. There was something more going on here. Why was she here?

He acted as though he didn't notice her flushed face and averted gaze. "Well, you came to the perfect place," he tried to reassure her. "For whatever the reason, and if need be, I'm sure you'll find all sorts of inspiration." He fixed his eyes on hers hoping for her to give away something, but she looked away and took a large mouthful of wine.

What was Duncan thinking by telling Will that she was here to try to write a book? It was a passing idea that had come to her a when she had called and asked to come. She had been so nervous he would say no that it was an excuse she babbled out hoping to sway Duncan's decision. It wasn't a new idea, she would love to sit and write her own book but she never seemed to have the time. There was always work to do and that was the priority.

Listening to Will and Duncan talk, Meghan focused on the fire. She was sure Will had wanted her to spill the reason she was there, which was—*let's face it*—to hide, but the way those eyes bored into hers… Man, that look made her want to spill her darkest secrets. Yet how could she? She didn't know anything about Will, except that he was a bodyguard, drove strange women around Scotland and he was hot. Oh God, so hot!

Rattled! her inner voice sang.

"Well, well now, who is this beautiful lass?" Three older men stood at the end of the loveseat. Both Will and Duncan stood to greet the trio.

"Stewart, Hamish, Raymond, may I introduce my granddaughter Meghan Kennedy," Duncan announced with pride.

"Well that's why we're here, Duncan," the tallest of the three said. "The name's Stewart Ross," he said in a no-nonsense tone.

Hamish MacGregor was the next to greet her. He had the bluest eyes and a warm smile. "If you need anything lass, you tell me an' I'll fetch it for you."

Will rested his hand on her lower back, instantly catching her attention. "Hamish owns The Black Ale." She tried to ignore the heat of his hand. "It's been in his family for over a hundred years." Hamish gave her a wink, confirming the statement.

"She's too young for you, Hamish, but then again you always had an eye for a bonny lass, no matter the age. I'm Raymond Campbell, but call me Ray. It's nice to finally meet you." He was shorter than the other two, and she could just make out a few bits of brown in his hair hidden mostly by grey.

"Och, but she looks like her gran, doesn't she?" Stewart commented.

"A wee bit, but she has Gordon's eyes."

"Those are my eyes, Hamish," Duncan corrected.

"But that colouring—'tis Ruth for sure," commented Ray.

"Ruth's hair was not that red, Ray. As you well know," Duncan mumbled.

Meghan began to get dizzy looking back and forth between the four men. She put up her hands and said quite firmly, "I have both my father and Duncan's eye colour, and I look more like my mum, but my temperament and apparently my hair...are from my grandmother, or so I've been told." With that said she batted her eyelashes at them innocently.

Hamish and Stewart began to laugh as Ray chuckled. "That you do, lass. And do you know you would be my granddaughter, if old Duncan here hadn't come along and stolen Ruth from me?"

She had never heard that before. Turning, she looked to Duncan for the truth, but all she saw was murder in his green eyes.

Meghan eyed Ray. She had met her grandmother Ruth only once, but it was so long ago the memory had faded. But she did know her grandmother had been a beautiful and spirited woman, so she had a hard time believing that this stocky little man had almost stolen her away from Duncan.

"Good thing for me you're not." She playfully waved her hand and chuckled the rest of her insult. "I'm not a big fan of heels."

"Meghan!" Duncan scolded.

Will coughed trying to hide his laugh. Okay so maybe she shouldn't have insulted him but she didn't like what the little twerp had said.

She raised her hands. "That's not what it sounded like...I meant..." She looked at the men standing in front of her and groaned inwardly. *Ah crap!*

"Look, it's just that we Kennedy women like our men tall, dark, handsome, with a" — she struggled for the right word — "commanding presence. Short and sweet just isn't our thing. But you seem funny. Funny's good too." She noticed that Duncan was still scowling. "What? I apologised." This time Will laughed outright.

"Oh for God's sake!" She was just about to give Ray a proper apology when Hamish cut her off.

"Tall, dark, handsome, with a commanding presence, eh? Does that sound like someone we know?" Hamish gave his friends a nod.

What was he talking about? All four men shifted their gaze behind her. She froze. "What? No, no. That's not what…"

"He is tall," Ray confirmed.

"And he does have dark hair," Stewart pointed out.

Meghan gaped, looking back and forth between the men, her heart starting to race.

"Hold it!" she said loud enough to get their attention. "You misunderstood what I…"

"No, we didn't," Ray beamed.

What was wrong with her? She had described her perfect man with him standing right behind her. But was that enough? *Nooooo,* she just had to say it out loud and in front of three complete strangers and Duncan.

Holy crap, it's hot in here.

"How about you, Will? Do you know anyone who fits that description?" Stewart asked.

"Yes, surprisingly I do." His response was mixed with a deep chuckle.

She could still feel his gaze, as her face continued to burn. *Stop,* she told herself, *Get control of yourself.* She inhaled deeply and plastered a grin on her face.

"Okay, I deserved that for my comment. I hope you have had your fun teasing me," she scolded. "I would have thought grown men would have better manners?" She shook her head at them. "Not nice."

"We're not teasing, lass," Stewart informed her with a straight face.

"Of course you are." She laughed softly. "Now if you will all excuse me, I'm off to the ladies' room. By the time I get back I expect gentlemen to be waiting." She turned to leave then stopped and turned back. "I also would like one of you to introduce me to some of your neighbours. I will be here for a…while and I don't want to have to search too far when I need polite company." Meghan's smile disappeared as she turned from the men. *Think before you speak. Think before you speak,* she lectured herself.

Chapter Five

Meghan's description of him hadn't been far off the mark. He was tall, and he did have dark hair. He wasn't sure if he would consider himself handsome, although he had never had a problem attracting the ladies. As for the commanding presence, well, that had been developed and sharpened during his years in the Navy. Except Meghan hadn't been referring to him, had she?

He grinned. The number of emotions that had crossed her face as she had struggled with her composure had been amusing, but he was impressed at how quickly she had gained control of herself.

Resting against the dark walnut bar, Will watched as Ray and Stewart introduced Meghan to some of the locals. Her manner was friendly and warm as she stopped a number of times to chat, while Ray and Stewart hovered behind her waiting impatiently.

"I'm leaving," Duncan announced. "Goodnight, Will, Hamish." He nodded.

"'Night?" Will responded. He was leaving without Meghan?

Before he could ask if that was his intent, Duncan commanded, "Will? Walk her home for me." The older man stared at his granddaughter. "There's a good lad. I'm afraid late nights are a thing of the past for me." And without waiting for a reply, Duncan marched through the doors.

Will looked at his watch, it was only nine o'clock. Since when had late nights become a thing of the past? Will scoffed. Just a couple of weeks ago his brother Gavin, along with Duncan, Hamish and himself, had closed down The Black Ale. He shook his head and sighed. Duncan was still at it.

Leaning his back against the bar, he once again focused on Meghan and wondered how she would react if she found out what Duncan was doing. Hell, he wasn't too sure about it himself. Then again he was thankful that Duncan approved. She was a beautiful woman, and the thought of spending the night with her had been lurking in the dark areas of his mind since they had met. Unfortunately, Duncan was a family friend and for him to take Meghan to bed just to satisfy his own need was disrespectful, not just to Duncan but to Meghan as well. And as strong as his attraction was for her, he was sure just one night wouldn't satisfy anything. There would be no one-night stand, not with her. The idea disturbed him because he didn't know how he knew that, he just knew. He would end up going back for more.

He studied Meghan closely. His training had taught him to assess people and situations in record time—it was essential in his line of work. The skill had saved his arse more times than he could count. He also found it handy while he prepared a location for his clients. Will examined her body language, hand gestures, and facial expressions, anything that might be an indication of some underlying fault. He'd misjudged a few people in his life, and he would never allow it to happen again.

Meghan's musical laugh pulled him from his trance. What was he doing? She wasn't a terrorist, and she wasn't a client, she was just a beautiful woman. A beautiful woman he had been judging for the past few minutes. This had to be some kind of new low for him. There was nothing wrong with being cautious, but Jesus, he had just met her.

Meghan laughed again as she made her way back over to the bar, Ray and Stewart arguing again behind her. She glanced around. "Where's Duncan?"

"He went home a little while ago." Her mood was light and he could see her cheeks glowed from the wine. He reached over and took her empty glass, placing it on the bar.

"He did? I hadn't noticed." She looked at the two men. "I should probably get going too. Ray, Stewart, thank you very much for introducing me to your friends." She turned and said goodbye to Hamish who was behind the bar filling up a pint glass.

Will held her grey jumper open for her when she turned back. He found it amusing that she was stunned by his simple gesture. She stood unmoving, just staring up at him, until he finally wrapped the jumper around her shoulders.

She blurted out, "Thanks." She slipped her arms into the sleeves, then tied it closed.

"Are you ready go?" he asked, pulling on his jacket.

"You don't have to leave. I can walk there by myself. It's only around the corner."

"Duncan asked me to walk you home." Then he couldn't help but tease, "I'd hate to upset a man with such a commanding presence."

The direct reminder was not well received. She wrinkled her nose as she gave him a tight smile. "Funny." Then turned and marched out into the night. Chuckling, he nodded to the men standing at the bar, and followed her outside.

"So," Hamish said, leaning over the bar towards his friends. "What do you think?"

Ray answered first, "I like her. She's got Ruth's spirit."

"Not to mention, she is loyal to Duncan. Did you see how quick she was to stand up for him?" Stewart added.

"And how about our young Will? He seems taken with her." Hamish pointed out.

"Can you blame him? She's a true beauty. She would be good for our young warrior. What do you think, Ray?" asked Stewart.

"It would be a good match, but he may find her reluctant."

"Why do you say that?" Stewart asked.

"There's no doubt that she is attracted to him. She just doesn't want to be," Ray said.

"Maybe she has a boyfriend?" Hamish added.

"Well, that won't work," Stewart bellowed.

The two men rolled their eyes simultaneously.

"Settle a wee bit, Stu. If there was a boyfriend why isn't he with her?" Ray reasoned. "I think there's another reason."

"Then we should remind Duncan of the contract, just in case," Stewart suggested.

"I don't think we'll need to." Hamish said, "Duncan practically ordered Will to walk her home."

"Do you think Will knows about the contract?" Stewart asked frowning.

"I'm not sure. But when the time comes he will. They both will."

"Well, gentlemen" — Hamish raised his glass — "here's to future weddings."

* * * *

"Did you have a good time?"

Meghan almost sighed listening to Will's deep voice, and she found his accent comforting. She found him comforting too, as if it was the most natural thing to walk next to him. Why was that? It was probably because her parents were both Scottish and hearing his accent reminded her of them. *Oh yeah!* she thought sarcastically. *That's it!* "Mmm, I did."

"I get the impression that there is another reason why you came to Little Glen other than wanting to write."

Like she would tell him the real reason. Smiling, she just shrugged as they walked together down the street.

"You don't look like someone who hides from their problems."

What the…? "I'm not," she answered too quickly. "I mean, I'm just here for a visit, to see Duncan…"

"Hey." He held up his hands. "Not my business. But if you're going to hide anywhere there is no better place then Little Glen."

How did he know she was hiding? Well not really hiding, it was more like spending time in a unknown location, where lunatics couldn't find her…she hoped. "Okay." She nodded. "That's good to know."

They reached the front of Duncan's house and she was about to thank Will for walking her home when he opened the front gate for her.

"I take my job seriously. Duncan wanted me to walk you home, and that's what I'll do right up to the front door." He winked at her, then nudged her up the path to the large wooden door.

She stood on the front step, then turned to say goodnight, but stopped when she came met Will's hypnotic stare. Her heart thumped in her chest the same time a strange fluttering began in her stomach. Maybe she was sick? Something she had eaten? *Oh please, let it be food poisoning.*

The pleading was short-lived. He moved his gaze over her face, stopping on her mouth, and her entire body heated up with anticipation. She was so entranced by the swirl of his mocha eyes that she didn't notice him moving closer until his lips touched hers. The touch was light and warm as he coaxed her mouth to move. As he continued to work his magic, her lids began to feel heavy from his intoxicating kiss, and closing her eyes, she sighed into his mouth. His kiss was captivating, and she felt herself slipping into a trance. She was barely aware that he had slid his hands to her waist until he pulled her closer, deepening the kiss. Only when she felt the weight of his large arms surround her did the reality of the situation hit her.

Fighting his sensual haze, she pushed back, breathless. She was stunned by the sudden intimacy and couldn't seem to put two thoughts together. She stepped back, needing the space to think.

"Meghan?"

Oh man, she liked the way he said her name. But, this wasn't the time or the place. She had to remind herself why she was there and that her time was limited. "I'm sorry, Will, I can't." She flushed as she tried to find the courage to look at his face.

"Why?" There was a heavy pause. "Meghan, look at me." His order had taken on a demanding tone. "Is there someone waiting for you, a husband, or boyfriend?"

"No, I'm not married, and I don't have a boyfriend."

His frown quickly receded. "Then why can't you?"

"I just can't. I told you, I'm here to see Duncan. I'll be going home soon." She hoped Ryan would be able to straighten this mess with Rob, then she wouldn't be lying "It wouldn't be right. Can we just be friends?"

His probing stare searched her face. The look was so intense that she felt herself become ashamed for not telling him the entire truth. Well, she hadn't told him a complete lie either, she would be going home soon, she just didn't know when. The other part was that she just wasn't ready to get 'involved'. Will was a scorching hot, hunky Scotsman and she couldn't afford to fall into a trap that she had just got out of. She had been such a naïve fool, and still felt that way even after all these months. She had placed her trust in Rob, had confided in him and he'd used her, had tricked her, and had lied to her. The Dickhead.

She wasn't ready to go through that again, not now. Although Will was awfully tempting, and if she had met him before the Dickhead then maybe, but not now.

She watched him, searching for some outward show of emotion. He showed her nothing. In spite of her lack of ability to read him, she had laid it out for him so he couldn't accuse her of leading him along. Besides, it was too late to change her mind now.

"I would rather be more than yer friend Meghan — but I'll take what I can get. For now. And as we are being *honest*" — his accent became thicker as he put a strong emphasis on the word honest — "wi' each other, then let me tell you this. I can be a patient man when I need to be, but I don't give up easily. And seeing how ye are going to make me wait I want somethin' to tide me over." With that said, he drew her forward, pressing his mouth to hers.

Despite his hard words, Will was extremely gentle as his arms surrounded her. She felt his heat quickly seep through her sweater as his lips covered hers. His mouth was hot and demanding, and for a second time she became so intoxicated by his kiss that she sighed when she felt Will tug her sweater open and pin her against his hard chest.

He was right, she thought dreamily. If this was the one time she had to kiss him, it might as well be a doozy, and with that thought, she wrapped her arms around his neck.

There was a deep rumble that she thought might have come from Will's throat but she wasn't sure, she was too busy enjoying the feel of him. *My God.* He was solid muscle and hot, she felt the heat radiating off him.

He slid his hand into her hair, cupping the back of her head at the same moment he squeezed her behind, pulling her tight against his long, thick…she inhaled. He instantly took full advantage of her open mouth, slipping his tongue between her lips, and entwining it with hers in slow passionate circles. On and on the kiss went. He gripped the back of her neck, gently caressing her skin. She felt his other hand squeeze her behind, the tight hold caused her jeans to pull blissfully tight against her heating body. He explored every inch of her mouth, skimmed the edge of her teeth, until he finished off by nipping at her lips. She was so enthralled by his touching and kissing that when he pulled away, she struggled to contain a cry of protest and found herself clutching at his jacket. Dazed, she quickly let go.

"Goodnight, Meghan." He stepped back, an arrogant flash of satisfaction covered his face. "I'll see ye soon."

Her jaw dropped open as she watched him walk away. A sharp breeze sent a shiver through her and she pulled her sweater closed. *He did that on purpose.*

She frowned, licking her lips, his taste filling her mouth once again. She had blown him off and he had said he was going to tolerate it for a while, but not too long? How much time would she have? And what would happen when the time was up? She wasn't scared in the least, actually she found herself curious as to what he would do. Whatever it was, she had the feeling that she wouldn't be able to concentrate on a damn thing when he decided her time was up.

Chapter Six

The next morning Meghan was up and out for her run before Duncan was awake. Not too surprising when she hadn't slept thanks to Will and that kiss. *That kiss! Holy what a kiss!* It was the most passionate kiss she had ever experienced...ever. Even when she was with Dickhead, not once had he kissed her like Will had. The way his tongue had swept inside her mouth and had sensually curled around hers, circling with excruciating slowness, the gentle way his arms had enveloped her, and that mix of male and light cologne. It had been a full-on assault to her senses.

Stopping suddenly, Meghan paused her music and scanned the area. "What the hell?" She looked at Will's house. How had she got here? Was she subconsciously hoping to see him again this morning? No, of course not. She was out for a run, to get some exercise and clear her mind. Drooling over Will and his hard body wasn't part of the agenda.

Starting up her tunes, she continued, eyeing Will's house. It was a large house for just one person. Why wasn't he married? He was a great catch, not that she wanted to do any fishing. Did his business have a lot to do with his relationship status? Personal protection sounded demanding, with the potential to be high-risk and unpredictable, then again so was the military. Yet what woman could resist a man in uniform? But would that uniform be enough to keep them? It would be a tough life. Or it could be as simple as Will not finding the right person.

"That's a joke," she snorted out loud. "He's probably found more than one."

Reaching the steep incline that led to the old ruins, Meghan caught a glimpse of a dark figure staring at her from a ground floor window.

Will. She stopped again and stared back. "Don't let him think the kiss got to you," she mumbled to herself. *Act casual. Ask for Lucy.* She pointed to the road with her hands in a questioning motion. Would he understand what she was asking? He walked from the window, and less than a minute later Lucy shot out of the front gates and up the road. The black dog bounded up to her, wagging its tail.

"Hey, Lucy, want to come keep me company?"

She laughed when the dog gave an excited bark and started up the road. She saw Will leaning against the doorframe, his arms crossed over his wide chest. She waved and he acknowledged her with a nod of his head. She started up the hill with Lucy a few feet ahead of her.

Will had had a feeling that when Meghan went for her run she would pass his house. Whether or not she meant to was a different story. He had chuckled when he'd first spotted her just down the road, looking around confused. Preoccupied with other thoughts? He knew the feeling.

He hadn't handled the situation as well as he should have done last night. But he had been surprised and fucking annoyed when she had turned him down. He had wanted her to come to him eagerly, to do whatever he wanted. He had in fact expected her to, though had no clue where that thought had come from. To top off the odd reaction was her sweet taste. He had known what she would taste like before he had even kissed her. How was that even possible? Something was happening, and he had no clue what it was, but it centred around Meghan.

His mouth began watering when he thought about the kiss they'd shared. That kiss meant to give her a taste of what she would be missing. What he hadn't expected was how hard it had been for him to end it. She was honey-sweet, and the feel of those pink lips had almost had him coming undone. The muscles in his chest flexed at the memory. He had actually trembled—a first for him. He had had to leave then, even though his body and soul had cried out for more. Leaving had been harder to do than ending the kiss and her stunned expression nearly killed him.

But she wanted to be friends, and friends didn't kiss on front doorsteps, so he had left her and had gone home for another cold shower.

When he spotted Meghan coming back down the road, he quickly grabbed another bottle of water from the kitchen and went to meet her. By the time she reached the gate, Will was standing in the road waiting for her. "Get up to the top yet?" he asked before she reached him.

"Nope," she said, slowing to a stop in front of him. "I'm not used to running hills." Her breathing was still quite laboured. "It's either a treadmill at my gym or the park close to my apartment." She breathed in deeply, then exhaled slowly. "I'll get there." She walked in small circles in front of him with her hands on her hips. He noticed how pink her cheeks were and how she was still fighting to catch her breath. It was easing, but very slowly. Frowning, he handed her the water. "This should help."

She breathed, "Thanks."

She opened the cap and took a long gulp. Her pink lips glistened from the water. A low moan echoed in his head.

"Why are you looking at me like that?"

"Like what?" He shifted his gaze from her wet lips.

"Like you're having a perverted daydream."

He crossed his arms. "Probably because I am."

"Oh!" Her eyes widened.

He laughed when she stepped back. "How did you sleep last night?"

She narrowed her eyes. "Great," she said slowly. "How about you?"

What a little liar she was. He could see faint shadows under her eyes.

"Unfortunately, I wasn't as lucky." He focused on her mouth and asked softly, "Do you want to know why?" He took note of her breathing, it had finally slowed. Actually, it might have stopped altogether.

"No."

"I'll tell you anyway." He kept his voice low. "All I could think about was how sweet your lips tasted and then began to wonder how the rest of your body would taste. Your shoulders..." He stepped forward and held her gaze with his own. The colour seemed to be fluctuating between green and blue. He pressed on, "Your fingers, the soft skin between your breasts, your inner thighs." He watched as her pupils grew large, taking over her now blue eyes.

"I..." She nearly shouted, then looked at his mouth, which he deliberately curled into a sensual smile.

"I've got to go." She turned and stiffly walked away.

"See you later, Meghan," he called after her.

She didn't acknowledge him.

Laughing out loud, he stared after her. He could have kissed her again, she wouldn't have stopped him. So, the stopping had been left up to him, which he hadn't wanted, but had done anyway. He had accomplished what he had set out to do, to make her yearn for his touch. This wasn't going to be easy, especially if she was as stubborn as Duncan. But he was expecting that and would adjust accordingly. He watched the sway of her hips as she headed back to town. Nope, this wasn't going to be easy — for either of them.

* * * *

"Do you have the list, Robert?" Emily purred into the phone.

He hated that she called him Robert. "No. I didn't get to her in time."

"Darling." She tsked. "Your time is limited."

He wanted to lie and tell her that it would be soon, but if she caught him in the lie...who knew what her associate would do. He sighed. "She left the country." But added quickly, "I doubt she'll be gone long. I've already emailed her."

"Why wait? Do you know where she went?"

"I have an idea, but I'm not positive."

"Where?"

He tightened the grip on his cell phone. Fuck, the bitch was persistent.

"Scotland," he revealed through clenched teeth. "Her parents are from a small village, but she never mentioned the name."

"What about the closest major city, did she mention that?"

"No, actually, she never talked much about it. I don't think she spent much time there."

Meghan had mentioned Scotland and that her grandfather lived in a small village somewhere in the Highlands, but she had never mentioned the name of the village or the surrounding towns or cities. He wouldn't have listened or cared if she had. "Like I said before she is very attached to her family and friends — she won't be gone long."

"These are the same friends and family that encouraged her to testify against you?"

He remained silent, squeezing his jaw so tight that the muscles burned.

Emily laughed. "Well, if I was in as much debt as you, I would start by finding out where she has gone, then pack a suitcase."

He sighed. "Yes, Emily."

Chapter Seven

It had been over an hour since Meghan had arrived at the Little Glen library. The building was quite small and appeared to be one of the newer buildings in Little Glen, which of course didn't mean much. Some of the newer houses or buildings dated back to the early 1890's. Regardless of its old stone walls, the interior of the library was in excellent condition and was well equipped with every modern convenience, plus it had a wide selection of books.

Meghan had been staring at the screen of her laptop from the time she had sat down at the only table. She had checked her emails, and had responded back to work emails first, then replied to her mother, of course, and her brother Ryan. Her friend Jessica had asked if she was ready to come home yet, even offering to pay for her plane ticket. Then she lastly deleted one other email, not recognising the sender.

Since then, she had tried to concentrate on work. She tried to focus, she really did, but Will and his sexy description kept invading her thoughts.

'All I could think about was how sweet your lips tasted and then began to wonder what the rest of your body would taste like? Your shoulders, your fingers.' She put her head in her hands. *'The soft skin between your breasts, your inner thighs.'*

Groaning, she dropped her head on the table.

"Not having a good day?"

Meghan stiffened and lifted her head to glare at Will. "Don't worry."

He put two cups on the table before holding up his hands. "I won't bother you while you are trying to work, but I make no promises once you step outside this building," he assured her.

"I'll make a mental note to pick up a sleeping bag," she mumbled sarcastically.

One dark eyebrow rose. "I have no problem tormenting you all the time." He rested his hands on the table and leaned towards her. "You want me to forget my promise?"

He would do it too. She heard the underlying threat to his words. She clicked her tongue in frustration. "I guess not." He laughed softly. "So, what do you want? Why are you here?"

"I'm here to do some research" — he placed one cup with a plastic lid in front of her — "and I wanted to give you this. It's a latte. You look like you could use it."

She looked at the cup, then to him. "Thank..." *Wait a second.* "What's the catch?"

"No catch, I went to The Black Ale to grab a latte and thought you might want one too," he said with a shrug.

"Hamish makes lattes?"

He nodded. "And anything else you can think of. The tourists like their choice of beverages, and coffee is a popular choice."

Studying the paper cup, she wondered why the simple gesture had her pulse racing and tried to ignore it. "Thank you."

"My pleasure." He sounded so sincere. *Was he?*

She snapped back to reality when he pulled out a chair across from her. "What are you doing?"

"Do you mind if I join you? Or if you feel I'll distract you, I can go to another table?" he teased.

"Was that meant to be funny because there is only one table?"

"It wasn't."

"Not really." A smirk tugged at her lips. It felt strange to be joking with him, after what had transpired last night and then again this morning. "But it's fine. I'm a big girl. I think I can handle it."

She regretted her decision immediately when he sat across from her and used that sexy smile of his. Now she'd never get anything done.

She was wrong and Will was right. The latte was just the kick that she needed and thankfully, he kept his promise. When she'd decided that she had put in enough time for one day, she began tidying up. When looked across at Will she noticed he had already put his laptop back into his carrying case and tucked his papers neatly into a zippered folder. He watched her from his side of the table with his legs stretched out before him and his muscular arms crossed over his chest.

"How long have you been packed up?"

He looked at his bulky black watch. "About half an hour."

"If you're finished, why are you still here?"

"I was waiting for you. I'll walk you home now that it's getting dark."

Dark? She turned to the window and saw nothing but black.

"I didn't realise I've been here that long." She hurried to collect her bag, stuffing her laptop in its case, then jammed her papers in on top of it. "Go, home Will. You must be starving, and I'm sure Lucy is as well."

"It's not that late, it's only six. I'll survive."

They headed out of the door, Will turned off the lights, threw the inside lock and closed the door.

"Where did the librarian go?"

"She went home about an hour ago. I told her I would lock up."

"Oh!" She felt a bit guilty about not paying attention to the library hours. "I didn't know the library closed at five."

"Don't worry. I often stay later than Grace. Besides, you looked as though you were getting a lot done, I didn't want to break your concentration." He swung his bag over his shoulder. "New kids' book you're working on?"

"Mmm." She gazed up. He was being nice again. First, the coffee, then leaving her alone to work, staying late so he could close up the library, and now walking her home. This was weird, no man was this selfless.

They walked side by side in silence towards Duncan's lane. She wanted to ask him why he was interested in her, there was certainly more fish in the sea and more willing ones to be caught. Scared of his answer, she asked instead, "Do you work at the library a lot? I would have thought with owning your own business that you would have all the tools you need at home. Or an office?"

"I have an office in London and a smaller one in Edinburgh. But I like working from here. I work at home in the mornings, and by the time the afternoon hits I need a change. So I go to The Black Ale and monopolise one of the booths or I head to the library. Sometimes I say to hell with it and take Lucy for a run or I stop in to see Duncan."

"So…you and Duncan are friends?"

"Yes." He paused. "Why are you so surprised?"

"It's just that I've never seen a younger man socialise with a man old enough to be his grandfather," she admitted.

"I've known Duncan most of my life. He was good friends with my grandfather, so we have a common history. He's very smart, lots of wisdom to offer, and I enjoy his company. You don't define your friends by a certain criteria, do you?"

"No." She shook her head. "I could never do that. I love each of my friends for who they are. I didn't mean anything by it. I'm glad you're friends with Duncan. But don't you find him grumpy a lot of the time?"

The rich sound of his laugh made her smile. "Yes, but I've gotten used to it. Though, since he found out you were coming he seems to have toned it down a bit."

"Really?" she mused. "That's nice to hear."

They walked in silence the rest of the way, and once again, they stood face to face on Duncan's doorstep. Meghan stiffened, preparing herself for what would happen next. Her heart raced and her lips tingled in anticipation.

"Good night, Meghan." He touched her waist with his warm hands, slowly pulling her forward. Her eyes closed, her heart leapt and he...kissed her forehead. "Sweet dreams." Meghan snapped her eyes open and stared up at him.

She was so dazed by his actions that, when he opened the door, he had to actually nudge her inside. Then as he reached for the handle, he gave her a wink, then closed the door.

What the hell? Dumbfounded, Meghan stood staring at the inside of the door. What had just happened and why was she feeling so disappointed? She had told him that they should only be friends. She had no right to feel disappointed. Did she?

Chapter Eight

Will's so-called patience was coming to an end. It had been two weeks of him keeping up a steady stream of torment. Meghan had run by every morning, and each time he'd been waiting for her. She'd stop and take the bottle of water he'd offered her, then the tormenting would commence. Some days he hadn't spoken to her all and had simply stared at her, which wasn't hard to do. He liked how her face got pink from her run, and the way her hair curled at the back of her neck. Other days he had been a little more to the point. One day he'd offered to give her a rub down. "All hard working athletes need a good rub down, now and again."

"Oh yah?"

"Mmm. It's good for the circulatory system."

"No thanks. I don't trust you not to do something...naughty." He'd noticed the taunt instantly.

He'd slowly moved to stand in front of her and had looked down into stunning sapphire pools.

"Naughty." He had nodded slowly. "You can count on it."

She'd backed away from him then, mouth hanging open. That time he'd got the impression that she had been seriously considering his offer. Sadly, she'd shaken her head and had slowly jogged back towards town. He had been close that day, but it had ended in disappointment just like the others.

There had been a few days when his frustration had been at such a dangerous level that he hadn't been able to be near her, the stubborn streak of hers annoying the hell out of him. Not to mention his ego was taking a beating. He had passed on going to the library those days. Which bothered him even more because he actually liked sitting with her, it was a peaceful break from the battle of wills they were engaged in. Although he wasn't the only one affected by this game of theirs. Meghan clearly wasn't having an easy time of it either, sometimes she would just glare over her laptop at him, shaking her head. He had a deep sense of satisfaction on those days.

Even though he was a patient man, he hated that he wasn't progressing as he thought he should be. It was time to turn up the level of play. Placing his full coffee mug on his desk, he went up to his room, threw on his running pants, a long-sleeved T-shirt, grabbed his shoes and headed back down stairs to his office and waited. When he saw her jogging towards his house, he stood at the window. As usual, she stopped and waited for Lucy.

He left his office, opened the front door and set Lucy free. He stepped outside and slowly walked to the front gate. He stretched his legs, then started up the hill behind her.

Will caught the thumping of music before he reached her. Her hair was up in a ponytail again, and the base of her neck looked damp. Her arms were pumping hard, helping to propel her forward. He noticed how she increased her speed every now and again, probably to match the beat of her music. She was working hard trying to climb his hill. He heard her inhaling deeply through her nose and exhaling through her mouth in an effort to control her heavy breathing.

He stayed behind her for a few more minutes when he noticed her breaths becoming raspy, as if she was struggling for air.

Meghan stopped, swearing silently. If it wasn't for her damn lungs she would have made it. She bent forwards, and rested her hands on her thighs. She felt weak, rubbery. She raised a hand and watched it shake uncontrollably. Yet it wasn't that that had her worried. She wasn't getting enough air. Her lungs... She tried to suck in air. Barely got what she needed. Her lungs were closing up on her, making the simple act of inhaling almost impossible. She heard a small whimper as she closed her eyes and dropped to the ground when her knees gave way.

She placed a hand on her chest. Why didn't she stop? She should have known when she felt that familiar heaviness. She struggled to get at her pocket, but her hands were shaking so violently now the simple task had become impossible. Oh God, she needed her meds. Needed them now. Dark edges curled around her vision. The invisible weight refusing to let air enter her lungs. She put a hand to her chest, forcing herself to calm down. She couldn't afford to panic. She whimpered out loud, she felt lightheaded. She yanked on her jacket pocket trying to tug the medicine free when her hand was pushed aside.

"I'm here."

Swaying, she tried to reach for her pocket again mindless of anything else but getting her inhaler.

"Easy, I got it." There was a sudden tugging at her pocket and she forced her eyes to open and struggled to focus. Will was in front of her on his knees, shaking her inhaler. He pulled off the cap, and handed it to her. "Here."

She grabbed it and inhaled the bitter-tasting mist, paused, then bent forward coughing as she tried to suck in more air. Again, she inhaled the mist. Better this time, more meds got in. For a third time she used the inhaler and the tightness began to ease, her vision slowly started to clear and she wasn't as dizzy. She stared at him while she worked to control her breathing, her limbs still shaking. He was alert and focused, his mouth was a straight line as the muscle in his jaw flexed.

"It's okay." She struggled for a breath. "It happens," was all she was able to get out before coughing.

"Is it always this bad?" He frowned, quickly adding, "Don't talk, just nod."

She tilted her head from right to left. "Sometimes?" She nodded.

"Then why do you try to run up this hill?"

She peered up at the ruins then back to him, shrugging.

Will knew where her gaze went, but that was the least of her problems. He watched and listened as she took long ragged breaths. At least she was getting air in now. The only thing he knew about asthma was it could be deadly under extreme circumstances. He felt so goddamn helpless. How could he help her? What could he...?

Instinct took over and he grabbed her hand and held it to his chest.

"Close your eyes, try to focus on my breathing. Try to breathe when I breathe." He shifted his position so he sat with his legs splayed open with Meghan kneeling between them. Covering her hand, he scanned her face as he kept his breathing slow and steady. She was still pale, even her normally pink lips were drained of colour.

She needed a doctor. And if she couldn't get this under control he could have her at Neil's office in less than five minutes. He ran a scenario over in his head and hoped that it wouldn't be too late. Shit, he hated that he couldn't give her the help she needed. He hated feeling so powerless. He clenched his jaw watching her. She looked so fragile, but he knew that she was a fighter. He wiped away a piece of hair that had fallen in her face, and then he gently pulled her forwards until her forehead was touching his shoulder.

"That's it, you can do it. Keep slowing it down, I'll stay here with you for as long as it takes." He then promised softly, "Until it's over."

Once she had control over her breathing, Meghan shivered. She was always freezing after an episode, and completely drained. She clung to his shirt as she rested against his shoulder. She sighed as he gently stroked her back. Feeling his slow deep breaths had helped more than she thought it would have. And he stayed. He didn't freak out like most people would, and he didn't leave.

"Are you ready to go? Can you walk?" His breath was delightfully warm.

She nodded and started to stand.

"Wait, let me get up first." He quickly stood, then helped to her feet. Swaying slightly, she gripped his shirt then heard him order, "Hold onto me." A second later he scooped up in his arms.

"Will." She coughed.

"Don't talk," he soothed.

"Will." Her voice sounded old, rough. "Put me down."

"No."

"I can walk."

"I highly doubt that at the moment." His sharp tone proved he was annoyed with her. "So stop arguing with me."

"I'm not a child, put me down." She put as much force into her demand as possible but it came out as more of a whispered plea.

He stopped in his tracks. "Ten minutes ago ye collapsed from lack of oxygen and now you want to walk back down the hill. No way. You and yer pride are going to have tae tough this one out. So hold on to me," he ordered.

Biting her lip, she did as he asked and held him tight around his neck.

"Once I get ye back to my house, I'm going to give the local doctor a call. I want him to have a look at you." His tone was commanding. She half smiled. He must have thought that she would argue with him again, and any other time she would have, but right now she was just too tired. Relaxing into him, she welcomed his body heat and allowed it to sooth away her chill.

Chapter Nine

Will sat silently on the edge of his desk and listened as Meghan explained what had happened during her attack. Neil Ramsey, the village doctor, gave Meghan a once-over in his office but only after Will stubbornly refused to leave the room. He couldn't leave her alone yet, he wasn't ready.

Neil quickly confirmed that she'd had an attack, and gave her some stronger medication. Handing her a prescription for refills, he stressed, "Take it easy for the next couple of days and get lots of rest. Call me if you have any problems but if not I'll see you next week." He stood, picking up his bag. "And hold off on the running until I give you the go-ahead. Okay?"

She nodded. "Okay."

"Good. Now go home and rest."

By the end of the exam, irritation had set in. Meghan had been running up that hill every day for two weeks. Two weeks! Was this the first attack, or was it one among many? And all so she could get to those bloody ruins? He wished Neil had told her no hills at all. It was the least she deserved for being so foolish.

Then again, having asthma, shouldn't she know better?

Will walked Neil to the door.

"Will" — Neil turned to face him — "tell Duncan he needs to keep a close eye on her for the next twenty-four hours, if she starts to cough or wheeze make sure she uses the inhaler I gave her, then give me a ring."

"Do you think she will have another attack?" Will found himself tensing at the thought of Meghan going through that again. What if the next time was worse? What if he wasn't there to help?

"Sometimes…not all the time, the attack appears to be over until a small amount of physical strain or excitement aggravates it again. Or it could be as simple as Meghan coming into contact with a trigger," Neil explained.

"Trigger? What, like dust or some type of pollen?"

"Exactly." Neil started to walk away, then called over his shoulder, "Don't forget. Have Duncan call me if anything else happens."

Will closed the door, and leaned against it. 'Have Duncan call him.' Will huffed. If Meghan needed to be watched for the next twenty-four hours, he would do it and he would be the one to call if there were any problems. There was no way he could walk away from her now. She could have another attack. This wasn't over and he had made her a promise to stay with her until it was. So, 'just friends' or not, they were about to spend their first night together.

He entered his study and found Meghan standing next to his leather couch, pulling her sweat shirt on. She was still pale and her movements seemed stiff as though they required all of her strength.

She sat back down and pulled on her shoes. Did she think that he would send her on her merry way?

"Where do ye think you are going?" It had been settled, he wasn't letting her out of his sight, she didn't have a choice.

"Home," she informed him, lacing up her shoes. "And I would appreciate if you didn't snap at me."

He walked over to stand in front of her. "You're staying here where I can watch you and help ye if you need it. And I wasn't snapping at you, I was askin' a question."

"Yes, you are snapping at me because your accent becomes thick when you're wound up." Her tone was quiet as she pointed out the one character flaw he couldn't always hide. She stood, swaying slightly until he held her by the waist. "Please, Will, I don't want to argue with you." She sighed, "I just want to go home."

The exhausted plea put a crack in his armour.

"If you feel the need to watch over me that's fine, can you at least do it at Duncan's house?"

"Wait here," he conceded. "I'll be two minutes. I just want to grab a bag with a change of clothes." He softened his tone as he reached to tuck a loose strand of hair behind her ear again. "Then I'll take you home."

They ran into Duncan as they entered the house. "I just heard, I was on my way." He looked her over. "My God, you're pale." He pulled Meghan into his embrace. He pushed her back and gave her a concerned frown. "I thought you said you hadn't had an attack in over a year?"

"I haven't. I don't know why I had this one. I was only running up the hill by Will's house, I guess it was too much for me today?" She shrugged, trying to act casual about it. She didn't want him to worry.

"The hill that leads to the MacKenzie ruins?" he addressed Will.

"MacKenzie ruins? What?" She glanced up at Will. "Do you own those...?"

Will's attention was on her. "They belong to my family." He then turned back to Duncan and confirmed his question, "Yes, that hill."

"I knew you were going to go out for runs, but that hill is very steep. That was a foolish thing to do, Meghan Kennedy. Were you trying to kill yourself?" he demanded.

"Of course not, that's a silly question."

"Then why were you doing such a silly thing? You should know better. And you—" He turned his attention to Will, who up until that point, had been looking smug and nodding his head in agreement.

"Me?" he asked, raising an eyebrow. "What about me?"

Meghan nodded. At least she wasn't the only one catching hell.

"Why didn't you call me and tell what happened right away? I had to hear about it from Neil, who dropped by to tell me."

Will's appeared calm yet his jaw was clenched when he answered, "My main concern was for Meghan and getting Neil over to have a look at her, not calling you." Then he added, "Did Neil tell you he wants us to watch her for the next twenty-four hours, to make sure she doesn't have another attack?" He looked Duncan in the eye. "So I'll be spending the night."

"He thinks she'll have another one?" Concern washed over his face.

Meghan automatically reached out for him. "Please don't worry. I'll be fine." She turned to Will and mumbled, "Big mouth."

His retort was to raise a single dark eyebrow at her, then focus on Duncan stressing, "Precautionary measure."

Duncan gripped Meghan's hands. "I will always worry about you, lass." He looked back at Will, asking, "Does he know what triggered it?"

"Running, I believe." Duncan nodded.

Meghan gawked at the two men. "Neil wasn't a hundred per cent sure if it was the running. He said I shouldn't run for a week and he'll let me know when I can start again."

"You're not running up that hill again, Meghan," Will ordered.

"He's right, no more hills," Duncan agreed.

She huffed and started for the stairs. "Oh, for God's sake."

"Meghan." Will's voice held an underlying warning to it.

She turned and faced him. "I'm not a fool." Then looked to Duncan. "And I'm not a child. I'll wait to hear what Neil has to say first, before I continue with my running. Now if you don't mind, I think I'll go up to my room and lie down." She knew that they were concerned about her. She just wasn't in the mood to be lectured.

Once in her room, she went straight to bed and climbed onto the puffy quilt. She rested back onto the pillows and took a few deep breaths. Not so bad now. She placed a hand to her chest and remembered Will's gentle touch and softly whispered words. The act had been simple, but the comfort it had given her had been beyond measure. What if she was wrong about him? What if he wasn't like Rob? That would be nice. It wouldn't be hard to fall for Will, in fact it would be too easy and if she wasn't careful it would happen without her noticing.

* * * *

She had slept the afternoon away, and vaguely remembered movement around her room but had been too tired to see who it was or what they had been doing. When Meghan finally woke, it was dusk and she felt as though she had been put through a meat grinder. Standing, she cringed when her limbs screamed, protesting the movement. So she grabbed the edge of the bed and stretched, finally admitting to herself — only — that she might have overdone it. After a quick shower, she changed threw on a pair of comfortable yoga pants and a T-shirt and headed slowly downstairs.

When she reached the bottom of the stairs, Will was waiting.

"I was about to come up and wake you." His dark eyebrows pushed together. "How do you feel? Still tired?"

"Yes, very tired. But not bad considering."

"Come on, we made you some soup." He held out his hand. She hesitated, then decided to take it, only because she was afraid her legs might give out on her.

Yah, blame your legs.

After forcing down a bowl of the delicious soup, the three of them went to the sitting room. Meghan watched some TV while Duncan and Will talked quietly together. When the point came that she couldn't keep her eyes open, she stood and said goodnight to Duncan and gave him a kiss on the cheek.

"I'm sorry I scared you today. I'll try not to do it again."

In his normal gruff tone Duncan responded, "See that you don't."

She looked to Will and rolled her eyes.

He smothered a smile and stood. "'Night Duncan." He followed her upstairs, and right into her room.

"Umm," she began. "What are you doing?"

"Following doctor's orders." Then sauntering past her, he settled his large frame onto one of the wingback chairs in her room.

"So you plan on spending the night sitting in that chair watching me? That's ridiculous...and a little creepy."

He laughed. "Sit in this chair, yes. Watch you all night, maybe a little, but I'd plan on reading a little too." She hadn't noticed the book he had until he mentioned it. "And after what happened today, no, it's not ridiculous."

"But it is creepy," she pointed out then snatched her pj's off the end of the bed and marched to the attached bathroom.

Once changed, she gave him a good frown as she pulled back the covers on her bed. "Will, I'll be fine."

"I told you I would stay with you until it was over." There was a velvety twist to his tone. "Go to sleep."

She watched him from the bed as he rested one of his ankles on the opposite knee.

Would you look at the size of those feet.

Her breath caught and she quickly looked in another direction as she climbed onto the bed. *He has big hands too, right?*

"Meghan? What is it?" His concerned tone had her focusing on his face, while hers heated up.

"I'm feet...I mean I'm fine," she quickly corrected. She groaned and pulled up the covers, then flopped her head onto the pillow, trying to block out the image of large feet and hands.

Meghan was alluring during the day, but when she was lying in her bed she was even more so. The book Will had brought with him was supposed to be a distraction. Unfortunately, all good intentions were thrown out of the window when she started to turn in her sleep. First, a long bare leg draped across the top of the blankets. He stared at the silky limb for a long time before he forced himself back to the book he was holding. Turning a second time caused the blanket to lower, revealing full breasts straining against her shirt. What broke his restraint was when she lifted her arms over her head and the movement pulled her T-shirt up, exposing the flat smooth plain of her stomach.

So much for reading. He tossed the book to the floor and placed his head in his hands. Instantly, images of her ran through his head like an erotic film. His mouth pulling on those lush breasts, kissing the quivering skin of her stomach, caressing her bare legs, cupping her slick heat.

Jerking up, he paced around the room, and automatically searched for her form lying beneath the covers. He ran a hand over his face. He wasn't dense. He knew when he was fighting a losing battle. Out of sheer desperation, he began reasoning with himself. She was in such a deep sleep that she probably wouldn't notice if he joined her.

No! He couldn't do that. It wasn't right. He should leave, it would be better for both of them that way. A dark thought caused him to frown. What if she had another attack and he couldn't hear her? Every muscle in his body clenched tight at the idea.

He paused. It was a familiar tightness that he had experienced once before, and he knew with his entire being that it was Meghan he had walked away from. A memory whirled into focus before him—Meghan, with tears trailing down her cheeks, her hands shaking as she waved one final time. That sad look on her face had nearly killed him. He blinked and the memory he never knew he had vanished. He studied the beauty lying on the bed. No! He couldn't leave her, wouldn't leave her. His mind was made up.

He sighed again. *"Shit!"* He mumbled softly as he approached her still form. *I won't even touch her,* he promised. *Just…stretch out beside her.*

That promise was broken the very second he joined her. It was pure instinct to pull her into his arms, and she came to him without any resistance. Would it be that easy if she had been awake? It didn't matter. He'd enjoy it and be out before she woke up. It had been an eternity since that last time he'd kissed her, so holding her would have to tide him over until she finally came around.

Whenever that would be. He didn't understand her. The attraction between them was strong, yet she was fighting it. Something was stopping her, that much was obvious, but what? Maybe he should speak with Duncan. He didn't like the idea of asking for help, especially from her grandfather, but Duncan might be able to answer a few of his questions.

He sighed when Meghan shifted next to him. No point in thinking about it until morning. Raising his head, he checked once again that Meghan's inhaler was still within reach. It was sitting in front of an old picture. He stared at the photo. He picked out Meghan right away. She appeared to be in her late teens and was standing next to her mother with her father and brothers behind her. The photo was definitely a favourite, the edges ripped and the corners worn, its appearance and location a dead giveaway of its importance.

Resting his head back, he focused on the woman next to him, content with the way her soft form moulded into his side. They were a good fit, even though she was under the covers and he on top. They fit. Meghan's head rested on his shoulder. He covered the small hand on his chest, gently stroking his thumb against her smooth skin. This felt right.

Meghan bolted upright, her heart pounding. It was just a dream. Her breaths came in short choppy bursts. Not real. She had dreamt that she had had another attack but this time it had been worse, she hadn't been able to breathe at all. She had been by herself on the hill that led to the ruins. Rob had come walking up to her laughing and dangling her inhaler in front of her, then Duncan and Will had been there laughing too. Saying this was what she deserved for not listening to them. She placed a shaky hand on her chest and breathed deeply.

She jumped when the bed shifted.

"Meghan? You okay?"

"Will?"

"I'm here." The bedside lamp snapped on and there he was, sitting next to her, concern on his shadowed face.

She blinked. "Wh-what are you doing here?"

"Sleeping, 'til you sat up. What's wrong?"

She scanned the length of him stretched out on top of the covers. He was wearing the same T-shirt and jeans, but was now haphazardly covered by the throw blanket she kept on the end of her bed.

"Are you okay?" He spoke each word carefully as he touched her thigh, her inhaler tucked inside his fist.

"I'm...okay. Just a dream." Her heart stopped. Her inhaler—he was holding her inhaler, ready to help her, again. Pulling in a shaky breath, she felt a slight vibration flow through her. "Why are you sleeping here?"

"I'm used to staying in this room. Duncan allowed me to stay here a few nights while I had some renovations done on my house. I'd hate to break a tradition," he teased.

"Will." She sighed. "You shouldn't be here. It's not good for..." She stopped before the confession tumbled out.

"Not good for what?" he prompted.

Not good for her. She couldn't be this close to him because it was so good, and that was bad. Very bad. She tried to get out of the bed. "Please, Will."

He reached out quickly and held her in place. "Relax. I was getting tired and I didn't want to leave you and go into the other room where I might not hear you. I can go back to the chair if you want me to?"

She studied the covers. She couldn't deny that she had been relieved when she had seen him. But this closeness...oh man.

"So that's what you're worried about?" He paused as she looked away. "That I might jump you and that you might like it?"

How does he know?

"No!" She snapped her head back to face him. "That's not what I said." Was she that obvious?

"You don't want me to go, do you?"

She was already having a hard time when it came to Will. Yet, despite all of that, she didn't want him to go. Shaking her head, she felt embarrassed by her weakness.

"Good," he sighed, resting his head back. "That chair is no' as comfortable as it looks."

She frowned, hating how casual he was about everything when she felt tied up in knots.

She slipped under the covers, knots and all, her muscles painfully tight as he turned out the lights. He rolled back, his shoulder grazing hers, and her body flinched. He swore under his breath before he pulled her into his side and forced her head in the hollow of his shoulder. "Relax, I promise I won't bite." His attempt to reassure her didn't help.

"You biting me isn't what I'm worried about."

"You should be. It's possible."

She stiffened.

"Shit!" He lifted her head with a single finger under her chin. "Meghan." Their lips were inches apart. She could feel his breath, warm on her face. "I'm not so selfish as to try to take advantage of you when you're not feeling well."

At that moment, she wished that he would, and as though he had been reading her mind, her heart stopped as he brushed his lips against hers in an excruciatingly sweet kiss. The pressure of his mouth on hers was brief. "That's it, I promise. Now go to sleep."

Like that's going to happen.

* * * *

Looking down at the paper in his hands Rob checked the name of the school again — Green Grove Elementary. This was the school. Jack must be six or seven by now. He hadn't seen him since before Meg's cop brother had arrested him. He remembered that the kid had light brown hair and Jessica's amber eyes. Jessica, now there was a hot woman, he should have hit on her instead. The only reason that he hadn't was because of the cautious vibe he had got from her, so he had set his sights on Meg, the wild child. Jessica had never trusted him, and she had shared that feeling with Meg more than once. If he was lucky, Jessica had kept her feelings to herself and not shared them with her kid.

This was his last resort, Jessica and her kid must know where Meg had gone. Going to Meg's apartment was a desperate act. Then running into Ryan had been bad luck and put him back on the cop's radar, something he had been trying to avoid since he had got out. He couldn't go to her parents, they would tell Ryan about his visit. He couldn't go to either Jody or Jessica, they too would tell the cop, so that left Jack.

Getting out of his black Porsche, he pulled his black leather coat closed against the damp fall air as the school bell rang. School was out for the weekend, and a wall of snot-nosed little midgets burst through the doors. Pulling the bright envelope from his pocket with Meghan's name on it, Rob crossed the residential street onto the school grounds. He didn't have to wait long before he spotted Jack and waited for the boy to pass him.

He plastered on a fake smile. "Hey, Jack," he called out.

The boy stopped before he had reached him and eyed him nervously. He had a friend on either side of him, and they too were looking at him with caution.

Great! He held up his hands, and stood still. He didn't want the kid to bolt on him.

"Sorry, I didn't mean to scare you. I'm not sure if you remember me, my name is Rob."

The boy nodded his head. "You're Aunt Meg's friend."

"That right. I'm Aunt Meg's friend," he said sarcastically.

"Aunt Meg isn't here."

Rob laughed trying to ease the boy. "Yes, I know. She's in Scotland."

The boy nodded his head, keeping a watchful gaze on him. Jack's friends stood valiantly by his side.

"Actually, that's why I'm here. I have this letter that I want to send to her but I lost her address in Scotland." He held out the letter and purposely turned the front of the envelope in Jack's direction, so he was able to see the name. "I went to see your mom at the hospital but she was too busy to help me. Could you help me?"

"Mom says I have to go home with Tommy, until she comes and gets me. I'm not allowed...Mom says I shouldn't..."

"Your mom is right. You shouldn't talk to strangers. But I'm not a stranger, besides I don't want you to come with me anywhere, I'm in a hurry. I was passing by and just thought you knew Aunt Meg's address, I know she is staying with her grandfather but like I said, I lost the address. And I don't want to bother Ryan. He's a real busy guy."

"Yeah, he catches lots of bad guys."

"Hmm. He sure does." He paused, the boy he wasn't as nervous now that he realised that Rob wasn't going to kidnap him. "So, do you remember the address? I'd like to mail this to her."

"I know she is in Scotland, Mom showed me where it was on our map. I can't remember the name of the little town but it's near high hills."

"You mean the Highlands?"

"Yeah, the Highlands. I don't remember the address. Mom has it in her book at home."

"Her address book?"

"Yeah, she had lots of stuff in there. She doesn't like when I touch it and always puts in up on the top of the fridge. I can still reach it though."

"You can?"

"Yeah, but it only has names and numbers in it. Real boring stuff, no pictures at all."

"Sure sounds it. Well, I guess I'll try visiting your mom at work again, or maybe I'll come by and say hi. You guys still live behind the school?"

The boy paused and slowly nodded his head.

"Cool! Well, gotta go, see you later, Jack." He turned from the boys, smiling. Address book on the top of the fridge. "I wonder how high the fridge really is?" Rob mumbled to himself.

Chapter Ten

Will scrubbed at his face as he stood quietly outside of Meghan's room. He needed to go home and get some sleep, God knew he hadn't slept last night. Jesus, kissing Meghan had been a mistake. That one little kiss had kept him awake all night while she had slept peacefully next to him. It was his own damn fault. But he kept his promise, holding her and nothing more — except for torturing himself.

Punishment fully deserved for exaggerating the truth. He was a grown man and his best excuse he could come up with to share her bed was that a chair was uncomfortable. Pathetic. It was a good thing she didn't know anything about the SBS. His years spent in the Navy had him used to staying in uncomfortable positions for hours at a time, so he was more than capable of sitting there the entire night. He knew, however, that if he was in the same position he would do it again.

Moving silently down the stairs, he threw on his jacket and was reaching for the front door when Duncan came out from the kitchen.

"Any problems?"

Fuck, where do I begin? "No. She's still sleeping."

"How about you? Get any sleep?"

"No. I told you I would stay up and watch her." Which was a form of the truth.

"So you did." Duncan nodded. "Were you comfortable?"

Will wasn't startled by the sudden question. There was no way anyone could have got in that room without him knowing, including Duncan. "Not bad."

"Not the first time for you though, is it? Your time in the Navy must have gotten you use to that sort of thing?"

Will nodded. "Mmm." Although watching Meghan was harder than anything he had had to do while in the Navy. "I'm heading home, get a couple hours' kip. I'll come and check on Meghan later."

"You don't need to do that. She'll be okay, I'm here."

Will fought to keep his irritation hidden. The idea of being kept away from Meghan didn't sit well. Then he caught Duncan's mischievous glint.

Still, he clarified his point. "I'll be back this afternoon." He then thought to ask, "Then if you have nothing planned I would like to talk to you about something important?"

Duncan must have caught his serious expression. "Is anything wrong boy?"

He didn't know how to ask so he just laid it out. "I want to ask you a few questions about Meghan."

"Like what?"

"Meghan is beautiful."

"Yes, she is," Duncan agreed before turning towards his office. Will frowned. Where the hell was he going? "Come in, boy." Duncan stood in the door. "Privacy is needed."

"It is?" he asked, closing the door.

Duncan sat behind his desk. "Continue."

"I enjoy spending time with her and I know she feels the same way…"

"Are you asking for my permission to date her?" Duncan leant back in his chair.

"Yes. No. She claims she isn't interested." Will gripped the back of the leather chair facing Duncan's desk.

"Maybe she isn't," Duncan pointed out, linking his fingers.

"She's lying."

"You're certain?"

Crossing his arms, Will nodded. "Absolutely."

"Well then" — Duncan smiled — "I guess you better sit down. I have a story for you."

* * * *

Meghan was having the worst time concentrating. She was supposed to be working, but her thoughts were swimming with Will and the dream she'd had. Not the nightmare but the erotic dream with her as Will's main course.

She'd dreamt that he had been finding the answer to his question about what her skin tasted like. His lips had brushed her fingers gently. Then slowly he had licked and nibbled his way over to a shoulder where he had pressed his mouth down and moaned. Then he had been at her breasts trailing his hot tongue between the sensitive valley, while tormenting her hard nipples. When he had finally reached her thighs she had been so achy and wet she hadn't been able to wait any long and had begged him to fuck her with his mouth. His hypnotic brown gaze had flashed as he had lowered his head...and damn it, hadn't she woken up, and in the same condition she'd been in her dream, wet and achy. She thanked God when she had realised he had already left.

What was she going to do? He was such a delicious temptation. She didn't want him thinking that she was starting to give in, even though she wanted to so badly.

The last experience with a tempting male was Rob Cummings. Tall, dark and slimy. He was so slick that she hadn't seen it coming. Swept her right off her feet and thrown her into a world of lies. She had known that something hadn't been right when picture ID and other identification had been missing from her wallet only to reappear a few days later. She'd wanted to believe it had only been her mind playing tricks on her, then her bank had called. Bounced cheques, money missing, all her savings gone. That day she'd gone home to her small two-bedroom apartment to confront him, only to catch him with some blonde bimbo—and in her bed! Yuck! That was the day she'd bought a new mattress and had given Rob the official title of Dickhead.

What a pain in the ass it had been. She had had to change everything, her banking information, her social insurance number, anything that had had any personal information attached to it. Ryan had helped her with the police report—having a cop in the family had its perks. That same week, Ryan had told her that Rob had been wanted in connection to ten other crimes, all with the same MO. Rob had then been arrested, but because there wasn't enough proof he had been given a light sentence of eight months and he had only got that because she had testified against him in court. Eight months? What that hell was that?

Short, that was what. And not nearly enough time for him to meet the real criminals and become someone's bitch.

After Rob, she hadn't had much left. Emotionally or financially. She'd been working non-stop to get back what had been taken. She rested her head in her hand, staring blankly at her laptop. Well, at least one good thing had come out of her time spent with Dickhead — she had realised that she wasn't the only airhead in Toronto who had fallen for his slick moves. Yet it had come with a price, she had wanted nothing more to do with men. Until now. Until Will.

She had mixed emotions when it came to Will. She liked him and he wasn't asking for anything. The only thing he wanted was…her. But she was scared. What if it happened again? Rob had treated her so badly and she had let him. She was still so ashamed of herself and terrified that it would happen again. No, it was safer if they were just friends — that way no one would get hurt. She would have to keep fighting the temptation and hopefully soon he would give up and find someone more willing. Although, the idea of Will finding another to torment had her heart sinking into her stomach.

Needing a distraction, she pushed out of her chair, deciding to go to the kitchen for a cup of tea. She was just passing the front door when it opened and Will walked in. She was so surprised to see him that she just stood there like an idiot, staring up at him. She had just being thinking about him and now there he was.

The darkest ring of brown in his eyes stood out as he stared back. Not saying a word, his sultry gaze drifted down her body, then back to her face. She shivered with excitement.

She forced herself to take a step back. "Don't do that." Her voice barely a whisper.

The corners of his mouth curled up. "Do I make you nervous?"

"No, it's just...you..." She couldn't seem to get the words out. His mouth was a sinful distraction.

He took a step closer to her, concern replacing his sexy smile. "You look much better today." She had never met anyone who could turn expressions on and off as quickly as Will. Even his eyes were back to the same dark brown that surrounded the toffee-coloured centre. "Any more bad dreams?"

"Nope." Her voice cracked as the flash of his wicked grin popped into her head. She cleared her throat then tried again. "No dreams at all."

His eyebrows pushed together as he nodded.

"Thank you," she blurted out. "For helping me yesterday morning and..." She bit her lip and felt her face flush. "And for last night."

He studied her. "You're not used to having anyone help you?"

"No, I'm not. I can take care of myself."

"I don't doubt it."

A silence fell between them. God, she was pretty, her face had a fresh glow, her cheeks were flushed with colour, and her lips were back to being a light pink. Better, much better.

Of course, last night was still lingering in his mind and seeing her brought it all back, her softness pressed up against him, her light breath feeling like a gentle stroke on his skin. His body reacted so swiftly to the memory, that he didn't have time to hide his desire. She shivered while he stared at her and he watched, amazed, as her turquoise eyes turned almost completely blue.

He was right. She wanted him. Just as much as he wanted her, the proof was there in her eyes. Why hadn't he picked it up before? Relief swept through him. Maybe he wouldn't need the contract after all, maybe he should just continue with the way things were? But he had done that for weeks now and hadn't gained any ground.

At that moment, Duncan walked out of the kitchen. "Will." He nodded and handed him a leather case.

He nodded in return, his throat becoming tight and painful.

The contract. Jesus, he still couldn't believe it was real.

"I didn't realise you were here to see Duncan, I would have gotten him for you."

He tucked the case under his arm, smiling at her. "I wanted to see how you were feeling." He nodded to Duncan. "Thanks."

Duncan returned the nod and walked away.

"I'll come back later, see how you're doing." He began closing the door when he saw her raise her chin.

"I'm fine, it's over. You can stop watching over me now."

God, he loved that feisty attitude. "I'll see you later." And closed the door on her frown.

Chapter Eleven

The Black Ale was all but deserted in the middle of the day, only Hamish and his wife were present. Hamish brought Will a drink, chatted for a few minutes, then went about his business.

Will didn't usually drink this early in the day, yet took a big mouthful of his pint.

'Don't bother reading if you don't want Meghan,' Duncan had warned.

Will rested a hand on either side of the case and stared down at the old leather. The marriage contract was inside. A marriage contract that was agreed upon by the MacKenzies and Kennedys over eight hundred years before.

"What's this?" he had asked when Duncan had placed the case in front of him. "I just want—"

"Meghan," Duncan had finished.

Will had studied Duncan. There had been no surprise, no displeasure, no joy, just acceptance. "But you already know that."

"Do you see me walking around with a white cane and a Seeing Eye dog? Of course, I know. You think I didn't notice the way you were looking at her. Which, by the by, was not proper, Meghan is my granddaughter not some hot-to-trot hussy."

Will had laughed at the description, despite the nature of their conversation.

"This is not funny, Will," Duncan had snapped.

"No, it's not." He'd cleared his throat. "I know she's not a hussy." Will had met Duncan's stare. "And you're right, I shouldn't have disrespected her or you for that matter. I'm sorry, Duncan. I was out of line asking you about this. Meghan is your granddaughter, you're just being protective. I'd act the same way if the tables were turned." Shit, who was he kidding? If the roles had been reversed and Meghan was his granddaughter, he would be reaching across the table and strangling the bastard.

"I never said I wouldn't help you. Respecting Meghan's decision would be the proper thing to do, that doesn't mean it's the right choice." Will had studied the older man, keeping his surprise hidden.

That was when he'd told Will what was in the leather case.

Will had laughed out loud when Duncan had told him, he hadn't been able to help himself. An eight-hundred-year-old marriage contract that still hadn't been fulfilled. It was the most ridiculous thing he had ever heard.

"Meghan deserves a man who is financially sound, who will protect her, respect her, and a man who will love her. I don't want her going through what she went through this past year."

"What did she go through?"

Duncan had sighed, clasping his hands as he'd leaned over his desk. "Now, I don't want her knowing that I told you this. I don't think she even knows that

Ryan told me what happened to her." He'd paused, waiting for Will's agreement.

Of course he had agreed.

"I'm going to make it short. You don't need to know all the details. Meghan was involved with a man who she had apparently been quite happy with, and he appeared to be taken with her. When she began to notice strange things happening."

By the time Duncan had recounted the whole story, Will had found that he had been fuming with a strong desire to fly to Toronto. He had wanted to hunt down this Rob and beat some sense into him. Men who preyed on women or children were scum and it sickened him that some men actually enjoyed it.

"Finally he was arrested and charged with ten counts of theft," Duncan continued.

"Ten counts?" Shit. He still hadn't been able to believe it. So, it wasn't that Meghan was an easy target. Rob had just been that good. Will's urge to pay Rob a visit had grown.

"Meghan was one of many."

Will had frowned. "But why Meghan?"

"I've no idea. Duncan had shaken his head. "So you see. This is why I want those things for Meghan. I want her to be happy."

Will peered out of the window next to the booth and systematically went over Duncan's list. He was far from rich, but his business was doing well. His protective instinct had clearly taken hold where she was concerned, and he had already proven he was being respectful. With the amount of patience he had shown over the past weeks, if he didn't respect her she would have already shared his bed and his conversation with Duncan would never have happened.

'A man who will love her.'

He had never been in love before. Mind you, he'd never had a chance to find out until now. He was always in between tours or training. It was never hard to find someone to share his bed, there had just never been enough time to see if love had been there. Did he love Meghan? He knew that he cared for her. There was no doubt about that—but love. He swallowed another mouthful of his pint as he contemplated the leather case.

He honestly didn't know. But he felt the blood rush through his veins and his adrenaline kick in. The same feelings would stir before he went out on an op, that feeling of excitement to get into the action and the dread of not knowing what the outcome would be.

When he hadn't answered the question, Duncan had asked another. "How would you feel if you saw Meghan with another man?'

Even now, the thought had him squeezing his hands into fists. There was nothing like a little jealousy to bring one's true feelings to the surface. Jesus, he had fallen right into that one.

Duncan had laughed.

"You find this funny?" Will had snapped.

"Now whose temper has been pricked?" the old man teased.

"My temper is fine."

Duncan had laughed harder. "You'll probably have a tough time with Meghan. She's a stubborn lass, it won't be easy."

"I've noticed that flaw, thanks," he'd bit out.

"It's not a flaw, boy, it's a good trait. You'll come to recognise the difference."

"Another pint, Will?"

Will turned his head to see Hamish standing next to the table. "Sorry?"

Hamish threw a drying towel over his shoulder and slid into the opposite side of the booth. "Duncan told you about the contract?"

"You know about it?"

"Oh aye! When that there contract was first agreed upon, the other men present were ordered to help fulfil it."

Exhaling he asked patiently, "What other men?"

"The MacGregor, the Campbell, the Ross, the Cameron. All lairds of their respective clans."

Will felt his mouth drop open. "You, Ray and Stewart all know about this?"

Hamish raised his greying eyebrows and leaned his elbows onto the table. "Why do you think all our families are so close?"

Shit. Will sat back. *It's true.* He had known each of those families his entire life, spending time with one or the other from as far back as he could remember.

"It's been this way since the day that" — he pointed to the leather case — "was written."

"Who gave the order?" Will studied the old leather.

"The Bruce."

Will levelled his gaze. "Pardon?"

"You heard me." Hamish slid out of the booth. "Go home, read it in private. Then come back later. Rangers are at Dundee. The lads will be here."

Will sat in the booth finishing off his pint before he left for the library. He hadn't planned on going today. He wanted to get home and get some calls out of the way. But after what Duncan, then Hamish had told him, he found he was making his way over before he could change his mind. Once there, he flipped open the case and pulled the old parchment free. He spent an hour reading it, looking up words in Gaelic that he was unfamiliar with, marking them down on the copy he had made.

With doubt still lingering, he finished translating the contract and began searching through the National Archives website. Will was proud of his heritage and he had thought he knew most of his family's history. He didn't, however, remember reading or hearing about any marriage contract.

Scrolling through the webpage, he caught sight of a formal document.

He recognised the first of the two names, Alasdair William MacKenzie. The second name was Fergus Kennedy, clearly Meghan's relative. Scanning the document, he froze. Then read it a second time. It was identical to the contract sitting in front of him. Sitting back in his chair, he ran his hand through his hair. "Holy shit!"

It was real. There was an eight-hundred-year-old marriage contract between the Kennedys and the MacKenzies. He studied the date again. It was signed June 1314. There was no way it was legitimate, it didn't matter that it was his and Meghan's names were on it. It was written eight hundred years ago, for a different Meghan and a different William. There was no way it was meant for him and Meghan...now...in this time.

Even if it was, it wouldn't help his cause. Meghan had been in a relationship with a man who had manipulated her. He didn't want to force her into a marriage, he wanted her to come willingly. He'd have to be patient with her. For how long though? This business with Meghan was driving him crazy. He was tormenting himself just as much as he was tormenting her. It was time he figured out a new strategy.

The reality suddenly struck him. "Fuck." He leant back in the chair and rubbed the stiff muscles in his shoulders. Was he actually contemplating marriage to a woman who wanted nothing from him but his friendship? He shook his head. He must be out of his mind.

Chapter Twelve

Meghan sat in the library still thinking about the hours before.

She had been packing up her laptop ready to head to the library when Will had walked into the front hall looking tired and distracted. He hadn't given her one sexy stare or word. He'd just handed Duncan a leather case and had nodded. When Duncan had left them alone Will had gazed down at her for what had seemed a very long time then had professed, "I'm glad you're feeling better."

She had been about to tell him to not bother, that she was a fully grown woman who could take care of herself, but had stopped when she'd noticed his look of concern.

"Be careful."

She'd stood staring up at him with her mouth hanging open. "Okay then."

He'd smiled at her stupid comment and had then gently cupped her cheek, "See you later." Then had left her standing there yearning for more of his attention.

Argh! The man was evil and a huge tease.

Looking at the clock, she sighed. She had been there for three hours and hadn't completed a single page. Time to go, there was no point sitting there if she couldn't give her full attention to the work in front of her.

After deciding on a walk, she first logged into her mailbox, and checked her messages before she left. Nothing but junk. Geez, a message from Jody or Jess, or even one from her mother would have been nice, but there was nothing but crap from the same sender. It was the fourth time she had received an email from this particular contact, and it was the strangest address, nothing but numbers. It was odd, she had never seen an email address like it before. And there was no way she would open it, she'd be super-pissed if one of those emails transmitted the E-Clap to her laptop.

After clearing the contents of her mailbox, she started packing up when Grace, Little Glen's librarian, stepped up next to her. "Leaving early?" Grace was a nice lady, in her mid-sixties, with short white hair. She had been the librarian in Little Glen for over twenty years, and therefore knew a lot.

"Yah, I can't seem to focus today. So, I've decided to go for a walk instead, maybe some fresh air will help."

"It usually does. Well, on your travels do you mind dropping this off to Will for me?" Grace handed her several sheets of paper. "He was in here early this morning using the printer and left these behind. I saw him heading over to The Black Ale about an hour ago."

"Sure."

Grace put the pages down on the end of the table while Meghan finished gathering her belongings. She was putting on her coat when she glanced down at the top page and noticed her last name. She saw Grace disappear behind a tall shelf and Meghan quickly snatched up the pages. One was a copy of an old document written in Gaelic and the other appeared to be the translation. She scanned the first. Guess her parents were right, learning Gaelic wasn't a complete waste of time.

By the time she was done reading she was so dazed, she had to sit down. She read the translated version just in case she had mixed up some words—like 'marriage'! She placed the papers gently down on the table and stared at them. Maybe she was mistaken? Maybe she had read it wrong? She picked it up and read it for a third time.

No, no. She had read it right. Her stomach suddenly flipped and a heavy weight made her gag. "Oh, my God." She swallowed hard fighting the urge to throw up.

This was a marriage contract and her name was on it. What the... How had he... "Oh my God!" Her head was spinning with questions. What was he doing with this? How did he even know about this thing? Was this why he kept pressuring her? Was this the reason why he was interested in her? To fulfil a stupid marriage contract?

Anger swelled in her chest as her stomach rolled. *Who in the hell does he think he is?* No one would force her to do anything. It wasn't 1314—arranged marriages were extinct. This contract would get him nothing but a good kick in the ass. God, she couldn't believe that he was doing this and she had been having doubts about him. She felt disappointed and foolish. *Guess he wasn't different after all.* Snatching up the remaining pages, she called out to Grace, "You said Will's at The Black Ale?"

"Aye, he and most of the town are there watching football."

"That's great," And waved as she pulled open the door, "Thanks, Grace."

Grace picked up the phone and quickly rang Hamish. When the phone was answered all she said was, "She's read it."

"When?"

"About five or six minutes ago." She paused to hear Hamish's reaction. "She's on her way."

"Is she now?" Hamish answered.

"She's worked herself into quite the state. Just thought I'd give you fair warning."

"And so you have."

"How is he?"

"Agitated, for about five minutes now," Hamish revealed casually.

Grace gasped in awe. "All this time and it's true."

"Aye, it's true." Hamish chuckled. "Ah! Here she is now."

Will felt a sudden release of tension when he caught sight of Meghan standing by the doors. He smiled. He couldn't help it, even though the glower on Meghan's face suggested that she was beyond annoyed, and by the way she was glaring at him, he was the cause. She squeezed a hand full of papers in her fist as she came to a stop in front of him.

He didn't move as she shook the pages in his face. "What the hell is this?"

"Pardon me?"

Impatiently she unwrinkled the pages and held them up for him to see. He blinked, keeping his reaction to himself. The Contract! How in the hell had she got hold of it? He focused on it as she bit out again, "What the hell is this?"

He had made only one copy and it was sitting in the centre of his desk at home. Correction—Grace had made the copy. *Grace Cameron. Son of a bitch.* He scanned the pub. Smirks were noticeable on Ray, Stewart and Hamish. Nosey bastards.

"Will?" she snapped.

"I'm going to assume by your yelling that you know exactly what it is." He kept his tone calm.

"This thing can't... There is no way... You can't be..."

He fought the grin pulling at his lips while she struggled with her words.

Hamish took pity on her and handed her a shot of whisky. "Here, girl, drink this, it will help calm you."

Heated green eyes flashed at Hamish. "I am calm," she gritted out. Then took the shot glass and downed the fluid in one swift movement.

Will burst out laughing as Meghan gasped. The shock on her face was pure entertainment as she coughed and gasped. She was obviously not used to Scotch. He gave her a couple of hard pats on the back as she yelled, "Hamish! Are you trying to kill me?"

The bartender shrugged. "Just thought you needed the help." Then placing both hands on the bar in front of him, he added with a merry tone, "Because the sooner you're done yelling at Will, the sooner we can get back to Aberdeen at Dundee."

"Well, I don't need your help. And I'll try to keep this brief so you can get back to your precious soccer game."

Her attention was directed back at Will, when Stewart corrected, "Football."

"What?" she snapped.

"It's not soccer here, lass, it's football."

"Of course! Football. What was I thinking?" Meghan turned back to face him, more irate then before, thanks to Hamish and Stewart. Looking up at him, she poked him in the chest. "There is no way this contract is—"

"Possible?" Will supplied, looking down at her finger. "Oh, it's possible and it will happen." She was a brave lady to be poking him in the chest, the last person to poke him in the chest had ended up getting a few broken fingers for his effort. Except this wasn't anyone, this was Meghan and he loved her feisty temper, it made him want to pin her to the wall and do wicked things to her. He focused on her mouth as he continued, "But how it happens is up to you."

"How it happens? What do you mean how it happens? Nothing is going to happen," she yelled, throwing her hands in the air.

He raised an eyebrow at her remark. This wasn't how this was supposed to turn out, she wasn't supposed to find out about the contract. He had decided not to use it after seeing her earlier. He wanted to win her on his own. But the time had come for Meghan to understand that he never gave up, or gave in, to anything in his life and he wasn't about to start now. He would get what he wanted, and at that moment, he knew with complete certainty that he wanted Meghan.

"Yes, it will." He laced the words with smooth confidence. "You can come to the realisation on your own and agree, or you will be told to. The choice is yours. I would rather you realised it on your own, but

I have no problem with the alternative. Either way, I win."

A person would've had to have been blind to see that she didn't like what she was hearing. She threw a hip out to the side and placed her hand on it, daring him, "If you think this piece of paper will make me do anything, you are living in a dream world, but I'd like to see you try."

He expected nothing less and was impressed by her courage. "Are you sure that's what you want?"

She raised her chin. "I told you I like to gamble. Give it your best shot."

God, she was beautiful when she was mad, her passion was overwhelming. This fiery side was making him hard. The sudden image of him riding her against a tree in the forest appeared before him. Her red hair was long, longer than she wore it now and it was hanging down her bare back as she clung to his neck. Her dress was gathered around her waist and her lovely legs were wrapped around him as he pounded into her again and again, her wet core squeezing him. His cock jerked to life as Meghan came back into focus.

What had just happened? He blinked, fighting his body. What had they been talking about? Gambling. "That's right, you like to gamble, then how about a little wager?"

"A bet?" She narrowed her eyes. "What kind of bet?"

He crossed his arms. "I bet that you fall in love with me."

"Yeah," she snorted. "Like that's going to happen."

"Well, then this should be easy for you."

She clicked her tongue.

"Not scared, are you?" He gave her pride a nudge.

She mimicked his stance. "What are the stakes?"

He smothered a smile. "If you win, you're free from the contract. But if I win…" He lowered his head until they were nose to nose. "I get you."

Will saw the doubt cross her face then decided to give her pride another poke, just enough to get what he wanted. "Think you can win?" Straightening to his full height, he held out his hand to her.

She eyed his hand suspiciously, then slid her smaller hand into his. "You bet I can."

He held fast as she tried to pull back, running his thumb over the back of her hand. The skin was so soft and smooth and for some reason he already knew what it tasted like. His mouth watered. "Good." He drew in her lavender scent. "You'll forgive me if I don't wish you luck. I don't want you to win."

Meghan's mouth dropped open in shock and she snatched her hand away. "You're an asshole."

Will grinned. "I have my moments."

Once again Hamish handed her another shot of whisky, she took it without so much as a thanks and again downed it as she had with the first. She swallowed the second shot hard and swayed slightly. Shoving the glass into Will's chest, she waved the printed pages in his face…again. "I'm taking these."

Will sighed, holding onto his patience at her last act of rebellion before leaving. Leaving! An unexpected annoyance filled him. He didn't want her to go anywhere, he wanted her here, with him. As she turned, her hair flew over her shoulder and before he could stop himself he reached out, grabbing a handful of her flaming hair, stopping her. Stepping up behind her, he toyed with the silky strands. "Going home?" he asked softly.

"That's none of your business."

She was right, it was none of his business and he didn't push her about it, but he needed to know. He squeezed his jaw. "Time's up, Meghan, I'm done waiting."

Except for the quick intake of air, she appeared unaffected by his warning.

Once freed, she straightened her shoulders and walked out of the door.

As Will watched her go, a sudden tension began building in his neck and shoulders. He could only assume that it was because Meghan was driving him crazy.

Someone coughed behind him, and remembering where he was, he stepped back to the bar and took a sip of his pint. Lowering his glass to the bar he looked over his shoulder at the spectators. Most had knowing grins and a few even chuckled. He called out, "So lads, I think I'm starting to wear her down? What do you think?"

Every soul in the bar raised their glass and cheered in agreement.

Chapter Thirteen

A few days after finding out about the contract and her standoff with Will in front of most of Little Glen, Meghan walked down to see Neil McBride. The local doctor was just down the lane from Duncan, his house doubling as the office for his small practice. A week had passed since her attack and she had promised that she would see him so he could give her the thumbs up for running again, plus she needed to ask him about the constant nausea and turning in her stomach. She'd had it since she had gone toe to toe with Will at The Black Ale. It was probably nothing more than nerves, but she wanted to be sure.

Nerves. Ha! What else would it be? Agreeing to be the subject of a love-bet would give any sane person a bad case of the jitters. Especially, if that person didn't want to fall in love.

Man, she needed a run and bad. She couldn't wait to get back at it. The past week had killed her. She needed to relieve stress, and she needed to sleep. She wanted to be so tired that she wasn't able to think and the past couple of days all she seemed to do was think.

Since that afternoon at The Black Ale she hadn't spoken to Will, or her own grandfather. Not only was she still angry at Will, but she was now even more so at Duncan after he'd admitted to showing Will the Contract.

She had met Duncan as he was leaving for pub, to join Will and the rest of the village. Before he'd found out about her and Will's bet from one of his friends, she'd told him first.

Duncan had taken his chair behind his desk and had sat in silence until she'd finished. She'd sat down across from him, waiting for him to tell her that what Will was doing was wrong and that he would stand by her side. To her dismay, he'd clasped his hands together and had exhaled a long breath, his guilt too obvious to miss.

"Duncan, did you know about this marriage contract?"

"Yes. I've known about it for a long time. My father told me and his father told him and so on and so forth. I imagine it was the same in Will's family."

"I don't understand how Will could have known about it and I didn't? My name is on that thing too. Mum and Dad never said…"

"I told him about it."

She'd felt her mouth drop open. Duncan had started this mess. She had shot out of her chair. "You told Will about this thing?" she shouted, crumpling the pages in her hand. "Why in the hell would you do that? How could you?"

"I was only thinking of you, I want what's best for you. I've noticed you two together, Will is good for you, he makes you happy."

"Happy?" she'd called out. "He drives me crazy and now that he has decided to use this contract"—she had waved the papers at him—"to marry me, with or without my permission, by the way. I want nothing to do with him, I don't want to see him or talk to him, nothing." She took a long breath to try to calm her nerves, then continued, "You had no right sticking your nose in my life. I came here hoping we would become closer, to let you know that even though you and Dad don't have the best relationship, it doesn't have to be that way with Ryan or me. Then you do this. I thought you would be mad as hell when you found out about this contract, that you would want to protect me, I guess I made a mistake...about everything."

She'd wanted nothing more than to go home, back to Toronto, but she couldn't thanks to Dickhead. She was trapped and she couldn't do a damn thing about it. So, after stomping around in a fit and crying on her pillow, she had decided to just suck it up. She would enjoy her time here with Duncan—when she started to speak to him—and would spend the rest of her time fighting Will, because with God as her witness this was one bet she would not lose.

Will. His handsome face came to mind, covered in shadows of desire. No shirt, pants undone, arms wrapped around her.

Stopping abruptly, she fisted her sweatshirt as her stomach rolled. She had never seen Will's bare chest yet she could describe—in detail—every hard inch of it, including a thick, dark pink scar on his upper chest close to his shoulder. How could that be?

She placed a hand on her forehead. Geez! The guy was driving her crazy and he wasn't even there. Carrying on her way, she tried to turn her thoughts from Will, but that heavy weight filled her stomach. She placed her hand over her stomach and swallowed hard. Look at what the idea of him was doing to her. Since meeting him she had felt things she hadn't felt in a long time—anger, nausea, frustration, nausea, confusion, all mixed with a hefty dose of desire and more nausea. He made her feel beautiful, that should count for something. She liked the way he focused those hypnotic eyes on her, and she was honest enough to admit that if it wasn't for that blasted contract she would have given in to him eventually. Now, out of spite, she wouldn't.

She didn't wait long for Neil to answer her knock. He gave her a friendly smile when he answered. "Well, you look better. Come in, let's have a look at you."

Once in his office/exam room, he settled himself behind his desk and took out a folder.

"So, how have you been? Any more trouble?"

"I'm good, I haven't…" She stopped when she heard a loud, almost persistent knock at Neil's front door.

"Excuse me, Meghan. This is the only problem with having a small practice in a place like Little Glen, patients come at all times of the day and night. I won't be a minute."

She waved her hand. "That's okay, I don't mind." He left the room and closed the door behind him. He wasn't gone a minute before he reappeared, exhaling a long drawn-out sigh.

"Is everything all right? Do you need me to come back another time?"

"No. You are fine, right where you are. I told you I would like to give you a clear check-up, so you can start running again. I was told you really enjoy it."

"Yes, I do enjoy it. It helps keep me in shape and relieves my stress level so I can work out problems in my head."

He smiled and nodded. "It's a nice change to have a patient who sees the benefits of exercise. But I feel it's my responsibility to tell you I was told not to let you run up any more hills."

"Who said that? Duncan?" She frowned.

"No, but knowing Duncan he would probably agree."

"Then who did?"

"Will." Neil paused. "Just a minute ago."

She stared at him. *Will was here?* Annoyance quickly replaced her surprise. He was checking up on her, she huffed silently to herself. Making sure she showed up for her appointment. That explained why Neil came back into the room annoyed, Will must have been ordering Neil to say 'no hills', telling him how do his job, just like he was trying to tell her who she would marry.

Neil rested his forearms on his desk. "Will has no say in this room. My exam will help me make my decision. Okay?" She nodded. "Now, let's have a listen, and find out if anything is going on in there."

After a thorough exam, Meghan answered questions about her past medical history, and her asthma in particular. Neil gave her the good news. "Well, your chest sounds good, and you look much better than this time last week." He wrapped his stethoscope round his neck. "I think what happened was a freak occurrence. You have my green light to go ahead and run. But..." His pause caught her attention. "I'd like you to keep away from hills. Just for a little while."

"No hills at all?" God she had got so close, she was almost at the top.

"I want you to wait. Walking up is fine, but hold off on the running."

"Running up the hill caused my attack?" she asked, surprised. "It's usually caused by certain types of pollen, or sometimes if the smog's bad enough. Running's a first."

"I think it was a combination of a couple of different things. You were pushing yourself too hard, you weren't getting enough sleep, and there could be a trigger on that hill. But now that it's colder the trigger shouldn't be a worry. You need to get more sleep and if you take your time and don't push yourself, running on an even terrain shouldn't be a problem. Can you lay off the hills for a month or so and find another place to run for a while?"

Crap. That really sucks. She had been looking forward to getting up that hill. She sighed. "I can find another route to take. Thanks for being honest." She hesitated. "Can I ask you another question? It doesn't have to do with my asthma."

She briefly mentioned how her stomach has been acting up the last few days and expected him to ask about the food she had been eating but commented instead, "Think maybe it has something to do with what happened over at The Black Ale?"

"Argh! You know about that?" Her face heated.

"Everybody knows about everything that goes on here. Try to not let it bother you, also try some peppermint tea, and if it gets really bad take these." He handed her a small box.

"What's this?"

"Just baby Gravol. One should do it."

"I don't usually take pills." She tried to hand them back.

"Keep them." He waved his hand. "They're not that strong, besides" — he nodded towards the door, where she knew Will was waiting on the other side—"you might need them."

She sighed, understanding his meaning.

Neil followed her to the office door and opened it for her. Will was leaning against the far wall, his large arms crossed over his chest. Straightening, he asked Neil, "How is she?" He frowned when he noticed the small box of pills she was holding.

Out of the corner of her eye, she saw Neil shake his head. She turned away from Will, trying to ignore his presence.

"Thanks again, Neil."

"My pleasure. Come see me in a couple of months or sooner if you have any concerns."

"I will." She turned and left the safety of Neil's office and walked like a woman possessed with a shoddy bladder back to Duncan's. Didn't matter though, she could hear heavy footsteps behind her. Then Will was there blocking her path. She deliberately focused her attention over his shoulder.

"Why are you running away from me?"

"I wasn't running, I have work to do, I'd like to get back so I can finish it." Not really a lie, she always had work to do, but she wanted to be away from him too.

"You're lying. You've been avoiding me, and you haven't spoken to me or Duncan in days."

"How would you know?" *Was her voice higher?* "And even if I haven't, it's none of your business."

"I went over to speak with Duncan this morning. He told me what you said to him. He didn't deserve that, Meghan, it was my decision to use the contract. It was my choice. Get mad at me, not Duncan. He loves you very much, he wants what's best for you."

Will froze when he saw the shimmer of tears. He didn't want to see her cry. He only wanted her anger directed at him. Duncan was regretting his decision to tell him about the contract, worried it had ruined his relationship with her. The moment Duncan had mentioned that Meghan was coming to Little Glen, the changes in him were immediate. Sure, he was still grumpy, but there was that spring in his step and the pride in his voice whenever he talked about Meghan. Will wouldn't be responsible for Duncan losing that, she had just come back into his life.

"And you're what's best for me?"

"Yes," he answered honestly as a tear slipped down her cheek. He hated seeing her cry, he would rather have her yelling and screaming at him, he could handle that, these silent tears were killing him. "I didn't mean to make you cry." He stepped towards her, but she backed away placing a hand on her stomach.

"Yes, you did. You want me to feel guilty about what I said to Duncan, and you got your wish, I do feel guilty and I will go home and try to set things right. Satisfied?" she snapped.

He sighed. "My only intention was to clear Duncan of any wrongdoing."

He couldn't blame her for feeling angry. He had dumped a bombshell on her. And then to hear that Duncan had been the one to tell Will about the contract?

"Let go of this stupid contract, Will. Things could get back to normal, back to the way they were," she pleaded, her turquoise gaze burning a hole in his armour. "Please?"

He was willing to give her anything, but not that. "No. Our bet still stands."

She threw her hands in the air and shouted, "You're driving me crazy. Do you really want to do this? You don't even know me."

He sighed contentedly, she was back to yelling. Much better. "I know enough."

"You don't know anything. I could be some loony who hacks up her lovers."

He couldn't help but laugh. "You won't have time. I'll be keeping you busy." He laughed louder when her eyes grew wide and her cheeks flushed to a soft pink.

"You think so, eh! You want to see the real me, well, get ready, you're in for one hell of a shock." She barged past him and stalked up the road.

"I can hardly wait," he called out.

Chapter Fourteen

Meghan headed out of the front door one sunny morning with anticipation growing in her stomach and one thing on her mind—getting up that hill. She felt a little guilty for trying again so soon after telling Neil that she would wait, but other than her constant nausea, she felt great. Well, she hadn't talked to Will in a while because of that whole contract/bet thing, but she had taken his advice and set things right with Duncan. Although it had taken a while to get up the courage to go and face him. She didn't want any bad feelings between them, yet she didn't believe that she was wrong and had told him so. "I know you want what's best for me. But you must understand I can take care of myself and when I want to get married I will."

In true Kennedy fashion, he'd given her a roundabout apology. "Fair enough, just as long as you know I think Will is the right man for you." Things had been fine since then.

Hitting the road, she decided she would go for her normal run, and once she reached the hill, she would see how she felt. If she felt good she would give running a try. If not she would take Neil's suggestion and walk her way up. But one way or the other she was getting up there today.

Grabbing her pocket for a second time, she gripped her inhaler, and once satisfied, she straightened Scott's old black baseball cap and headed down Duncan's lane. The cap was the only thing she had wanted that had belonged to Scott and she used to wear it all the time, but now only wore it when she felt like it and that was only when she went for a run. She didn't care what it looked like or how bad of a shape it was in, it had been Scott's favourite hat, so that made it her favourite hat.

By the time she reached the base of the hill by Will's house she felt fine and decided to give it a shot. She hesitated for a moment and wondered if Will was up and if so was he watching her? *Argh!* Why did she care so much? Better to question why did he care so much? She rubbed at her stomach when it rebelled, then flipped her hood over Scott's ball cap and continued.

Will leant back in his chair, clasping his hands behind his head. He had got up early to finish off some work before he left for London that afternoon. He'd made it a habit of not only to research where his new clients wanted to go, but also research his new clients — their personalities, any type of behaviour problems, their careers, and their friends and family. He needed to know everything about their life. He wanted to be ready for anything.

As he reached for his coffee, he spotted movement outside. A flash of red hair stuffed under a beat-up baseball cap drew his attention.

He clenched his jaw. If she was thinking about running up that hill...he'd what? Threaten her with a marriage?

He sighed and waited for the inevitable. What was with the baseball cap? Was she hiding, hoping that he wouldn't notice her?

"Not bloody likely." Damn, he was glad to see her, even though she was trying to kill herself.

She paused for the briefest of moments, flipped up her hood, then continued. He shook his head. He should just let her go. She'd made it clear that she could take care of herself. Yet there she was running up that hill again, taking the chance of having another attack. With each step she took, Will's neck and shoulders contracted almost painfully. The memory of her sitting in the middle of the road struggling to breathe had him pushing out of his chair. "Bloody...stubborn..." He slammed down his cup.

Once in his room he threw on jeans and a T-shirt then decided that she was trying to kill herself or spite him. It was the only logical conclusion. What really ticked him off was the fact that she knew it was wrong. He had no idea if Neil had put any restrictions on her. That day at Neil's office, he had merely suggested to Neil that hills should be removed from Meghan's normal running routine. Neil must have agreed to him or she would have tried before now and she wouldn't be hiding under a beat-up old hat.

He grabbed his jacket and keys as he headed out of the door, then jumped in his Land Rover and drove up after her.

By the time he reached her she was walking. Her earphones were in so she was unaware that he was behind her. He slowly pulled ahead of her and stopped—blocking her path. He got out, crossed his arms over his chest and waited for her. He wanted to throw her into his truck and take her back home or maybe he should put her over his knee and spank some sense into her. Now that idea had merit, a good spanking might just be what she needed.

Meghan caught the look on Will's face before she reached him. The man was, for lack of a better word, pissed off. She slowed her pace as she closed the gap.

"What are you doing?"

"Walking," she said, stating the obvious.

The muscle in his jaw flexed.

"Wrong answer, eh?"

"Try again." His tone was deathly quiet. "I saw you run by the house. I was under the impression that hills are a no-no."

How could he have known that? "Did Neil…?"

"Neil didn't say a single word to me. But I'm right, aren't I? I can tell from the look on your face."

Am I that easy to read? She watched him study her face as he closed the space between them. She pulled at her middle, felt waves of nausea swell high.

"Not always. But your face wasn't the only thing that gave you away."

Meghan did her best to hide her embarrassment. She had no idea that she had said the question out loud. "What else gave me away?" She might need the information one day.

"The hat. And the hood."

She glanced up and saw he was scanning her head.

"Meghan?"

Why did he have to do that, say her name that way? She met his questioning stare fully expecting to pitch her cookies, but strangely nothing happened.

"Are you okay?"

"I think so," she lied.

His nostrils flared. "Why are you so goddamn determined to get up this hill?" His tone wasn't as unsettling, but his intensely focused look did make her a little nervous. Although she didn't know if was a good nervous or a bad nervous and to be on the safe side she took a step back, so that she wasn't within his reach.

Will noticed when she stepped away from him. How could he not? Her fear insulted the hell out of him. He clenched his teeth tight then forced his body to relax. "You may not care if you have another attack. But I do."

"It has nothing to do with that." She paused, and suddenly found the ground very interesting as she admitted, "I just wanted to see the ruins."

He sighed. He couldn't tell what she was feeling. The hat hid her face from his view. "You're not scared of me, are you?"

She raised her head and answered firmly, "No. I'm not."

He nodded, pleased with her honesty. "So why did you back away from me?"

She opened her mouth, paused then blurted out, "You have a real intense look, like you want to snap me in two."

Taken aback, he repeated, "Snap you in two?"

"Yah!"

He shook his head. Where did she get that idea from? He focused back on the subject at hand. "Tell me why you are so intent on getting up to those ruins."

That insulted look on his face was sobering. Maybe…she was wrong. He was such a big man. She just assumed the nervousness was due to his size, but maybe it was… Her heart pounded and she felt hot, in a yummy-wet sort of way. Oh man, was she turned on by his intensity?

No, she couldn't be. And yet all she could feel was how her body was reacting to him. Her nipples were hard, scraping the inside of her bra, her inner thighs were heating up. She closed her eyes, fighting the delicious swirl in her belly.

"Open yer eyes, Meghan. Answer my question," he ordered, his accent caused goose bumps to tickle her arms.

"I'm not sure," she said firmly. "The last time I was here was with my brothers. We tried several times to get up there without Duncan knowing, but it never happened. We got caught every time and then we left. And so much has happened since then. I just feel the need to get up there."

"Why didn't you want Duncan to know?"

"He said it was too dangerous for us, that some of the outer walls were giving way and he didn't want us getting hurt." She shrugged. "It just made us to want to get up there even more. Maybe I want to get up there now for my brothers, or maybe I want to spite Duncan for all those years ago, or maybe I just want to see what it looks like from the top. To see what the former owners saw, to stand where history took place. I don't know. All I know is that I'm getting up there today." She was breathless by the time she was done.

Now that he knew what was in her heart and her head. The reasoning probably sounded a little crazy, but she had been honest. If she was lucky, he'd think she was nuts and forget about the prehistoric contract. She saw his baffled look.

Yup, he thinks I'm crazy.

Surprisingly hurt, she huffed, "Whatever." Stepping around him, she put in her earphones, dismissing him.

A heavy arm snaked around her waist and he dragged her towards him until she stood between his long muscular legs. He was so close, she could smell his musky scent mixed with a spicy aftershave, and she felt the heat from his hands seep through her sweatshirt. He gently squeezed her waist, but she could only focus on his mouth and remembering how nice it was when those warm lips pressed against hers. He frowned and gave her a harder squeeze. Sighing she removed her earphones.

"Get in." He nodded to his Land Rover. "I'll take you up."

She started to protest but he cut her off. "This isn't up for discussion. I'm not sure I understand your reasoning but it's clear that you need to get up there. So, either you let me take you up there or I'll take you back home. But you will not run up that hill."

"I was walking remember. You asked me what I was doing and I said…"

"Meghan," he growled.

She didn't like having only two choices, especially when she had no say in them and she didn't like the way he was giving her orders, but she did want to get up there today. Did it really matter how she got there?

Although part of her wanted to know what Will would do if she still refused. Would that intensity rise to the surface again? And would she once again be turned on by it? "What if I said no? That I was still going to get up there, but I was going to walk not run? I am allowed to walk, you know." She raised her chin.

Will drew her up against his chest until his cheek rested against hers. He hadn't shaved and his whiskers felt rough against her skin. "I don't care what Neil said. If you try to walk or run up this hill I will put you over my knee and spank some sense into you."

She sucked in her breath. His tone wasn't as firm but the effect was the same, her heart jump and her skin tingle.

She pulled her head back to see if he was telling the truth. He raised a dark eyebrow in silent warning.

Oh man! Now that was quite the naughty image. Will's big hands spread over her behind. His lips kissing away the sting. Oh wow! That was a first for her and not really her thing but she would probably make an exception for him. She bit her lip to keep from laughing.

"Well, is it a spanking or will you let me drive you up there?"

"Fine," she sighed. "Let's go."

"Are you sure that's what you want?" A sexy smirk tugged at his lips. "You looked as though you might be having second thoughts." She pushed away and walked to the passenger side door with Will's deep laugh echoing in her ears.

Chapter Fifteen

"What happened here?" Meghan asked, scanning the vast area where the MacKenzie castle once stood.

"What do you mean? It's been this way since before I was born." He looked down as he stood next to her. The morning sun made her eyes stand out like prized gems, and her cheeks had a healthy glow. He felt his body respond to those two simple features. Not five minutes ago, he had been ready to spank her, and now he grew hard with just one look. So much for those years he had spent learning to control his body.

She responded to him by frowning back. "Don't look at me like that. I just want to know how they became ruins? Why isn't a castle standing here instead?"

Will turned away before he laughed. Her feisty attitude was something he wasn't used to but liked all the same. "From what I've read of my family's history, the MacKenzies were feuding with another clan and these ruins are the result of that feud."

"Who was the other clan?" He could hear the eagerness in her question.

"The MacDougalls."

"Oh." She sighed, disappointed.

Will couldn't help but laugh. "Do you really think two feuding clans would also have a marriage contract that would unite them?"

She shrugged. "One can dream." Walking into what would have been the centre of the keep Meghan tilted her head back and gazed up at the last remaining tower. "It's strange."

"What is?"

"I feel like I've been here before. But I know that I haven't." She paused turning to give him a puzzled frown. "Have you seen a picture of what the MacKenzie castle used to look like? Or maybe a sketch or something?"

"A charcoal sketch," he confirmed.

"Did it have only three towers?"

"Yes." He stepped closer as she studied the ground.

"The keep only needed protection of three towers because the mountain it was built into protected if from behind," she mumbled in a low voice.

"Meghan?"

Her head suddenly snapped up. She turned and walked to the back of the keep—the edge of the rock face. There was a giant hole where a wall had been and nothing but trees and mountain now filled the view. "Stairs were here once." She pointed. "They provided an easier access to the forest for hunting and as a means of escape if needed."

Will pulled her back and peered over the side. He caught sight of something square in shape and covered in moss. Kneeling down, he reached out and tugged on the moss. It pulled away revealing a roughly carved stone step.

Will stood and brushed off his hands. He scowled at her. "I had no idea these were here. How come you did?"

"I...I have no idea." She really didn't, he could read the truth on her face. "A picture just...popped into my head."

Tugging on her arm, he pulled her back from the edge. Once back at his Land Rover, he broke the silence. "What else did you see?"

She turned to face him. "You really want to know?"

"If you have seen more hidden gems, like those steps, then yes."

"You honestly didn't know about them, did you?"

"No," he answered honestly. "I didn't."

She stepped towards him. "I've never been up here before, Will, I swear."

"I believe you." He rested against the hood of the Land Rover. "Go ahead, tell me what else."

For over an hour, Will had listened quietly as she described the old MacKenzie castle. The castle she had never seen but felt as though she had lived in. At one point, Will asked her to describe the outside of it and she must have satisfied him because he nodded once she was finished. She couldn't believe he hadn't called her crazy and walked away from her the second she had pointed out the steps. It was freaky how she had known they were there, especially when the owner hadn't.

Once she was done, Will pushed himself off his SUV, and walked over to her, studying her intently.

"Well? Am I certifiable?"

He chuckled. "No."

"Did I describe the sketch?"

"Perfectly."

She pulled off her hat and pressed her hand to her forehead. "Bizarre."

"You okay?"

"No! How could I possibly know all of this?"

There was a relaxed expression on his face as he reached for her hand. "Don't know." He started dragging her behind him.

"Where are we going?"

He just grinned over his shoulder at her. He stopped at the only part of the outer wall that was still standing, and pointed out a narrow set of stairs with a handrail on one side.

"This outer wall was reinforced and these steps added a few years ago, to keep the tourists interested." He extended his hand for her to precede him.

Stand on the wall of an old keep? "Cool!" She was so eager to get up that she tripped half way up the narrow stairs and would have fallen over the open side if Will hadn't been right behind her. He grabbed her about the waist and pulled her back against his chest. Hitting him wasn't any softer than it would have been if she had hit the ground. He was rock-hard, a great mass of unyielding muscle. His sudden closeness became disturbing yet her stomach didn't roll and she had no desire to throw up, which was strange considering what had happened between them. Her body involuntarily shivered. His large arms tightened around her and that was when her heart skipped a beat. "I'm okay, you can let go."

"Not yet." His breath warmed her ear. "Did you notice that your body fits mine?"

Of course, how could she not. It was like they were designed for one another. "Will." She sighed.

"Did you think I was going to make this easy on you?" He chuckled, letting her go, "Every chance I get I'll be touching you so you better get used to it."

"I don't want to get used to it."

"Maybe that's true, but I know you like it."

"I don't...like it."

"Really?" There was an amused ring to question, and she realised she was still resting against his chest. She grabbed the handrail and hauled herself away from him as though he were on fire.

The view from the top of the remaining section of the outer wall was breathtaking. It was a clear crisp morning and the sun that was shining down from the east bathed Little Glen in an orange hue. Meghan felt her lips curve into a smile. "It's beautiful."

"Very beautiful," Will agreed.

Meghan shot a glance over her shoulder and realised that Will was looking at her and not the view. Her entire body froze as his gaze trailed over her face and hair.

She forced a scowl, but felt her cheeks heat up before she could turn away and walk along the wall.

He followed her to the end where it met and joined the last standing tower. "This door was added the same time as the stairs," he informed her.

"Does it open?"

"No, it's sealed. The inside of the tower isn't safe, the stairs have fallen away."

She turned back to the view. Will moved to stand behind her and pointed through two large trees in front of them. "If you look between these trees, you can see Letham Loch in the next valley."

Pushing up on to her toes, Meghan swayed trying for a better view. Unsuccessful, she stepped to the side and tried a second time just as a stone shifted. Looking down, she watched as the stones beneath her feet gave way and tumbled into the trees below.

Chapter Sixteen

Will clamped his arm around her waist when he heard the stones shift under her feet. He easily held her weight as he took a cautious step back. "We have to get off this wall," he announced softly. "Stay behind me — step where I step." Then without any hesitation he moved in the direction of the stairs. He didn't give her a chance to argue, he moved too fast and practically carried her.

By the time, they had reached the last few steps Will allowed himself to breathe. His heart thumped in his chest. He silently thanked God that he had thought to hold her as she stood on her toes.

Once they reached the last step, she pulled her hand from his, mumbling, "I think...I dropped my iPod?"

Will felt his entire body stiffened just as he spun to face her. "What?"

Christ, she nearly falls off the wall and she was worried about her damn iPod!

He exhaled and shook his head. He was only beginning to calm down, but there she went stirring other emotions around. The feelings that Meghan caused were uncharacteristic for him. He was disciplined, trained to be an efficient soldier and he took the same approach with his business and his life.

Then Meghan had come along. Her fiery temper bemused him, her beauty astounded him and her stubbornness annoyed the hell out of him. He had to force himself to concentrate on work or he would think about Meghan. When he was sleeping he dreamt about her or he would just lie awake in bed thinking about her. And lately, when they weren't near one another, he felt...agitated. *Christ, women were pain in the arse*. Only a woman could do this, screw with a man's mind and emotions and be none the wiser as to what she had done. He took a step closer and repeated his question.

Startled by his quick movement, she took a step back. "I said...I dropped my iPod over the side." She tripped on the stairs and fell hard onto the bottom step. Her hand went to her lower back. "Damn." She rubbed her back. "What is wrong with me today? I'm never this clumsy!"

Will's frustration dissolved as he knelt on the ground between her feet. "You okay?"

"Yes." It was apparent her pride was answering for her.

Will sighed. "You are, are you?" Then, moving her hand aside, he began to rub the tenderness away from her back. He shifted his hand and splayed his fingers wide, taking in as much of her smooth skin as possible. "Feel better?"

Her hips shifted slightly as she nodded her head. "Mmm."

With his face level with hers, he didn't miss when her black pupils became huge in her now indigo eyes.

Heat pulsed through his groin and he pushed between her thighs. "You can't moan like that." It was killing him and the position they were in... His nostrils flared as he snapped his teeth together.

She squeezed her eyes shut, trying to block him out. "Don't," she pleaded.

"Meghan." His voice was raw, Jesus, he could hear the need when he said her name.

She shook her head but her body trembled.

He refused to stop, however. "I want you to look at me when I kiss you," he ordered, running his thumb along her bottom lip. "Open your eyes and look at me."

He nodded when she followed his order, then slowly he bent his head and covered her mouth.

He kept his mouth firm on hers, stroking her lips, then gripping her lower back, he jerked her forwards, pinning her open body to his stiffening cock. He nibbled at her bottom lip perhaps a little too hard. When she inhaled from the sting, he was able to slide his tongue into her sweet mouth and capture her low moan at the same time.

Christ, she tasted so good. A forbidden pleasure that he had been waiting for, and now that she was there and open to him, he would take all that he could before she pulled away. He possessively gripped her behind, squeezing the supple flesh with one hand as he slid the other up her side to cup the back of her head. He tangled his fingers in her hair as he sealed their bodies together. His tongue continued to mate with hers, he thrust against her centre, needing her to feel as hot and achy as he was feeling. He was rewarded with a sexy little groan as she instinctively wrapped her legs around his hips. That was what he had been waiting for, her acceptance.

Tilting her head back, he kissed a trail down her neck to her collarbone, then back up, all the while tasting her skin with his tongue. Her damn cap got in the way again as he bumped the brim with his forehead. He grabbed the brim, asking, "Do you mind?"

She pulled the hat off and her soft crimson locks fell free, framing her face. Her lips were pink and swollen and her neck was flushed. Her hands gripped the front of his jacket, pulling him close. "Don't stop," she demanded in a whisper.

A growl of pure satisfaction rumbled in his chest. He quickly reclaimed her mouth, his teeth scraping her bottom lip as he slid his hand up under her sweatshirt. He loved the feel of her skin all hot and silky. A need unlike anything he had ever experienced ran through him, it was in full control of his mind and body and it only wanted Meghan. It had craved her for so long—hell, it even felt as though it had missed her.

Panting, he pulled away from her. "I want you, Meghan. I want to fuck you long and slow, until you are left breathless. I want nothing between us but sweat, nothing under you but my bed, and nothing on top of you but me."

"That will take too long." She shook her head. "Now…has to be now." She pulled at the button of his jeans.

He raised her head with a single finger under her chin, unconvinced over her sudden acceptance. "Meghan?"

She placed her hand over her heart. "I don't understand this need I have. It's been so long…been so…lonely."

She felt the same way that he did—a pull that she didn't understand. He could hear it in her words, see it on her face. All he could do was nod, then he pulled her to her feet before he allowed her to unbutton his jeans.

He jerked her close and kissed her neck, sliding his hand into the top of her jogging pants. "Shoes off." He felt her struggle, then kick off one then the other. He tugged on the top of her pants, pulling them over her hips and down her smooth thighs.

"It's cool," she breathed out as he ran his hands back up her legs, reaching for her panties. She gripped at his shoulders, steadying herself. "Maybe we should…in your truck?"

He pulled off his jacket and threw it on the ground. "You won't notice the cold in a minute." Then pulled her down onto his lap once her panties were off.

As she straddled his lap, he kissed her again, thrust his tongue into her mouth so he could taste her desire and need. She rocked her hips against him, her sweet wet heat teasing his cock through his jeans. Reaching between her thighs, he cupped her mound, groaning when he felt her slick lips. He brushed her clit with his palm, moving over it in a slow circle, then he drove two fingers deep. Her cry was soft. Her ragged breath warmed the side of his mouth. Again and again he impaled her with his fingers and each time she kissed him harder — held onto him tighter. He would have smiled at her breathless whimper if he hadn't been rock hard and hurting.

Fuck, he was hurting. It was her scent, it was driving him wild and he liked the feel of his palm wet from her lusty need.

"Now?" he found himself asking — though didn't know why.

"Yes." She nipped at his ear. "Yes, now. What are you waiting for?"

His lips curled into a cruel smile as he laid her back, supporting her in his arms. He shoved down his jeans enough so that his cock was freed and pushed between her legs. He clamped onto the back of her thighs. "Higher." She did as he ordered then sucked in a breath when he drove deep.

They both became still. Their breathing heavy, their cheeks touching.

Will felt his chest squeeze so tight that the air was driven from his lungs. God in heaven, this felt right. He had a feeling it would but hadn't realised it would be this overpowering. He shifted and positioned his arms at the side of her head, dragged his lips across her cheek.

Just then Meghan drew in a shaky breath and trembled.

"Meghan?" He kept his voice low.

"I won't love you."

He felt his lips twitch in response to the challenge, then pulling his hips back he plunged in deep. Her gasp filled him with satisfaction. Punishment for her comment? Damn right.

He pushed up so he could look down at her as he drove into her over and over again. Her body welcomed his invasion, her slick channel gripped him, clenching tight as he withdrew. Her eyes clouded over as he continued, her nails scraped his shoulders and back. God she was maddening, he was angry and hurt by her words and she loved every minute that he punished her for it.

What a sight she was. Hair spread wild on the ground, lip caught between her teeth, face flushed, her legs wrapped around him then she arched her back. The sight was breathtaking and very sexy and he felt his cock swell even more.

As they continued the steady pace their lips brushed against one another, and locking eyes with her, he finally responded, "You will."

She tried to shake her head. He wouldn't let her. "No, I-I..." Her words came out in a rush each time he drove into her.

"Yes." He nipped her bottom lip. "Stop arguing and kiss me."

She did, long and hard and with as much passion as he kissed her.

The kiss heated his blood, filled his cock and he quickened his pace and pounded into her, with his fingers in her hair and their mouths glued together. He felt her grip his butt cheeks, her nails scratching the skin as she pulled him tighter. He ground his hips against her and she turned her head, panting, "Close. Don't stop."

He moved his hand between their bodies, his fingers searching for and finding her sensitive clit. He stroked once and she moaned, raising her hips. Damn, this was getting tough. He didn't know how much longer he could last. Her thighs flexed, drawing his attention to their joining bodies. He watched as he entered her. Felt the way she clenched around him and the heat. Christ he loved the heat. The pressure in his groin mixed with pain. She was such a delicious torture. He gritted his teeth together as his body tightened, became painfully hard with each thrust. He never wanted this to end.

He added pressure as he teased her swollen bud. Then she dug her fingers into the back of his head and cried out, "Almost. Will, fuck me."

He followed her command. He fucked her hard. Her scorching muscles milked him mercilessly — then he was coming. He came hard, groaning into the side of her neck as his hips pounded into hers.

It didn't take any time at all for the haze to clear. But not before Will tangled his fingers in her hair, pressed his lips to hers and kissed her soundly. The intensity of it had her gripping at his neck again.

"Come on." He stood up first then reached for her, pulling her to her feet. He stared at her as he quickly pulled up his boxers and jeans. That was when reality slapped her in the ass. Heat flew through her, as she stood half-naked in front of him. She was able to hide her face as she searched the ground for her panties and yoga pants. She couldn't believe what had just happened. She had begged him to make her come, to fuck her, even moaned it out loud.

"Here."

She snatched away her panties when she saw them dangling from his fingers. She quickly tried to pull them on but stumbled. He caught her by the arm, steadying her. She peeked up at him, her cheeks still on fire. He didn't laugh or smile at her, hell, he didn't even frown, he simply reached down picked up his coat, wrapped it around her shoulders and turned so his back was facing her.

She dressed as fast as possible, then handed him his coat before she tugged on her ball hat, and pulled her hair through the back. Her stare drifted over to the road leading down the hill.

"Thinking about running away?"

"Yes."

"Don't." There was an underlying warning to the word.

She didn't care what he wanted. It was the truth. She did want to run away from him and everything that had just happened.

He held out his hand and waited for her to take it. When she didn't, he sighed. "I'll drive you down the hill, and then you can run back to Duncan's. Okay?"

She nodded and walked to his Land Rover without touching him—she had done more than enough of that today.

* * * *

Minutes later they were sitting parked in front of his house, a heavy silence filling the area between them. Will spoke first. "You okay? I didn't hurt you, did I?"

"No."

"No for which one?"

"For both." She blurted out. "We just had sex on the ground?"

"Yes we did," he agreed. "You liked it as much as I did?"

She blinked at his question. "Of course I liked it," she snapped. "But I wasn't finished."

"So finish."

"We had unprotected sex on the ground."

"Mmm. Yes we did. But," he quickly continued, "I can honestly say that was a first for me."

Meghan snorted. "Yah, and I'm the Virgin Mary."

He turned, squared his shoulders. "Not once have I ever had unprotected sex. I was too selfish."

"That makes no sense."

"If I was to get some woman pregnant I wouldn't have been able to live the life I had at that time. My job was dangerous, I couldn't stand the thought of leaving a family behind because of it, so I would not willingly allow myself to be put into that situation until I was ready."

"Oh." She hadn't been expecting that.

He ignored her and asked, "What about you?"

All the bluster went out of her then. Now it was her turn to convince him that she had always been careful. "No." She looked him dead in the eye. "Never without a condom, and I've been on birth control since my late teens. I was always too scared."

He gave her a hard stare, then sighed. "Being a first for both of us I don't think we really need to worry about unwanted diseases. Can I assume you are still on birth control?"

She nodded.

"Well then, we don't have to worry about any little feet running about yet."

"Mmm." She snapped her head around. "*Yet!*"

"That's right." He winked.

"No. There will be no 'yet'." She threw open the door, then jumped out. She knew that he was teasing, but she didn't even want to go there. She stopped abruptly after stomping five paces. Her breathing increased as her heart thumped wildly. *Oh shit! He better be teasing.*

"Meghan." Will was behind her. His tone held a trace of humour. Urgh! She hated that.

"What?" She turned in time to see him step towards her.

She held up her hand, stopping him without words as she backed away, giving him what she hoped was a warning.

He sighed, then called, "I'm leaving for London this afternoon."

"And why am I supposed to care?"

Her sharp words didn't seem to affect him. "Duncan has my cell number in case you need anything."

Anger had her spinning around. She shouted over her shoulder, "I can take care of myself. I don't need you!" And she began a slow jog back towards the village, furious with herself.

As she ran out of sight, Will roughly ran his hands through his hair. He turned, walked into the house and slammed the front door closed. "Fuck."

Ending an earth-shattering moment in a fight. Jesus. Leaning back against the door, he closed his eyes. Meghan's face was suddenly there. He snapped his eyes back open. "Fuck." All he could think about was Meghan. Her supple mouth, her heavy breathing, her body wrapped around his, the desperate way she'd held onto him. And he had held on just as tight if not tighter. He was never spontaneous and certainly not when it came to sex. He always knew who he would be with, where they would be and how long he would spend with her. And he always...always governed their time together. Meghan had him focusing on nothing else but her. No other woman had made him do that, he was always the one in control.

Though he didn't like the idea of leaving for work, he was beginning to think getting away from her might be good. He needed to clear his head and think about other things.

His chest constricted when he thought about being away from Meghan.

Sighing, he climbed the stairs to his bedroom. He had to go, people were depending on him. It wasn't like she wouldn't be safe, Duncan was there and so were others who would help her at the drop of a hat. But he didn't want others helping her. He wanted her to want only his help. Christ, that made no sense, he sounded like a jealous ten-year-old.

Stepping into his bathroom, he pulled his shirt over his head and dropped it to the floor. Confusion mixed with agitation, the need to stay close to her had him gripping the sink, anger swelling his chest to the point of pain. He was wound so tight all of a sudden that he had to fight the urge to rip the sink from the wall. He studied his reflection in the mirror. This wasn't him— he never acted this way. He took a deep breath and released the sink. Her face flashed in his mind, again. "Fuck." She was driving him crazy.

Chapter Seventeen

Five days had passed since Meghan had seen Will. With him away in London she now had had the time to figure out how to handle their little sex-capade. Little. Ha! There was nothing little about it. She had been so desperate for him, had craved his kiss and touch, as though she had been denied it for years. That feeling had scared the crap out of her. Oh, and she couldn't forget the way she'd given into him so easily. She groaned. He'd barely touched her and she had turned to mush. So much for the strong Kennedy willpower—apparently, that particular skill was useless where Will was concerned.

As was the normal daily occurrence, her stomach heaved. She slowed to a walk and placed her hand on her middle praying for the sensation to end.

Will's face shadowed with a dark hunger filled the void before her. Even now she was still embarrassed. She wished she had been able to control herself. She didn't like the memory of lying on the ground acting like an animal. Then again she wasn't the only one who had been there and Will had acted the same way—they had been desperate and needy for nothing else but each other. She had never felt that way before and she never wanted it to happen again, though deep down the craving was still there, eating away at her.

Disappointment rolled around in her stomach with the nausea and embarrassment. She'd really enjoyed their time spent at the ruins. They were finally getting to know one another. Will had been very patient with her crazy notions about the old MacKenzie castle and he had listened to her. She wasn't one to share personal thoughts with many people, yet with Will, she felt like she could tell him anything.

For five days, she had repeated the same daily routine—running, work, meals and bed. Not much of a life. Although her boss was pleased with the amount of work she had finished and decided to give her more responsibility even though she was half a world away. That should have cheered her up, but it didn't and she knew the reason why...she missed him. She missed his tormenting in the mornings, his company in the afternoons and his overall comforting presence. Even if they weren't in the same building and she was mad at him, she knew that he wasn't far away. God only knows where he was now. She only knew that he wasn't there. Bile filled the back of her throat and she swallowed hard to push it back down.

Holy! She wiped the sweat from her forehead. She was making herself sick just thinking about him. Maybe she could call him—it might make her feel better—she could if she wanted. She had peeked into Duncan's address book to see if Will had been lying. He hadn't, and she had been truly relieved when she had seen his name and cell number.

"Damn it." She really had no right missing him, yet couldn't seem to help herself.

Fighting the weight in her middle she started up with a slow jog, when she spotted Mary heading up to Will's house. "Good morning, Mary," she called, coming to a stop next to the older woman. "Where are you off to?"

The older woman gave Meghan a warm greeting. "I'm off to Will's to see to Lucy. She'll be needin' to get out."

"Didn't Will take her with him?"

"Oh no. He can't be dragging that beast with him while he's working. So I see to her while he's gone."

She was surprisingly annoyed that Will would leave Lucy alone overnight in that huge house. *Poor girl, she's probably lonely,* she huffed in her head. Well, she knew what that felt like.

"How long is he gone for?" Meghan saw the amused look on Mary's face and clarified her questioning. "'Cause if he's going to be gone for a while, I don't mind taking Lucy over to Duncan's house. Then you don't have to worry about her and I'll have my running buddy back."

Mary frowned, thinking about Meghan's suggestion. "I'm not sure how long Will is going to be away. He usually tells me when he leaves and when he will be returning. But this last time he left without telling me when he was coming back. He never does that."

Was she the reason he left abruptly? She hoped so. "Then it's settled, I'll come with you to get Lucy and her things. She'll stay with Duncan and me until Will returns." And she wasn't doing this because she felt guilty. She was not guilty.

Mary started to giggle. "What do you think Duncan will do when that huge beast walks into his house?"

"I'm not sure. Though I'm pretty sure it will be entertaining," Meghan joked. "Would you like to walk back with me and see first-hand?"

"Of course! I wouldn't want to miss that."

* * * *

Will exhaled as he hung up the phone, some of the tension lifting from his shoulders. This was the best he had felt in days. He was still agitated but it had lessened after talking to Mary. He'd called Mary for two reasons. One, to apologise for throwing Lucy in her lap without letting her know when he would be back. And, two, to ask her to watch her for another couple of days. His last job had kept him longer than expected in London, and he still had to stop at his office in Edinburgh.

When Mary had informed him that Meghan had taken Lucy over to Duncan's house to stay with her, he had been relieved. Especially after she had yelled that she didn't need him. At first he had been angered by her comment—he wanted her to need him. He realised later that she had been mad at herself for giving in to him. She couldn't hide the passion she felt, it was clear in her eyes. Those eyes. The way they turned blue, then became heavy as he kissed her. That was why she had turned so mad, so quickly. She'd wanted him as much he had wanted her. He smiled to himself, he would bet a marriage on it.

* * * *

The Black Ale was a dark hole in the wall, a real dump compared to his normal standards. Rob sat in a booth next to the row of windows, giving him a clear view of most of the little village. This was the fourth day that he had driven up from his hotel in Perth, looking for a way to get to Meg. She was so close. He could almost smell her lavender body wash. If he could just get her alone, he could get her cell and get the hell out of this shit hole.

That was the problem, she was never alone. Someone was always with her. When she wasn't with her grandfather or some other local, she had that damn black dog with her. Getting to her with the locals around would not be a problem, her grandfather maybe, depending on how much he knew about her past. The dog was a different story — you couldn't charm a dog, they either liked you or they didn't. He had found that out the hard way a couple of nights ago.

The old man had left, heading over to the local pub, leaving Meg alone. His luck had held when he'd tried the front door and it had been unlocked. Once inside he'd followed the sound of running water and had started up the stairs. His pulse had quickened with the thought of coming face to face with her. Although, he wasn't sure if it was the thought of her perfect body naked in the shower or the thought of having to wait so many months to get at her that stirred in his cock, all he knew was that he wanted to touch her. He'd been stopped halfway up the stairs, coming face to face with that huge black dog. There was a lot about dogs he didn't know, didn't want to know, he hated dogs, but the one thing he did know was if you turned and ran instinct alone would drive them to chase. As he'd stood facing the dog, anger had swelled in him, he had been so close to her. That was when a deep low growl had echoed down the stairs. He'd watched, frozen to the steps, as the blue-black fur on its neck had risen, and white fangs had become visible when its lips had curled up. Lowering its head, it had begun stalking him down the stairs and right out of the house. Fucking dog.

"Good day to you Robert."

Rob snapped his head around at the interruption. *The bartender, what was his name again?*

"Have the usual?" The bartender stood at the end of the booth eyeing him. Harry? Henry? Hamish.

Plastering a fake smile on his face, he greeted the man, "That would be great, thanks, Hamish." The older man gave him a stiff nod, then left to get the drink. This bartender was a pain in the ass. He asked too many questions and watched everything that he did. Rob noticed a few of the locals staring at him. He nodded a greeting and leant back, hoping to give the impression that he was there on vacation. Travelling through England and Scotland was his excuse, looking for a quiet little town to buy a place so he could rest and relax. Fucking small towns—there was no anonymity. Someone always knew your business.

"How's the house-hunting going?" the bartender asked, placing the beer in front of him.

"Not bad." Rob casually toyed with the glass. "I'm having a hard time getting what I want."

"I could recommend a few good estate agents. They'll find what you're looking for."

Pretending to consider the suggestion, Rob turned to look out of the window and caught sight of bright hair. It was hanging down her back in long soft curls. Her jeans clung to her firm thighs and tight ass. He watched as she stopped at the entrance to the library, turning in his direction. Rob made no move to hide. There was no point, not with the bartender standing beside him, and he would be surprised if she could see him from where she was standing. "No thanks, I've found what I want. Just waiting for the right moment to make the deal."

"Where is the cottage? It can't be here in Little Glen, nothing is available here."

Rob turned and gave the man a smile, knowing full well the bartender had seen him watching Meghan. "No, the cottage isn't here. I'm just here enjoying the view."

"Can see that," the older man mumbled. "Let me know if you need anything."

Rob turned back to the window.

Chapter Eighteen

Meghan stared out of the large windows of the Little Glen library. A multitude of coloured leaves covered the ground. The village looked so peaceful. She wished she felt that way.

Something just didn't feel right, she felt...sick and lonely and blue. Other times she felt creepy—like something or someone was behind her, but when she turned there was no one in sight.

She hated this feeling. It felt like she would never be happy again. She had felt like this after Scott had died, and the only thing that had seemed to help had been going for a run, but not even that would drive away the constant turning in her stomach now. She rested her head in her hands. She felt awful. Was hungry but couldn't eat, was tired but couldn't sleep. She had no idea what was wrong with her. Neither did the local Doctor, so he had decided to send her to see a specialist in Perth about her stomach problems.

"Are you all right, m'dear?"

She jumped at Grace's sudden appearance. "Oh...I..." She pulled her hand away from her turning stomach. "I'm okay."

"You don't look okay. Have an upset stomach, do you?"

Was that a smirk on her face? Meghan couldn't help but get snippy. "No, I'm fine."

The older woman moved away from the table with her stack of books, the smirk turning into a full-blown smile. "Try peppermint tea. That should help."

"Already tried that, you old..." The mumble was cut off.

"What was that, dear?" Grace stuck her head out from behind a shelf.

"Nothing." Meghan forced a smile.

"Ginger ale."

Huh? What was that old bird talking about now?

"For your stomach. That should help also."

"Ah...okay, thanks, Grace."

After packing away her notes and checking her emails, she found herself surfing the net. She didn't know what she was searching for, until she typed in 'Royal Marines SBS'. She wasn't sure what to expect or what the job even entailed.

She read the details on the unit, several times in fact, just to make sure she wasn't reading it wrong. Will had been a part of a British Special Forces unit. The list of duties shocked her as she read them out loud. "Counter-terrorism, personal protection, coastal reconnaissance, helicopter-borne assaults? He did all those things?" And those were only a few of the many talents members of the Special Boat Service had.

"Holy crap!" she groaned. Now she knew why Will had looked startled and insulted that time in The Black Ale. She had thought he had made a mistake and had meant to say SAS. Her faced heated even though she sat alone. "It's official. I'm a tool."

Startled by the volume of her own voice, she looked around and saw Grace scowling at her. Good thing she was the only person in the library. Who was she kidding? She was the only person in here on a regular basis.

"Don't you be rolling those eyes Missy. Just 'cause you're the only one here doesn't mean you don't have the follow the rules. Now keep it down!" Grace commanded in a firm, motherly tone.

Whoa! "Sorry Grace!"

The librarian nodded with satisfaction.

Meghan continued reading. She couldn't believe it. This was the kind of thing she had only seen in movies, she had never met anyone who was a member of this type of organisation. She remembered when she'd first seen him on the hill, leaning against his Land Rover, and that sudden thought that he could snap her in two. She covered her face. *My God* — she had been right. And she wanted to spite him just to see what he would do. Which was clear at this point, he could do more than just snap her in two.

Except, he hadn't and it was clear that he had been insulted that she would think so.

After packing up her laptop and saying goodbye to Grace. Meghan took her time as she walked back to the house, thinking about Will and his previous job. He used to be a member of a highly trained military unit, which meant he had probably seen his share of combat. He was probably capable of doing things she couldn't even begin to imagine.

Strangely enough, his role in the SBS didn't keep her attention for long. How could it when her thoughts kept turning to how he had made love to her? He had known where to touch and how much pressure to exert. His mouth had been a wicked distraction, while his hands and body had overwhelmed everything else. He had melted her heart and had set everything else on fire. She had tried to fight that fire, but the feeling had been so all-consuming that she had just given into it. "Oh God!" She drew in a shaky breath. She had given in to him quickly, too quickly. Just like with Rob.

It doesn't matter. She began a fast pace back to the house, as though she could outrun that lingering embarrassment. It didn't matter that she was attracted to him beyond any reasonable sense of the word. She had to keep away from him. Had to fight that feeling growing in her chest. Nothing could happen between them, her life was waiting for her in Toronto. At that moment a rolling wave in her stomach had her gripping her middle and blindly reaching for Duncan's front gate.

The front door flew open and Duncan raced down the path. "Meghan!" He gripped her shoulders.

"I'm fine," she lied, forcing herself to straighten. "Just a stitch in my side."

"Like bloody hell a stitch!" Duncan grumbled, helping her into the house.

Once she had been seated in his office, he left. But was back a minute later with a cup of tea. "It's peppermint. It should help."

Geez! What was with this town and peppermint tea?

"Thanks." She took the cup, resting back.

"Better?"

She nodded sipping the hot tea.

"Well," Duncan began. "While Lucy slept on my favourite leather chair, I was thinking that after your appointment tomorrow, we should have lunch and you could pick up those gifts you wanted for Ryan and your parents. Make a day of it. What do you think?"

"I don't know about the lunch part but the shopping sounds great." She didn't want to hide the fact that she was feeling giddy. It was a great idea. She hadn't done anything like that since before she had arrived. Spending the day shopping with Duncan sounded like fun.

"I know you haven't been feeling well, but you've got to eat. Besides you've got caught up in the same old routine since you first came. Work and running will only get you so far, young lady. You have to include time for fun too," he instructed.

"You're right. And I think I'll have fun spending the day with you."

"Good." He flicked his hand. "Now out with yah. I have a call to make."

Meghan raised her eyebrows at his order. He ignored her, searching through the papers in his desk drawer. Holding her cup of tea, Meghan gave him a good frown as she stood. "I'll be upstairs."

"Fine." Duncan closed the drawer and plopped his address book down. As he reached for the phone on the side of his desk, he gave her an order, "Take that beast with you too, please. She's happier when she's with you."

Chapter Nineteen

"Glad you made it." Duncan extended his hand.

Will nodded silently at the older man. He was still surprised that Duncan had called him, surprised even more when Duncan had told him why he had called. Now that he was there, he only wanted to know one thing. "How's Meghan?"

Duncan shook his grey head. "Why don't you see for yourself?" He nodded to the shop across the street. "She's shopping."

Will caught sight of her flaming hair as she walked around the shop. The two men crossed the street and stood outside. Will couldn't take his eyes off her. She didn't look sick, though she was resting her hand on her stomach. But other than that she looked incredible. Her hair was hanging down her back in long loose curls, shimmering against the dark brown of her coat, her face was bright with a sweet smile tugging at her lips.

As he watched Meghan stroll around the shop, the reflection of a man appeared in the window. He was on the other side of the narrow street, staring into the same shop. Will's training automatically kicked in and he took note of his height and build, his hair colour and how he held himself. Meghan's hair briefly caught his attention, but he fought the urge and adjusted his focus to watch the man standing behind him.

The longer the guy stared at Meghan, the darker the look became. He had seen that stare before. On men who were broken and twisted. It was the look of a man who wanted what he saw and would use whatever method necessary to get it. Arms flexing, Will turned, glaring back over his shoulder, and, whilst flashing his best death glare, he ordered, "Move on." He smirked, satisfied when the stranger stiffened and hurried down the street.

He met Duncan's questioning stare and cracked a smile. "Still got it."

The muscles in his arms along with his back and neck eased as he studied Meghan. He'd been wound tight since the moment she'd walked away from him the week before, affecting him in every way. He had been unusually sharp with his team and sometimes had just been plain miserable and it had only become worse when Duncan had called. Now that she was near, he felt fine. He took a deep breath and felt his body begin to relax. Then like an idiot, he couldn't stop smiling.

"Oh! For God's sakes, go on in, boy," Duncan grumbled. "You aren't listening to me anyway."

Will faced his friend. "Pardon?"

"I've been trying to get you to answer my questions, but you're too busy gawking at my granddaughter. So please go to her and get it over with. Whatever happened between you two can't be that bad. Then we will be able to have a decent conversation."

Will didn't need any more encouragement. He assumed that her embarrassment and his hint about future children still hung between them, but right now it didn't matter, he felt better just seeing her. Everything else could be fixed later.

The small antique store was quaint with its old wood shelves and delicate floral wallpaper. They only sold smaller antique items but the selection was nice. She slowly walked around the store while she waited for Duncan, finding a few expensive items. One in particular was a lovely silver frame with hand-carved flowers around the edge. She had a photo of her family that she had brought with her. It had been taken before Scott had died. Her stomach rolled and she pressed her hand to her middle in an effort to control it. Eyeing the size of the frame, she knew the picture would fit.

The outer door opened but she ignored it and asked the clerk, "How much is this frame?"

"I'm sorry, Miss, it's not for sale."

"That's too bad." She paused as a strange calming sensation swept over her. "I-I—" She sighed. "Have a picture that would look great in it."

"The one of you with your family?"

Meghan stopped breathing, recognising the familiar voice.

"On your bedside table?"

She would never forget that voice. It made her heart jump every time that she heard it. She turned. "Will," she breathed out his name as her head filled with erotic images of him moving above her, in her.

"Meghan." He nodded then slowly scanned her face, stopping on her mouth.

"Hi." She blinked, trying to control the heat spreading through her limbs. "What are you doing here?"

"I was on my way home when Duncan called and asked if I wanted to join you two for lunch." He gestured towards the door, and Meghan thanked the young sales clerk before she left.

"So?" Duncan stepped up, staring at her. "Ready to eat?"

Placing her hand on her stomach, Meghan looked from Duncan to Will and back. "I-I think so."

Will reached for her shopping bags. "How about something light? Soup? There's a nice café a block or so away. They probably have peppermint tea."

She glared up at him. "You too."

"Me what?"

She shook her head. "Nothing."

"Well?" Will pushed for an answer.

With her hand still pressing into her middle she fully expected to become nauseous at the thought of food. That was what had happened every other time, but that wasn't what happened this time. Her stomach grumbled loud enough for both men to hear.

Will's chuckle made her smile. "I'll take that as a yes."

* * * *

After lunch, the trio strolled along the street. Meghan stopped at a couple of shops and ended picking up a nice scarf for her mum.

"I see your shopping is going well?" Will eyed the new addition to her shopping bags.

"Yeah, too well. I have only one more stop to make, and then I'm done."

"And tell Will where it is you have to stop," Duncan piped up.

"Duncan, don't start. I've already explained." Will's confusion was easy to see. "Duncan thinks I'm crazy. I need to stop at a supermarket to get the last of my gifts."

"A supermarket?" he asked, confused. "Like Morrisons?"

She nodded. "I want to pick up certain items for Ryan and my parents that only a grocery store will carry."

"What kind of items? Sweets?"

"Well, I'm no' taking you shopping at a bloody grocery store, Meghan Kennedy. So, say goodbye to Will," Duncan ordered. "It's time we went home."

Her mouth dropped open at his overbearing remark. She couldn't believe he was acting this...stubborn. She put her bags on the ground and began buttoning up her coat. Smiling at Will's puzzled stare as she pulled on a pair of gloves, she then reached for her bags and did as she had been told. "Goodbye, Will." Then walked away — in the opposite direction.

"The car is this way, girl," Duncan said.

Meghan turned to face Duncan. "Yes, I know." She raised her arm and pointed. "But I saw..." She turned to Will. "What was the name of that supermarket?"

"Morrisons," he supplied.

"Thank you. I saw a Morrisons this way."

"Ah" — Will rubbed his chin trying to hide his smirk — "it's actually back that way." He pointed in the same direction as Duncan.

"Stop trying to help."

He laughed, crossing his arms.

"I want to finish my shopping. This was your idea, remember," she pointed out.

"Lunch and a little shopping for yourself." Duncan snapped. "I didn't mean for you to send home a full grocery order."

"It's not a full grocery order." She met Will's surprised expression. "It's not. He's exaggerating."

Duncan snorted. "I do no such thing."

"Ha! Yah, right!" She turned.

"Stop this foolishness," Duncan called as she began to walk away again.

Will watched, amused, and found it even funnier when Duncan ordered her back. The determination on her face was very clear. She was going to the supermarket to buy gifts for her family. It sounded bizarre, but she was Canadian—maybe that was normal for her.

Meghan and Duncan stared at each other, neither one relenting. In a dramatic huff Meghan turned and started walking away for a third time. That was it, he was done. "Meghan," Will called out then added in a firm tone, ordered, "Wait there please."

"Why are you fighting her?" He faced Duncan. "Let her go if she wants to."

"No. She wants to buy them food for their gifts. Does that make any sense to you?" The old man threw his hands into the air.

"I told you earlier, Duncan," Meghan called out as she walked back to join them. "There are certain things here in Scotland that we don't have in Canada, and the few stores that do carry them charge a small fortune."

Will nodded, he understood now. Meghan was buying Scottish brand-name foods to send back to her family as a treat from their homeland.

"If Ryan wants a can of soda he can bloody well go to a store at home and buy it himself. You should'na have to send him one from here."

"I'm still going." Meghan informed. "I know you have a hard time understanding, but I want to do this. Mum and Dad and Ryan will love all the treats. I know they will."

It was clear to him that Meghan was trying to be patient, but Duncan wouldn't be swayed. She shrugged and began to walk away *again*.

"Wait, Meghan." Will caught up with her. "Will you let me talk to him before you go?"

She stared at him for a moment, and sighed. "Fine. Good luck."

Will walked back to Duncan. When he had received Duncan's call that morning all he had thought about was getting to Meghan, to make sure she was okay. He hadn't thought he would have been playing referee between her and Duncan in the middle of Perth.

"Duncan, let me take her to get the rest of her gifts."

"I won't wait around while she wastes her money," he snapped.

"You don't have to. I'll wait for her and we won't be long after you," he offered.

"I don't like her wasting her money. She's a smart girl, I know she watches her money closely. This seems so silly to me." The concern for his granddaughter was evident.

"Stop overreacting, it's not as bad as you think. She wants to spend her money on the people she loves. Would you rather she just throw it away or spend it solely on herself?" Will pointed out.

"Meghan is selfless. She would rather spend it on others." Duncan paused staring at Meghan. "You'll bring her straight home." Duncan wasn't asking, he was telling.

"Yes."

"Fine, I'll see you then." Duncan nodded, a cunning smirk on his face. Will stared in disbelief. That crafty old bugger had set them up—and in less than five minutes.

"Well, holy shit!" Will shook his head as he headed towards Meghan. *Very impressive.*

"He's leaving me, isn't he?" He could hear anxiety mixed with annoyance.

"No, I told him to go home and let you shop. I'll take you home once you're done."

Her expression turned wary as she watched Duncan walk away. "Maybe I should just go with Duncan."

"I thought you wanted to finish your shopping?"

"I do. I want to mail all the goodies home as soon as possible. I'm just not sure…it would be a good idea." She wrinkled her nose.

"Do you have to fight me over everything?" He sighed, frustrated when she didn't answer. "Meghan, we'll be in a supermarket. What could possibly happen?"

"You know. You'll start talking naughty to me…because we're not in the library. And then things could happen, like at the ruins."

"True. But I can't imagine the store's employees would allow us to have sex in the middle of the fresh produce aisle." He paused, giving her a wicked grin. "Or maybe they would. I can ask if you like." He laughed when her jaw dropped open. "Okay. What if I promised that nothing will happen while we're in Perth? Would that make you feel better?"

"Yes it would." She gave him a serious frown. "But what about when we get back to Little Glen?"

He wiped the smile from his face. "You know the answer to that."

"So, you'll keep your thoughts and..." She waved her finger up and down the length of him. "Everything else to yourself here and in the library? Those are the only two places I'll be left alone?"

"You won't be alone, I'll still be there." He shrugged. "I just won't be talking dirty to you and I'll do my very best to keep everything else contained."

"Of course you will." She rolled her eyes. "Why shouldn't I trust the man who wants me to lose our bet?"

He took her bags with one hand. "I never break a promise once I give it, but if I were in your shoes, I wouldn't trust me either." He held out his other hand as he met her turquoise stare.

In the end, Will clasped her hand in his and gently pulled her along the pavement. They would be standing there all night, waiting for her to make up her mind, if he let her. "Was that meant to comfort me?" she called over his shoulder. "'Cause it didn't, you know."

He grinned. "Just giving you fair warning."

Chapter Twenty

Meghan rummaged through the bags of groceries on the floor of Will's Land Rover. She had bought a mountain of food for her parents and Ryan. Maybe a little too much? She grabbed a chocolate bar and pulled it from the bag. Her mouth started to water as she stared at the brightly coloured wrapper.

"Chocolate lover, huh?" Will said. Meghan turned to look at him. He was watching the road as they drove back to Little Glen.

Meghan looked back to the bar. "Yeah."

"Go on, have it. It's not going to kill you."

No but it might make her puke all over his nice leather interior. She waited for her stomach to heave. When nothing happened, she didn't question it and tore open the wrapper so fast she almost dropped the milk chocolatey goodness on the floor. Ignoring the deep chuckle coming from her right, Meghan licked her lips, already tasting the rich chocolate.

"Do you think your family will like your gifts as much as you do?"

"More!" she mumbled, savouring the smooth texture of the chocolate, then threw the empty wrapper back into the grocery bag.

"More!" Will repeated. "After what I just witnessed. How is that possible?"

Meghan laughed. "My mum will use the Cook In sauces with bologna. Which is gross, I don't recommend it, then she'll hit the chocolate. Ryan will drink most of the Irn-Bru pop I'm sending him in one sitting, and Dad will go straight for the crisps. It will be quite the feeding frenzy, I'll be sorry to miss it." She exhaled slowly.

She had been there for almost a month now. She had hardly realised how much time had passed since she had last seen her family. Guess she should thank Will for that. She had been so preoccupied with him that she hadn't really thought about her family.

"What about your other brother? Which treat will he stuff himself with?"

"What?" She turned to face him, the all too familiar weight began squeezing her chest. "How do you know about Scott?" she asked carefully.

"Duncan mentioned two grandsons and I saw two teenage boys in that picture you keep on your bedside," Will informed her. "What's Scott's favourite?"

"Nothing." She fought the urge to slump her shoulders and concentrated on the view out of her window.

"Scott won't like the sweets or crisps you're sending?" he asked.

"No, he liked the dark chocolate bars—you know the really big ones?" She gestured the size with her hands.

"I know them." He paused. "Megh—"

"Scott's dead." She cut him off. "He died ten years ago. Just after we came back from visiting Duncan."

She continued to stare out of the side window. He really had had no idea about Scott. He had been serious when he had asked what treat Scott would like. She had assumed Duncan had told Will about Scott's death. Maybe it was still hard for Duncan too? She'd never ask him, she couldn't take the chance that he would look at her with the same pity as everyone else. Although the thought of someone else still being affected by Scott's death ten years after the fact was comforting. She was so tired of feeling like she was the only one.

"I'm sorry. I had no idea."

She didn't want his pity. It was ten long years ago. She had worked hard to put aside her feelings about that day. She never wanted to forget what happened, but it still hurt to remember.

"Why would you? I haven't told you much about my family." She shrugged.

Heat surrounded her hands as he gave her a little squeeze. She chanced a look as he focused on the road.

"No, you haven't." He quickly glanced at her. There was no pity or sympathy in those hypnotic eyes, just understanding.

"Can we talk about something else?"

He nodded and released her. "Duncan said you haven't been feeling well."

She groaned. "I don't want to talk about that either."

"Too bad," he countered. "What did the doc say?"

When she didn't answer he said her name in a quiet warning.

She faced him as he watched the road. "You're really bossy."

"Yes," he agreed. "I'm still waiting for my answer."

She huffed. "He doesn't know why I feel sick all the time."

"What kind of sick?"

"Like I want to throw up."

He casually pulled the Land Rover over to the side of the road and turned to face her. "Are you pregnant?"

"What?" she squeaked, shaking her head. She cleared her throat. "No, I'm not."

He gave her a hard frown. "You're certain?"

She nodded, turning away.

He turned her face back. "How are you certain?"

She threw her hands up. "I took a pregnancy test and it was negative. I told you I was on birth control."

"But you took the test anyways?"

"After what you said and because we...you know." She nodded her head. "It freaked me out, I needed to be sure and I had to rule it out. I have no idea why I feel so nauseous all the time. And I can barely think about food let alone eat it."

"You had no problem eating lunch today and you just ate that chocolate bar." He pulled the Land Rover back out onto the road.

Meghan sat back and stared out of the front window. "No, I didn't have a problem. I was starving."

"You don't look sick now. How do you feel?"

She placed her hand over her stomach. "I feel fine." She sat for a minute tuning into her body, waited to feel the heavy weight to rear its head.

"Well?"

"That's strange? For seven days I've felt as though I wanted to throw up and now it's gone."

"Seven days?" He gave her a thoughtful frown then abruptly changed the subject. "How's Lucy?"

She had forgotten all about Lucy. She should have remembered to tell him that she had brought Lucy over to Duncan's. But with her appointment and Duncan being unreasonable, and with Will all of a sudden showing up, she'd forgotten all about poor Lucy.

"Fine." She shrugged, and quickly confessed, "I didn't like the thought of her being alone all night." Heat spread to her cheeks. "You have been gone for seven days. That's almost a month in dog time." She chuckled.

"I had some unexpected problems with my last client and I had to stop in at my offices before I could leave." Then he teased, "If I didn't know better, I might suspect that you missed me."

She let her pride speak for her. "I don't care how long you've been gone for. You shouldn't have left Lucy like that. I was ticked off at you, that's why I dog-napped her."

"First you tell me you didn't like her being alone, and now you're telling me that you dog-napped her? Does that mean you plan on keeping her?"

Meghan gave him a sideways glance and shrugged. "She might not want to leave. She has had it pretty good at Duncan's. Lots of treats, runs and walks more than once a day, lounging on leather chairs, sleeping on beds, who could blame her for wanting to stay with us? You did after all abandon her."

"Now I've abandoned her?" He laughed. "And whose bed did she commandeer?"

"Mine, unfortunately. She takes up the whole bed and when I kick her off she just hops back up in the middle of the night."

"That's my Lucy. Besides the stealing of bed space, how is she?"

"Good. She's a real sweetheart."

"Sweetheart? That's one I'm not used to hearing. Most people are scared shitless of her."

"Why? She's a good girl. You know I haven't heard her growl once since I met you?"

Meghan didn't know what to make of his thoughtful gaze and it was weird how he studied her before answering, "I've noticed that."

Chapter Twenty-One

For a week Will watched Meghan. He watched her body movements, her expressions. Took mental notes on how she responded to him when he was close and what she was like when she was unaware of him. And after the week was up he paid Duncan a visit.

"Will!" Duncan stepped aside allowing him entry. "What brings you here?"

"Meghan."

"She's still at the library, something about a rush on a deadline."

"I know where she is." He levelled his stare on the older man. "I need to ask you a few questions about her."

Duncan frowned, closing the door. "I have a feeling we might need a drink. Come on." Duncan marched into the den not bothering to wait for him.

Once Duncan had handed him a Scotch and had settled himself in an old wingback chair, he asked, "Now, what's this all about?"

"What's wrong with Meghan?" Will asked, taking a seat across from him.

"How do you mean?"

He placed his glass on the floor beside his feet. Clasping his hands, he rested his elbows on his knees. "When I'm with Meghan she's fine, no nervous stomach or nausea and she eats. But, when I'm not there, she looks uncomfortable and I swear to God she looks as though she is about to throw up. This wasn't happening before, but it is now, so I'm asking you, what the hell is the matter with her?"

"Just like you said, nervous stomach."

"Bullshit," Will snapped then ran his hand through his hair. "It looks like..." This was crazy, but it was the only thing that made any sense. "Like she gets nausea when I'm not with her."

"Well, at least it's happening when you're not there. It's good to know you're not the one making her sick," Duncan pointed out.

"Damn it, Duncan, that's no' the point."

Sighing, Duncan gripped the glass in his hands. "I was hoping she wouldn't have this much trouble, but I should have expected it, she's a Kennedy after all and if we are anything, we are stubborn."

"Yes, you are and so is Meghan, but what does that have to do with anything?"

The older man exhaled slowly. "Meghan's sudden bouts of queasiness are your fault."

The muscles in his shoulders tensed up. "How's that?"

"Now don't go getting your back up. She is doing her share to you too."

"Doing what to me?" He clenched his fists.

Duncan gave him the okay-I'll-spell-it-out-for-you sigh. "Meghan's absence is causing you to behave this way."

Will snapped his head up. "What way?"

"The entire time I've known you, even when you were a wee lad, you could always control your actions, when other children even your own brothers, could not. Yet here you sit about ready to beat me senseless."

"Duncan, I would never—" He was cut off before he had a chance to finish.

"This behaviour is out of character for you, as are Meghan's bouts of nausea out of character for her."

Will exhaled as he stood. "Jesus, Duncan, out with it."

Duncan swallowed the remainder of his Scotch. "Have you ever heard of a binding spell?"

"A what?"

"A binding spell," Duncan repeated seriously.

Will went to Duncan's side, then bending down, focused on his eyes.

Duncan leant back. "What are you doing boy?"

"Looking to see if you're pissed,"

"I'm not pissed."

Will stood back. "Then what the hell are you talking about?"

"Enough!" Duncan ordered. "Sit down."

Will took a deep breath but remained standing. "Okay. Go ahead."

"A binding spell was woven into the words of the marriage contract."

"A spell." Will took another deep breath. "Duncan," he began carefully. "Spells aren't real."

"Yes, they are."

"No..." Will frowned.

"Have you noticed that when you are away from Meghan you are agitated?"

Will paused, remembering his latest job. At the time, he had chalked it up to frustration over the problems with his new client. Yet, when he thought about it, he hadn't stopped thinking about Meghan the entire time he had been gone and the more he had thought about her, the more agitated he had become.

Duncan continued, "And you noticed Meghan. When you aren't near she feels sick. But once she sees you, she's fine again."

Will shook his head. "That doesn't mean anything. She probably has a bug."

Duncan was already shaking his head. "It's the binding spell. The moment you both read the marriage contract, the spell took hold. Neither one of you will feel at ease when you are apart, only when you are together will you have peace."

Will sat down, replaying his time spent with Meghan since reading the marriage contract. There had been some force drawing him to her before he knew of the contract but once he had read it, the need to be with her had grown. As for Meghan, he couldn't remember her having any bouts of nausea before reading the contract but after he had noticed more than once how she would place her hand over her stomach, her face becoming pale.

My God. He wasn't actually beginning to believe this nonsense, was he?

"James did tell you about the different families of the highlands, didn't he, boy?"

"Granddad told us a lot of things." Will sat back. "Bedtime stories mostly, about brownies living in our house, banshees appearing outside the house of someone who was about to die, the story of the Sleeping Fian Warriors and how kelpies live in Letham Loch."

"Well, I know the Fian are out on one of the Isles, not sure which one though. The locals out there are tight-lipped." He rubbed his chin. "Haven't seen a kelpie in years. They like to travel from loch to loch, so that's not unusual. But those brownies..." Duncan scowled. "They can be nasty little beggars if you're not careful."

Will opened his mouth but closed it when he realised Duncan was serious. The man actually believed what he was saying.

"Well?" Duncan pushed. "Did James tell you about the 'sight' some families have?"

Shaking his head, he waited for Duncan to explain.

"There are a few families in the Highlands that have extra abilities. The Cochrans have the gift for seeing the future. You see, at the Battle of Bannockburn the MacKenzie's son William was killed in battle. He had been betrothed to the Kennedy's eldest daughter Meghan. It was rumoured that the two were already in love and planned to..."

"Wait," Will interrupted. "I know this one. But he dies in battle, and she was left alone, right?" He remembered Sarah complaining about that part the next morning at breakfast.

"So James told you of the binding?"

Will shook his head. "He never said anything about a spell or a binding. I just remember the part about the battles."

Duncan raised his eyebrows and nodded his head. "You being a soldier, that makes sense." He went and poured himself another drink. "After the battle was won and the lairds all gathered around the Bruce, a young woman was called to tend to Alasdair's wound. Her name was Kassandra Cochran. She is the one who foresaw you and Meghan, and who wove the binding spell into the Contract. It was widely known that her gran used the binding spell on couples who were strongly attracted but reluctant to marry."

Duncan was back in his chair when Will focused on him. "What happened to the other Meghan?"

Duncan shook his head. "'Tis the sad part. It's said she died shortly after she heard of William's death. The story is that she either tripped down some hidden steps at the back of the MacKenzie castle or she threw herself down. Regardless, she was found at the bottom with a broken neck."

Will calmly reached down and picked up his drink, swallowing the amber liquid in one gulp. *Holy shit!* Meghan had taken him straight to those steps.

"Are you all right boy?" Duncan asked. "You looked a little shell-shocked there for a minute."

He stood. "I'm fine." And headed to the front door with Duncan trailing behind him. "I have to go to London for a few days." He turned, dropping his stare to meet Duncan's. "Call me if it gets bad."

Duncan knew that he was referring to Meghan and nodded. "I'm going to ask her to take care of Lucy while I'm gone." He sighed. "Maybe it will help." Will opened the door and began down the front walk.

"That's it?" Duncan demanded as he stood in the open door. "You believe everything I just told you? I expected you to at least give me some kind of an argument. Tell me I'm crazy. That's what people usually say."

"No. No argument and I don't think you're crazy." Will pulled open the front gate.

"But you did at first," Duncan called. "What changed your mind?"

Will didn't bother answering, he simply called, "I'll be back as soon as I can."

Chapter Twenty-Two

"Come on, Lucy," Meghan called over her shoulder. The black beast bounded out of the front door after her.

Her stomach rolled again. *Hooray, another day of constant nausea.*

She exhaled slowly, shaking her head. Her stupid stomach had kept her awake most of the night, until her thoughts had drifted to Will. She had dreamt he had come into her room. She had watched as he had taken off his black jacket and had tossed it on the bottom of her bed, and how the sleeves of his black T-shirt had clung to the muscles of his biceps and shoulders. He had sat on the bed, taking off his boots, then he had swung his legs on top of the covers.

"Will?" She hadn't been sure why she had called to him like that. She had already known it was him.

Turning towards her, he had slid his warm hand under her shirt and across her belly. "I'm here." She remembered sighing as he had rolled her onto her side to face him and how nice it had felt when he had touched her. He had pushed down her covers so he was able to slide his hand up her bare back. She liked the heat he gave off and she liked how he fitted their two bodies together. Her insides had begun to stir, to heat up, she had wanted him inside her body, had wanted him to make love to her.

"Will," she had pleaded, tugging on his shirt.

"Shhh." He kissed her mouth lightly. "Not tonight, you need to sleep."

She'd thought that had been a weird thing to say. "But I am asleep."

The breath from his soft chuckle tickled her skin. He kissed her again, this time on the forehead. She pressed her face into his neck, his scent calming her. She felt so comfortable, so warmed and even a little...loved.

When she had woken this morning she had felt cold and alone and the waves of nausea that followed had yet to calm.

She rested her hands on her hips, breathing through the queasiness. Was this ever going to stop?

Lucy sat in front of her wagging her tail. That big toothy grin was the best part of her day. "Okay, fur-face. Let's see if this helps."

Having completed her normal route, she was on her way back when the grey stone tower caught her eye. It was a beautiful afternoon—the view from the outer wall of the ruins would be breathtaking. She came to a stop at the beginning of Will's road. The last time she was up at the ruins she had acted like an animal. Had begged Will to fuck her. She didn't want to go through that feeling of being completely out of control. She shook her head. What did it matter—he wasn't even home. He was still in London, so nothing would happen anyway.

"God damn it," Will growled, throwing his laptop case onto his desk.

Crossing his arms, he kept his gaze glued to Meghan as she ran past. She was oblivious to him and his reaction. With her arms and legs pumping hard, her concentration was solely on the road in front of her. He noticed her hair was pulled through the back of that ragged-looking cap as she moved up the hill.

He had come back late last night in a bad mood. He remembered the side effects of the spell, hadn't stopped thinking about them the entire time he had been gone, and had turned towards Duncan's rather than going home. He had needed to know if she was the cause but more importantly he needed Meghan.

The moment he had pulled her body to his, all of the anger that had built up over the past few days had vanished. However, watching her run up his hill, risking another attack that could very well take her away from him, caused his anger to flare to a dangerous level.

Will watched as she continued up the hill. He couldn't go to her, not like this. He was too mad and his bad luck in London weighed in as well. He had lost Shawn Mackay, one of his best guys, which was really saying something considering he was ex-SAS. A company that specialised in protection work in war-torn countries had offered him top dollar to join their ranks. Will's company, S&G Protection, just couldn't compete. He was lucky that most of his guys had started families, and weren't willing to travel anymore. But Shawn, who had lost his wife and didn't have a family, had nothing holding him back. Hell, who was he kidding, if he hadn't started his own business, he too would have joined ranks with a similar company. He missed the excitement, that kick of adrenaline that only the fear of death could bring.

The scrambling had begun after that, he had to find a replacement for his next job. And after all the phone calls, his last resort had been his younger brother Gavin. An ex-Royal Marine Commando. Gavin had chalked up a number of tours in Afghanistan and other various places, then without giving a reason, Gavin had released and had been sitting around doing nothing ever since. He wasn't sure if working with family was going to be a good idea, but he'd find out soon enough.

Not the best couple of days and all he wanted was to come home and see Meghan. To smell her flowery scent, touch her soft lips. She had wanted more than that last night and he had almost given into her whispered plea, but her drowsy—'But I am asleep'— had quickly sobered him.

Jesus, that was the only time she hadn't fought him and that was because she'd thought she was sleeping.

He watched her start up the steep incline towards the ruins. "Stubborn brat."He squeezed his jaw.

The urge to give her that spanking he had threatened suddenly seemed like a good idea. She clearly didn't understand his warning. He had said he didn't like her running up the hill, that attack of hers had scared the hell out of him. Although since then he had made a point of doing a bit of research and now he knew the details of her particular illness.

He moved his head back and forth, trying to ease the muscles in his neck. This was not a good day to push his buttons, but if she wanted to get up the bloody hill so badly, then by God he would make sure she did. There would be no driving her up today, she would run the entire way. He would make sure she did, then maybe her obsession would come to an end. Obviously, she didn't worry about the people who cared for her or how her reckless acts affected them. That would change today. Today she would know how it felt to be scared.

He was running up the hill, in less than a minute. He didn't bother to change and went out wearing what he had on, jeans, his fall jacket and his boots. He didn't need proper running shoes. He had trained in boots for so long that he had got used to their weight. He caught up to her in no time, slowing to her pace. His gaze slid down her back stopping on her backside. His hand tingled when he remembered cupping that juicy bottom.

God damn it. Never had he been so easily distracted. This stubborn brat was making him crazy. His unwavering concentration was something that he was proud of. He never lost focus on a task once he had his mind set on it, and it was unsettling that Meghan was the cause of his lack of concentration.

Man, her legs felt like weights! They weren't burning like the last time, but still, she should take it easy. Being cautious was necessary, if she happened to have another attack, Will wasn't there to help her. So her inhaler and common sense were the only defence she had. She grabbed the outside of her pocket feeling for her inhaler. It was still there, just like it had been two minutes before.

She slowed her pace, the heaviness pulled even more at her legs until she slowed to a walk. She pulled her ear buds out and surveyed the hill. "Not too bad, Meg," she said out loud, pleased with her effort.

"Not good either." She jumped and quickly turned. "Will." That familiar fluttering returned to her stomach and she started to smile when she saw the hard look on his face as he loomed over her.

Easing back a few steps, she babbled, "I-I didn't see your truck. I thought you were in—"

"London? I was. But now I'm here, with you. On this hill. Again." He bit out each word, the muscles flexing in his jaw.

"Ah...okay." She kept her tone light. "I just finished and was going back home to have a shower." She began to walk back down the hill.

"Not today, you're not."

She blinked at his sharp tone and found him standing in front of her. She stepped back, startled by his speed.

"You're going to finish your run today." It wasn't a statement, it was an order.

"I am?" For the first time since meeting Will, she was actually nervous of him. Was it deliberate or—he cut her off.

"Yes, you are. You want to get up this hill so goddamn much that you are willing to risk having another attack? That's fine with me." He took a step closer, crowding her. "You like to gamble. Let's roll the dice."

Oh yah, she totally wanted to run now...in the opposite direction!

He was scaring the crap out of her, but she couldn't allow her fear to show. She would never allow her fear to show ever again. "No! I think I'll just go home."

"You don't have a choice today." He crossed his large arms. "There's no backing out. I'm here to make sure you finish this run." He raised his arm and pointed up the hill. "Now get moving."

"No!" She stood her ground.

A smirk pulled at the corner of his mouth. "Of course if you think you can't do it?" He teased.

Damn, he could play her so easily and she fell into it every time. Glaring up at him, she pushed her earphones back in and turned on her music. "You're a dick." She turned and started back up the hill.

The heavy pounding of her heart vibrated though her body. She shouldn't be doing this. Her body had told her enough, yet her pride forced her to keep moving. She felt for her inhaler.

Will! Urgh! He was so good at poking her pride, and she was so stupid to let him. She called over her shoulder at him, "I wasn't pushing myself. I took it easy on the way up."

"I don't care," he snapped directly behind her. "Keep going."

"Fine." It was fine. This was what she had wanted, climb this steep hill. To get up to the ruins and say 'I did that'. Of course she had never thought it would happen like this but what the hell. And with that, she put on a burst of speed.

Which didn't last long. "Damn it," she mouthed silently.

Her breathing was fast, ragged even, and her legs felt like they were going to give out on her. She couldn't go any farther—her feet suddenly tangled together and she flew forward. The ground came up fast. She barely had time to pull her hands out when two vice grips locked onto her upper arms, stopping her with her nose an inch away from the dirt road. Will pulled her upright.

The heat of Will's chest seeped into her back. She tried to ignore it but it didn't help when his breath tickled the side of her neck. "Don't stop. You're almost there." Then shoved her out in front of him. "Move!"

Then slapped her hard on the butt to emphasise his point.

"That hurt!"

Meghan shot him a nasty glare over her shoulder, her hand still rubbing the sting he had caused. He knew that she was pushing herself hard, running faster than she should be. He also knew that he was scaring her, but he didn't care, she needed to know how it felt. How his chest had tightened with the memory of her bent over struggling for air. Or what might have happened if he hadn't been there to help her. The idea of her gone from his life was not something that he would ever allow.

They reached the top a few minutes later. Will followed Meghan as she slowly walked around the ruins, listening to her heavy breathing, willing it to slow. His wish was granted and he finally took a breath himself when she began hopping from foot to foot, punching the air, humming the tune to a bad boxing movie. The urge to burst out laughing was hard to fight, but he forced a hard look. "How do you feel?"

She looked up from under the old beat-up hat, her face bright with satisfaction. "Tired and a little shaky, but good."

He nodded. "It's done. You've run up the hill. I don't want you to do it again."

A snort came before the words. "You can't make me do anything I don't want to do. If I want to run up this hill again I will. But I will say thank you for pushing me."

Shit! How did he know she would say that? Sighing, he quickly clasped her hand in his and started pulling her towards a flat rock in the centre of the clearing. Its light grey colouring suggested it that might have been part of the old keep at one point.

"What are you doing?" she asked, trying to pull her hand free. Will ignored her question, tightening his grasp.

Once at the flat rock, Will sat and began to slowly pull Meghan closer. She stared down at him, turquoise eyes swirling with confusion.

"You're no' going to like me very much after this. But not for too long. I won't let you." Will knew the precise moment when she realised what his intentions were.

"What! No!" Meghan gasped. Will was going to spank her. He was going to put her over his knee and spank her. He had said he would, but she had never believed... He said he would never... He lied? She tried desperately to pull her hands free, but he was so strong. She stared at his face. It appeared as though he didn't want to do it.

"Please, Will. Don't." She began to panic. "You're such a big man. I don't think I could...you could do a lot of damage to me. Please."

"I don't give threats lightly. I said if you ran up this hill I would spank some sense into you. And that's exactly what I plan on doing." His face was hardened now, set on the task at hand. Meghan dug her heels in, but the wet grass stopped her from holding her ground and he easily pulled her forward.

It was going to happen. He was just too big for her to fight off. She whispered a plea, "Please, Will. I'm sorry. I didn't mean to start this."

A snap of his wrist and she found herself standing between his bent legs. "Then why did yeh?" He squeezed her hips. One quick jerk and she would be lying across his knees. "The truth this time."

"I…wanted to… Oh! I did it out of spite, all right," she shouted. "I don't like being told what to do, I didn't care if you knew or not. I won't let someone else push me around or take advantage of me." She placed her hands on his large arms. Maybe she could pull herself free somehow.

He didn't seem to notice her struggle. "You think I'm trying to take advantage of you?"

She stopped. "Well, maybe not," she admitted slowly. "But you are pushing me around and I don't like it." Crap! In her haste to explain, she'd got him confused with Rob.

He mumbled a curse. "This has nothing to do wi' anyone pushing you around or telling you what to do. This is about your lack of common sense. You were told 'no hills' by a doctor. He wasn't being overly cautious. He said it because he's concerned for your well-being." He gave her a shake when she slid her eyes from his. "Look at me! What about Duncan? What about the other people who care about you? Don't you care how they would feel if you ended up in hospital while you're here, just because you don't like being told what to do? You're being very selfish."

Meghan studied the ground. Was she selfish? The thought had never occurred to her, she honestly didn't think about her actions or how they affected anyone else except herself. She didn't want Duncan, or anyone else for that matter, to worry about her, and the hospital was always a possibility, if the attack was bad enough. Crap, he was right. She was being selfish. Why of all people was it Will to point this out? Why did it bother him so much? Was Will one of those people who cared about her? Or was he just here to punish her on their behalf?

"You're right. I don't want to worry Duncan," she confessed, trying to pull away. His grip only tightened. "You made your point, you can let go." Panic rose when he shook his head.

Meghan fought him like a demon and when he'd finally had enough he gave her a quick jerk forward and had her sitting on his lap, straddling his thighs. His hands gripped her waist keeping her pinned in place. A tremor shook her.

"Enough," he growled against her ear. "Calm down."

"Will, please..." She suddenly wrapped her arms around him, pressing her face against his neck.

He sighed, a guilty weight sitting in his chest. This was not how he wanted to make his point, but made his point he had. He prayed silently she wouldn't be terrified of him now. He would never have touched her but she didn't need to know that. He just hoped she would understand why he was doing this.

Resting his chin on the side of her head he slid a hand to the back of her neck and stroked the exposed skin. "I need you to promise me that you won't run up that hill again."

"Promise?" Her breathing had slowed but her body was still tense.

"Yes." He pushed her back so he could see her face. "Promise me."

She lowered her head, the brim of her baseball hat blocking her features.

"Damn it, Meghan." He sighed. "Is that so much to ask?" He cupped her cheeks and raised her head. "I need to know that you won't try this again."

Her thin eyebrows pressed together as she whispered, "Why?"

Yes, why? It wasn't something he couldn't describe to her and have it make any sense. It was a heavy need that rested in his chest, close to his heart. He had to know she would be safe. He had to know that she wouldn't try this again because if something happened to her he was fairly certain he would go crazy and turn into a dark shell of a man. "Just promise me."

She lowered her head again. "Why do you... damn it," He huffed. "I'd like to see your face when I talk to you." And he took hold of the brim of her ball cap. "Take this thing..."

"No." She forcefully slapped his hand. Her quick movement surprised him and he let go of her. Taking full advantage of her freedom she shoved against his chest and fell to the ground. A low whimper escaped when she landed hard onto her bottom. She glared up at him from under the hat, anger glowing in her now green eyes. "Don't ever touch this hat."

The bite to her words caused Will to frown. He sat forward, resting his elbows on his knees as he looked down at her. Not a few minutes ago he had thought she was becoming scared of him and now she looked ready to do some spanking herself. Even so, her odd change in behaviour wouldn't deter him from his goal.

"Give me your promise." He forced a hard edge to his words. "No hills."

They stared at each other for a few minutes, until she sighed, "I promise I won't run up this hill again."

Will shook his head. Christ. That could have gone better. He studied her still sitting on the ground. "I didn't know the hat was so important to you. I wouldn't have touched it if I had."

A curious look came to her face. "Well, it is important to me."

"As important as you are to me?" He watched her face become pink. He shook his head. "It didn't feel nice, did it? Not having any control over a situation. Not knowing what the outcome would be? Scary, wasn't it?"

She was quiet for a moment then nodded. "Yes, it was."

"Good, now you know how it feels." He stood, grabbed the front of her hooded sweatshirt and hauled her to her feet. "God, I hope you aren't going to be this spiteful when we're married." Her mouth gaped open in disbelief, then snapped shut as he straightened her top. "And for the record, the only way I'd spank you is if you were wearing a red leather bra, matching thong and asked me real nice."

She inhaled sharply, her eyes huge. He chuckled, stepping beside her. "I see you still like that particular idea."

"No...I don't."

"Oh yes you do," he called as he walked away.

Chapter Twenty-Three

Raising her focus from her laptop, Meghan stared out of the library window with the feeling that someone was watching her. Again. It wasn't Will. No way. He was upfront with his torment, and this feeling was different than the feelings Will stirred — this felt sneaky and underhand. Besides, she hadn't seen him since her run yesterday. The run that had gone from a relaxing excursion, to a physical fitness test, to a lesson in respecting others and had finally ended up with her wearing a red leather bra with matching thong and Will smacking her on the ass.

She snorted out loud. *He must be living in a dream world if he thought that she would actually wear red leather. Red looked terrible with her hair colour. As for the spanking...* Her skin tingled and heated with the thought of Will's hands on her. "Oooh!" She groaned. What was the matter with her?

It bugged the hell out of her that Will had been right. His methods had been completely barbaric, but would she have listened if he had tried another way? No, she wouldn't have. She wasn't blind to her faults. She knew how stubborn she could be. Still, that didn't mean she liked to admit she was wrong. Though, she would make a conscious effort to think about the people she cared about before she did anything rash again.

I hope you aren't going to be this spiteful when we're married?

"Oh God," she groaned into her hands, hearing Will's deep accent in her head.

Married to Will. Her heart, along with her stomach leapt—a nice change from wanting to spew. "Nooo!" she whined. She couldn't want things like that. Placing her head in her hand, she fought to block out his outdoorsy smell and unshaven chin as she logged into her mailbox. Waiting for her was a long email and a very cute joke from her friend Jessica and attached was a picture of little Jack, holding a painting he had made for his Auntie Meg.

Her computer hummed a tune as a real-time message appeared on her screen.

Ryan: Hey, Megs. Got a few questions for you.

Meghan: Well, hello to you too, Ryan! You're at work early?

Ryan: Yah. Listen, some things have been going on here that I think you should know.

Meghan. Okay?

Meghan sat back when she read the screen. Ryan had caught Rob outside her apartment. Said he had just dropped by to say hi and that there were no hard feelings. No hard feelings? What crap. Something wasn't right. Rob never just dropped by.

Meghan: Did you arrest him?

Ryan: No. Just gave him a warning to keep out of trouble.

Meghan: That's it?

Ryan: He has to commit a crime in order for me to arrest him and no matter how much I want to make him hurt for what he did to you, wanting to talk to you isn't a valid crime.

Meghan gawked at the screen then pounded out her next thought.

Meghan: Can't you think of something to arrest him for? Be creative.

Ryan: Meg. He will slip up, just let me do my job.

Meghan: Okay. Sorry.

Ryan: Listen, I need to know... Did you tell him it was over?

Meghan: Of course I told him it was over.

She felt her lips press together in irritation.

Meghan: I shouted it at him for God's sakes. And if he didn't get that, you arresting him for theft might have given him a clue or two.

Ryan: He's left the country and word has it he's in Scotland.

She gasped out loud.

Meghan: Please tell me you're kidding.

Ryan: We've sent alerts over to the major cities and I made sure Perth received one as well. If you see him call the police.

Call the police! There were no police in Little Glen. It was too small. She crossed her fingers before she asked her next question.

Meghan: Is he looking for me?
Ryan: Promise me you'll call the police if anything happens.

Oh shit! She jumped when the outer door opened and slowly let out her breath when Will walked in. She looked past him and out into the village as he approached the table.

"Meghan?"

She shifted her eyes to his when she heard his question.

"Is everything all right?"

She nodded, then turned her attention back to Ryan's line of text.

Meghan: Yes. I'll call them.
Ryan: I'm sorry I can't be there.
Meghan: Please don't worry. I'll be fine.

Ryan said his goodbyes, promising to email her soon.

Meghan sat there for a minute just staring at the screen until Will's breath warmed her neck. "Things not good at home?"

She jerked forward. "Everything's fine." And switched off the real-time chat box, displaying the picture of Jack holding his painting.

"You're not a good liar."

She took a steadying breath. *Please say he didn't see that.*

Thankfully, he changed the subject. "Cute kid. Not much of an artist though."

Her back and shoulders cooled as he moved around to sit across from her.

Focusing all her attention on her laptop she stated matter-of-factly, "Jack is six, and the world's greatest painter."

"What art critic told you that?" Even though she wasn't looking directly at him, she knew he was smiling because her skin prickled to life at the sound of his amusement.

"He told me."

His chuckle echoed around the library.

She bit the inside of her cheek to keep from smiling and turned her attention back to her mail. There was a new message in her box from Jody. Now there was a good yet slightly bizarre friend. They had grown up going to high school and university together. Jody had an amazing way to make everything fun, she missed that. However, it seemed that fun would now span the Atlantic. Jody was coming to Scotland, this Friday in fact, for the weekend. Jody was a music agent for a Toronto-based record company, who wanted a feel for the European market. So they were sending Jody and their new up-and-comer over to test the waters.

"Holy crap, that is awesome!" She clamped her hand over her mouth expecting to hear Grace snap at her.

"She left when you were engrossed in your email." Will chuckled.

She grinned at him, then continued reading. A mutual friend, Kris, had become Jody's client. Kris had gone to university with them and had studied business to appease his family. Which had never made any sense to her. He was a gifted musician and wrote all of his own songs. It was nice to know that he had finally given into his first love, music.

"That must be good news?"

She looked up from her laptop into Will's hypnotic stare, suddenly wondering if he could read her thoughts. She hoped not, because the memory of his body covering hers filled the space between them. Her skin began to heat and tingle. Her body tightened, becoming achy like she was back there with him, digging her nails into his shoulders, holding on tight as he rode her hard.

"Are you having a dirty dream about me?"

Meghan focused and drew in a breath. The look was wicked and dark, carnal desire shadowing his handsome face.

"Yes." She blinked and gasped at her own answer. "I mean, no!"

"Take a breath," he encouraged smoothly.

She did. "I mean yes. It's great news. Two of my closest friends are coming to Edinburgh this weekend." She focused back on the screen of her laptop—a much safer option than his steamy 'I know you want me to fuck you' look.

Thank God Jody was coming. She would be able to get away from that naughty grin and those turbulent eyes for the weekend. Clear him from her thoughts for a few days. She needed this, to be close to her friends, to relax and to not worry that she could lose a bet and end up married.

She typed in her response and agreed to meet at Jody's hotel on Friday afternoon. Today was Wednesday, so that gave her a day and a half to figure out how she would get down there. She better start kissing up to Duncan ASAP, just in case.

A giddy feeling bubbled up in her chest, and she smiled, she was so excited she wanted to dance around the room.

As she began packing up her belongings, a new message popped into her inbox. Her fingers paused above the keyboard. Same as before, the sender was just a bunch of random numbers. Not again. She sighed, annoyed, but opened the message, knowing full well she shouldn't. The message was brief and to the point—

'Go home, Meg. Or better yet let's go together.'

Holy shit! Did Rob send this? She peered out of the window again, this time only seeing grey shadows mixed with the last bits of sun reflecting off the trees. Was he there watching her? Man, she really hoped she was overreacting. Just in case she wasn't, she created a folder in her mailbox and moved it over. Just in case.

"Going back home to hide?" Will raised one dark eyebrow.

"I'm not hiding." She tried to keep her tone light, he wasn't going to ruin this day.

"Then why no run this morning? Wanted to avoid seeing me?"

"Boy"—she shook her head at him—"can you get any more conceited?"

"Yes. But I'm right. Aren't I?"

"Can you blame me? You made me feel like a child. I was scared and humiliated."

"You were acting like a child." He stared her straight in the eye, seemingly unfazed by her shout. "Scaring and humiliating you was unfortunate."

"Unfortunate? What would happen if you lost control? We both know exactly what you're capable of."

His expression darkened and his words were spoken just above a whisper, "Let's get a couple of things straight. One, I don't want you to know what I'm capable of. And Two, I would never…" His voice hardened to emphasise his point. "*Never* lose control with you."

Goose bumps appeared on her arms as her skin tingled and she was unsure if she was cold or scared or…? Crap! What was wrong with her? She must be some kind of freak to be turned on by the dark side of a man, especially this man.

"If you don't like the way I behave, then can I assume the bet has been taken off the table?"

"No you can't." His tone was harsh. "The bet still stands."

"Why?" She jammed her hands onto her hips. "So you can win a bet? I get the feeling sometimes you don't even like me."

"I don't?"

"Of course you don't. It's so obvious that a blind man could see."

"Really? Why don't you explain it to me? My vision isn't too clear today."

She felt her jaw drop open. "Are you kidding? Where do I start?" she snapped sarcastically. "You called me stubborn, and selfish. You think I act like a child. You force me to run up a hill, and then at the top you scare the hell out of me by threatening to hit me if I ever try it again. You follow me to the doctor's so you can lecture me on my relationship with my grandfather. You're forcing a marriage contract on me that is older than God himself. And you sit there looking at me, like you have no idea what I'm talking about." She pulled in a mouthful of air.

"Spank you."

She blinked. "What?"

"I said I would spank you, not hit you. There's a difference."

"Are you kidding?" she bellowed.

"No, I'm not. Hitting you would never happen. But spanking, that's still up in the air."

"What am I doing? Why did I even bother?" She needed to get away from him, far away, and the sooner the better. She shook her head, mumbling, "Why didn't I just stay away from you?"

The next thing she knew Will was crowding her, forcing her to face him.

"It wouldnae have mattered." He gave her a little shake. "I would have found another way to get close to you. And if that didnae work, I'd find another and another." She knew that he spoke the truth. If anyone could get near her it would be Will, one of his many skills, she supposed.

The heat he gave off melted her willpower. How was she supposed to fight that dark suggestive look that caused her skin to tingle and her insides to burn lusciously? She focused on his mouth, remembering the way it had covered hers, remembered how her body had come to life the moment their lips had touched.

Even though she wanted to fight him, her body betrayed her the moment he reached for her. Her breasts ached, her nipples hardened to stiff peaks, and eager moist heat pooled between her legs. She had never experienced this before. Not with anyone. This only happened with Will.

"You want me," he stated, just above a whisper.

Despite wanting to fight her desire for him, she let her shoulders slump and nodded She caught sight of an arrogant grin before his mouth came down hard on hers.

A whip of electricity snapped between them, the moment that their mouths touched. And just like at the ruins, she didn't have any say in the matter, everything seemed to be happening and she had no way of controlling any of it. Then again, she really wasn't sure she wanted to.

His mouth moved over hers, his whiskers lightly scraping her skin. He slipped his tongue between her lips and stroked the inside of her mouth. His mouth was warm, sweet with a masculine taste and she savoured his tongue as it teased and caressed. The forceful touch making her hotter and wetter. She ached for more. She had to have more. Sealing their bodies tight, she wrapped her arms around his neck.

Meghan's nails dug her into his scalp in her need to pull him closer. Will couldn't stop the groan that escaped. Fuck, she was killing him. One minute she had been thinking he hated her and the next she was in his arms. What was he going to do with her?

Pulling his mouth away, he stooped down and gripped her just below her behind. He kneaded her firm bottom through her jeans before ordering, "Hold onto me." He lifted and parted her thighs in one fluid movement, then wrapped her legs around his waist without her aid. He sat her on the table, keeping his body glued to hers as he forced her to lie back. He sucked in a breath when she shifted her hips, the apex of her thighs teasing his cock. He thrust forward, receiving a sexy little whimper for his effort.

"This table is the perfect height," he pointed out as he nibbled on her neck.

"Perfect," she breathed, tugging on his shirt. "Let's use it."

Will grinned as he stood back and pulled off her brown leather boots. He dropped them to the floor and reached for her belt as she sat up and reached for his. She fumbled with the buttons on his pants, her now lustful sapphire gaze was hooded by her long lashes. Her swollen lips curled slightly at the corners when she slipped her hand inside and rubbed her hand along his hard cock.

Growling, he yanked off her jeans and covered her half-naked body with his own. He pushed up her top, kissed her stomach, loved the way the muscles clenched when his mouth touched her. He moved to her breasts, cupped their weight, and sucked her large pink nipples through the sheer fabric of her bra, leaving damp spots.

"Will," she demanded, running her hands up under his shirt. "Stop teasing me."

Without breaking contact with her mouth, he shoved his pants down far enough that his cock jumped free and pushed against her panties. He hissed in frustration this time. He was so close, only the lust covered piece of material between her legs was all that was stopping him from taking what was his. He gripped the lacy fabric and tore it free, then plunged deep, her narrow muscles closing tight around him.

Meghan's gasp never had time to escape. Will's mouth covered hers the second he ripped her panties off. She moved her legs high around his waist as he drove into her over and over. The table rocked with their loving. Their breathing was fast and choppy. She leaned her head against his as he kissed the side of her neck. God this was hot. She felt so wanted, so desired, so sexy. She raised her hips to meet his, and sucked in a breath when the friction of their bodies stroked her clit. She repeated the movement and moaned when Will curled his hand around her behind and held her in place, thrusting into her in quick, hard strokes.

Slowing, he pushed up onto his forearms and her breath caught again, but not because of him touching her body, but because of the rush of emotions that ran through her when he gazed down. She fought like crazy to block it out, fought to focus on what Will was doing to her body and how much she was enjoying it.

"Stop fighting me." Will brushed his lips over hers as he moved even slower.

She shook her head. "I'm n-not…" She sucked in a gulp of air when he dragged his body over hers. Her hips jerked when he repeated the slow movement.

"You are." He nuzzled the side of her neck, ran his hands into her hair, holding her head still. "Why? Am I that bad of a person? Do you find me hideous to look at?"

"No." Her head bumped the side of his head as she shook hers. Of course she didn't think he was a bad person, and she loved to look at him. He was beautiful, the perfect example of a man. "I-I just…" she began, but was interrupted when he thrust back into her. "Mmm," she moaned.

The tension built with each stroke of his cock, each kiss of his lips. Soon that familiar tingling heat was spreading lightning quick through her core and thighs, then to the rest of her body. He gripped her face, crushed his mouth to hers, slammed into her like he knew what her body was going to do before she did. She arched her back when the throbbing started, trying to pull him in farther, but he straightened and clamped his hand around her thighs and plunged hard. Again and again. The pulsing didn't end, it grew stronger, more powerful each time Will drove into her. Then her body began to shake, it scared her a little, this intensity he was causing. She reached for him, prayed silently he would come to her, protect her from herself. As he moved down to cover her body she exploded into a million pieces. At the same moment Will gritted out a curse, his body slamming into hers one last time before he pressed his lips into the side of her neck. And there she stayed for a few minutes, cradled in Will's arms, his large body warm and protective, and she wished with her entire being that it would last a lifetime.

* * * *

As the clouds covered the old village, Rob hid in the shadows of the trees across from the library, watching the couple. He had purposely moved to that spot to wait for Meghan to leave for the night. He needed that fucking cell and he was at the point that if she didn't give it to him, he would take it. He was just about to cross the street when that Scot had shown up again. Fuck. He was always with her. And he hated that the fucking Scot was touching her and he hated that she was touching him, but what he really hated was the fact that she was enjoying it. Even from where he stood, across the street he could tell she more than 'liked' this guy. Meghan was very conservative when it came to sex, no kinky shit with her, he should know, he had tried many times with her. Yet this guy was able to throw her on a table and fuck her brains out.

She was different with him too. The way she touched him. She had feelings for this guy. Christ, even with his track record he could tell when a woman was in love, and Meghan was in love with this guy. "Mother fucker," he mumbled. Stepping farther back into the shadows he decided that was what he hated most of all.

Chapter Twenty-Four

Will stood on Duncan's front step, staring blankly at the door. He hadn't seen Meghan since the previous afternoon in the library. She had hidden the day away at Duncan's. He didn't like it but knew why she had done it. She was embarrassed that they had had sex again, though he wasn't sure why, she had no reason to be. She had a beautiful body, which was all that more attractive with her hair all messy and her lips swollen. But he'd given in and had turned away when her face had flushed.

When he'd faced her, she had been jamming her laptop in her bag, her face still pink.

He'd closed the gap and had reached for her. "There is no reason for you to be embarrassed." She had shaken her head. "Meghan," he had begun, "What we did was—"

"I'm sorry, I..."

"I'm not sorry," he confessed in a hard tone. "I'm nae sorry for this time or the last, and I won't be sorry when it happens again."

"Will," she sighed.

"No." He set his jaw. "I will no' feel sorry for enjoying sex with ye and neither should you." He glared down at her. "We are good together. You can feel it. I know ye can, when are you going to stop hiding and face the truth?"

Her mouth had opened as tears had shimmered in her eyes. He'd reached for her when he had seen how pale she had become, but she'd backed away placing her hand to her middle. She'd cleared her throat and had nodded. "I have to go."

He sighed, remembering how her hand had trembled as it had fisted the material of her top. He should have come before now, she was probably having a hard time with him not there. But, she needed time to sort things out, so he had given it to her.

Now here he stood outside Duncan's house, hoping she would accept his offer of a ride to Edinburgh so that she could see her friends. They both had a reason to be there, and the idea had seemed logical, but now... '*For Christ's sakes, you don't even like me!*'

She couldn't have been further from the truth. Meghan was everything that he wanted in a woman. He just hadn't known it until he had met her.

He knocked on the door once, before he walked into the dimly lit hall. He followed the sound of an argument to the kitchen and stopped in the doorway, as Duncan battled it out with Meghan.

Her hair was clipped up at the back with the odd loose strand hanging down the sides of her flushed face. The white long-sleeved T-shirt she was wearing was too big for her small frame and the sleeves she had pushed up her arms slid back down as she rubbed at her middle. He laughed when she shouted at Duncan. "You are the most stubborn man I know."

She narrowed her green eyes at him. "Do you ever knock?" she snapped.

He raised an eyebrow at her snippy attitude. She was an angry mess and a delight to watch.

"No, Will doesn't need to knock," Duncan answered for him. "He is welcome in my home whenever he wants. And don't snap at him when you're annoyed at me." Duncan rose from his place at the table, addressing him. "Would you like a drink? I was about to pour myself one. God knows I need it."

"No, thanks. I just came to talk to Meghan. But, I'll come back when it's safer."

"There will never be a safe time, so you might as well talk to her now. We're done here." Duncan glanced back at Meghan as he left the kitchen. "The answer is still no."

"Oh! We are sooo not done," she called as Duncan left the room. She looked up at him and he took note when she moved her hand from her stomach to her hip. "What do you want?"

He cleared his throat in an effort to cover his laugh. "Actually, I came to offer you a ride to Edinburgh. I have a job this weekend. I'm leaving Friday morning, and coming back on Sunday."

"Well, that's real nice." Her tone oozed sarcasm. "But my grandfather, in all of his infinite wisdom, has forbidden me to go."

"Forbidden? Really?" What was that old man up to now?

She snorted. "I'm still going." Then she cupped the sides of her mouth and called around him, "And my friends won't get me into any trouble."

"Yes they will," Duncan called back.

She threw her hands up. "You see. This is what I get for trying to do the right thing. I tell him the truth about who I'm going to see and he tells me I can't go."

"He thinks your friends will get you into trouble."

She nodded. "It wasn't like I wanted him to drive me all the way to Edinburgh, just into Perth, I can find a bus or something from there."

He cocked his head. "Will they?"

"Will they what?" she huffed.

"Will your friends get you into trouble?"

"What! No, of course not."

He gave her a hard stare until she relented.

"Maybe…once upon a time in high school, but not now."

His interest was suddenly piqued. "What happened while you were in high school?"

"Ha! Yeah!" She snorted. "Like I'm going to tell you the trouble I got into in high school."

"Then let's make a deal. If I can convince Duncan to let me take you down to see your friends, then you have to tell me what trouble you got into in high school. Deal?"

"Oh no!" A strand of silky hair fell as she shook her head. "I'm not making any more bets with you."

"Scared?"

"Of what? You?"

He chuckled, enjoying her shocked expression.

"No."

"Really?" He focused on her mouth and pushed her pride. "That's okay." He held up his hands. "I can see you can't handle being such close quarters with me."

"I can handle being in a car with you for a few hours." She clicked her tongue as she raised her chin. "Fine! I'll tell you what happened *if* Duncan agrees."

* * * *

"A deal is a deal, just like a bet is a bet. You don't welch out on bets do you Meghan?" Will asked, poking her pride. Again!

"I'm no welcher." She exhaled. "It's really nothing big. I did things that most kids do, I guess. I didn't get into serious trouble."

"You're stalling."

Meghan groaned as she looked out of the front windshield. She was hoping Will would have forgotten about that and that there drive would be calm and torment free. She still couldn't believe it had been so easy for him to convince Duncan. She should have just lied to Duncan, then she wouldn't be having this conversation. Sometimes respecting one's elders was a real pain in the ass.

"Tell me." A smiled played at his lips.

"I think Duncan is referring to the time when Jody, myself and a few other friends broke into the local pizza parlour and accidentally burnt it down."

"You broke in, then burnt it down?" he clarified.

"Well, duh! It wouldn't have happened if it was the other way around. Anyway, it was a total accident. Troy's parents owned it and he forgot his key. We all had the munchies, and he said he would make us a pizza. Then we forgot about the pizza and it caught on fire." She ended with a shrug.

"Munchies?"

"It's not what you think." She grinned. "Or maybe it was."

She turned at his heavy sigh. "And that's what Duncan was talking about?"

"I think so. Or…maybe it was the time we borrowed Jess' mum's car and drove into Toronto so we could each get a piercing?" She laughed. She had forgotten about that.

"Piercing?"

"We only got caught because her mum saw the car was missing and reported it."

"You stole a car!" His astonishment was unmistakable.

"No, we borrowed it," she corrected. "Besides, I just drove it, Jessica borrowed it and it was only for a few hours. I don't understand what the big deal was. Nothing happened. I'm a good driver."

"You stole a car," he repeated.

"Borrowed," she clarified again.

"So you could get a piercing?"

"Yes. You can let it go now. It was a long time ago."

"Not yet." He paused, then asked, "What kind did you get?"

Turning to the view out of her side window, Meghan smiled to herself.

"Meghan?"

"I got a tongue stud. Is that enough info for you?"

He lowered his voice so it was as smooth as silk. "Now why would a good girl like you get a tongue stud?"

"Who said I was a good girl?"

Her lips tingled as she watched his gaze drop to her mouth. "Why did you take it out?"

"It wasn't the image I wanted while looking for a job."

She broke eye contact. She had to. It felt like her lips were swelling up, getting ready for his kiss. She studied the view again. Had they passed Perth yet? She couldn't remember. All she could focus on was Will and his sexy mouth and hard body and he smelt so good. God, this was such a big mistake being so close to him.

"So is that it or should I be worried about becoming an accomplice?"

"Funny." She wrinkled up her nose at him. "Those were the most serious. Everything else was minor compared to those two."

"There were more?"

She shrugged. This couldn't be good, Will was learning way too much about her.

"Well, I'm beginning to understand why Duncan didn't want you to go."

She snorted. "I'm not like that now. And I wasn't the only kid who got into trouble. I'm sure you got into trouble when you went to school?"

"Sure, but nothing like that. I went to a military school, the worst I did pales in comparison to what you did."

"You make it sound like I belong on the Ten Most Wanted List. I lived in northern Ontario. There weren't a whole lot of things to keep kids my age busy. I played a few sports in the summer, but in the winter when it was too cold to go out...that's when we got into trouble." She wasn't sure why she felt the need to explain her actions—it was such a long time ago. "Enough about me. Did I tell you I Googled the SBS?"

Will turned to face her. "Where did that come from? I thought we were talking about your short-lived crime sprees?"

"That's old news. I did the crimes and did the time."

Here we go again. Will gripped the steering wheel. He had been through this before and the outcome had never been good. The women he had dated while he served never liked the fact that his job came first and everything else second. Mind you, he had never told any of them what he truly did — they hadn't needed to know. Although it was different this time, he was no longer a member. "Why Google? You could have just asked me."

"I was curious about your last job. I've never heard of the SBS before."

"Really? I hadn't noticed," he teased, remembering their conversation that night at The Black Ale and how she had thought he was SAS.

"I'm sorry," she breathed out. "If it makes you feel better, I feel like a real tool."

"Don't worry about it. It's not something I share with many people."

She gave him a sideways glance. "Yeah! I bet."

They were silent for a few minutes before she quietly asked, "Why'd you leave? You seem like the type of guy who would enjoy that kind of life." He saw her staring at him through the corner of his eye. "You probably can't answer that, can you?"

No, he couldn't. He chuckled and gave her a roundabout answer. "It was time to go. The operations were becoming repetitive."

"Repetitive? I have a hard time believing that. I saw a list of some of the missions the SBS had been involved in. You didn't have a run-of-the-mill job."

"No, I didn't." He grinned.

She studied him. "You miss it, don't you?"

He saw the compassionate look on her face. "Sometimes."

"Did you really do all those things?"

"What things?" He sat and listened to her reel off a number of different tasks that his old unit was responsible for. He was impressed, she had really done her research.

He nodded. "Those were part of the job."

"Wow!"

They sat in silence for a few minutes, then he noticed her eyebrows were knitted together. "What's going on in there? I can hear the wheels turning from here."

"I'm thinking about the SBS." She glanced over at him, apparently still deep in thought. "It explains why you act the way you do."

He raised his chin. "And how's that?"

"You like to be in control of situations around you and can adapt if necessary but you will still try to push things your way. You have lots of patience when it suits you, but when you've reached your limit, you use your size to either intimidate, or brute force to get the desired result."

"Is that all?" he asked drily.

"No." Surprised by her answer, he listened as she continued, "You like things organised. I've seen your little stacks of papers lined up when you're at the library. You have to have order." She paused. "You can't leave it behind."

He pulled the Land Rover to the side of the road and gripped the wheel. "I was a soldier for most of my life, it's not something ye can just turn off. What the hell do you expect?" He glared at her from the corner of his eye. "Is 'at all you see when ye look at me?" he asked quietly.

Meghan stiffened in her seat. "I didn't mean to start anything."

"Well, you did, so finish it."

"I-I... Please don't get me wrong, I think it's great that you were in the Army..."

"Navy," he corrected.

"Right, the Navy." He could see the guilt on her face and he knew most people found his former job interesting. She was just curious, he shouldn't take her observation so personally. But damn it, the way she described him, it made him sound so cold and unfeeling.

"It's just…this is all I know about you."

He turned in his seat to face her. "True, but you do'nae have a very good memory. You know I have the ability to show concern, compassion and respect, all of which were for you." He paused. "You know I enjoy watching football and I enjoy spendin' time with your grandfather, and the other old geezers that live in Little Glen. I have a dog, Lucy. I believe you've met her a few times."

"Will, I didn't mean—"

He cut her off. "This is what ye wanted, to get to know the real me. I'll tell you something else about me. I enjoy sitting in th' library working across from a moody redhead who chews on her lip while she works on her laptop. I enjoy her company even though she is hiding somethin' from me. I enjoy her company even though she is lying to me. I want to help her, but I respect her enough to wait until she asks for it." He glared at her as she lowered her head and stared down at her hands. "And I hate that she is fightin' this intense need we have for each other. I want tae force her to come tae me, but I can't do that. I don't want to hurt her." He cupped her chin, raising her head. "Ye can't tell me that need between us is only one-sided, because ye know damn well it isn't."

The pulse pounded in her neck, he could see it from where he was sitting. He lightly trailed a finger over her flushed skin.

"No, I-I don't know what you're talking about." She began to shake her head.

"Still fighting, huh?"

Her breath caught when he leaned towards her and cupped the back of her head. "What are you doing?" She asked breathless.

"Refreshing yer memory?" Her exhale warmed his face as he pulled her forward. He stroked the curve of her lips, and she opened for him without any protest, allowing him entrance to the warmth of her mouth.

For someone who had given him nothing but grief, Meghan didn't seem to care when he roughly plunged his tongue into her mouth, and she didn't care when he undid her seat belt, dragged her across the Land Rover and onto his lap. She just slid her arms around his neck and held tight.

Her mouth was minty sweet, her body warm and restless. She shifted her bottom, causing his dick to throb, his body to crave. His jeans became excruciatingly tight, holding him firmly in place. She moved her behind along the length of his shaft. It felt so fucking good. He groaned into her mouth, whilst he held her hips still. She chuckled and tried to move again. God, she was maddening, a sexy contradiction. Teasing him, but embarrassed after they had had sex. Wanting him, yet fighting it every step of the way.

He tugged on her hair so her neck was exposed and he fastened his mouth over the sensitive skin. He trailed his mouth up to her ear, nipping at it playfully, and smiled when a shiver ran through her. He loved to hear her heavy breathing. He kissed the side of her neck again, toying with her hair. Inhaling her light flowery scent, he claimed her mouth forcefully, sliding his tongue inside to join with hers. Her movement became more restless and he couldn't seem to stop himself as he slid his hand under the knitted jumper she wore and touched warm skin. A receptive moan came from deep in her throat as she turned so he cupped her breast. He gently palmed the lush mound, teased her nipple by swirling little circles over it with his palm.

Will battled against the haze fogging his brain. He had to stop this. It was bad enough, this greedy need he had for her, but when they kissed and she melted in his arms... He exhaled when she rocked her hips once again. He was almost past the point of control. He was a touch and kiss away from peeling off her tight jeans and forcing her to straddle his cock.

He forced his mouth away, brushed his lips against hers. "Do you remember now?" Her eyes now sultry blue pools, stared back and it was all he could do to keep himself from throwing her into the backseat.

"Vaguely." Her mouth was swollen and glistening from his kiss.

"Well, let me give you another reminder."

She held him off by putting her hands against his chest. "No, no, I'm good," she blurted out, wriggling to get free.

He grinned when he saw her face turn pink. He released her and she slid off his now throbbing shaft, causing him to shudder from the friction. Meghan had clearly enjoyed their little session and was as restless now as he was. When would she stop fighting him?

Taking a deep steadying breath, he waited for her to put on her seatbelt. This was a good start. She had let him pull her onto his lap without a fight, a promising way to start the weekend. He probably had the emails from her friend Jody to thank for her change. Spending time with her friends would do her some good, and from the high-school story, this Jody sounded like a real character, he was looking forward to meeting her.

Chapter Twenty-Five

Will struggled for control. Hiding his anger was harder than he had thought it would be. Then again he didn't think he'd ever get this angry. Clenching his jaw tight, he watched Meghan run to her friend and throw herself into his arms.

His fucking arms!

He wasn't caught off guard very often. But, since meeting Meghan, it seemed to be a regular occurrence.

"Son of a bitch!" he swore under his breath. It hadn't occurred to him that her close friend would be a man. Will had just assumed that Jody was a woman. Not a goddamn Pretty-boy. He tried to remember what she had said about Jody on the ride down there. She had mentioned three people specifically — Jody, Jessica and Troy.

The last two were clearly gender specific. That left Jody — a name that could be used for either sex. He honestly didn't remember if Meghan had referred to Jody as a she or he. Had she done that on purpose?

Will's hands curled into fists when she kissed him. Jealousy. A new experience for him and so far he didn't like it. He did however like the image of his fists smashing that GQ face into a broken and bloody mess.

Pondering the sadistic, but satisfying thought, Will slowly walked over to the pair, and realised his new emotion was nowhere near under control. This was pathetic. He did not get this angry without being severely provoked. It must be the spell.

Right then Jody made the lethal mistake of giving Meghan another affectionate hug. Spell? Nah! He still wanted to rip the fucker's head off.

"Aren't you going to introduce us, Meghan?" The question came out harsher than he had intended. And no, he wouldn't apologise for it.

He didn't like the way her blond-haired, blue-eyed friend smiled down at her and he didn't like how his hand lingered on her lower back. There was a history there. The nature of that history was still in question.

He flexed his shoulders. Christ, he wasn't ready to think about that. Honestly, it would be safer for Pretty-boy if he didn't think about it. Or the lie Meghan had told him. She had said that no one was waiting for her in Toronto. No husband and no boyfriend. Will had taken at her word. It had never occurred to him that she might not have told him the truth.

Meghan turned and looked over her shoulder, she was beaming. Until she saw his face, then a confused frown appeared. Pulling her away from GQ boy, Will forced a nod and offered his hand. Meghan made the introductions. Her friend gave him a nod which quickly turned into a warm smile accompanied by a slow and deliberate once over as they shook hands. Jody Wilson? He knew that name.

Will studied Jody, as Jody sized him up. Maybe sizing up. Maybe not.

Meghan stilled. She had seen that look on Will's face before, he was annoyed. Of course she was usually the one who annoyed him, but this time it was directed at Jody. She watched him cross his large arms over his chest, the hypnotic brown of his glare becoming almost black.

She glanced back to Jody who had a stupid smirk on his face. Meghan had seen that look before too. *Shit*, Meghan groaned inwardly. Not again. Will was getting the wrong impression, he wouldn't understand. Fear for her friend had Meghan stepping in front of Will, gaining his attention. "Thanks for the ride, Will. I'll see you on Sunday. What time?"

He studied Jody over the top of her head before turning his dark stare on her. Without so much as a word, he grabbed her hand, pulling her away from Jody.

"Will?" She tried to pull free but it proved impossible.

"I need to talk to ye in private." He stopped by a comfortable set of chairs on the opposite side of the lobby, out of earshot from Jody.

"What's wrong with you?" She kept her voice low. "One minute you're all happy-go-lucky and the next you look ready to kill someone?" She watched as his death stare drifted over her shoulder to Jody. *I knew it.* She gained his attention when she poked him in the chest. "Don't you hurt Jody."

Exasperated, he exhaled. "I think ye should stay at my sister's house with me."

"What?" she asked, surprised. "Why? I've already booked a room here. And Jody's staying...here..." She trailed off. *Wait a minute.* She watched him glare over at Jody again, the muscle in his jaw twitching.

Two words—holy and crap. *Will is jealous...of Jody.* She bit her lip and fought like crazy to keep from laughing out loud. The idea of Will being jealous was laughable. No, no, it was more than that...it was absurd. She huffed. Will, jealous of Jody... She straightened. Will was jealous of Jody!

An idea suddenly popped into her head. An idea that could easily solve a little bet she had got herself into, not to mention that damn contract.

Startled, she blinked up at Will's glare. This was too good to be true. Jody's help would be required and he would give it to her, there was no doubt about his loyalty.

"I'm serious, Meghan."

She blinked, raising her eyebrows. Did he just growl at her?

Meghan continued to watch him. He was losing control of the situation and was now trying to bend it in his favour.

"And I'm seriously staying here with Jody." Guilt crept into her stomach when his frustration became evident. She hated to do it this way, but he wasn't leaving her any choice.

Will was mad as hell and on the verge of throwing her over his shoulder and carrying her back to his Land Rover. But there were too many bloody witnesses. He didn't want her to stay here at the hotel with Jody. He observed Pretty-boy, took note of the amused smirk. He focused back on Meghan, her hands were sitting on her hips. This wasn't going well.

"Fine...but my sister is havin' me and my brothers over for a brunch tomorrow," he blurted out. "You're coming with me. So be down here by ten."

"Now you tell me," Meghan huffed at his order. "Why didn't you tell me on the way here? I might have plans, you know."

"Do ye have plans?" he snapped out the question.

"Well, no, we were just going to spend time together seeing the sights. But that's not the point—"

"You have plans now," he gritted out. "Ten o'clock."

"No." She raised her chin.

"Pardon?"

"No, I'm not going." Her red locks skimmed her shoulders as she shook her head. "You can't just order me around. Besides, I want to spend time with Jody."

The muscles in his jaw twitched. "Fine," he relented bitterly. "Bring him."

He knew what he was doing and it was stupid and immature. His only excuse was that he didn't want this guy anywhere near Meghan. She belonged to him and the idea of them simply talking stirred around urges that were dark and turbulent.

"Will, you can't just..." She paused, then sighed softly. "Do that."

That worn-out look and sigh were almost his undoing. She wasn't eating and Duncan mentioned something about her not sleeping that well either, all thanks to the spell. Fighting with her about her spending time with her friend could very well make her feel worse.

She shifted almost timid-like—he then averted his gaze to her drawing her lip between her teeth. Meghan was anything but timid and she had no problem looking him the eye and telling him how she truly felt. So why the change?

She peered back over her shoulder to where Pretty-boy stood waiting.

Something was going on here, his instincts were never wrong, he just didn't care. All he could think about was Meghan. A rumble formed in his chest. He stifled it and the urge to drag her from the building, and instead drew her forward, pressing his mouth to hers.

His lips were hard, punishing and he wouldn't apologise for it. Her flowery scent and the soothing warmth of her body would not distract him. Her hands encircled his neck, a feather-light touch that had a way of calming the desperate anger swirling inside. He groaned and possessively wrapped his arms around her, pinning her to his chest.

That was when the kiss turned from punishing to sensual and Meghan opened her mouth for him, the tip of her tongue teasing his lips. An encouragement he didn't need but enjoyed all the same. His tongue swept inside her sweet mouth and entwined with hers, circling in slowly thorough strokes. A slow heat burned between them and before it went any further Will forced her away from him.

Will held her tight to keep her from swaying.

Licking her lips, she met his stare with defiance.

He glared down at her as he gave her a command. "Be good, Meghan."

A flush tinted her cheeks and neck. Crossing her arms she poked the bear. "Why would I want to start now?"

She turned her back on him and paraded her way back to pretty-boy.

Exiting Meghan's hotel, Will pulled his phone free and hit the speed dial to his office in London. "Hugh?

I need a background check." He recited Jody's full name.

"I know that name," Hugh said. There was a brief rustling of paper then. "Ah! Here it is. Jody Wilson. Public relations for One Mean Kat Productions out of Toronto."

"Shit!" He knew he'd heard that name before. He navigated through traffic and opened the door to the Land Rover. "I want a full employee check on this guy and anything else you can find out. Email me when you have it."

"You think this guy is going to stir up trouble this weekend?"

"Absolutely."

* * * *

Meghan laughed out loud when Will disappeared through the front doors. That kiss had made her lose all sense of time and space. Meghan giggled. She couldn't believe it, Will was jealous of Jody. Actually, he had looked as though he had wanted to kill Jody. She shouldn't be smiling. It had scared the hell out of her. But she needed to get Will to back off and Jody was the answer.

She could see why Will would be jealous. Jody was a good-looking man, short sandy blond hair—styled in the latest fashion of course—beautiful cobalt eyes, lightly bronzed skin. He wasn't as tall as Will and certainly not as wide through the chest and arms. Jody kept in shape and used his body to attract. Will's strength was a requirement of his job, yet his strength wasn't just physical, there was something else, something deep inside him that projected an inner strength as well.

Stop it. You're going home remember, nothing can happen. Her stomach heaved and twisted as though the room was spinning.

Jody gave her a crooked smile. "What was that all about?"

She swallowed hard all of a sudden, fighting like hell not to hurl all over his suit.

"Meg?" Jody wouldn't let it go easily—he was almost as stubborn as she was. He would want everything in detail, right down to the kiss he had just witnessed.

"Let me check in," she breathed through the waves of queasiness. "And bring my bag up to my room. Then we'll go out and I'll fill you in on everything."

She knew that he had a million and one questions, but he only asked, "Is it juicy?" as he followed her to the reception desk.

"You might say that."

"Will it explain why you're green all of a sudden?"

She pursed her lips. "No, I have this weird stomach thing going on."

He wrinkled his blond eyebrows in doubt. "Okay." He nodded. "Just as long as you keep your distance. I don't want you pitchin' your cookies near my Armani."

Ten minutes later, a silence fell between them as they stood side by side waiting for the elevator doors to open. Staring up at the floor numbers, Jody commented, "Will seems nice."

"No." She continued to focus on the numbers.

"No?"

"No."

"Okay," Jody conceded.

She turned her head slightly. "Are you in the mood to do some role playing?"

A mischievous grin claimed his mouth. If Jody was anything he was predictable. He raised a single eyebrow, still grinning, "Always."

The elevator doors slid open and they stepped in together. "How about playing my lover?" Meghan waited for a response.

This man was one of her closest friends, he had seen her through very hard times, and she had returned the kindness shown to her in full measure. If she asked him for his help with Will and his outrageous bet, she didn't have a doubt in her mind that he would give it.

Frowning, Jody leaned against the back wall of the elevator. He crossed his arms over his chest, staring at the doors deep in thought. "I'm not sure." He paused, then gave her one of his dazzling smiles. "It has been a long time since I've played a straight man."

Chapter Twenty-Six

After Meghan had dropped off her bag in her hotel room and had freshened up, she popped a baby Gravol in the hopes it would get her through the evening.

Jody suggested that they go for a walk around the city and find a place along the way for dinner. They ended up stopping at a small bistro that had a large picture window at the front, comfortable chairs and a relaxed atmosphere. And the food...it looked great and smelt even better, not that she could bring herself to eat any. It was, however, the perfect place to sit and talk. Jody filled Meghan in on everything going on back home, and mentioned that he had seen Ryan.

"Ryan didn't tell me shit though, has he heard anything about where Dickhead might be?" Jody eyed her still full plate with a concerned frown.

"Well," she began. "Ryan saw him outside my apartment and then informed me he's here in Scotland."

"Oh, yeah." Jody's words were said between clenched teeth. She had known Jody for too long not to notice that he did not like hearing that. "Think he'll be able to find you?"

"I never told him about Little Glen. But who knows." She reached for her wine glass and stopped when her insides turned over in an act of rebellion.

"What does Rye think Rob wants with you?"

"I'm not sure. You know Ryan. He might not tell me if he thinks it will freak me out. He did email me the other day, saying things at my apartment were cool. So, that's good. But I still don't know why Rob was even there. I don't remember him leaving anything."

"He wasn't back for 'something' but for 'someone'," Jody pointed out.

"What? That's crazy."

"Really? Let's recap, shall we? You caught him cheating. He stole your life savings and God knows how many other women's savings. Your brother arrested him and he went to jail. I'm surprised you need the history lesson." He levelled his blue gaze on her and said soberly, "Meg, he wasn't there for a social call."

Inspecting her wine glass was the only way to avoid Jody's penetrating stare. She didn't want to talk about Rob. It made her nervous just thinking about him. Especially since all the creepy feelings she's had lately.

"What's with you? You're not eating or drinking?"

"Not sure," she lied, then changed the subject. "So, when is Kris getting here?"

Jody sat back. "Are you worried about Rob?"

She pressed her lips together.

"You can't avoid this thing with Dickhead forever. You'll have to deal with it sooner or later."

Shaking her head, she groaned, "I know." She should have known better, Jody wasn't easily distracted. "But there's nothing I can do right now, and Ryan said he would take care of things. You know Ryan never backs out of anything."

"Meg, I'm just worried about you. You should have listened to me about him."

"I do to. I wish I could change the mistakes I've made, but I can't."

Meghan leant forwards and rubbed her temples. She would eventually have to face Rob, unless Ryan figured out what he wanted and beat her to it. She didn't like that idea any better than facing Rob herself. Ryan had turned into a very large and intimidating man, but he was still her brother and cop or not, he shouldn't be fighting her battles for her.

For some reason Will's image popped in her head. What she wouldn't give to introduce Will to Rob. One look at Will's dangerous glare and Rob would be shaking in his designer suit. That, of course, would mean telling Will about her relationship with Rob and that was the last thing she wanted. He already knew too much about her, he didn't need to know how blind, foolish or weak she had been.

"So?" Meghan asked, changing the subject for a second time. "Where did you say Kris was?"

Jody shook his head and let her have her way. "He should have arrived at the hotel by now."

"Our hotel?" It had been a long time since she had seen Kris. She'd missed his easy smile and fun-loving humour.

"God, no! He's the star, darling, nothing but the best for him now. He's staying in a five-star hotel in the ritzy area of town."

"What was I thinking?" she mumbled sarcastically, then stopped. "Five-star? Really?"

"Yup. Our little boy has come a long way." He chuckled then continued, "Ah! You know Kris. He couldn't give a shit where he stays. Actually, he wanted to stay at the same hotel as us. Except the security company that was hired to accompany him asked that he stay at the other hotel. They said something about the hotel having a better layout or something about more exits. I'm not sure. I'm here to push his new album, that's it. Security is not my department."

"Of course it isn't. Who cares about your friend's safety?"

"Hey, I care. I read the report on Kris' security. The owner was some Special Forces guy who recently left the Army, and started up his own personal protection company. Apparently, he opened his first office here and soon opened a larger one in London. The company has a great reputation and is in high demand in the UK."

Meghan's mouth dropped open. Was it Will's company that was protecting Kris? No, couldn't be. "You don't remember the name of the owner, do you?" *Please say it's not him.*

"No, I don't."

She sighed.

"But I do have his card." She stiffened as Jody pulled the card from his wallet. "I was given one just in case I need to contact him for some reason." He handed her the card.

"What are the odds?" she whispered, staring down at the crisp white business card. 'WA MacKenzie' was neatly typed in black ink, with the numbers to both offices in Edinburgh and London printed in the bottom right corner.

"What's wrong?"

"Royal Navy," she said, handing Jody back the card, and rested her head in her hands.

"What?"

"He left the Royal Navy, not the Army."

She couldn't escape him. She'd thought she would have a weekend to herself to spend time with Jody, and hopefully, a little time with Kris. Then Will had made plans for her to have brunch with his sister, and dragged poor Jody into it. Then she found out that it was his company protecting Kris.

"How do you know that?"

"What?"

"About the owner, how do you know he was in the Royal Navy?"

She shrugged. "He told me."

"Ah, your chauffeur?" A sly smirk pulled his lips. "He's the owner of S&G Protection."

"Is that the name of his company?" She'd never thought to look — she had been solely focused on his name.

"You didn't know?"

"No. I didn't think…it never came up. And Will is not my chauffeur. He was coming here anyways because of a job. Now I know who the job is…" She trailed off.

Jody watched her closely. She looked away, knowing very well that he was one person who could read her like a book. Jody raised his hand and caught the waiter's attention. The young man quickly came to the side of the table.

"What time do you close?" Jody asked, looking at his watch.

"We close at midnight, sir."

"Great! We'll have another bottle of wine and get my friend here a shot of tequila." He winked at the young man. "I'm trying to loosen her tongue and tequila is the fastest way to accomplish my goal."

The waiter frowned at Jody then gave Meghan a questioning frown.

Even as her gut lurched at the idea of drinking tequila, she reassured him. "He's completely harmless, and I would love a shot of tequila." *Can't make me feel any worse*.

"Of course I'm harmless," Jody said with mock anger. The waiter still had a doubtful look on his face but he left to fetch the order.

"It's not going to take until midnight."

"You never know."

Jody was right of course. It wasn't quite midnight, but it had taken a while to tell Jody what had happened since her arrival in Little Glen, including the idea about Jody being her lover. In true form Jody had been very thorough in his questioning, even asking what she thought Will's perception might be.

"Well, I want to say his perception is diluted." Then she snapped out, "How the hell do I know what he's thinking? I'm not a mind reader."

After nursing half a glass of wine, Jody was finished with all of his questions. He leant back on his chair and folded his hands behind his head, studying her.

"So, what do you think? Pretty crazy?" she asked, toying with the stem of her wine glass.

"Not so crazy. I would say...inventive."

"Excuse me?"

"Will has found something he wants and he is using the tools given to him to get it. I mean...come on...an eight-hundred-year-old marriage contract, that's brilliant!"

Meghan's jaw hit the table.

"I wonder where I could get one of those."

"Jody!" Meghan shouted. She peeked over his shoulder to see only a few people staring at her. "Didn't you hear what I said?" She leaned over the table. "If I refuse to honour our bet, he will use the contract and force me to marry him."

"Oh, I heard you. But, for the record I still think it's pretty slick. The man has a gift."

"It's an evil gift, Jody," she whispered low under her breath. "Evil."

Jody threw his head back and laughed.

"Stop laughing," she whined. "Help me. I don't want this. I don't want him to want me."

"Really, I'm having a hard time believing that."

She blinked at him. "What?"

"You get this dreamy look on your face every time you..." Jody's mouth dropped open as he pointed a finger at her. "You've had sex with him."

"I... What?... No."

"You lie," Jody accused happily.

"Jody, please." She exhaled.

"You naughty girl."

"That doesn't matter."

"Doesn't matter? Of course it matters." He stopped grinning at her and asked, straight-faced, "Was he good? I bet he was."

She tried to hide the smile, but this was Jody, it was nearly impossible to hide her feelings from him. "Yeah," she ended on a sigh. She couldn't help it.

"That good, huh?"

"It really was."

He stopped and leaned across the table, taking hold of her hands. "Did you stop to think that Will might actually be in love with you? That this old marriage contract is just an excuse?"

She shook her head. He couldn't be in love with her, they barely knew each other. "I don't... How can I... It can't be." She struggled for a breath.

"Stop selling yourself short. Why couldn't he love you?"

A heavy silence hung between them. What if he was right?

"He's a Special Forces guy or...whatever. He was trained to pick things up fast, right? He would have to be very perceptive to be a good soldier, wouldn't he?"

"Stop it. I know what you're doing."

"Someone has to do it." He squeezed her hands.

She stumbled on her words. "I don't...think... What if he..." She was so scared it was true. She wasn't ready. Things had gone so badly the last time.

"Meg, breathe," he ordered and she willingly complied. "Now, do you think Will is the type of guy who would steal your heart just to steal your money?"

"No, he would never do that."

"Then it's safe to say he's not Rob." He paused and squeezed her hands again. "Actually, most men are not Rob."

She shook her head. She had to keep Will away. She had to be ruthless. "Are you going to help me or not?"

Jody exhaled. "If you're sure this is what you want?"

"I'm sure," she said firmly.

"All right. Then if you want this plan of yours to work, we better get our stories straight. So, tell me lover, how do you like it? Missionary? You on top?" He lowered his gaze and winked. "Doggy?"

"Jody!"

He shrugged. "Well, I'll need to know this, won't I? Just in case he asks."

"What? He won't ask you that." She paused. "Will he?"

"Straight guys might. How do I know?" He picked up his wine glass and swallowed the remaining liquid. "You know this wouldn't happen if he was gay."

"Will...gay!" Her side ached by the time she was done laughing.

"I would be happy to confirm that for you if you like."

She giggled. She would love to see the look on Will's face. But he couldn't know Jody was gay, or her little plan wouldn't work.

"Maybe he's gay and doesn't know it yet."

"You're funny. Although, it would solve this problem I've gotten into. But, unfortunately he's not gay. Didn't you see that kiss he gave me in the lobby?" She didn't know why she felt the need to bring that up.

"Meg, every person in the lobby saw that kiss. If I didn't know better I would think he was marking his territory." He stood up and started putting on his coat then helped Meghan on with hers.

"Marking his territory?"

"He was letting everyone there know, including you, that you belong to him."

"That's crazy. He only did it because he's jealous of you," she said, looking up at him as they walked down the street together.

"Well, I am devilishly handsome. What woman could resist me? Not even you, my good friend, are immune." He grabbed her hand and placed it in the crook of his elbow. "So, doggy's out. What else do you like?"

"I never said doggy was out."

Jody whistled, wrapping his arm around her shoulders. "You are a naughty girl. Now, how about the mile-high club, are you a member?"

The Bannockburn Spell

Chapter Twenty-Seven

Will stood by the window in his sister's guest room and looked at his watch again. It was past midnight and past time he went to bed. He just couldn't sleep, he kept thinking about Meghan and wondering if she was as uncomfortable as he was. He ran his hand through his hair.

He'd been severely agitated when he'd arrived at Sarah's, but the beautiful new addition to the MacKenzie clan, Abbey, had changed that quickly enough. Sarah had helped too, and she had filled him in on the lives of his two brothers and parents. She'd also noticed his mood right away. Not caring, she'd casually stated, "So, I've heard you met Meghan."

He had been floored to learn that she knew about Meghan and she had confirmed when he had asked if Duncan had called her.

"No, not me. Dad and Mum."

"Am I the only person who didn't know about this contract?"

"What do you mean? You were there when Granddad told us the story."

He huffed. "I left to help Gran, remember?"

"Oh, I forgot about that."

Will shook his head. "You'd think one of you could have told me that it was real."

Sarah had sighed when he had frowned. "I only found out it was real when I heard Dad and Gran talking one night. That was back at the end of school and then you left. You've been gone for twelve years. A lot has happened." She had then reached for her tea cup.

"And you didn't think to tell me about it?"

"I was told not to." She toyed with the handle of the cup.

He'd stopped his pacing and had sat next to her on the couch. "I wasn't gone that long."

"The occasional phone call and email hardly counts as a visit."

"I was working."

"You don't have to explain. I know. I'm just saying you missed a lot of stuff. So don't be surprised that we know more than you about what's been happening."

"Who else knows?"

"I'm sorry," she had said softly, a guilty frown covering her face. "I couldn't keep it to myself."

"Rich and Gavin?"

She had nodded.

He was okay with that. They would give him a hard time over it but in the end he knew that they had his back.

"Ah! Just so you know they were there when Duncan called Dad."

He had sighed.

"If it makes you feel better, Gavin has no problem changing your name with his."

He had felt the hair on the back of his neck stand on end and his hands had clenched into fists. "Oh yeah."

"He mumbled something about a dry spell. Rich though, he didn't bat an eyelash." Will had smiled when she had snorted. "Mum and I didn't think you would ever meet her."

"Why?"

"Mum thought something might happen to you...you know, while you were working, and I just assumed you never wanted to settle down. Glad I was wrong about that." She elbowed him in the ribs.

"What about Dad?"

"Dad was more optimistic and said"—she dropped her voice low mimicking his father's rough accent—"'We'll jist have tae wait an' see.'"

* * * *

He paced around the room and studied his watch again. Did his family know about the spell? If they did, did they know how damn uncomfortable he was? And Meghan. God, she had it worse than him. He squeezed his jaw so tight it pulled into his temples. It kept her from eating and sleeping.

He checked his watch for a third time. "Fuck it."

He was at Meghan's hotel in ten minutes. He pulled to a stop across the street. He sat there for a minute or two, his shoulders and neck pulled into knots, and wondered if his being there was a good idea until he saw her push open the front doors. His decision was made when he saw the panic on her face and how she shook her hands as they hovered above her stomach.

Shit! He got out and jogged across the street trailing behind her as she half-ran down the sidewalk. He called to her but she didn't seem to hear him. Slowing, she turned the corner into a dimly lit street.

"Meghan?" he called out again.

She swirled to face him, her hand on her chest. "Will?"

He walked straight up to her so that she could see his face clearly. "I'm here."

She gave him a shaky smile. "What are you doing here?"

"Can't sleep." He pulled her jacket closed. "Why are you out here?"

"I feel…" She rubbed her stomach, then gave him a puzzled frown. "I can't sleep either and thought some fresh air might help."

"Sounds reasonable. How about I walk around the block?" He gestured with his hand and they continued walking around the block until they were standing back out front of the hotel. "Feel better?"

"Yes, thanks." She gave him a confused look. "Why did you come here? If you couldn't sleep. Why not just stay at your sister's?"

"Sarah's a light sleeper when her husband is away and I didn't want to wake my niece."

"That's nice. But why come here?"

He shrugged and told her the truth. "'Cause you're here and I thought you might not be feeling well." He pointed to her stomach. "Was it bad?"

Her cheeks flushed as she lied, "Not really."

"Want a cup of peppermint tea?"

"No." She creased her brow. "I'm good."

"Ready to go to bed then?"

She blinked nervously at the doors to the hotel, then lied again, "Yes."

He sighed, hating that she was lying to him, but was secretly pleased she wasn't any good at it. "Come on, I'll walk you up."

Standing outside her room, she slid in her key card and opened the door. The second she stepped into the room her hand went to her middle.

"Meghan?"

She looked at him over her shoulder, her red hair very bright compared to her now pale complexion.

"Would you like me to call Jody?" He hated the idea of it, hated himself even more for offering, but if it helped her, he'd suffer through it.

"Why?"

He cocked his head to the side. That was not the response he was expecting.

She gaped at her own answer. "I mean, I don't want to wake him. He's had a long day."

He nodded carefully. "Okay." He stepped back and saw her knuckles go white as she gripped at her shirt.

Finally he asked, "Would you like me to stay until you fall asleep?"

She gave him a hard frown, then answered, "No," as she nodded her head yes.

Will kept his relief hidden as he entered behind her. She kicked off her shoes and threw her coat on the chair. She slipped beneath the covers with her clothes on. Will was about to ask why when she began to struggle about, then she pulled her yoga pants free from the covers, throwing them onto the end of the bed.

He chuckled as he draped his coat on top of hers, then sat down on the side of the bed and took off his boots. Before he snapped off the light he inspected Meghan over his shoulder. She was staring at the ceiling, a worried frown covering her pretty face. "You okay with this?"

She swallowed hard. Light smudges shadowed the skin below her eyes. "Yes, but no tonsil hockey. I'm really tired."

He chuckled at her choice of words but agreed as he reached for the light, "Okay, no tonsil hockey."

Lying next to her, Will crossed his feet, listening to her sigh, then felt the bed rock as she flipped onto her stomach, then with a loud huff, she rolled onto her side. When he finally had enough of her fidgeting, he reached for her.

"What are you doing? I said I was tired."

"I know you're tired." He lifted his arm. "Now come here." He tugged gently until she settled her head in the hollow of his shoulder. He wrapped his arm snugly around her. "You sleep better like this."

"How do you know?" She tentatively placed her other arm on his chest.

He didn't bother telling how she had slept in his arms twice before, he just gave her an order, "Go to sleep."

* * * *

"And where have you been, young man?" Sarah teased as he entered her kitchen. She was sitting at the table drinking her coffee and feeding Abbey breakfast.

"Out." He walked over to his beautiful niece and kissed her cereal-covered face. "Did you wake your mum early again?" He laughed when she gave him a toothless grin.

"Out!" She snorted. "I can see that. But where out? Stalking a certain someone?"

He opened a cupboard and grabbed a mug. "I wasn't stalking her." He poured some coffee. "She needed some help."

"Is everything all right?"

"Mmm." He swallowed a mouthful. "The contract gives her a nauseous stomach."

"I'm sure," Sarah mumbled. "And if that didn't do it, I'm sure your little bet would."

Will frowned. "You don't know about it…?" Will caught himself too late.

"Know about what?"

Silently, Will leant back against the counter and sipped his coffee.

"No," Sarah demanded, "you can't do that. You have to tell me now."

It only took two minutes of Sarah pouting, until he caved and explained about the spell woven into the contract. The funny thing was that she didn't even question it, Sarah fully believed what he said was true. He asked her why.

"It was in the bedtime story," she reminded him. "So you went to Meghan so she wouldn't feel uncomfortable. Will…" Sarah reached forwards and clasped his hands. "That is so fairy-tale romantic."

He snatched his hands away. "Oh, for the love of…"

Sarah giggled as she sat back. "I have a question for you. What if she refuses to honour the terms of your bet? You can't force someone to marry you even with the help of a spell."

"I can't?" he teased.

"Will."

"A bet is a bet. As for the spell, I'm not sure. But if what Duncan says is true, it will definitely help me out."

Sarah gave him a serious look. "Do you love her?"

Good question. He knew that he wanted her in his life. He knew that she was meant for him because of the spell. But that didn't mean it was love. He wasn't really sure what love was. How was he supposed to feel? Were there certain rules to falling in love or was it 'a learn as you go' type of deal? One thing he did know was that he hated the thought of her being away from him, of Jody touching her, kissing her. A dark, aggressive sensation leached its way into every cell of his body.

"Well?" Sarah persisted.

He stood, keeping his now dark mood to himself. "I'm going to go shower. Then I'll come back down and help you get ready for brunch." He turned to leave when he remembered. "I forgot. Meghan and Jody are coming too."

Sarah gave him a knowing smile. "Of course they are."

As he climbed the stairs his phone vibrated. It was Hugh with the information he'd requested on Jody. He read what appeared to be a normal personnel file. Jody had a degree in Business and was hired straight out of school. His outgoing and likeable personality made him perfect for public relations. He worked and played well with others and was a natural leader. Jesus, not even one screw-up, the man was painted a saint.

Hugh added a personal note to the bottom of the text.

'Just thought you might want to see these most recent photos of their company vacation in Jamaica.'

Will stopped halfway up the stairs and laughed. "Holy shit."

Chapter Twenty-Eight

A loud knock on the hotel room door caught Meghan's attention. She checked her watch. Jody was early. That was odd. He was the type of person who followed his own clock, which was usually fifteen minutes behind everyone else's. After setting the hairdryer down she reached for a towel. Another loud knock sounded at the door. Meghan laughed. "Okay, Okay. I'm coming."

She pulled open her door and teased, "My God, it must be some kind of a miracle..."

She stopped mid-sentence and froze.

Will's wicked mouth curled into a smile that made her insides all mushy. His swirling brown eyes became dark as they slowly moved down the length of her, setting her skin on fire. "Good morning."

Crap! Her cheeks heated quickly. Not only did she wish that she had grabbed a larger towel, but she wished she hadn't been so needy of him last night. Man, she really hated that. Thankfully, he had been gone when she had woken this morning, which had saved her some embarrassment.

She quickly looked him over then glanced away. Why did he always have to look so yummy? It was making her little 'Jody is my lover plan' harder to put into play.

She went ahead though and exhaled a long disappointed sigh. "I thought you were Jody."

"No." He gave her a strange grin. "I am definitely not Jody." He crowded her, commenting, "You know, that towel doesn't cover much."

She swallowed hard. "Like I said, I thought you were Jody."

"So you did." He stepped into her room.

"You're early. I was just getting dressed."

"By all means. Don't let me keep you. Unless…?"

Her startled expression was obviously enough to cause a burst of laughter.

"Finish getting dressed. I'll wait."

But she just stood there ogling him as he took off his jacket. His white, short-sleeved collared shirt was tailored to fit over his wide chest, detailing his sculpted muscles. The material seemed to be ready to split at the seams as it clung to his thick arms.

She forced herself to look at his face, and clearing her throat, she asked, "You're going to wait here?"

"Yes."

"There are perfectly good chairs in the hotel lobby."

"Yes, there are. But I'm already here." Sitting his large body on the side of the bed, he turned to fix his mesmerising gaze on her again. But it was different this time, more intense, pulling at her. She could feel her legs wanting to move, to step towards him. She wanted him to peel the towel from her, to feel his big hands on her back as she pressed her breast to his waiting mouth. She wanted that so much that she could feel her body spark to life.

She quickly turned and walked back into the bathroom. Damn. That was close. She had almost made the mistake for a third time. Would it be a mistake to give into Will? She closed her eyes, battling confusion. Her heart knew that it would be good to give in, but her memory was relentless in reminding her of the past. "Shit," she whispered, covering her face.

She looked at her watch. When the hell was Jody getting here?

Meghan was ready five minutes later. She stepped from the bathroom just as a knock sounded at the door. "That's Jody. Ready?" she asked, sliding her feet into small heels. She reached for her coat and purse and noticed Will was giving her a hard look. "What's wrong?"

"Nothing." He seemed distracted as he studied her.

She blinked up at him, a nervous knot forming in her stomach as she toyed with her black sweater. "Is this okay? Maybe I should wear something else?"

"Why are you so worried? Hoping to impress someone?" he teased.

She lifted her chin and glared at him. "I want to look nice for Jody, of course." She huffed as she tugged on her coat. "I just wanted to know if my outfit was okay. You don't have to be such a douche about it."

Will burst out laughing.

"It's not that funny."

Then he surprised the hell out of her by saying, "You look fine. Jody will be…pleased."

Jody will be pleased.

What the hell? That wasn't the answer she was hoping for and she actually had a hard time breathing afterwards. This was insane. She had no right to feel disappointed or hurt by his comment. This was what she wanted, for Will to believe that she and Jody were lovers, wasn't it?

By his answer, he must already think so. After the kiss he had given her yesterday in the hotel lobby and how he had stayed with her last night she thought that he might have needed at least a little convincing. An ache in her chest made swallowing difficult. She had to stop feeling this way. They couldn't, wouldn't, ever be. God, her mind knew this, when would the rest of her?

* * * *

Will pulled to a stop in front of a large three-storey townhouse. It was very old, just like the other houses in the area. Jody held the door open for her, reaching for her hand. She took it of course, even though it felt strange. They didn't seem to mould together like hers and Will's had. Will sauntered past them, and held the wooden door open, then stepped in behind them and called out a greeting.

A high feminine laugh filled Meghan's ears and she watched as Will's sister walked into the front hall. She gifted Will with a kiss on his cheek and smiled warmly at her then Jody. She was a beautiful woman with dark brown hair that appeared almost black, cut into a stylish bob. Her brown eyes were similar to Will's but didn't have the same intensity. She had flawless light skin, which accented her high cheek bones and full red lips. Her designer skirt and blouse had Meghan feeling a little underdressed. And when Will made the introductions and Sarah shook her hand, she couldn't help but notice her manicured nails. God, she felt like a little kid standing next to her. Why in hell had she agreed to this?

"It's really lovely to meet you both. I'm so glad you could come." Sarah gestured them towards the living room. "Please come in and meet Richard and Gavin." Meghan stopped in her tracks just inside the living room. Two very large men stood in unison and grinned at her.

"Hi," she said carefully, watching the men studying her. Why the hell were they staring at her like that?

"This is Richard," Sarah introduced the man closest to her. He had black hair and dark eyes and an intense gaze that made her uncomfortable under his close scrutiny. "And this is Gavin." He was the tallest of the siblings, with hair the same colour as milk chocolate and golden-hazel eyes, which were filled with amusement. Both were tall and athletic, and like Will, they both had wide full mouths, intense eyes and were very handsome. Ha! Who was she kidding, they were gorgeous.

"Boys, this is Meghan Kennedy and her friend Jody Wilson."

Gavin stepped forward first and extended his hand to Jody, then turned to Meghan. He gently shook her hand. "Nice to meet you, Meghan."

His infectious grin gave the impression of a fun-loving troublemaker, but when Meghan met his gold-hazel eyes she found that his stare was just as intense as Will's, he was just a little more subtle about it. And there was no mistaking the air of self-assurance radiating from him.

She returned his smile. "Hi, Gavin."

He winked.

Richard stepped up next. She peered into his dark, penetrating stare realising very quickly that there was a dark side to Richard. Will did too, but he was better able to mask it. In a nutshell, Richard made her uneasy. Jody, who stood next to her, casually slid his arm around her waist, tucking her into to his side. Her body stiffened against the close contact.

"Richard," Jody acknowledged, giving the man a sharp nod. Meghan felt Jody's hand on her waist. This was weird, Jody's intimate touch felt…icky and the heat and weight just felt wrong.

"It's nice to meet you, Richard." Meghan held out her hand in greeting.

Richard gave Jody an odd look before reaching forward and gently taking her hand.

"It's lovely to meet you, Meghan." Instantly, his dark stare was replaced with a breathtaking smile, giving him a wickedly handsome appearance. "You are a very lucky man, Jody." His dark eyes twinkled as they remained on her. "Meghan is quite beautiful."

She slowly pulled her hand back. His comment was unexpected and embarrassing. She blinked at him and watched as he narrowed his dark glare on Jody. And she suddenly wondered if he was aware of her little charade.

"Yes." Jody grinned, showing his white teeth. "I am lucky."

"Wonderful," Sarah sang. "Why don't you all sit and I'll get the Bloody Marys." Sarah turned to touched Will's arm. "Could you help?"

He nodded and followed her to the kitchen. She closed the door and grabbed his arm. "She is beautiful. And that hair. Gorgeous!"

He grinned like an idiot, pride swelling in his chest.

"But I have to say. I think you're reading this wrong, I don't think Jody is her lover."

"What makes you think that?"

Sarah tsked. "Didn't you see? She doesn't like it when he touches her."

He nodded. He shouldn't really be surprised, Sarah was just as observant as his brothers.

Rich walked in, closing the door behind him. He stepped next to Will and point-blank said, "Somethin' not right with those two."

"See, I told you." She waved her finger.

"You told him, I suppose?"

Sarah nodded sheepishly. "And Gavin."

Will shook his head. "Okay." Will rested his hip against the table. "What's your theory?"

"She doesn't like his touch. And he's not what he seems. He's not acting himself."

Will smiled this time. Richard was a police officer and a damn good one too. So Will wasn't surprised that he had picked something up.

"You probably made him nervous with that death-stare of yours." Sarah bit the top off an olive. "You're not at work and my sitting room is not a holding cell where you have to stare down every crook."

"I stare down everyone I meet. Why would I change now?"

Meghan turned when she heard Will laugh.

"Mmm." Gavin said, "I better make sure they aren't starting without us." With a wink he stood and left the room.

"How are you doing?" Meghan whispered.

"How do you think I'm doing?" Jody sat back and swiped at his face. "This is killing me. Three Scottish studs all in the same room and I can't do a damn thing. This is heaven and hell all rolled into one." He pointed at her. "You owe me big time, Kennedy."

"You got it. So do you think they're buying it?"

"They will when you stop flinching away from me."

"I know," she whined. "I'm sorry. I just can't help it, it feels weird." She shivered.

"This isn't a walk in the park for me either. But if you want this to work you'd better suck it up."

Gavin closed the door behind him, and stopping next to Sarah, reached for an olive. "You do know that Jody is gay, right?" He popped the olive into his mouth.

"That's it!" Sarah snapped her fingers. "Thanks, Gavin, we've been trying to figure out what's going on."

Gavin frowned at Will. "But I thought you knew?"

"I know," Will confirmed. "Found out this morning."

Sarah smacked his shoulder. "And we've been racking our brains."

"It does make sense," Rich mumbled. "So why are you allowing this?"

"Allowing." Sarah snorted. "She isn't his property, Rich."

"She will be." Rich looked at him and nodded. "We all know the story."

"But she isn't yet," Sarah reminded them in a sharp tone.

"Well, if things don't work out..." Gavin smirked, then tossed another olive in his mouth. "I love redheads."

Will gave Gavin a touch-her-and-limp-for-a-month look, then confessed, "She's scared for some reason. And if it makes her feel better to put on this little show, then so be it." He shook his head. "Come on, we're being rude."

Will grabbed the tray and walked behind Sarah. "It's such a shame about Jody," she sighed, whispering over her shoulder. "It's always the good-looking ones."

Will laughed.

Chapter Twenty-Nine

Sarah had outdone herself. As usual, the food was plentiful and tasty. Will lowered his coffee cup and listened as Gavin asked Meghan questions about her family and Duncan. She flinched when Jody rested his arm on the back of her chair and lightly traced his thumb back and forth along her shoulder.

Will hid his smile by taking another sip of his coffee. He wasn't worried about Jody in the sense that he was competition, yet he still found that his shoulders and neck tensed every time Jody touched her. And he didn't know if it was because she didn't like it or because he didn't like it.

Her laugh caught his attention. She seemed to be having a good time and it was nice that she had hit it off with Sarah and his brothers. If they didn't like her, he would have known without so much as a word. Just the way they had greeted her had spoken volumes. Even Rich, the unpredictable one, had been civil to her, which was a rarity.

Will's attention was drawn back to the table when Sarah asked, "So how long have you two known each other?"

"Long time, since high school," Meghan answered. She kept her attention focused on Sarah until Jody spoke up and pulled her close to his side.

"Meghan is the only one who knows all my evil little secrets. Isn't that right, pookie?" And, with a wide charming smile, he glanced in Will's direction and winked. The guy actually winked at him! Will gave him a stiff smile and glared at Gavin when he heard him cough in order to cover his laugh.

He felt a sharp poke to his shin and noticed Sarah giving him a big fake, but sweet smile. He chuckled back but stopped when she straightened in her chair, listening. He heard it too—a soft cry trailed its way down the stairs.

Sarah quickly stood. "Abbey must be awake from her nap. Why don't we go and sit in the living room again. Abbey will want to see her uncles."

It sounded like a great idea, meeting little Abbey. Meghan loved spending time with kids. They were so honest with their feelings. They saw the world as this amazing place and would never consider that it could be mean and cruel. She loved that innocence.

Abbey was no different. She had to be the cutest baby she had seen and she was lucky to have all three of her uncles wrapped around her chubby little fingers. The men greeted her when Sarah carried her in, giving her loud kisses and making her giggle. But she squealed when she saw Will. The baby pulled away from Sarah, reaching towards him, opening and closing her small fists, willing him to come to her.

Chuckling, Will stepped forward and plucked Abbey away from Sarah. The squeals stopped once she was in Will's arms, and she rested her head on his shoulder. That was when Meghan's heart caught in her throat. She would never have guessed how good Will would be with kids. She had never thought about him and kids at the same time, but now...it made her heart ache with regret.

She chatted with Jody and Gavin and Sarah, while Will and Rich entertained the baby. Everything was calm until Will put Abbey down and she made her way over to where Meghan sat and struggled to crawl up onto her lap. Smiling, she pulled the baby up and gently rubbed her back. At first the baby just stared at her, then she pulled at her hair, then she puked milk on her.

"Oh, Meghan, I'm so sorry! Oh! She's ruined your top!" Sarah cried out as Jody jumped off the couch.

Laughing, she sat forward, feeling the white milky vomit ooze slowly down her sweater. "Isn't this a rite of passage? Doesn't everyone have to be burped up on at least once in their life?"

"I have no desire to go through that rite of passage." Gavin covered his mouth. "It's gross."

"Gavin!" Sarah said, shocked. "Come upstairs, Meghan, and I'll find you something to wear, while you soak your top."

Meghan laughed again as she rubbed the puke from her sweater. It had happened so quickly. One moment the baby had been playing on her lap and the next she had been hosed down with baby vomit. Not what you'd expect from a brunch—but then again this was her first brunch.

She gazed in the mirror above the sink, checking to see if her bra had sustained any damage and if her hair had any traces of milky residue. There was a knock at the door and, thinking it was Sarah, Meghan didn't think twice about telling her to come in. She really liked Sarah, which had taken her by surprise. Meghan had been picturing an uppity snob. She was glad she had been wrong, and after all, her daughter had thrown up on her—now that was bonding.

She continued her scrubbing when she called to Sarah, "I think I've got most of it out."

When there was no reply Meghan lifted her head to look in the mirror. She froze as her face heated up. Will stood a breath away from her. She had no idea that he was even there, but now that she did, his heat slowly seeped into her back. God it felt nice, too nice. But instead of sharing her thoughts she mumbled, "Will. You shouldn't be in here." He cocked his head and stared at her with an unreadable expression.

Will fought like hell to not touch her. When she called out to come in he had expected her to be dressed. His breath had caught when he'd seen the gentle sway of her breasts as she had scrubbed at her sweater. She was so sexy, standing there in just her skirt, bra and small heels. It was like the beginning of an erotic fantasy. Her bottom was held nice and snug in her grey skirt, her back was smooth and her shoulders held a tint of pink to them from her blush and all he wanted was to kiss that flushed skin, soothe her embarrassment. He caught her turquoise gaze in the mirror, amazed how the colours separated, the green fading and the blue becoming dominant. The hairs on the back of his neck stood up when those blue beauties stared back.

"If I shouldn't be in here, then who?" he asked as she turned.

Her lips parted and she leant back against the sink, her flushed chest rising and falling with her deep breaths. "You know who." She raised her hands and placed them on the counter behind her, causing her back to arch slightly. His body reacted lightning quick — the ache in his groin grew with each breath she took.

"Ah yes. Jody." He closed the gap between them. "But is he really the one you want?"

Her silk-covered breasts rose with another breath. "Will."

He shouldn't be here. He had to take her back to her hotel, then run through drills for tonight. He didn't have time for this game of hers.

Her lips caught between her teeth and her delicate eyebrows pushed together in a confused frown. She shifted her hips, which sent a vibration through her body, causing the plump flesh to swing gently.

"Bloody hell," he swore, then pulled her close, fastening his mouth over hers. Her long sigh made his chest swell and his groin hardened. Their mouths fused together in heated kisses. When his tongue probed between her plump lips, she welcomed him eagerly by sucking on his tongue. He was losing his control fast. He pinned her against the sink, moved his hands over the smooth skin on her shoulders and down her back. He knew he had to stop, except the taste of her was so addictive, he just needed a little more.

He ran his tongue over her sweet mouth, trailed his hands down her hips and back, skimming over her sides and around to her stomach, the silky skin quivering as he traced his fingers just below her breasts. That was all he could take. If this went on any longer, he would be pulling up her skirt and fucking her on the bathroom floor.

He pulled away from her mouth and dragged his lips across her jaw line to her ear where he whispered, "You want me. Don't you?" He flicked her ear lobe with his tongue and he felt her shudder.

She nodded. "But Jody."

He clenched his jaw and exhaled. Finally, she admitted to wanting him and she had to bring up Pretty-boy.

"What about him?" He nipped at her ear this time. "It's not him who's in here with you. It's not him who makes you wet."

"But Jody…" She trailed off in a whisper as another shiver moved through her.

Fine, if she wanted to keep up the show, he'd play along. "I want you, Meghan." He paused then shook his head. "But I won't share you. I'm not the other man." He forced her back, glared into her flushed face. "Go find someone else's cock to tease." Her gasp and confusion made a big dent in his armour but he held firm.

"Get dressed." He turned, keeping his voice hard. "Jody's waiting for you."

Chapter Thirty

"I had no idea Kris was this popular." Meghan stared in amazement at the faces waiting in line. She had always known that Kris would do well when he finally started his music career, she just had no idea it would take off so quickly.

Jody ushered her through the front doors and took her coat, giving it to the coat check girl. The club was dark and the heavy bass from the music caused a strong vibration that moved up her legs and into her chest. Or was it a sudden urge to want to stomp some planks and shake her badonkadonk?

She bobbed her head as she scanned the club. The grey walls gave the place an industrial feel, with black, white and chrome accents scattered throughout. There was a long bar on the far side of the enormous room, and there was a stage that looked out onto a packed dance floor. Beyond was a sea of round tables and chairs. On the wall opposite the bar were round booths cordoned off with long black velvet ropes marked with reserved signs. At the end of the booths was a small set of stairs leading to a raised platform where the DJs could survey the dancers.

Meghan began to move her hips to the beat. "It seems like forever since I was in a good club." She couldn't even remember the last time she had been to one. Probably when she realised that staying out all hours of the night wasn't practical when she had to be at work at eight the next morning.

"It's not bad. It's a smaller venue, so it won't be too crowded tonight," Jody said next to her ear so she could be heard over the music. He placed his hands on her waist and began directing her towards the reserved section.

Leaning over her shoulder, Jody said, "I have a surprise for you."

"You do?" She searched in the direction he had pointed. "Tanya! I didn't know she was here." She waved at Kris' wife Tanya.

"It was Kris' idea. He knows you like to dance and we don't. So he thought you might like a dance partner tonight once he's finished his set."

"Tanya is a great surprise! Now I don't have to drink you two under the table again."

"Yes, Kris mentioned that as well. Something about male egos..."

She laughed.

Will thought that his eyes were playing tricks on him when Meghan had first walked through the door. He wasn't surprised to see her. He knew she was coming tonight because he'd seen her name on the guest list. What he wasn't prepared for was her chosen attire.

He had been casually scanning the club when he'd happened to catch a glimpse of a stunning redhead.

She was wearing a short jean skirt with knee-high black boots, making her legs look like they went on forever. His jaw dropped open when he realised the redhead was Meghan. He got hard just looking at her, which wasn't unusual. It just stirred different urges in him, dark urges. The woman was the embodiment of sex, of hot open-mouth kisses, and sweaty bodies. His gaze was drawn to that skirt as she walked towards the booths. The seductive sway of her hips made his chest tighten and he remembered how silky those thighs were, and how they had opened eagerly for him. Looking around, Will saw that her walk hadn't only caught his attention, there were many others who were also appreciating that sway — including members of his team.

He would have never thought that she even owned clothes like that. Then again, he couldn't picture her burning down a pizza parlour, getting arrested for stealing a car or having a tongue piercing either. But she had done all those things, so why was this so shocking?

Will watched as Meghan greeted his client's wife with a hug and noticed how her tight-fitting black top rose slightly when she raised her arms, revealing the smooth skin on her back.

Fuck! What the hell was the matter with him? This was not the time or place to lose focus. A major client with the potential of repeat business was at stake here, nothing could go wrong tonight. He took a slow deep breath. Nothing would go wrong. His team was in place, the client would be kept safe and Meghan, in her high black boots, would not cause him to lose focus.

After joining Tanya and ordering drinks, she gazed around and noticed Will standing by the end of the bar. A tight-fitting black T-shirt was stretched over his thick arms and wide chest, a pair of black combat pants that had pockets on each thigh, and black boots. He seemed to always wear boots.

His gaze was watchful as he scanned the crowd, a controlled strength surrounded him. He was ready...for anything. A fluttering started in her stomach, and she quickly looked away before his gaze came her way. Why did he have this effect on her? Just the sight of him in his black T-shirt and his no-nonsense stance had her tingling all over.

She chanced a peek in Will's direction once again, only to find him staring back. His mocha eyes were dark and mesmerising, she could feel their pull from across the club. Then turning his attention away from her, he pressed his fingers into his ear and searched the far side of the club.

She sighed when the lights started to dim and the music began.

This whole thing with Will was confusing and maddening. She had no reason to feel guilty, just like he had no reason to be mad. From the beginning she had told him that she wanted only to be friends. But did he listen, nooo. Did she let her pride get the better of her, just to prove she could win a bet, yesss.

She crossed her legs, not bothering to apologise to Jody for kicking him. It was sad that she had to resort to lying in order to win. But so be it. She wouldn't let herself fall into the same circumstance as before.

Meghan huffed and tried to concentrate on Kris and his group, when Jody placed his hand on her knee to still her swinging leg. "Stop huffing and pay attention to Kris. He'll be pissed off if he finds out you were too busy staring at your Navy boy instead of watching him."

"I'm paying attention," she snapped.

"Then why do you keep frowning every time you look over at the bar?" He grabbed her leg once again but with more force. "And stop kicking me with those hooker boots."

She stopped her leg, not giving him an apology. "I'm not frowning," she stated point-blank. "And these are not hooker boots. I can't afford the boots they wear."

She saw him shake his head and laugh. "You know what I think?" Jody said lightly.

"No. And I don't want to know."

"Yes you do. I think you two need to fight this out in the sheets."

"Jody," she flared.

"Well, I'm right. There is so much sexual tension between you two, and it's being wasted on petty schemes and male egos." He elbowed her when she turned away. "And I'm not talking about a quickie. You need a full night of mind-numbing, body-pounding I-ain't-walking-for-a-week sex. It would be good for both of you, release all that pent-up stress." He gave her a sly grin. "And close your mouth, you look ready to earn your way to real hooker boots."

Snapping her mouth shut, she crossed her arms under her breasts again and turned back to Kris. He was singing about how tough love was.

Yeah, no shit!

She forced herself to focus on Kris, but her mind kept wandering back to what Jody had said. The idea of having more than a quickie on the ground or at the library with Will wasn't exactly a new idea. Jody was right, it would be mind-numbing. And not walking for a week. A girl could only dream!

Not that it mattered. She couldn't take the chance. She was afraid of falling for Will, and bet or not, contract or not, she had a life that was a world away. She couldn't afford to make another mistake.

Jody was still watching Kris on stage when he leaned into her. "Well?"

Meghan didn't take her eyes off Kris, as she shook her head. "It can't happen."

Jody sighed. "You're so fuckin' stubborn."

"I'm being sensible for the first time in my life. I thought you of all people would understand."

"I do understand, and I know why you're scared. But he's not Rob. You need to go for it, Meg, even if it is only for one night. A good all-night hump has a way of changing your point of view." Jody teased by adding, "This is of course from my own experience, which is vast."

Meghan snorted. "I appreciate your concern and I always enjoy listening to you brag. It just can't happen. Please let's just enjoy Kris' show." She turned her attention back to Kris, avoiding Jody's stare.

* * * *

Kris came out to join them twenty minutes later, and following him were three men dressed identically to Will. Meghan didn't recognise the first two but the last was Will's younger brother Gavin. The three men followed Kris into the reserved area and stood nearby. Smiling, Kris walked up to Tanya and cupped the side of her face, whispering before kissing her. Next, Kris shook hands with Jody, then roughly pushed him aside and hauled Meghan up to his chest and nearly crushed her with his arms.

Pulling back, he asked, "What's so interesting at the bar?"

"How in the hell...?" she blurted out.

Kris' deep laugh echoed around them. "Just because there are spotlights on my face, doesn't mean I can't see what's going on out in the audience. I come all this way, looking forward to see you, bring Tanya with me especially to surprise you and you watch the bar instead of me?" He gave her a weak imitation of a scowl.

"Whaaat? Me ignore you...never," she teased.

"Guilt trip didn't work, huh?"

"Nope! You were great though." She laughed. "I'm so happy to see you up there, doing what you were meant to do. But next time I promise to make you the centre of my attention. After all, you are a rock star now."

"I'm no rock star. Just plain old Kris Shaw. A man who needs to sit and have a drink with his beautiful wife and his distracted friend."

After a round of drinks were delivered to their table, Gavin positioned himself close to Meghan at the edge of the booth. He leaned over, giving her a sly grin. "Miss me?"

Meghan couldn't help but smile back. He was a very attractive man, then again all of the MacKenzie brothers were attractive, but the youngest had a fun-loving nature and could probably charm the pants off any unsuspecting woman. "Well, of course, isn't it obvious?"

"Ah! I knew it. Couldn't stop thinking about me all day?" He gave her a wink.

She sighed. "It's true. I have been thinking about you all day. What other man would I be thinking about after meeting you? You're gorgeous, with that tall strong body and those eyes. Why, I'd have to say you're almost god-like. I was even thinking about putting you on a pedestal." She laced her words with a heavy dose of sarcasm and looked up with an innocent pout. "So all the female race could kneel before you and worship at your feet."

"Okay, okay." He laughed holding up his hands. "You're a little viper aren't you?"

She shrugged. "Not always."

Jody choked on his drink then laughed. "Yes, always!"

* * * *

"Which hen is she?" the tall blond asked.

"What?" Rob snapped. He couldn't understand a fucking thing this guy was saying. Why couldn't he just speak normal English?

"Which broad is she?" the blond asked again.

"The redhead with the band. Jean skirt, black top and boots." Rob glared at the VIP section. He dropped his gaze to those boots. He loved those boots on her, specially the backs of her thighs. So smooth and supple, thanks to the weight loss. He'd told her that she would look hotter if she lost weight. He was right. Nothing worse than a hot chick with cottage-cheese thighs.

"Och! Very nice!" the blond's friend mumbled. "Keepin' her for yourself? Or can we all share?"

"When I have what I need, I don't care what you do with her."

"You are bitter. What she'd do then?"

"None of your fucking business. Just do what you're getting paid for. I'll meet you outside when you have her."

Chapter Thirty-One

This was fantastic! She was having a great time. Hell, she and Tanya had even got up to dance a few times. And even though they were followed by Donnie, a huge linebacker of a man who was a member of Will's team, it didn't stop them from having fun.

When the song they were dancing to finished, Tanya locked elbows with her. "Come on, let's go grab a couple of drinks."

Donnie blocked their path. "Ladies, are we headin' back to the booth?" His Welsh accent was so thick.

"Nope, we're heading to the bar," Meghan said, and started in that very direction when Donnie stopped Tanya.

"Mrs Shaw, you'll have to either stay here or head back to the booth."

Tanya was about to argue with the linebacker when Meghan said, "No problem, I'll go place our order and be right back." She turned and started towards the bar, calling over her shoulder, "I won't be long."

Will watched as Meghan squeezed in next to a tall blond and one of his two friends standing close to the end of the bar. Will had noticed them when they'd first arrived, standing in the back shadows with a fourth man, glaring over at the reserved section. They had split up shortly after the client had ended his set, now three were at the bar and the fourth — Will scanned the club — was standing by himself, in the shadows of the wall. His attention was directed solely at the bar.

Will turned back to Meghan, his gut tight. Something wasn't right here. These men were not here to have a good time, or to enjoy the show. They were here to stir up some trouble and Meghan was somehow in the middle of it.

Leaning forward to speak with the bartender, Meghan inadvertently gave them a good view of the tops of her legs. The blond nudged his friend and they nodded approvingly before surrounding her.

Moving closer to Meghan, Will stopped a few feet away, scanning the club, giving the impression that his attention was elsewhere. His instincts screamed at him to get her the hell away from them. He squeezed his jaw, then took a deep breath. This better be more than just old-fashioned jealousy. He paused, waited for his body to tell him something when his gut pulled into a knot. This was not jealousy. It was his body's way of telling him to be on alert. He'd had the sensation many times in Iraq and Afghanistan. He didn't ignore it then, so he sure as hell wouldn't ignore it now.

Shifting his glare, he studied the three men as Gavin's voice travelled into his left ear. "Everything all right, Will?"

He knew Gavin was still in position by the client, as were the other members of his team still in theirs. None would move unless he told them to.

"Not sure," he answered, keeping his voice low. "I'll let you know."

"Roger."

All three men were a fair size and could very easily overpower Meghan and do God-knew-what to her. He had seen the dark need in their eyes as they watched the hypnotic sway of her hips while she moved back and forth to the music on the dance floor. Will had almost fallen into a trance watching her. He had wanted nothing more than to drag her away to a dark corner and get his fill of her. His entire body hardened at the thought of him pinning her to the back wall, her fingers pulling on his hair, her wet sex gripping his. A sudden cheer from the dance floor cracked his dirty daydream and it faded. But his body didn't seem to notice. *Damn it!* He didn't need this tonight.

Crossing his arms, he moved closer and thanks to a lull in the music, he listened as the tall blond start talking to Meghan. He was well-built, with short hair and dark eyes, and he gave the impression he could handle himself in a fight.

"How about comin' home wi' me, angel? I can take you back to heaven when we're done."

Will shook his head. Man, what was this guy doing? He flat-out didn't like this guy anywhere near her, but come on, couldn't he come up with a better line than that?

"Heaven!" Meghan broke out in a fit of giggles and had to grab the bar to steady herself. She wiped away fake tears then turned to the blond, "I didn't know this was a Comedy club too!"

Will actually chuckled. She was such a smart ass. Watching closely, he shifted his stance as the blond glared down at her.

"Look, I'm flattered. I think. But why would I leave? I'm having too much fun here."

"I really don't care how much fun you're havin'. We were paid to bring ye tae meet with an old friend and meet him you will. Then after we'll have that fun."

Meghan stepped back. "What friend?"

The blond leant down, so his nose an inch from her face, and spoke so softly that Will couldn't hear what he had said. What he didn't like was how Meghan's face turned white as her eyes darted around the club.

Panic. It covered her lovely face. She turned away and faced the blond. "I'm n-not going anywhere."

The blond leant down again and clamped his meaty hand around her arm. "Oh yes, ye are." He roughly hauled her forwards.

Meghan couldn't believe what was happening. Just as the tall blond grabbed her arm and began pulling her towards him, Will appeared, inserting himself between her and the would-be attacker. He now stood like a wall in front of her, his wide shoulders blocking her view. She placed her hands on his back wanting to get around him but he stepped back, pinning her against the bar. His order was deathly quiet when he threw an order over his shoulder. "Do. Not. Move."

"This is none of your concern. On your way." The blond flicked his head to the side.

Will took one step forwards and...wait, did he just snort? "None of my concern," he repeated.

"Aye! Someone wants a word with her."

"And who would that 'someone' be?"

Meghan felt her entire body stiffen and she prayed the man wouldn't answer. When he didn't she sighed with relief.

"Oi!" Said the shortest of the three men. He had a shaved head and thick dark beard and looked real mean. "You heard him." The muscles in Will's shoulders suddenly flexed and became solid as the man with the shaved head balled his fists. "Mind yoor fucking business." All three men suddenly lunged at Will.

Meghan flinched as the men attacked. She sucked in a breath when they surrounded Will and she couldn't see him. Oh God! This was her fault. Rob was here for her and Will was getting hurt because of it. She was about to step forward to help when she heard a crack. The man to the left of Will stumbled back holding his nose, blood running between his fingers and down his arm.

Taking a hit to the face, Will growled out a harsh curse, then slammed his elbow into the face of the man on his right, knocking him to the floor. With only the blond left standing, Will advanced, the man meeting him halfway. It was unnerving how fast Will could move, his precise blows wielding maximum results. The guy didn't really stand a chance, even she could see that. Will was too quick, too strong. By the time the man had made another attempt, Will was on him, and as if reading his mind, landed three hard punches before he could act.

In a last attempt, the blond, bruised and bleeding, swung wildly. Will caught his forearm in mid-air, quickly grabbed his wrist and wrenched it back. As the man fought to get free, he jerked his head back. Will easily avoided the attempt to injure him and simply took the blond's legs out from under him and forcefully slammed his chest into the floor — the wind and fight knocked out of him.

Everything had happened so fast. The only thing Meghan could do was stare at the bodies sprawled on the floor. Her gaze slid to Will. He stepped back, blocking her from the attackers. The muscles in his neck and shoulders flexed once, then relaxed when his team picked up the men and helped them to the door.

She sagged against the bar, using it as a crutch. Will turned to face her. "You okay?"

"Y-Yeah." She lied, of course. Her knees felt like they were about to give out and her legs and arms felt shaky. The opposite of Will. He appeared normal, as though nothing out of the ordinary had happened. It was just another moment in his life. He had simply dealt with it and moved on. Well, it wasn't that simple for her. It had scared the hell out of her when the big blond had told her that Rob was there and had clamped down on her arm. Rob! Jesus! What was she going to do?

Will touched her arm. "How's it feel?" He gently ran his thumb over the tender skin. "I can't see anything, but it feels like it's beginning to swell."

He leaned across the bar and motioned to the bartender. A minute later he was handed a small bag of ice. Then, taking hold of Meghan's hand, he led her through the crowd to a side door and into the club manager's office. There was a one-way window that looked into the club from behind the bar, a desk with a leather chair and couch and a bathroom.

Will closed and locked the door. He pulled her into the small attached bathroom and turned on the overhead light. He inspected her upper arm then gingerly placed the bag of ice on top of the raised skin.

Meghan stared at him from under her lashes. "Your cheek is swollen."

"It's fine."

"Doesn't it hurt?"

Will shook his head. "What's going on? Why were those men paid to drag you out of here?"

She looked at his chest and shrugged. "I don't know."

The muscle in his jaw twitched.

It wasn't a total lie, not really. But she couldn't tell him that. She met his accusing glare. "I didn't start anything. I just went to order a few drinks. They came to me." The words tumbled from her mouth.

"Yes I saw that. But why did they come to ye?"

"I don't know."

"Want to know my thoughts?" He continued without giving her a chance to answer, "I think trouble has followed ye over from Canada." He paused, studying her. "Or, some rich bloke saw you and wanted you for the night."

"What does that mean?"

He ignored her. "I believe the first theory. Although wearing all of that" — he pointed down the length of her — "my second theory has merit as well."

"What's wrong with my clothes?"

He laughed dryly as he pulled out his ear bud. "Are you kiddin' me?"

"No." She jerked her arm away from him. "Are you implying that if I was wearing something different that they wouldn't have approached me?"

"Yes. You're not leaving much to the imagination when you're giving boners away for free," he said, firmly crossing his muscular arms. "But my gut is going with option number one." His frown deepened.

She ignored the second comment. "Oh, I'm sorry, Father Will, I didn't realise we were in *church*," she snapped, pushing past him. His large body blocked her. She stepped back and watched his glare became shadowed.

"Let me go."

He didn't answer her, he just fixed his swirling dark eyes on her.

Folding her arms over her chest, she mimicked his stance. "Will." She hadn't meant his name to come out on a sigh. "You don't honestly believe that I provoked them? Do you?"

He closed the small gap between them. "By wearing that" — he pointed to her semi-sheer top — "and that" — then pointed to her skirt — "oh yeah. But what pushed them over the edge are those." He stared down at her knee-high black boots. "You know the effect clothes like these have. So ye should nae be surprised when someone makes a move for ye. You're lucky I was close enough to stop them."

"You can't be serious!"

"Those three could have dragged ye away afore' anyone could have stopped them," he barked out, his accent thick.

"Oh, for God's sakes. You're being ridiculous."

She gasped when he quickly pinned her against the wall. He placed a hand on either side of her head. "Am I? What if they were able to get ye intae a confined area? Like this room?" His questions held an threatening edge but she wasn't scared. Turned on was a better description.

He leaned into her, lowered his face, his mouth an inch away from hers. "Ye don't have much room to move. Still think I'm ridiculous?"

Damn it! She couldn't think of a thing to say, she was distracted by his lips and the memory they sparked of how they felt pressed against her neck.

"They would be able tae do whatever they wanted to ye, for as long as they liked. The door is locked. The crowd at the bar and the music would cover any sounds, like screams or moans…" Her skin heated and tingled to life at the idea. "No one would know ye were missing until after the deed was done," he said softly. She swallowed hard. Her body tingled in anticipation, waiting for him to make her moan.

Will watched as Meghan pulled her full lower lip between her teeth, her breathing becoming heavy. She was openly responding to the closeness he had forced on her, not hiding like she would normally do and it was all he could do to hold himself back. He had been hard since the moment he had seen her and now that she was standing this close, her mouth inches away from his, her flushed breasts pulling at her sheer top, he could feel his control starting to slip away.

"Meghan." The low growl was meant to be a warning, but when she slowly licked her lips, he secured her body against the wall and fastened his mouth over hers. He roughly cupped her face, tilted her chin up with his thumbs, pressed his hips into hers — keeping her trapped by the wall and his body. She gripped at his forearms, held tight, her nails digging into his skin as he deepened the kiss. When she sighed, he slid his tongue in between her trembling lips to tangle hungrily with hers.

This wasn't the plan he had come up with. He was supposed to be playing her little game, make her think he wouldn't be the 'other man'. That he wouldn't touch her. Which was a lie. He would go against his deeply held beliefs and he would become the 'other man' for Meghan. He would cheat and lie and steal for her and he wasn't ashamed of it.

He couldn't stay away from her. It was like telling himself he didn't need to breathe. What had he been thinking? The binding wouldn't allow it, and would simply make their situation worse, which explained why he was flat-out angry after the episode in Sarah's bathroom. He had tried to push her away, hoping it might make her come to her senses, but the spell had kicked in and had made his life hell for it.

It was the beginning of the end for Meghan. She knew it as soon as Will kissed her. His mouth was relentless as he pinned her to the wall and explored her body with his hands. They skimmed down her waist and hips, outlining her shape. He slid a single hand around to her behind and she couldn't help but moan when he squeezed her cheek and roughly pulled her close. But he didn't stop there, he then continued farther down the back of her thigh until he reached the hem of her skirt. Without any hesitation, he jerked the material up around her hips and lifted one leg pulling her up against his hard shaft.

Meghan moaned out loud as Will moved against her. The heat between her legs spread through her with supernatural speed. She ached for him, inside and out, and wanted to tell him, but he wouldn't stop kissing her. So Meghan did the only thing she could think of, she tugged at his T-shirt, wanting to stroke his hard muscles, needing him to feel as hot as she was.

She ran her hands under his shirt, enjoying the heat of his skin. His muscles tensed when she touched the rough hair of his chest. She liked the combination of soap and aftershave, mixed with his musky scent. He stopped kissing her, and when Meghan opened her eyes to see why, she noticed his gaze was directed down. He rested one forearm on the wall beside her head while he brushed his knuckles over her black silk panties.

"Not red," she pointed out for some stupid reason.

"No." He slipped a finger inside the elastic but only enough to trace along the curve of the see-through material. "But just as sexy."

She sucked in air, felt her belly clench and her core liquefy into a fiery rush. She cupped the sides of his face, pulling him down, claiming his mouth in a deep, probing kiss. She whimpered against his lips when he pulled his hand away and she arched trying to keep him in place. He didn't laugh or make a comment of any kind about her naughty behaviour. He simply tugged the silky material aside and slid his fingers into her slick folds. He teased and caressed in slow rhythmic circles, her swollen bud so eager for his attention. He deepened the kiss as he increased the pressure between her thighs and slipped one finger deep. "Fuck me," he breathed out coarsely.

Just like every other time she was with Will, her body reacted on its own. Her back arched trying to draw his finger in deeper, her limbs shook, and her hands ran up his neck and into his hair. She wanted more than this, she wanted him. Her hips began to rock in harmony with his torment, the leisurely movement, almost deliberately trying to make her squirm. She didn't mind, in fact she loved it. Loved his hands on her. Loved his fingers inside her. Then he stopped kissing her and pulled away.

"Open your eyes, Meghan. Look at me." His tone was raw, demanding, but she did as he asked.

"What's wrong?"

"You want me?" He continued to make her hips rock as he spoke.

"What...I..." Her breath was short and choppy. She couldn't talk—this felt too good.

"You need to say it, Meghan." He growled low. "You want me." He slid a second finger in to join with the first, locking his gaze with hers. "I know you do. You can't hide it. I can see it, feel it."

Sobering, she blinked up at him, a twinge of fear closing her throat. Yes, she wanted him and no, she couldn't hide it, not now that he had triple-X-rated proof. She couldn't admit it either though, not out loud where he might hear. So why say anything? Why not just show him?

Hips still rocking, she reached for the button and zipper of his pants.

"Meghan," he warned. He lowered his face, his mouth so close to hers. She pulled back and slid her hand under the waistband of his boxer briefs and encircled his hard silky cock.

"Is this clear enough?" She stroked down the thick length, watched him close his eyes in surrender.

This power was all-consuming. She gripped and stroked his engorged shaft until his nostrils flared and his breath became laboured. Amazing—she had the ability to make this large formidable man lose his control. She lightly kissed the tight muscle of his jaw, just wanting to taste his skin. This heat that flowed between them was so hot and incredibly sexy, and the fact that a crowd of people were so close, gave her a thrill. What wonderful mixture of feelings, and she knew she could easily become addicted to them.

"If you keep 'at up, it won't matter if you never speak again." His accent was thick, rough.

"Just as long as it stays up," she breathed into his mouth, grazed her tongue along his lower lip.

Without giving her warning, he grabbed the backs of her thighs, lifting her high.

She drew in a startled breath and flung her arms around his neck. "In a hurry." She purred as he turned her to the counter.

He could only growl. She still hadn't said that she wanted him. Still hadn't told him why those three men had wanted her. But he didn't care anymore. The only thing he cared about was Meghan. She wasn't the person he thought she was. She was better. He was constantly surprised by her. Under normal circumstances he wouldn't have liked it in the least. Now he expected it from her and actually looked forward to seeing what she would do next.

Her gasp broke through his haze as he roughly pushed her legs apart. He tried to be gentle but his control was almost completely gone, his sole focus was on Meghan and being inside her.

He kissed her cheek then her jaw. He loved her fingers in his hair. "Want me, Meghan." Her body became stiff. "Want me like I want you." He kissed her neck. "Want me with your body and soul."

Shivering, she pressed her face into the side of his neck. Was that fear or desire, maybe both? "Will...I..."

He pulled her close, trailing his lips across her cheek to her mouth, rubbed her back, touched her hair — anything to soothe her stiff body. "I told you I wouldn't make this easy," he reminded her, pressing his mouth to her ear.

"Please, Will," she pleaded in a whisper.

He sighed. "Should I let it go for tonight?"

"Yes, please."

"Done." He ran his hands up the front of her smooth thighs. The same spot where he had seen Jody touch her. He had seen it from where he had stood at the bar and it didn't matter that Jody was gay. He was still a man and he had touched Meghan. He gently rubbed over the area, erasing Jody's touch and replacing it with his own.

She released her hold on his neck, enough for him to reclaim her mouth and the heat instantly flared between them. Skin pressed against skin, tongues swirled, teeth nipped.

His normally comfortable combat pants were tight and a bloody nuisance, blocking Meghan's body from him. He pushed them down with her help, his cock pressed between her damp lips. The urgent banging on the outer office door didn't stop Will as he kissed her sweet mouth. He made the conscious decision to ignore it. Her heat was drawing him forward, calling to him and he had to have her. Had to press his body to hers, had to feel her heat as they joined. Her legs circled him the same moment she scraped the back of his neck. She pulled him forward and deepened their kiss.

There was another series of loud thumps against the door. Pulling his mouth away, Will paused, holding his breath.

"Will!" Gavin pounded against the outer door. "Put your goddamn ear bud back in."

Chapter Thirty-Two

Whatever the problem, Will knew his team could handle it. But the pounding continued. "Shit." Will forced his small ear bud back into place with one hand as he tightened his hold on Meghan with the other. "What?" he snapped.

Meghan sat up straight on the counter, blinking at him, wide-eyed and confused.

"The three you bounced. They're back and started in on the client and the rest of his party."

"What do they want?"

"Meghan." There was a pause. "I'm assuming she's still in there with you?" Gavin wasn't stupid, he knew where she was.

Fuck! He should have stopped. He should have kept his distance from her. But, no he had to have been drawn in by her mouth and body, he had to have let her screw with his mind, make him lose control. And tonight of all nights, this was his first job for a large record label. If word got around that things had got messed up, it could screw him out of having a chance with any other labels.

"Yes." He glared down at her. "She's with me." Then he growled out a quiet order, "Get the client out, now."

"It's being done as we speak. What about Meghan?"

"Stay there, I'll be right out." Pulling away from Meghan was the hardest thing he had ever done. But he did it and tucked in his T-shirt, plus put everything else back into place and zipped up his pants.

"What's wrong?"

He didn't have any patience for her now, no matter what state of undress she was in, no matter how tempting she was.

"Get dressed," he instructed. She was still staring at him, her eyebrows wrinkled together. "Now!" he ordered.

She flinched at the harsh word and quickly slipped off the counter.

"Looks like yer three friends were able to get back in."

"My three friends?" She looked up as she was straightening her jean skirt.

Meghan started to panic. She watched the muscles in Will's jaw clench—she instantly wanted to step back but was trapped by the bathroom counter. It had taken the sight of him doing up his pants for her to bring her back to reality. Then his frown and the sharp tone suggested something more. "What's going on? Is something wrong with Jody and—"

"You've already forgotten about the three guys at the bar?" He stood scowling down at her.

"No, I just...you said friends."

"I don't fucking believe ye," he snapped. "Ye toy with people, screw wi' their thoughts and feelings and you go on wi' life as though nothing has happened.

Well, here is a dose of reality for ye — those three guys have come back for you."

"I didn't realise...I told you..." She struggled with her words, trying to get them out too fast and became tongue-tied.

He abruptly cut her off. "Why do they want you? Who wants ye bad enough tae pay these bastards to fight their way back into a club just to get tae you?"

Tell him, the voice in her head screamed. *Before he gets hurt.* But her pride won out. "I don't..."

"Fuck." He clenched his hands into fists. "Stop lying to me."

She opened her mouth.

"Don't." He stalked across the room only to stop and turn back. "I knew from the minute I saw ye tonight, lookin' like a..." He stopped before he actually said the word but it hurt all the same. "With the hair and make-up and wearing those clothes, that there would be trouble. Because of you, I had my guys pullin' double-time, watchin' out for ye and the client. You've turned out tae be a big pain in the arse. None of this would have happened if you weren't here."

Whore! He thought she looked like a whore or maybe a slut, or something else just as bad. It didn't matter which one it was, they all fell into the same category. Meghan felt the blood rush to her face as she stood looking at him, feeling small and humiliated. She wanted desperately to turn invisible, hide from him and his insults. Not five minutes ago he had been stroking her, kissing her, taking her to heaven and now there was nothing but pain. He wasn't wrong though, it was her fault Rob had followed her there. He wanted her and if she had just stayed in Toronto none of this would have happened.

Will deserved to be angry. It was because of her problems that he kept getting jerked around. Yet he had just treated her the same way Rob used to. Taking his time to build up her confidence, making her feel radiant, just so he could smash it down minutes, sometimes seconds later, breaking her into tiny pieces of nothing. How was it she had let herself fall back into the same pattern? She knew why, because Will seemed different, Jody said he wasn't like Rob. But he was. All men were.

Will's deep frown caused his brown eyes to darken. She shifted her gaze to look just over his shoulder, and allowed her eyes to become unfocused. It was easy to wipe the expression from her face—it was an old habit she had got into while she had been with Rob. She had taught herself to hide any sign of embarrassment or hurt, because showing it gave him satisfaction. Oh God. It was really happening, she was repeating the past. She had worked hard to keep it from her life, yet here she was again.

A heavy weight grew in her stomach, and her lungs started to burn. She didn't know if she was going to be sick or have an asthma attack. So she closed her eyes, waiting for her body to choose.

"When ye decide to open yer eyes Gavin will be waitin' for you outside the office. You will go with him when he thinks it is safe, and he will take ye to yer hotel where you will stay. I will pick you up at noon tomorrow and drive you back tae Little Glen. Understood?" His commanding tone wasn't as harsh, but it was abrupt and to the point. She wanted to tell him to go to hell, but all she could do was nod in agreement.

When she finally heard the office door open then slam closed, she opened her eyes. The tears were coming, but she fought to keep them back. She would not cry. She still felt nauseous, and the burning in her lungs increased, her breathing becoming a little laboured. But she would not cry. No man was worth this feeling. Taking a deep breath, she straightened her shoulders. "No one has the right to do this to you. Not even Will."

Chapter Thirty-Three

Gavin's scowl greeted him when he slammed the office door. "Was that really necessary?"

"Was what necessary?" Will bit out. He had completely flown off the handle. Christ, he could still see the hurt look on her face.

"You put your ear bud back in, you dick. And even if it wasn't, I was still able to hear you yelling at her through the door," Gavin said harshly.

"Mind yer own business, Gavin."

"No I won't, she didn't deserve that." Gavin blocked his path. "Besides, I didn't have a choice. *We* didn't have a choice."

"Shit."

"Yeah, shit."

From the moment he put his ear bud back in the entire team had heard what he had said to Meghan, how he had treated her.

"I know there is some bizarre shit going on right now, but this is not you," Gavin reminded him.

Ignoring the statement Will asked, "Is the client out?"

His underlying issues with Meghan would have to wait. Keeping the blond and his two friends, plus some mysterious fourth guy, away from her and getting the client to safety was the main priority now.

"Yes." Gavin crossed his arms clearly irritated. "He and his party are on their way back to their hotels."

"Jody didn't stay?"

"No."

With curiosity getting the better of him Will asked, "Did Jody ask where Meghan was?"

"Yes he did. I told him she was with you."

"And?" Will prodded.

"He said, and I quote, 'About time she took my advice.' Whatever the hell that means. But he laughed, so I'm assuming that was good."

What advice? He looked back at the door to the manager's office. He didn't want to talk about Meghan or her make-believe lover. "Where are they?" He changed the subject.

Gavin turned his head and nodded towards the bar. "They've taken up your old stop." Will saw the three men as he and Gavin scanned the club from outside the manager's office door.

The blond, and obvious leader of the group of numpties, was at the end of the bar, it was a good vantage point. There was a clear view of the entrance and both exits. Meghan would be seen the moment Gavin tried to get her out. Scanning the bar a second time, Will looked for the remains of his team. Four had left with the client and his party, that left three at the club—himself, Gavin and Donnie. Gavin would take Meghan back to her hotel, leaving big old Donnie and himself against the three. Will could handle them alone but would use Donnie's size to block their view of Meghan.

"Immediate action?" asked Gavin.

"Donnie." Will spoke low. "You and I will distract the targets, while Gavin escorts Meghan back to her hotel. You know the drill, no stopping, not even for her coat or bag, I'll do that. Just get her out. Got that, Donnie?" Will asked.

"Nice and simple," Donnie confirmed in his rough Welsh accent.

"I like simple, less confusion that way." Gavin's voice dropped as he levelled his glare on the three men.

"Donnie. Let's keep Blondie awake. I have a few questions for him about his employer. Clear?"

"Clear."

"Right then. Let's show these bastards the door." Will flexed his shoulders as a rush of adrenaline flooded his veins. He walked towards the targets and curled his fists. Now that Meghan wasn't standing behind him he wouldn't have to hold back, he would be able to finish what he had started.

"Oh my God!" Meghan whispered, placing her hand to her chest. Heat flooded her face.

Gavin had heard everything, so had the rest of Will's team. All of them. She stood staring at the back of the office door, frozen in place.

Wasn't it bad enough that Will thought she looked like a whore? Did his entire team need to know how he felt? Even if they didn't share his opinion, how could she leave the room, knowing they had heard what he had said to her? She swallowed hard. She hated feeling this way—embarrassed and ashamed of herself.

Her hands shook as she smoothed the thin fabric of her top. Gavin, of course, walked in catching her at her worst. He stood frowning at her for a second, then gave her a playful wink. "Don't you dare, I happen to like it. Especially if you're going to be kneeling at my feet," he said wiggling his eyebrows.

She knew he was only trying to make her feel better, but the attempt fell flat.

Stepping in front of her, he gave her the sweetest smile. "Will is not himself right now." He let out a long sigh. "Don't judge him by his actions here tonight."

Shaking her head, she mumbled, "I wish he..." She shook her head as a deep anger began to brew.

"Wish what?"

I wish he'd left me alone! she screamed in her head. She wouldn't be feeling this miserable if he had. "Nothing. Is it time to go?"

Gavin gave her an understanding wink, then spoke in a quiet tone that demanded attention. "Once Will and Donnie are in position distracting the targets, they'll give me the go. Then I will walk you out and take you to your hotel."

Meghan nodded, not saying a word, afraid she wouldn't be able to hide her anger.

Anger was good, it was also new. Normally, she'd just push the hurt and embarrassment aside and continue on like nothing had happened. Not this time. She had taken enough crap from the men who had entered her life, and that included Will.

Now Gavin, he was different, he had won a small special place with her. Not only defending her to Will, but he had tried to make her feel better.

She was ready to go and get as far away from Will as possible, and decided that there was no way in hell she was going back to Little Glen with him. She would have to leave once she got back to the hotel, just in case Rob or his hired help showed up. The faster she got the hell out of there, the better.

She inhaled slowly, fighting a wave of nausea. Rob. Hired thugs. She placed her hand to her stomach. Will calling her a whore. What a mess. How could she have let this happen?

Gavin obviously thought she was worried about leaving with him because he said, "Don't worry, you'll be fine. I haven't lost a client tonight."

Meghan opened her eyes and saw Gavin grinning down at her.

"You've lost clients?"

"Not tonight," he said straight-faced.

"Am I the only one you've escorted out?"

"Yup, so I have a fifty-fifty shot. Wish me luck?" he teased.

Meghan chuckled but stopped when Gavin stilled, listening. He reached for the door handle, commanding, "Stay on my right side, don't let go of my arm. If I stop, you don't, keep moving and don't look back. I'll be right behind you. Go straight to the front entrance unless I tell you otherwise. Okay?"

Gavin's sudden change caught her full attention and she nodded. "Okay."

"Good." He covered her hand as he placed it the crook of his elbow. "Let's go for a walk."

Chapter Thirty-Four

"You're brilliant, Kennedy!" She pressed her palms into her forehead and leaned against the wall of the elevator. "How could I be so freakin' stupid?"

She felt like crying, she just couldn't, she was too mad at herself. The second she reached her room she had changed and packed in record time and was ready to walk out of the door when she realised...no purse, no coat. The coat...no problem, the purse however... How could she have left the club without her purse, or her coat for that matter? And of course her small wallet was in her small purse. No money, no credit cards meant no way back to Little Glen. The entire night had been a complete disaster and this just topped it all off. The only thing she had done right was to slide her key card into the side of her boot. A lesson life taught a few years ago. Always keep your money and your keys separate. She wished she had put some cash in her other boot.

"And my driver's licence," she whined. "And my credit cards."

The door slid open and she flew down the hall and banged on Jody's door. She shifted her weight from side to side, and before she had time to cross her arms, the door flew open.

"Meg!" He pulled her forward into a bear hug. "Are you okay? What happened? I saw Will take you into the manager's office after he beat the crap out of those guys who grabbed you, and then all of a sudden they were rushing us out." He stopped, frowning. "What's going on?"

"It was Rob."

"What was Rob?" he asked carefully.

She stepped in his room and closed the door. "He sent those guys after me."

"What?" he roared. "That's it. I'm calling the cops."

"Stop it, Jody. I'm fine. Will...helped me."

He put down the phone. "Then maybe I need to call him. Ask him to sort Rob out."

"No!" She grabbed his hand and flat-out begged, "Please, please. I-I...don't want him to know, he would never understand."

"Okay, easy, calm down." He squeezed her hand. "Jesus, you're turning white. Sit down." He forced her onto the bed, then squatted down in front of her. "I suppose you don't want me calling the cops either?"

She shook her head. What the hell was she going to do? There was no way Jody would let her leave now. She had screwed herself by telling him the truth.

"You didn't happen to grab my purse on your way out, did you?"

"No, I didn't. You left it there?"

She prayed. "Unless Tanya or Kris grabbed it? Could you call them and see if they have it?" He nodded and reached for the phone. It only took two minutes for her prayers to be crushed.

"It's only a purse."

She huffed. Typical male answer. "Jody, my wallet is in the purse. My licence, my money, all my credit cards, my Photos IDs. Everything!" Her voice had got a little squeaky and she felt very close to having a meltdown.

"Okay," Jody said calmly. "No problem, let's call the club and see if anything has turned up."

The manager had his staff search the reserved area with no luck. And her coat was gone too. She left the description of both with the manager and her number at the hotel.

She was beyond screwed. With no money and no credit cards, not only would she have to go back with Will but she couldn't pay her hotel bill or buy any food, plus she would have to report all her cards missing, again — the second time in two years. What a kick in the ass.

It served her right. This was what she got for being weak — her punishment for not sticking to her plan and keeping Will at a distance. She should have just lied to him at the beginning and told him there was someone else, then things wouldn't have got so complicated. Complicated! She snorted — things couldn't get more complicated if she tried.

"There's something else going on?" Jody asked, walking her back to her room.

"What makes you think that?" Meghan didn't look at him. He could read her too well.

"That look on your face when I first answered the door. I've seen it before." They stopped outside her room. "Look at me, Meg." She felt him staring down at her.

Don't. He'll know right away. Don't do it! You're in for a lecture if you do. She raised her head. "Let's just say I'm a glutton for punishment."

Once Meghan had started telling Jody, she couldn't seem to stop. "And now I'm stuck with no *money*." She put emphasis on the money part in the hopes he would lend her some. It wasn't something she would normally do but she was desperate. "I can't pay my hotel bill, plus I've been labelled a whore. Whore!"

Pulling out his wallet, he shook his head. "You're not a whore and you know it." He gave her all the cash he had in his wallet.

"No." She pushed his hand away. "I didn't tell you so you could take pity on me. I don't want your money," she lied. "This is my problem I'll handle it."

"I know. This is a loan, I want every cent back, with interest...forty per cent." He shoved the bills at her. As she reached for the fistful of cash, he snatched it back and glared down at her. "You better not use this money for a bus ride back to your Grandpa's."

Holy shit, how did he know that?

He grinned. "I'm serious Meg. If Dickhead is out there, waiting for you to leave, God only knows what could happen."

"I won't. Thanks, Jody." She gave him a quick kiss and backed into her room, hoping he wouldn't see that her pants were on fire.

There had only been a couple of times that Jody could remember when he had butted into Meghan's life. The first had been after Scott had died. She had needed help snapping out of her grief. The next time had been when she hadn't been able to face the fact that Rob had been using and abusing her. This would be the third time, and he felt about as guilty for butting into her life again, as he was sure she was, for hiding the fact that she was going to high-tail it back to her grandfather's...alone. After he'd asked her not to...that lying bitch. His chuckle ended in a sigh. No. There was no way he would allow her to leave this hotel when Rob had made an attempt to kidnap her. Thank God she was such a bad liar.

Crossing the lobby and heading towards the pub on the far side, he saw Will stop at the front desk. So he was back for more. This guy didn't know when to quit. Jody smiled to himself—he couldn't help it. They were perfect for each other.

He joined Will at the front desk. "So you have it? Meg was not looking forward to having to replace all her cards again."

Will glared over his shoulder at Meghan's Pretty-boy. "Again?"

"I think we need to sit and have a drink."

"No, we don't. I'm just dropping these off for Meghan." Why would Jody want to have a drink with him? Maybe he knew what had happened between him and Meghan at the club, wanted to warn him off. He almost snorted out loud. It would never happen, he wasn't going anywhere.

"I want to talk to you about Meghan. There are a few things that you will need to know about her."

Things he would need to know about her? "What things?" He kept his expression blank.

"Let's sit over there." Will followed Jody's gaze as he nodded towards the small pub attached to the hotel. "That way we can both watch while she tries to sneak out of the hotel."

"Sneak out?"

"You heard right. Come on."

Will watched as Jody moved two chairs to one side
of a small table so that they faced the elevator doors
and sat down. Will placed her small black purse on
the table and hung her coat on a chair before joining
Pretty-boy.

"We might as well order something, what would
you like?" Jody asked.

"Coffee, one cream."

"Coffee, good idea. I think I'll have the same." Jody
went off to the bar and placed the order. Will stared at
the small black purse. Meghan was going to sneak out.
He clenched his jaw. In the middle of the night, with
Rob sending hired heavies looking to nab her? Now
he knew why he had kept her purse. He hadn't been
able to understand his feeling until now. Guilt had
made him turn around and drive back there to give it
to her. Guilt, and that constant need to be with her.

"Coffee, one cream." Jody placed the cup in front of
him.

"Tell me who Rob is."

"Straight to the point, eh?" Jody settled back into his
chair. "Rob is not a very nice person. He is in the habit
of using women for their money then dumping them
after he cleans them out." Jody sat back and crossed
his legs. "Of course I didn't find this out until the trial,
none of us did. He is a real slick prick."

Will already knew this from Duncan, but he wanted
to hear Jody's perspective—he had been there, he'd
witnessed what had been done to Meghan. "You're
saying he robbed Meghan?"

"Yes, in a way. You see, Meghan isn't the type of
person who craves money. She enjoys working, loves
her friends and family, and has the occasional
shopping frenzy across the border in Buffalo. But
other than that, she doesn't want anything. Rob on the

other hand wants everything, has always had everything. And for some reason he wanted Meghan even though she didn't have very much."

Will took a sip of his coffee. He already knew she was selfless, he had seen the shopping bags full of gifts for her family, and the only treat she had given herself had been a bloody chocolate bar. "So why Meghan?"

"Mmm." Jody replaced his cup to the table. "You know I've thought about that a lot and the only thing I could come up with was that he wanted Meg. She's got this feisty appeal that people...men" — Jody winked at him — "find appealing. I mean beside her beauty. I think he wanted to have power over her, crush her spirit as it were, and he nearly did. I thank the day she caught him cheating on her, it was the kick in the ass she needed." Jody studied him. "How did you find out about Rob?"

"Her Grandfather told me a bit and I wanted to beat some info out of one of his employees but he passed out before he could answer my questions."

"Mmm." Jody smirked. "Too bad I missed that."

Will leant forwards and rested his forearms on the edge of the table. "Guess I don't have to ask about the show you two put on today."

Jody laughed. "My acting skills are a bit rusty. I love Meg, but there is only friendship between us. I have known her since high school, we were nothing but friends then and we are nothing but friends now."

"What kind of friends?"

"Not the kind you're thinking. Just friends, there are no fringe benefits." Jody grinned. "I'm surprised. I was under the assumption you knew?"

Will nodded. "I know. I just need the confirmation."

They sat in silence for a few minutes, drinking their coffee. All Will could think about was Meghan. Now he knew why she was scared. Things were starting to make sense—her stubbornness, the constant frowns and the wariness in her eyes when she was around him. She was scared for falling for someone like her ex, and tonight he had made it worse by yelling at her and blaming her for his own problems, and calling her a...

Shit! That was why her face had gone blank and her eyes had become unfocused, it was a defensive reaction, she had been hiding her emotions and protecting herself from the situation.

She was doing what she could to protect herself. And this wasn't just about tonight, she had been fighting him since they had first met. Of course she didn't stand a chance even without the contract or the spell. He knew right down into his soul that he could never let her walk away from him. Fuck, he was in deep, very deep.

"So," Jody continued, "Meg's plan didn't make you change your mind about this marriage contract."

Jody knew about the contract. Will should've been mad as hell, he wasn't though. "No, it didn't."

Jody nodded, then asked, "Is it legit? This contract?"

Will left the question unanswered.

"Listen," Jody said quietly, "Meghan is closer than family. She's stood by my side through pretty rough times. And not once did she question our friendship when I told her things that made most people turn away. Do you know how rare that is? I don't want her hurt again." Jody's direct stare didn't go unnoticed, Will just didn't react.

"I can't promise you that she won't get hurt. But I'll do my best to prevent it."

"I hope so, because after what happened tonight, you have a lot of work ahead of you."

At that very moment the elevator door chimed and slid open. Both men turned to see Meghan step from the lift. Her hand dropped from her stomach as she glared at the men. She was shocked and clearly angered that they were expecting her to leave. Will locked eyes with her stormy green ones and raised an eyebrow questioningly. And only when Jody laughed did he finally crack a smile.

In a performance worthy of an award, Meghan stepped back into the lift, dropped her suitcase, and hit the panel of buttons. When the doors didn't close fast enough, she punched at the buttons again, getting frustrated. Flashing green eyes focused on Jody and Will watched as Meghan mouthed the words 'dead meat'.

Unfazed, Jody waved calling out, "Goodnight, Meghan! See you in the morning." Jody's laugh rang through the lobby. "Man, she was pissed off. Did you see the look on her face?" Jody laughed again. "I might be dead meat but it was totally worth it, don't you think?"

Will, still smiling, stood, grabbing her coat and black purse. Jody wasn't too bad. For a Pretty-boy.

As Will started for the lift Jody called out, "Do you love her Will?" He turned back to Jody when he caught sight of a man leaving through the main door. The guy looked over his shoulder at Jody just before the door closed behind him. There was a whole lot of nervous blanketing the guy's face. He'd seen that guy before—but where? Had he seen him here, at Meghan's hotel or some other place? Tonight at the club? Standing at the back hidden by the shadows? Maybe, it was too hard to tell, he hadn't got a clear look. But wherever Will had seen this guy he was positive Meghan had been there as well and his gut was telling him this guy was the source of Meghan's turmoil.

Chapter Thirty-Five

Meghan's decision to leave for the bus in the morning had absolutely nothing to do with the fact that Will and Jody had caught her trying to sneak out. It was late and she was tired. Okay, that was a total lie. Whatever.

"Jody!" She whipped the extra pillows off the bed. He looked so freaking smug sitting there with his new BFF. How could he do it? Jody had betrayed her with the one person she was trying to keep away from. And in typical Jody fashion, he had laughed his head off. "Well, he won't be laughing when I shove my fake hooker boot up his ass," she mumbled, pulling back the feather bedspread.

Sleep was the best thing right then and it would be stupid to leave at night when she had no idea where Rob was. Besides, a good night's rest would give her time to dream of revenge against Jody. That pecker-head deserved it too, and once she was finished…

All of a sudden her stomach lurched, causing her to sit on the side of the bed and put her head between her knees. "Ohhh, God!" *Sleep, yah right.*

A knock at the door made her jump. Brushing the hair from her face, she shuffled to the door, fighting waves of nausea. It was most likely Jody. She didn't want to see him, she was feeling like crap again and his betrayal just made it worse. "Come to beg for forgiveness. Ha, where's my boot." He was wasting his time. She was in no mood to talk to him now. "Jody! I really have no..." She flung the door open and snapped her mouth shut.

Will! Oh, man. She didn't want to see him either. She gripped the door handle as she leaned into the door. "Why are you here?"

"I need to talk to you." He studied her face intently. "Stomach bothering you?"

How did he always know? "I'm fine."

"Stop lying to me."

"I'm not..."

"You looked ready to pass out when you opened that door." His tone wasn't sharp but it did have a demanding edge to it.

Frustrated, she snapped back, "So? Why do you even care? It's none of your business."

The scowl dropped from his face, as she caught sight of the slightest twitch in his cheek.

"I've had enough of you talking at me for one night." She exhaled. "Goodnight, Will." She closed the door on his face.

She had taken one step when she heard Will's roar, "Meghan."

She flung the door back open. "Shhh! Are you crazy? There are other people on this floor."

He said nothing, just stood there glaring down at her. Then his stare dropped and raked over her thin white T-shirt and pink striped boy shorts. "That's a bad habit you have, opening doors before covering up."

"What are you, the fashion police? You came here to nag me about my clothing again?" This time she slammed the door.

She heard his curse mixed with his long sigh, before, "Meghan, sweetheart, open the door please."

"Sweetheart! Ha!" she called. "Now you're sucking up? It won't work. I'm not opening the door. Come back tomorrow morning and you can yell at me then. I'm going to bed."

She stomped to the bed. *How dare he come here after what he did and said. Then he thought to lecture me about my clothes, again!* "Who the hell does he think he is?" Pulling down the sheets she continued her rant, "And please, for a man, any man to comment on a woman's clothing is ridiculous." She called back to the door, "As long as a man isn't colour blind he's pretty much set."

She climbed into the big bed. Still, why had Will made such a huge deal tonight about her clothes, they weren't bad enough to have deserved 'whore' or whatever else. Her chest tightened at the memory about what he had said. She had to keep reminding herself that he hadn't actually said it. Yet the impact was the same.

Will's deep chuckling caught her attention as she reached for the light. She froze and stared at the door.

"Meghan." His voice held a hint of…what was that? "You left your key card in the door."

"Bull." He was bluffing, he had to be. She glanced over at the phone that sat atop the desk in the room, she always left her key card next to the phone, it was a habit. But there was nothing by the phone. Pushing up onto her knees, she blinked, still nothing. Her heart froze for a beat, then two. It wasn't there. She stood up on the bed, staring in disbelief and heard the beep of the door indicating that it was now unlocked.

"Oh my God!" she whispered.

What was she going to do? She paced around on the bed in small circles trying to think. The extra security latch! She jumped off the bed and landed with a thud on the floor. By the time she had stood, Will was standing in front of her with a questioning smirk on his face. "Did you just jump off the bed?" He looked from her to the bed, the blankets and sheets were in pile in the centre, thanks to her stomping around on it in a nervous tizzy.

Flustered, she stepped back and jammed her hands onto her hips. "Get out!"

He simply shook his head. "That latch wouldn't have kept me out."

Deep down she knew he was telling her the truth. The idea both excited her and frightened her.

"Just..." She sighed feeling the energy drain from her limbs. "Tell me why you're here and leave."

"I came here to give you these." He held her coat and small purse forward.

"My coat...my purse!" She grabbed the small black bag from him and opened it, checking inside to make sure the contents were still there. Sighing, she looked at him, "Thank you. I thought I was going to have to cancel all of my cards again and get new ones."

"Again?"

She met his hypnotic stare. "Because your ex stole your last ones?"

"No, I-I..."

"Stop right there." He held up a hand. "I don't want another lie from you. I would rather wait until you are ready to tell me the truth."

She shifted her gaze to the wall behind him. "Fuck," he growled. This was enough. He didn't want this Meghan, he wanted the real Meghan. The flaming beauty who filled him with frustration and desire. "Why is it ye fight me every other time, but now you stop?" He stepped in front of her so she had no choice but to look at him. "I expected you tae scream your head off at me after what I said to you tonight, but you've suddenly turned into a coward."

She slapped him hard across the face. "I am not a coward. And just because I'm not yelling at you doesn't mean I'm not angry."

"Then stop acting somethin' you're not. And start acting what ye are."

"And what am I, Will?" she snapped. "Wait, let me start you off, a whore maybe? Or maybe you were going for something more subtle like slut or maybe skank. Is that what I should be acting like?"

Though he hadn't actually said the word, it had been clear then and it was clear now that the hurt he had caused was deep. Will shook his head and apologised, "I should never have thought that, let alone say it. It was unfair of me to blame you for something you had no control over. You didn't deserve that."

Her thin eyebrows pressed together, the fluster suddenly gone. "I'm not a whore."

"I know you're not."

She shook her head. "Then why...?"

"I don't know. But I am sorry that I hurt you and when I figure out why I reacted that way, you'll be the first to know." He searched her face. "Feel better?"

She stared at his chest, then answered, "I'm still...mad." Then she gave him a confused scowl. "You did that on purpose."

He nodded. "If you're mad at me, don't hide it. Yell, scream, swear 'til you're blue in the face, but please don't hide it. Whatever it is, we'll fix it." He studied her frown. "Still going to sneak out of here?"

Her small frame stiffened, then relaxed as she admitted, "No. I just want to go to sleep."

He nodded once. "And will you be coming home with me tomorrow?"

Defiance flashed in her turquoise stare.

He held up his hands. "I won't stop you if that's what you decide. But I did promise Duncan that I would bring you back."

"Duncan doesn't need to know how I get back."

He laughed dryly. "You do remember where I live, where Duncan lives? As soon as I arrive without you, Duncan will be pounding on my door wondering where you are."

She paused, then sighed in defeat. "I hate that you're right."

"I know." He turned and moved to the door.

As he reached for the handle Meghan called his name. He turned back, noticed how her hand twisted at the material of her T-shirt above her middle.

"Yes?"

Her eyes silently pleaded with his, her cheeks became pink. She seemed to recognise that she felt better when he was near. He didn't want to go either, his body screamed at him to stay but she needed to ask him to stay, he needed to hear her ask. Hell, he didn't care if she ordered him to stay, just as long as she admitted that she needed him.

"You're leaving?" The colour drained from her face.

"Yes." He waited patiently. "Why, was there something you wanted?"

"No, I-I'm…good." Her breath was choppy as she exhaled. "Goodnight."

He nodded and pulled the door open. "Goodnight."

The door wasn't even fully closed when he heard Meghan gag, then the bang of the bathroom door as it bounced off the wall.

Will entered her room quickly and found her bent over the toilet. "Shit." He ran a washcloth under some cool water and went to her, pressing the cloth against her forehead as she coughed.

When she sat back on her heels, he held her tight, making sure she didn't fall. "Better?"

She nodded. "Yes. You can go."

He helped her to stand. Her face was white except for her lips and her hair was glued to her forehead thanks to the damp cloth. Tugging a strand of hair behind her ear he gave her an honest answer, "No, not this time."

Thankfully she didn't fight him and he kept a close watch on her as he turned back to the door to lock it and throw the extra security latch. By the time he had taken off his jacket and boots, Meghan was already under the covers waiting for him.

Both were silent as he turned off the light and rested his head against the pillow. He lifted his arm and waited. She curled into his side a second later. "Thanks."

He stroked her hair and rested his cheek against her cool head. "You're welcome."

"I'm still mad at you."

"I know."

They were quiet for some time, just laying together when Meghan whispered, "Will?"

"Mmm."

"Why don't I feel sick when you're with me?"

* * * *

Rob's cell vibrated in his pocket as he stepped out into the damp night air. He had been crossing the lobby when he had heard Meghan's friend, Jody, call out to her. Jody had been sitting with that Scot like they had been best of friends. Then Rob had seen her, looking surprised and pissed off. His dick had hardened, and his mouth had watered for a taste. Fuck, he liked that feisty streak, he almost wished he hadn't broken her of it. Although, it would be fun to do so again.

He remembered the way Meghan had moved her hips on the dance floor, her arms raised above her head, exposing her flat belly and smooth skin. His cock jerked at the memory. He looked up at the windows covering the face of the hotel, wondered which room she was in and if that Scot was fucking her. Gripping her hips, pounding into her tight cu — his phone vibrated again.

Exhaling, he withdrew it from his pocket, knowing who it was before he even flipped it open.

"Good evening, Robert," Emily purred. He could almost feel her forked tongue licking at his ear. "Or should I say good morning?" She chuckled lightly. "I trust the men Serge sent to assist you were successful?"

"No, they weren't. They had their asses handed to them by the band's security." As much as he enjoyed the silence from the other end he couldn't help but rub it in the smug bitch's face and added, "Twice!"

"Well, that is surprising. Serge must be focusing more on his export business than helping out old friends. I'll have to remind him how important loyalty is to me." She sighed into the phone. "It also reflects poorly on you." What sounded like a low moan echoed through the phone.

"The hell it does. It wasn't me who fucked it up."

"No. But you are behind on your payment to me. It's a good thing I sent Ivan over. He's going to remind you that when you embark on an agreement with another party, you must hold up your end of the contract."

Rob stopped in his tracks when he saw Emily's giant approach him. "Go with Ivan, Robert. He has something for you," she ordered.

Following Ivan across the street to a dark sedan, Ivan opened the trunk and pointed to a small box. "While you open the box, why don't you say hello to your father?"

A second later his dad was on the line. "Rob?" The old man's voice was strained.

"Dad? What's wrong?"

Ivan shoved his shoulder. "Open it."

He reached for the lid of the white box. "Dad, are you okay?" He flicked the lid off the box and sucked in his breath. Blood covered the inside of the plastic-coated box. A man's finger was tucked neatly into a crimson-covered towel. "Dad! Dad?"

"You have to pay her back, Rob. Get the money off that bitch and pay Emily back." There was a clear groan of pain on the other end. "I mean Meghan...get the money off of Meghan."

The phone was taken from his father. "I hope you understand how serious I am, Robert? I know your father certainly does."

"You fucking bitch," he roared into the phone.

Ivan grabbed the back of his neck and growled into his ear, "Watch how you speak to her."

"Oh! Did I forget to tell you how attached Ivan is to me? He doesn't like it when people are nasty to me. And he doesn't like when I get upset. So, do yourself and your father a favour and get me my money!" She ended in a snap before the phone went dead.

Ivan shoved him away from the car and replaced the lid. After closing the trunk, he moved around to the driver's side. "Get the money, or the next gift you receive will be your father's hand." The giant stopped and rested his arms on the roof of the car. "I've been doing this a long time, and have met some pretty nasty fuckers in this business. Emily is different, she's not like the others, but I can tell you she has no problem following in her father's footsteps. You don't want to cross her. Which is why I'm here. When Emily is happy, I'm happy because she keeps giving me that tight ass of hers. So, I'm going to give you some tips on how to make Miss Kennedy give you those account numbers." Ivan cocked his head. "How are you with kids?"

Rob frowned over the odd question. "What do you mean?"

His charcoal stare had an evil flicker when he laughed. "Get in and I'll explain. But first we are going to pay Serge a visit. Emily paid him for a service and he will see it through. Then maybe we won't have to bring in the kid."

Rob closed the door to the dark sedan, feeling a little nervous. "What kid?"

Chapter Thirty-Six

Will had gone when she woke, just like the day before. Her stomach suddenly heaved when she realised he wasn't beside her. It was so strong that she had to run to the bathroom and gag into the toilet. Again! After she washed her face and dressed, she packed her small suitcase, trying to make sense of why she felt fine whenever Will was near. Of course that was the problem. It didn't make sense. How could she feel so sick that she wanted to throw up, simply because Will wasn't with her? Or better still, how could Will's presence hold off those rolling waves in her stomach? How could she feel...not sick, whenever she was with him?

It was painfully obvious that whatever was wrong with her was directly linked to Will. The sudden bouts of nausea, the eight-hundred-year-old contract, their bet, her attack, and she couldn't forget the sex. She sat on the edge of the bed and covered her face. The attraction they shared for one another was so strong, it bordered on animalistic. When he touched her or kissed her she couldn't get enough, and when he wasn't kissing her she needed to be near him and not because she felt sick without him but because she just wanted his company. She felt at peace in his presence, even though he was driving her freaking crazy.

It didn't matter what he did to her or how he made her feel, it would never work between them. Not only was her home and family an ocean away, but she couldn't bear it if Will found out about her mistakes. He was already so close to finding out. She didn't want to see that look of disgust in those bewitching eyes, not when she had acted all tough and independent around him. She sighed and stood, checking the room for any forgotten items. She was a fraud, she knew it, she could even admit it to herself, she just didn't want Will to know it.

* * * *

This had to be the worst car ride of his life. Shit. Getting his old SBS team to break radio silence was easier than trying to get Meghan to talk. Maybe even easier. He had hoped that admitting he was wrong and spending the night would have helped a little. Then again he knew he had more to do than just apologise for calling her a whore. His treatment of her was inexcusable. Never in his entire military career had he handled a situation as badly as he had last night.

At least he was able to figure out why he acted the way he had. As she had slept curled into his side, he had come to a few startling truths. The desire Meghan had stirred in him had shattered his armour so quickly, so completely, yet he loved every steamy minute of it. All he could think about was her, nothing else had mattered at the time, not the creeps harassing her, not the client, not her fake affair with Jody, nothing. Then he realised, she was the only woman he had every truly wanted. He wanted her. He craved only her.

The spell and contract crossed his mind more than once. Was he reacting this way because of them? The answer had come swiftly and had cracked like a whip in his head. No! He would have felt this way without the contract or spell, he knew this was true because he felt this deep in his heart and soul. Then he acknowledged the last and single most important truth—he loved her. Had been falling in love with her before they'd each read the contact, before the spell had tangled their two souls together. The contract and spell had amplified the feelings he had already had. Or maybe they had simply forced him to see them clearly.

He couldn't forget about their little side bet. He wouldn't think twice about using it if that was what it took. Of course telling Meghan of his newfound insight would not go over well right now. He was going to have to be patient with her, even though he knew she would fight him the entire way. But in the end, he would win, because there was no way he would fight this hard just to watch her walk out of his life.

Meghan purposely kept their conversation to a minimum. She didn't want to talk to him, or engage in any type of exchange. She would start seeing him as a man, the man she wanted so much that she couldn't think straight. She didn't want to think at all—that would lead to feeling again and she was trying desperately to keep her emotions hidden. Even though he had admitted he had been wrong she was still hurt by his words and actions. She had been willing to give herself to him last night, and he had pushed her away and had insulted her in the process.

Despite Will's treatment, there was something else bothering her. With everything that had happened last night, she knew that Rob was the cause—although his presence at the club, hadn't bothered her as much as what had happened between her and Will. The idea of Rob being so close should have her scared shitless, and she was worried, but not as much as she was worried that Will might find out about him. What would he do if he knew? What would he think of her then? Her heart almost seized up and she turned to look out of the side window.

She frowned. "Where are we?"

The SUV slowed to a stop and Will turned off the engine. He rested his elbow against the window looking out at the water. "This is Letham Loch, and that's"—he pointed to a group of houses not too far away from them—"the village of Letham." They were quiet for a minute. "Beautiful, isn't it?"

Meghan took in the dark water and the surrounding mountains. It was beautiful. Made all that more picturesque by the sight of two boys sitting in their small row boat, fishing rods dipped into the water. "Yes, it is."

"Softening you up?"

"Was it meant to?"

"Yes." Will climbed out.

Meghan tensed as he circled the front of the Land Rover and opened her door. "What?"

He leaned his weight casually into the door and held his hand out.

"I don't want to get out," she informed him curtly, then began toying with her seat belt.

He stood still, not making a sound.

"Are you just going to stand there"—she met his gaze—"staring at me?"

He cocked his head.

She huffed. "Fine! I'm coming." Then she slid from the Land Rover, without touching him.

He led her to the edge of the water and stopped. "The stream that runs by Duncan's house leads to this loch. There's also a trail that follows it and circles the loch." He pointed to the opposite side of the lake, then waved to the boys. "It might not be a good place to run right now, but once the ground dries up it will be. And it's always a nice walk."

"It sounds it." She also waved to the boys, who giggled in response. "I'll have to try it out, sometime." She strained to see if either boy was wearing a lifejacket.

"Worth the extra minutes? Meghan?"

"Mmm. It is." She didn't see anything resembling a lifejacket but the boat was turned at an odd angle from where they were standing.

"Do you fish?" He must have noticed her watching the boys. Meghan tensed as the small boat rocked back and forth as the boys moved around inside.

"No." She shook her head too quickly. "I don't like the water." *How deep was this particular loch?* She had heard somewhere that lochs had a tendency of being very deep, and some might be joined deep underground.

"Then why the frown?"

Shaking her head again, she left the question unanswered. What was she supposed to say? That the idea of those two little boys not wearing lifejackets worried her? Even though she had never met them. She mentally shook her head. This was crazy, she was panicking for no reason. For all she knew they could be great swimmers.

Scott was a great swimmer.

She ignored the cruel reminder. These kids lived there, and the locals always knew the nearby lakes, or in this case, lochs. She had been a 'local kid', growing up in northern Ontario. She had developed a kind of instinct. She knew which lakes were deep and which ones were not—she knew where to avoid rocks and shallow areas.

Scott was a local kid.

Pressing her hand to her forehead, she turned and started back towards Will's Land Rover. She really shouldn't worry, she just couldn't help herself. It didn't matter that she was thousands of miles and ten years away from what had happened to Scott.

Will appeared in front of her. "What's the matter with you?"

Squinting up at him, she opened her mouth, then closed it. He was so handsome and the perfect distraction from her overactive nerves. She loved how he stood there in his dark navy sweater, loose-fitting jeans and black boots trying to intimidate her with his scowl. Casual and sexy, her favourite.

Even though she was still mad at him her fingertips tingled as she fought the urge to smooth out his creased brow. "You are so handsome." She realised what she'd said when he straightened in reaction. Waving her hand casually she blurted out quickly, "But you already know that." Her cheeks and neck burned.

"What?"

"I said you already know that."

"No." His nostrils flared. "The first part."

She felt her pulse start to quicken and she felt a little lightheaded. *You idiot, Meghan,* she scolded herself. She tried to step around him. "All this anger I have is making me tired. Can we go back now?"

He didn't buy into her flimsy excuse and there he was again, formidable and gorgeous, blocking her path. "There is something going on." He stepped forward, closing what little space there was left between them. "Tell me." His warm breath accompanied the soft demand and she couldn't help but remember how nice it was to sleep wrapped in his arms. She craved his touch, his kiss, his skin on hers. God, how she craved him.

She blinked, entranced by his beautiful scowl, surprised for the first time that she didn't put up a fight. She really wanted him. But... She stopped the doubt before it became a fear. Couldn't she just have him, for one night, just one? What harm could it do to her?

Lots!

"Meghan?" He gripped her coat when she tried to step away.

"I'm so tired." She placed her hand on her forehead. "I just want to go home." He studied her intently and she felt guilty for lying to him. "Seriously." She jammed her hands into her pockets. "Just tired."

His nostrils flared as he exhaled, she knew he was angry at her explanation but all he did was sigh. He opened his mouth, about to say something—that was when a sudden splash cut him off.

Chapter Thirty-Seven

Meghan froze, fear turning her blood cold. She stared at the now empty boat. *No! Not again!*

It couldn't happen twice. Not in the same lifetime, it wasn't possible.

It had been only a few seconds since they'd heard the splash, but fear quickly consumed her. Will turned from her and slowly walked to the edge of the water. His intense stare was directed at the dark water when neither of the two boys came back up.

Meghan followed, stepping up beside him, waiting.

Four. Five. Six. Seven. The seconds passed by painfully slowly.

Will tossed his sunglasses to the ground and stepped into the loch. He pulled his sweater over his head and threw it onto the ground, leaving him in only a T-shirt, jeans and his black boots.

Heavy weighted knots formed in her stomach. *This couldn't happen, not again.* "No. Not again." She wouldn't allow it.

As Will waded out into the water, his attention focused on the boat. Meghan shrugged out of her coat and quickly followed. She gasped when the water reached her stomach.

Will shot a look over his shoulder. His face had a hard edge to it. His eyebrows were dark slashes above intense eyes. He flexed his arms and shoulders as he continued to wade out into the loch. "Meghan," he snapped. "You can't swim, get back to the shore." He quickly dismissed her, pushing off the bottom of the loch. His powerful arms pulled him smoothly through the water towards the boat, his shirt clinging to his wide shoulders.

Meghan struggled to follow. She was amazed by Will. He was so calm, so focused. The complete opposite of her. Meghan felt like she was going to fall apart at any moment and it wasn't because of the vibration from her chattering teeth, she was truly terrified.

A loud gasp came from the far side of the boat, followed by an anguished cry. Meghan watched, stunned when Will's pace increased as he rounded the boat. By the time she'd reached Will's side, her body was screaming from the cold. The sharp pin pricks on her skin were relentless and seemed to increase with each breath. Meghan grabbed onto the boat next to the boy as Will spoke softly to him. Will's hushed words went unnoticed as the little boy wailed for his brother.

"Liam! Liam!" the boy cried. "My brother, Liam? Where's Liam?" Meghan's heart ached. She turned to Will but he was pushing away from the boat.

"Take him back to the shore." His tone was very calm, too calm. "Meghan!" he snapped out again. "Did you hear me?"

"T-take him b-b-back to the sh-hore," she repeated back to him.

"Do. It. Now," he commanded.

Then she watched in awe as Will slowly drew in a deep breath and without a sound, slipped beneath the surface of the water.

Getting the boy back to the shore was easier said than done, thanks to the freezing water. Her arms and legs felt like lead weights, and her skin felt as though it was turning into a block of ice. Still, the little tiger fought her all the way back, not wanting to leave without his brother.

Once back on dry land, Meghan knelt next to the child, and tried desperately to calm him while she watched for Will to surface.

The noise level around her grew quickly, thanks to the boy's crying. A group of people had gathered around them and before long the little boy was plucked away from her.

She focused back on the water, she couldn't look away. Where was he? The small boat had drifted away with the force of the wind, the paddles floating in the same direction. She scanned the spot where the boat had been, the spot where Will had gone under.

"Surface, damn you." She guessed that he had been under for about forty-five seconds, maybe longer. The water was freezing though. How was he staying under this long?

Meghan watched, rooted to the ground and waited. Her heart paused.

Fifty seconds. *Remember his training*. If anyone could save the boy, Will could. He had been in the SBS, and B stood for boat, and boat meant water. He was a powerful swimmer, it had taken no time at all for him to get to the small fishing boat, and the way he had slipped below the water…looked like an old habit.

It had to be over a minute by now. She swallowed hard. Oh God! Where was he?

The crowd shifted away from her. She watched as an older man shook his head and she heard him say, "Too long."

Another person mumbled, "The water is below freezing by now."

With her heart feeling like it was being squeezed, Meghan began to beg. *Please God. Not another.* "Not Will." She felt hot tears on her face. *Please, please not Will.*

The crowd suddenly moved to the shore. "Oh no!" a woman gasped, covering her mouth. "This is so sad, that poor boy's mother and that man was so brave." There was a sniff and then another and another.

That was it. She couldn't take any more. She didn't want to hear the sad voices, didn't want to see the pity or tearstained eyes, and she didn't want to feel this pain. Not again. She couldn't handle it again. She turned from the loch and the crowd and started to run. Her heart was breaking with every step she took. Breaking, because another boy had drowned and because Will was now gone from her life. She picked up speed and circled around the loch following the trail Will had just pointed out to her. Will.

Hot tears slid in an endless flow down her face. She flew past a tree that was strangely familiar. She stopped dead in her tracks and turned to face it.

A sharp vision flooded her mind of Will pinning her against that tree. Pulling up her long dress, his kisses covering her face, claiming her mouth. His hands were warm and his arms were strong and his thick shaft plunged deep, taking her, making her his for all time.

'I love ye, Meghan.'

'I love you too, William,' she'd said. *Her accent heavy and just as erotic as his.*

'Come back to me,' she'd pleaded, pulling his mouth closer to hers, tugging on the dark hair that hung down the back of his neck.

'Of course I will, love.' He cupped her cheek gently. 'There is no William without Meghan.'

With that said, the memory vanished, taking Meghan's heart along with it.

Sobbing at a memory she hadn't known she had, Meghan ran until she broke through some trees and out onto Duncan's lane. She looked over at his little cottage wanting, no, needing the warmth of family, but she knew it wouldn't help this time. Nothing could help her. Nothing could save her. She was lost. Lost and alone and so unbelievably heartbroken that she knew she could never be with another person.

Words filled with anguish tore through her head as she continued to sob. 'No William without Meghan. No Meghan without William.' Again, the words were hers but spoken in a strong Scottish accent. She didn't understand why, all she knew was that the words made sense.

So she ran, flat out. She passed the centre of town and the library and The Black Ale. Every place reminded her of Will. She cried harder, ran faster. She flew past his house, despite her urge to stop and stare at it, and climbed the hill to the ruins.

She reached the top panting, her head spinning, her vision flickering with white flashes of light. She automatically reached for her inhaler but of course it wasn't there. It was in her coat pocket and she had taken it off to follow Will...

Clutching at her stomach, she bent forward sobbing, her throat raw from crying. Her chest was tight and she was having a hard time breathing but she was certain it wasn't from the running. Will. He was gone. Gone from her life, forever.

'No Meghan without William.' The words screamed in her head.

Then again, 'No Meghan without William'. She paced around the ruins holding her head, the phrase spoken over and over and over, until she stopped at the top of the ancient steps.

Stepping closer, she looked down. She knew where every step had been carved into the earth, knew where they would lead. Knew how steep they were. Knew if she made one wrong move, the darkness below would consume her.

She inched to the edge, her foot swung out over empty space. She knew those steps had taken away her pain the last time. And she knew that there was, 'No Meghan without Will.'

"No!" The command was shouted from behind her just as she was jerked away from the edge. "Don't you fucking dare." The words were growled next to her ear as her assailant pulled her to the ground. As she struggled like a wild woman, the arms around her tightened like a vice-grip. 'No Meghan without Will. No Meghan without Will.'

Then—"No Will without Meghan," rumbled from her attacker's chest.

Her chest froze, her heart froze. She froze. That sounded like Will. No. She shook her head, it couldn't be. "Will?" she held her breath, almost afraid of the answer.

"I'm here."

Meghan's struggling stopped when Will nuzzled the side of her damp head, the tension releasing as she slumped back against his chest. He kept his arms tight. They had to be. He shook so badly, he needed to hold her until he had it under control.

He took a deep breath, still feeling his heart in his throat, the image of Meghan standing at the top of those steps, ready to throw herself over, fresh in his mind. He inhaled a shaky breath. What would he have done if Hamish hadn't seen her run past The Black Ale? Jesus, he'd thought it was bad enough when a woman told him about her running away in tears, but to see that look of distress on Hamish's face as he pointed up the hill towards the ruins, for the first time in his life he had actually panicked.

After his shaking had finally stopped, Meghan's began. From fear or cold or both? She was shaking so violently that he didn't bothering asking her and stood without giving her any warning and carried her to the Land Rover. He didn't want to take the chance that she might make a move closer to those steps. That would never happen again. He would do whatever it took to block that side of the ruins, never would he go through that fear again.

He drove down the hill with the intent of taking her to Duncan's but rebelled at the idea and pulled to a stop in front of his house. He quickly pulled her inside, then locked the door behind him. She fought him as he led her up the stairs and until he let her see his true anger. "Meghan." He gripped her shoulders harder than he should have. "You will not leave me. Not now." *Not ever.*

He hauled her inside his room and closed the double doors. "You're staying here wi' me, until we figure out what just happened." He let go of her when he reached the fireplace. He held up a hand the second her lips twitched. "I'm in no mood for a debate, so don't bother."

To his surprise she nodded and gazed down at the floor, her cheeks flushing. "What did just happen? I don't...I've never done anything like that before. Not even when..." She trailed off.

Of course he knew why she had almost stepped off the edge. His head flooded with everything that Duncan had told him about the William and Meghan from long ago—the spell, the contract, how William had died and how the other Meghan had killed herself because of his death. As he had driven up the hill he had prayed that his instinct was wrong that she wouldn't be standing there. His heart had stopped when he had seen her. He didn't understand any of this. It was like his Meghan was possessed by the older Meghan's spirit. How was that even possible? Yet when she had mumbled, 'No Meghan without Will,' there had clearly been a Scottish lilt to her words.

Jesus, this was insane. He would have to tell her about the spell, it wasn't fair not to, not after today. But not yet, only after he had got her warm and dry would they go see Duncan, and together they would figure this out.

Will stood silently, waiting for her to look at him, when she didn't, he raised her head for her. "Not even when what?"

She answered with a question, "How's the...how's Liam?"

His nostrils flared in irritation but he answered, "He's fine." He focused on a wet strand of hair and peeled it off her face, then tucked it behind her ear. "He's a little waterlogged but no worse for the wear. I'm more concerned about you."

"I-I'm okay."

He sighed, trying to control his temper. Why did she always have to play the tough girl? Her breathing had slowed down and at least she was aware of her surroundings now, but she was still shaking and that wasn't good.

Chapter Thirty-Eight

Meghan stood trembling in the centre of Will's large bedroom. Rich dark green paint covered the walls and large antique prints were hung around the room. A king-size bed made of dark wood, with matching side tables, ran against a long wall. A fireplace finished in an old stone and framed with the same dark wood sat opposite the bed, with two chairs residing in front. The room belonged to a man, but even with its dark woods and furnishing, the room was comfortable, cosy even.

Will squatted in front of the fireplace as he tended the glowing flames. His T-shirt, still damp from his swim, clung to the muscles of his back and shoulders, exposing every hard ripple and bulge.

Shivering, she squeezed her arms tighter across her chest. The heat of the fire surrounded her, but the cold had already seeped through to her bones.

Then again, it could be shock.

Two boys had almost drowned in the same manner as Scott and Ryan had and she had almost thrown herself down ancient steps because she had thought

Will had drowned too. Of course it was shock, what else could it be?

She swallowed hard. She could still feel it, that pain carving its way through her chest into her heart. She felt hollow, alone. So utterly empty without Will filling the gaping space in her soul. But he was here. He wasn't dead. She blinked hard, not trusting her own eyes. Then slowly as though he might disappear, she reached forward and touched his shoulder. The muscles flexed as he turned his head the slightest amount to watch her. She felt the damp shirt first, then the cold was replaced by his heat, sweeping into her hand. She sighed, relieved that he was alive and not some cruel fantasy her mind had created.

With one fear slipping away she concentrated on the other two — almost drowning and trying to kill herself. Holy shit, she didn't know which one was worse. There had been no drowning this time, thanks to Will. He had saved little Liam. A feat she'd never achieved with Scott. Will was amazing, the speed in which his large arms had sliced through the water, his focused determination, the calm way he had controlled the situation. And what had she done? Stood on the shore, like an idiot. It didn't matter that she had been reliving a nightmare or that her legs and arms had felt like lead — that was no excuse. She should have moved faster, been right on Will's heels. If that little boy hadn't screamed, she would probably still be standing there like a fool.

Guilt sat heavy and nauseating on her chest, it flowed through her veins, dug itself into her bones. Today's events brought her past mistakes back to the surface. She worked hard to not blame herself for what had happened the day Scott had died. She really tried, she just couldn't do it. The grief and guilt were always there, sitting in the back of her mind waiting for an opportunity to tear her in two. And today they had got their chance as she had relived her one single greatest failure.

No one had blamed her for what had happened that day. In fact, the opposite had happened. Her parents had been thankful that she'd saved one of their sons and had tried to convince her that she'd done everything she could have done to save the other. That she was only human.

She stared through Will when he stood and faced her. He said something then walked away.

Only human. Maybe if she had been a super-soldier like Will she would have been able to save Scott. She wasn't though, and the events of the past were unchanged. Scott was dead. Her parents had lost a son, and she was still weak.

Had the almost drowning of those two boys and the memory of her failure to save Scott played a part in her running to the ruins and trying to become a human javelin? Maybe. But the pain she had felt today had been different. It had been so strong, so overwhelming, she had felt like she had been being pulled to the bottom a of a giant black pit, that she knew she wouldn't be able to crawl out of, hadn't wanted to crawl out of, not if Will was gone.

What did that mean? She cared for Will, without question, but enough to want to kill herself if he'd died? A high laugh echoed in her head. Care? Who was she kidding? If she only *cared* for Will, the idea of him being gone shouldn't have upset her so much. Her heart sped up, began slamming in her chest. Oh God, did she...was she in love with him?

No. She rebelled against the idea. She wouldn't let it happen again, she would not fall blindly. It couldn't happen, she had to go home, to Toronto, to her family and friends... Her stomach heaved so violently at the thought that she clutched at her middle from the pain, falling to her knees.

Will appeared beside her a second later, wrapping a towel around her, mumbling, "Jesus, I leave for two seconds. What happened?"

She caught his worried frown. "Why do I get sick every time I think about going back home?"

He swore under his breath and pulled her up. His sympathy was mixed with a dark scowl. "Your lips are blue." He ran the pad of his thumb along her bottom lip. The simple touch sent heat flying through her, but not enough to stop her shaking. "We need to get you warm. Take those wet clothes off."

She nodded and moved towards the bathroom.

He quickly grabbed her arm and pulled her back in front of the fire. "No. Here in front of the fire, it will help warm you faster."

True. She felt her cheeks heat. "W-Will you t-turn?"

"No." He reached for her pants, undid the top button and lowered the zipper. "You can't even form a word without stuttering. And what happens if I let you go in there and you fall again, then what?" His voice dropped, accenting the lilt to his accent. "No. You'll stay here wi' me, where I can help ye."

Her heart thumped when he squatted in from of her, pulled off her shoes and socks, then reached for the waist of her pants. "Will...I..." God she felt like such a child, confused and embarrassed over her actions, shy about the feelings growing in her for Will. Nervous about standing naked in front of him.

Will stood to his full height when he heard her plea. He sighed, taking in her now pink face. She was processing a lot right now and his gut was telling him there was something more than the spell making her sick and her trying to kill herself.

He locked onto her shoulders when she leant back. "Listen to me very carefully." He softened his words, trying to soothe her sudden fear. "You are cold. Your lips are blue and you cannae stop shivering. You need to get warm." He pulled her closer to his heat. "I know you feel nervous about me helping you, and I'm not going to lie, I want to see you naked standing in front of me, so I can look you over from head to toe and all the sweet spots in between. But my main concern, right now, is gettin' you warm." He reached for the hem of her shirt and pulled it over her head. "The rest will have to wait until you've thawed."

He exhaled, relieved when she stood back, then shifting her hips she pushed down her damp pants, kicking them out of the way.

Once Meghan was stripped down to her bra and panties, Will quickly discarded his shirt and jeans leaving only his boxer briefs. He snatched the heavy cover off his bed, threw it over his shoulders, then pulled Meghan to his chest. He wrapped his arms and the cover around her, trapping in their body heat. He felt her arms slip around his waist, splaying her fingers wide on his back. "You're so w-warm." Her teeth chattered.

"You are not," he teased lightly, willing his heat into her. He weaved his fingers into her wet hair, and forced her head against his chest. "Relax," he soothed. "Close your eyes and take a deep breath. Feel my body warm you."

She did as he ordered and relaxed into him.

This skin on skin contact was killing him. He fought his body for control. He wanted Meghan safe and warm, his body however, demanded that he threw her down on his bed and make love to her until neither of them could breathe.

He could never do that to Meghan, not now he had fallen... He lifted his head from hers and exhaled. Holy shit! He hadn't been sure before, but now he was. He loved her. *Jesus, all this time trying to get her to love me and I fell in love with her first.* He grinned to himself.

Now for the big question—did Meghan feel the same way? He knew she hated the idea of him dead, if killing herself didn't prove it, than her mumbles about—'No Meghan without Will'—sure did. But did she *love* him? He squeezed his arms tight around her, felt her warm breath caress his skin as she sighed.

Yes. She did love him, though he doubted she would admit it, hell, she might not even realise it, and the spell was taking its toll on her, which meant she was still fighting the idea of them being together. He should probably give her time alone to figure things out, but what damage would it do to her? He wasn't willing to take that chance, not after finding her on her knees holding her stomach.

He felt a strange melting around his heart at the idea of her loving him, but he couldn't get ahead of himself. This was Meghan, and if she was anything, she was stubborn.

He pressed his lips into her drying hair. "Warmer?"

She sighed.

He groaned inwardly as her breasts pressed against him. "Meghan—"

"Did I ever tell you how much I like the way you say my name?"

Caught off guard by her comment, he paused. "No...you haven't."

"I like the way you say my name," she repeated. "With your accent and your deep voice, it sounds so..." She slid her hands up his back. "Sensual."

Meghan wasn't cold anymore. She was delightfully warm and quite content being cocooned in Will's arms. Now fully thawed, she snuggled closer, enjoying the contact and the security. Will's masculinity surrounded her, his large body was pressed tightly against hers, the steady beating of his heart and his musky scent all made the world outside disappear. No kids were drowning, she wasn't trying to throw herself down ancient steps, no problems with ex-jerks, no doubts about the present or the future—just the two of them, wrapped in a protective blanket.

She should've been pulling away, putting distance between them. But she didn't want that, she knew that now. She wished it hadn't taken today's events to make her come to her senses. She wanted Will. It was that simple.

She wanted to talk and laugh and spend time with him, when she didn't have to worry about the future. She wanted their time to be free of all her crazy restraints. She wanted the desire she had for him to take over and allow him to touch her and kiss her without any fear of reliving her past. She wanted him to make love to her again like on the ground at the ruins or on the table at the library—that crazy out-of-control loving where nothing and no one mattered but the two of them. Oh yah! She really wanted that. She shivered.

"Still cold?"

She ran her hands down to his waist. "No."

"No?"

"I..." She wanted him, so much. Wanted to tell him, but she couldn't get the words out fast enough and babbled, "I've tried to stay away from you. I didn't want to start something that would end once I leave." She shook her head. "It was a stupid rule I put on myself. It was meant to make things easier for me." She stroked his chest, caught sight of a scar close to his shoulder. Heat from his skin tingled her fingers as she traced the puckered outline. "I need you to understand. I've never wanted a man as much as I want you. But the last guy I was with..." She paused, not knowing how to explain without giving her mistake away. "Wasn't very nice. And I was...he..." She stopped, not knowing how to continue and fought the heat spreading like fire across her face.

The blanket dropped to the floor as Will raised her head. "He hurt you."

She gave him a quick nod. "I'm afraid, Will."

"Afraid of what?"

"Of you...of this...of what might happen between us." Confessing, she stated, "I want to make love to you. I want you to look at me. But I'm afraid. And after the way I reacted today, thinking you were..." She couldn't finish.

"You're afraid that one night won't be enough, that you will want me, us, for longer?"

"Yeah!" she admitted in defeat.

"So, that's why the show with Jody?"

She shook her head. "You knew all along, didn't you."

He gave her a tender smile. "There's nothing to be afraid of."

"But I..."

"We'll deal with the future when it comes. Besides, I'd hate to miss my chance at making amends for my behaviour last night."

She stiffened and tried to tug away but he held her tight. "I don't want anything between us when we make love." He paused, as though letting her get used to the idea of them spending the night together. "I have no real excuse for my behaviour, I behaved like a child. I was mad at myself and took it out on you. You looked so incredible, so sexy and I could only think about how much I wanted you, nothing else. It scared the hell out of me and I reacted badly. I'm sorry."

Tears formed and she couldn't have stopped them if she had tried.

He smoothed away the crease between her eyebrows. "Do those mean I'm forgiven?"

Yeah, absolutely! But instead she shook her head and sniffed. "There is one more thing you have to do before I can forgive you."

He nodded. A determined look appeared on his shadowed face as he squeezed her shoulder. She lowered her face and softly kissed the centre of his chest, then raised her head. "Finish off what you started." She pushed up onto her toes and kissed the side of his mouth. "Then, and only then, will you be forgiven."

He grazed her cheek with his palm, and tangled his fingers into her hair. "It will be my pleasure."

"Good. Because you can continue right...there." She placed her finger on the spot below her ear. Will took hold of her hand, and as he placed it on his chest, he pressed his lips against her heated skin.

Chapter Thirty-Nine

Meghan savoured the light pressure from Will's lips, resting her cheek on the side of his face. Why did this always feel so right, so familiar? They had only known each other for a short time yet they were so in tune with one another. Will's stubble was rough as he skimmed his mouth along her skin, kissing a slow path along her jaw line to the opposite side of her neck. When the intoxicating sensation stopped, she opened her eyes and drew in a quick breath.

The flickering glow from the fire played with the shadows on Will's face. But she could still see desire. He didn't try to hide or tame it, he allowed it to etch into his dark face, raw and wild and open for her to see. The muscles in his chest hardened under her fingertips. The knowledge made her heart beat wildly and a needy fluttering filled her stomach. The fear that had controlled her life over the past few months had vanished. Nothing else mattered, only this sharp carnal sensation. She welcomed it, savoured it, let it surround her, as he pulled her forward, sealing their bodies, his mouth coming down hard on hers. He wasn't gentle when he forced his tongue between her lips and searched for hers. Once found, he stroked greedily taking everything she gave and more.

This urgent need controlling her was new. She was ravenous — Will could make love to her many times and it would never be enough. She was also terrified because she had never experienced anything like it before. It alarmed her that he could stir such a strong emotion in her, and how he easily pushed past the barriers she had built to protect herself.

Blocking out her fears, she concentrated on the way his skin heated her trembling hands. Lightly touching his skin, she ran her fingertips along the inside of his belly, his hard erection struggling against the tight material of his boxer briefs. Will's body was perfect. He had the hard rippling muscles guys worked at for years to obtain and the type of body women drooled over — and he was sharing it all with her. She pulled away from his mouth, needing to see him, to feel his strength, to taste the passion she had dreamt about.

She pressed her mouth to his chest and slipped the tip of her tongue between her lips, tasting his skin. He tasted crisp and clean, like the outdoors, but there was that distinctive taste of male that made her crave more. She caught his dark stare as she moved slightly and kissed his chest again. He loosened the clasp of her bra and he slowly slid the straps down her arms, dropping it to the floor. As he brushed the undersides of her breasts with his fingers, he sucked in another breath when she moved her mouth above a nipple, brushing her tongue across the tip. She grinned, she couldn't help herself.

Meghan traced her lips across his chest enjoying the taste of his skin as he picked her up and carried her over to his bed. He laid her down and covered her body with his own.

Will studied her for a long moment, brushing his thumb along her swollen lips. "There's been something I've wanted to do for a while now but we always seemed to be outside or in a public place." He gave her a wink as he tugged on her hand.

"What's that?"

"I have a few questions that I need answered." He raised her hand to his mouth and gently kissed the tip of each finger and ended by placing a wet kiss in the centre of her palm.

"Do you remember what they were?"

Shifting his weight, he lowered his head and kissed her shoulder, giving the area a little nip when he was done, then moved to her other shoulder to repeat the torment. With his mouth still burning her skin, he challenged, "Do you remember what comes next or should I show you?"

Of course she remembered. She thought about that day all the time. How his face had darkened, the sexy curve to his mouth and how his eyes had swirled hypnotically, willing her to step forward and lean into him.

She ran her moist fingertips between her breasts, because she knew she couldn't utter a single word.

"That's right," he murmured, and lowered his head to the soft skin in between.

She tunnelled her fingers in his short hair, shivering when he licked at her skin. She cried out when he tugged on her tender nipples, then arched her back when his hot mouth replaced his touch. His hot breath seared her skin as his tongue flicked and teased the dark pink tip. Just when she couldn't stand any more torment he closed his mouth hungrily over the peak, sucking her vulnerable tissue into his mouth.

She moaned and squirmed. She couldn't help it, she even giggled when he lifted her breast kissing the underside. He gave her a wicked grin as he nibbled his way to the other. He didn't tease her this time, he simply covered the waiting tip and swirled his tongue in slow circles. He ended the exquisite torture by closing his teeth around her now throbbing nipple and sucking hard, pulling forth a moan.

Gripping the back of his neck, she felt that delicious ache surge between her legs, growing hotter, more demanding. She never knew that making love could be like this, the way her body responded to Will, the way she craved his touch, his kiss.

Next he trailed his lips down her ribs. She gasped as his stubble scraped her skin. He stopped on her lower stomach and gazed up at her.

"Like that, do you?"

She nodded. He gently rubbed his chin back and forth over her belly as he gave her a command, "Show me the last place I'm supposed to taste."

Following his command, Meghan opened her legs and touched the inside of her thigh.

"Are you sure that's what you want?" His hot breath skimmed over her skin as he spoke. "I'm open to a substitution."

She stroked her fingers over the damp material between her legs. Her sensitive folds throbbed from her touch but ached for Will's.

Giving her a throaty growl, Will placed moist kisses on the inside of her thighs, his breath sending shivers down her legs. His fingers were rough when he yanked off her thong and with a flick it flew across the room. Then he was back up, wedging his hands, then forearms under each thigh, holding her in place.

With her behind now resting on his forearms, she was raised off the bed, her body open wide, erotically exposed to him. Normally she would have felt shy, even a little embarrassed, but she found with Will she was impatient. "Will," she pleaded. "Don't tease, that's not fa—"

Air whooshed from her lungs and her back arched. She held her breath with each deliberate flick of his tongue, sighed when he parted the folds and deliberately licked her in long slow strokes. She pulled at his hair when he drove his tongue deep, making love to her with his mouth. Over and over, he thrust into her, only to stop. Then sucking her clit deep, he moaned low in his throat.

Will gripped tight, holding Meghan's hips still. Again, he licked her slowly, making sure to circle her clitoris along the way.

Meghan moved her hips against him. It was instinctive and he loved that, but he ruthlessly held her still, not giving an inch. He wasn't ready to, she tasted too fucking good. So hot and sticky-sweet. She was his own personal piece of candy. "Again?"

"Yes...again." She breathed out. Once again he tasted her glistening lips, sucked her sensitive bud into his mouth and moaned.

She cried out, pleading for more. "Again, Will. Please again," she called out. "Make me come. Please, please."

He wanted to make her come. He wanted to feel her muscles clamp down, wanted to hear her cries of pleasure. Wanted to watch her body shake from his torment. An ache so deep had him sliding two fingers into her tight opening, curving them up, stroking her sweet spot with each pump. He gave into her plea and once again moaned, sending a long vibration through her clit.

She came quickly. Her muscles contracted, her hips rocked, her body shivered. She cried out, trying to pull from him, but he snatched her back, not allowing her freedom until she had ridden the full course of the orgasm.

Will chuckled softly, listening to her ragged breaths. He gave her one more wet kiss before he moved up her body. He enjoyed the taste of her flushed skin and watched the slow sensual way she relaxed onto his bed. He watched the restless way her hips shifted back and forth touching the inside of his knees. The hunger he felt for her was razor-sharp. All he wanted was to be in Meghan, to feel her around him. There was nothing else but Meghan.

A sweet, lust-filled smile covered her face. She locked her fingers around his neck and pulled his mouth to hers. The kiss was long and slow and deep. Her tongue stroked and coiled around his in painfully slow strokes. The kiss continued until Will couldn't handle the torment any longer. He had to have her, had to make her his, there and then, not at the ruins or in the library or club but there in his room, surrounded by his scent, under his roof.

Pulling his mouth into a straight line, he fought his body as he gazed into her weighty stare. She was such a beautiful woman, so soft and tempting, so feisty and stubborn, and all the more tempting with the flush to her skin and her hair spread wildly on his sheets. She brought out emotions in him he had never thought he was capable of having. Jesus, she took his breath away.

"Will..." She brushed her fingers up the side of his cheek, scraping her nails through his whiskers.

He turned from her and quickly decided he couldn't wait any longer. He reached across to his nightstand and opened the top drawer, then pulled out a silver condom wrapper. He tore it open and covered himself before settling back between her thighs.

Resting one arm beside her head he stroked the side of her face, needing to touch her. "Do you want me?"

She blinked up at him and nodded.

"Not good enough." He lowered his face, her mouth a breath away. "Say the words."

She pressed her lips tightly together. She was still fighting even after admitting her fears of them being together, and the way she had just begged him to make her come.

"Stop fighting me." He nipped at her bottom lip. "Give me the words. I deserve them don't I?"

A crease formed, drawing her eyebrows together, but she gave him what he need to hear. "I do," she admitted. It was the truth. He could see it mix with her confusion. "I want you."

He moved her hand to his cock. "Why can't you look at me when you say it?"

Her defiance kicked in and blue sparked behind her lashes. "I want you, Will. Here, now..." She sighed, pumping in slow strokes. "Anywhere."

Will ran his tongue over her now swollen bottom lip. "I want you too, love. More than you can ever imagine." And with that said he captured her hips, lifted her high and plunged into her waiting body.

He buried his face in the side of her neck and stopped once he was fully embedded, then simply enjoyed the feeling of her muscles clamping around him. She was wonderfully tight, so much so that blood pounded in his ears when he fought the urge to slam into her. "Christ almighty," he groaned. "Okay?"

The nodding of her head and her sigh came at the same moment and Will gritted his teeth when she shifted her hips and proceeded to wrap her legs around his waist. The movement pulled him in deeper. "Fuck."

He couldn't wait any longer, and linking his fingers with hers, he roughly pinned them above her head.

Slowly pulling out, Will watched as she parted her silken pink lips, pulling air into her lungs, then exhaled in a whoosh as he plunged into her again.

"You're so tight." He kissed the corner of her mouth. "I don't want to go slow." He increased his tempo, needing to feel her warm breath on his face and her hands gripping his.

"I don't want you to go slow."

He grunted in satisfaction as he drove hard into her. Again and again. Faster and faster, he surrounded himself in her narrow heat, felt her hot, slick muscles pull at him.

God, he loved the sound of her moans and how they mingled with the slapping of their bodies. He loved how she raised her hips meeting his each time he sank into her. And he loved how uninhibited she was with him. Her passion sparked the wild, undisciplined side of his personality to life. He felt dangerously insatiable. He couldn't get enough of her.

Gripping her hands above her head, he felt her sleek muscles begin to contract and her breathless moans caused his own body to tense. He released her hands and locked onto her hips, pushing in deeper. He ground against her sensitive clit, and caused the erotic friction between them to grow. She wrapped her arms around his neck as he gritted out next to her ear,

"Come with me. Now." He wasn't asking, he was demanding.

Her body started to throb after his command, like she was waiting for him. Her muscles quivered then pulled at him, until the pulsating drove him over the edge and, slamming deep one last time, he exploded inside her.

He loved that scorching sensation as it flew through his body. And he loved that Meghan was the one to cause it. He loved the way her body arched against his as she came. And he loved the way she clung to him after, how her arms and legs tangled with his, her hot breath tickling the side of his face.

Chapter Forty

"What happened this afternoon?" Will's voice was low as he nuzzled the top of her head.

"We just finished. You need a recap already?"

He gave her a squeeze. "Smart arse."

She giggled, she couldn't help it. She couldn't help a lot of things when it came to Will. She wouldn't change it. This was the best she had felt in a long time.

They were stretched out in his big bed, her head on his shoulder, her hand resting on his chest. It was so...peaceful.

"I assumed when you said you didn't like the water that you couldn't swim."

"I can swim."

"Yes. I saw that. But tell me, if you don't like the water, why did you follow me?"

She tensed not knowing if she should tell him or not. "The two boys, they almost drowned."

"Yes, but you were terrified beyond any normal sense." He paused. "Was that for me or the boys?"

Now that she thought back she felt like a fool. Will was a highly trained soldier who had served time in the SBS, you couldn't get a better person to perform a water rescue. Yet, as she had stood on the side of the loch and had stared at the dark water, his training hadn't mattered. How could she tell him that he meant so much to her that if anything happened to him it would destroy her? There were no words, none that would do justice, anyways. Still, she wasn't ready to tell him about the change in her, it was too soon. She needed time to sort it out in her head first. So she gave him a simple, "Both."

"This has to do with your brother, Scott, doesn't it?" He silently waited for her to answer, weaving their fingers together.

"Did Duncan tell you?"

"No. It was the look on your face at the loch. You were shocked and scared, then mumbled 'not again'. I put the two together."

Hesitating briefly, she finally confirmed, "Why do you have to be right all the time?"

Will brought her hand to his mouth and lightly kissed her knuckles. "When did he drown?"

She took a deep shuddering breath. "Ten years ago in the lake by my parents' house."

He brushed his lips against her forehead. She felt so safe, so secure in his big arms. It almost seemed as if he were trying to protect her from the memory.

Closing her eyes, she began, "I can still see that day perfectly in my head, even after all this time. The water was dark and there were these trees by the boat launch, they were so big and the branches hung low enough to touch the water." She swallowed. "Ryan was sitting on the white bench in Dad's boat drinking a can of Root beer and trying to burp out his name. Man, that was gross."

Will chuckled.

"And I remember giving Scott a lecture as he strapped on the knee board."

"What was that about?"

"I told him no stunts. He needed lots of room to do all his flips and stuff, but there were too many boats on the lake that day. He didn't complain or anything and just threw off his hat so it wouldn't get wet."

"Your black baseball hat?"

"It was his favourite," she quietly informed him. There was silence for minute or so.

"Do you want to keep going?"

"Not really, I don't like talking about it."

"Okay." He kissed her head.

She began babbling anyway. "It was really hot that day, and Scott had packed a cooler with bottles of water and pop. I stopped close to the shore so I would be out of the way from any other boats. I just finished my lecture and we were just getting ready to head back out when the other boat hit us. I'm not sure where it came from, or how I missed hearing it, all I remember is hitting the water." She paused, swallowing hard. A lump always came to her throat when she thought about it.

He wrapped his other arm around her as she fought to continue. "The boat that hit us was much larger. The impact actually flipped Dad's boat. When I surfaced, I saw Dad's boat going under and remembered thinking how mad he was going to be. I looked around expecting to see Scott and Ryan right away. We're all good swimmers and we all wore life jackets. But I could only see Ryan. He was face down in the water with blood pouring out of his head. Someone helped me get him to shore and gave him CPR. Then I went back to the water to find Scott, but there was only the other boat." She paused, taking a deep breath. She tried hard to keep her voice from cracking. "Then I remembered that Scott was already strapped to the knee board. The rope attached to the board had wrapped him up somehow, and when the boat went under it pulled him under too. I tried to" — Meghan swallowed hard — "to get to him free…but the rope was twisted… By the time I got to him, it was too late."

She remembered the feeling when she had realised that Scott was dead, seeing the hollow stare of his green eyes. The pain had been so heavy, so consuming that she had felt it crushing her heart and lungs. "That part was the worst, because…I knew he was… I never got the chance to…" That was it. She couldn't go on. She exhaled a shaky breath now that her tale was done and waited for Will to say something, anything.

"I'm proud of you. That was difficult, but you finished."

She bit her lower lip, not sure what to say to that. "I'm… I don't…" She sighed, "Thank you." She relaxed into him.

"Feel better?"

"Yes, but a little blue. I miss him. Every day I think about him."

"That's normal, I would think. I would feel the same way if it had been Sarah or one of my brothers." He pulled her tight against him. She loved the way she fit against him. It was like she was meant to lie next to him. His arms flexed when he asked, "Was it the memory of Scott's drowning that made you want to hurt yourself?"

Trying to pull back, she realised right then why he was holding her so tightly. "I don't…want to talk…"

"Stop. Calm down and answer my question."

She didn't want him to know that it had been the idea of him dead had driven her to those steps. It freaked her out too much.

"Answer me, I need to know," he pleaded. The words were rough and held too much emotion.

She cracked.

"No." She felt the tears well up and she sniffed. "It was the thought of you dead that made me do that. But it wasn't me, not really."

"Explain please."

"I've never done anything like that before. Never thought about it, and I've clearly never acted upon it. It was like...I had been through it before and by throwing myself down those steps was the only way to take away my pain."

"So you never experienced something similar when Scott died?"

"No! Weren't you listening? Never." She lowered her voice and confessed. "I was just really sad for a long time."

"Okay." He loosened his grip and rolled her onto her back. "I just wanted to be sure." He wiped away the tears that had pooled below her lashes. "Because I never want to go through that again. Promise me you will never do that again."

She shook her head. "Will, I just said—"

He covered her mouth in a hard kiss, then growled against her lips, "I need to hear your promise. Give it to me."

His body flexed above her, tension gathering in his muscles as though he was getting ready for a fight. Her heart suddenly melted. "Are you that worried about me?"

He dropped his head onto her shoulder. "Yes, I'm that worried about you. Please answer me."

She tugged on his hair until he lifted his head.

"I promise."

He kissed her, gently this time, his lips brushing against hers. "I'm sorry you had to go through that today." The words were tender, as was his kiss. His arms were a sanctuary, keeping the past and present at bay.

"Me too! But it hasn't been all bad, right now...and before, when you ordered me to come with you, that was pretty good."

He snorted, "It was better than just good, it was bloody amazing."

"Well, I do have a gift for the amazing," she teased.

"Yes, you do." He suddenly flipped and she found herself straddling his hips. "How about showing what else what you can do?"

Grinning, she pushed the hair out of her face.

She melted into him, savouring the taste of his mouth, the feel of his strong muscles under her palms. She touched the scar on his chest. It was thick and jagged, the darkened skin extended over the muscles. It was right where she knew it would be. *How was that possible?*

Tracing the outline with her fingers she asked, "How did you get this?"

"I.E.D. fragment." He reached for her, pulling her down.

"Oh," was all she got out before he kissed her. He tangled his hands in her hair while he tasted her mouth. His body hot and solid beneath hers.

She sighed. It was her turn to make love to him, to give him the same amount of pleasure he had given her. She broke their kiss, pushing back.

"I took horseback riding lessons one summer. Would you like to see how I can ride?"

The growl came from low in his throat. She drew in a breath as he gripped her hips, sliding her along his cock, parting her moist lips. She shivered when the pressure vibrated through her, sparking a dirty craving deep in her core. "But not yet." And lowered her mouth to his chest.

Will's slow hiss made her body stir even more. She loved knowing she could make him feel as hot and as hungry as he had made her feel. So she continued, encouraged by his hands and moans, she kissed and licked every inch of sensitive flesh she could find. She enjoyed how his solid muscles rippled beneath his hot salty skin.

Saving the best for last, she trailed light kisses down to his stomach, and grasping his shaft, pumped up and down in slow rhythmic movements. He reached out and fisted a hand in her hair. She locked eyes with him, and lowering her mouth to the tip, she licked at the pearly white drop that appeared. A low rumble came from his chest when she closed her mouth around his cock and slid down to the base. She sucked hard, drawing him deeper into her mouth, squeezing with her hand at the same time. He tasted incredibly good, salty and manly. She increased her speed, repeating the torment again and again, stopping to swirl her tongue over the tip only to suck him back in.

When he finally stopped her, he wasn't gentle about it. He hauled her up his chest and spread her thighs wide, forcing her to straddle him. He paused as the tip of his cock began to stretch her swollen lips.

"Will!" she demanded, slapping his chest.

"I don't have a condom on."

"Birth control, remember. I'm still on it."

His nostrils flared. "Sure?" he asked, his voice strained.

"Yes, damn it."

That was all the clarification he needed, and he drove his hips up as he forced hers down. The penetration was so deep that she rolled her head back and moaned out loud.

Instantly the erotic pressure was there in her belly, tingling the tops of her thighs, compelling her to rock back and forth and the feeling to grow. She wanted it to consume her, wanted Will to consume her, needed him to be the one who caused her to feel this way. Her body swayed as her hips bucked. Will cupped her breasts, pinching her nipples, then he gripped her waist, forcing her to move faster. She fell forwards, propping her hands against his chest.

Then he pulled her down, at the exact moment her muscles clamped around him. She cried out as he held her body still, pumping into her hard and fast, drawing her spasms out longer, making the feeling deeper, more intense. But she had to move, couldn't stay still any longer, and pushed back as he surged into her. "Ah God! That's it," Will gritted out. "Fuck me love, make me come." He held her still, stopping her thrusts, and he pumped one last time, groaning out her name as he came deep inside her.

Chapter Forty-One

The moment he woke Will knew she was gone. He sat up and scanned the room. No soft body in his bed, no clothes, no Meghan. Clenching his jaw, he slid off the bed and grabbed his watch. Six-thirty. When the hell did she leave? He rubbed his face and stopped, frowning. He could still smell her on his fingers, on his bed, in his room, it was faint but it was there. Sighing, he padded to the bathroom and turned on the shower.

He stepped beneath the warm spray. He didn't like it, waking without her. He wanted to wake her up by making love to her. Feel her arms wrap around his neck, taste her candied lips. Ironically, he was usually the one to leave in the middle of the night—not once had it been the other way around.

After the second time they had made love, Meghan had fallen asleep on her side facing away from him. Without thought, he'd pulled her back against his chest and had wrapped his arms around her. He'd been lightly dozing when she'd shifted her position, rubbing her lovely bottom against him, and that was all it had taken. He'd grown hot and hard in a matter of seconds and he'd tenderly kissed her awake at an unhurried pace. They had made love in the same way. Her arms and legs wrapped around him, as he pumped into her in long slow strokes. He'd petted her wet lips, teased her clit. Watching her face, hearing her soft moans had been all he had needed to find a release of his own.

Still, he didn't like the idea of her leaving without waking him. Was she embarrassed about last night? She had been the other times, was this why she'd sneaked out?

Reason finally set in and Will considered the possibility that she might be concerned about Duncan. He had briefly thought about calling Duncan last night, but he had become so engrossed with Meghan's sweet lips and body that calling Duncan just hadn't been that important.

After dressing he headed straight for the kitchen, needing a coffee. Meghan had surprised the hell out of him. Not because he didn't think she would be an incredible lover. Meghan was a passionate woman by nature. What had surprised him was the trust she'd given him. She'd told him about her brother's death and had been honest when he'd asked why she had tried to hurt herself. It had been hard for her and up until last night she hadn't shared much personal information, nor had she been truthful to him when it came to her feelings about him. He felt humbled that she'd finally trusted him enough to be honest with him. Well, almost. He was still waiting to hear from her about her ex, but that could wait until she was ready.

As for her sneaking out this morning, that topic would get answered as soon as he saw her. He wanted to go to her now but knew she would be sleeping. He could wait until this afternoon to see her, when she would be at the library. And if by some chance she wasn't there then he would go find her.

* * * *

"You left without waking me?"

Meghan jumped when the words were spoken next to her ear. "What?" Turning, she realised Will had squatted down next to her chair, putting him at eye level.

God, he looked so good. Dark jeans, a white T-shirt peeking out from under a light winter jacket, a scarf hanging loose around his neck, and, of course, his boots.

"Why didn't you wake me?" He casually draped his arm along the back of her chair. "I could have given you a lift to Duncan's. I'm assuming he's the reason you left?"

She should have, it was damn cold early this morning, especially since she hadn't had a coat and Will had kept her so warm. A nervous fluttering began in her stomach as he stared at her. Yesterday had been a real eye-opener. She had realised that her feelings for Will were deeper than she had first thought, and she had woken in a panic. Her face heated as she focused back on her laptop. "I-I should have called Duncan. He knew about what happened with the boys."

"Meghan." Silence. "Look at me, please." Did he have to be so polite? She obeyed his request. "Why do you hide yourself away every time we make love?"

"I don't hide."

"Okay. Let me rephrase. Why are you embarrassed after we make love?" He watched her so intently that she shifted her gaze from his. He gently tugged on her hair to get her attention. "I'm not letting it go, so you might as well tell me."

"Because" — she huffed — "I'm not normally like that." She waved her hand.

"Like what?"

"So…so…voracious when it comes to sex."

He chuckled at her description.

"But when I'm with you…I feel overwhelmed with need." She gazed at his chin. "It scares me, that's all."

He traced the curve of her jaw with the back of his finger. "I know what you mean."

"You do?"

He dropped onto his knees, and straightening, he turned her chair to face him. "Yes, I do." And with that admitted, he kissed her.

She closed her eyes and felt his arms snake around her, pulling her to the edge of the chair, forcing her legs apart. She hooked her arms around his neck while he thoroughly explored her mouth.

Ending the kiss, he traced his thumb along her lower lip. "Have dinner with me tonight?"

Breathless, she could only nod.

"I'll pick you up. Seven okay?"

"No."

He raised a dark eyebrow.

"What I mean is, I need to make it up to Duncan for not calling him. Could you come have dinner with us instead?" Then she thought to add, "That way you can take some of the heat off me."

He laughed. "You want me to be your buffer?"

"Not only that, but because I took heat for you this morning, Duncan believes that at least one of us should have called him and that you are just as guilty as me."

He nodded. "I can see his point. Okay I'll be there at seven." He gave her a quick kiss. "Now get back to work."

"Seven," she puffed out as he stood.

Giving her a wink he opened the main doors and was gone.

Excitement crept into her belly as she faced her laptop. Seven. She searched for the time and grinned like an idiot. Four hours to kill until she saw him again. She mentally shook her head. What the hell was wrong with her? He was just another guy, right? No, he wasn't just another guy. He was William MacKenzie, ex-super-soldier, body guard and hunky Scotsman. All he needed was a cape, a pair of tights and some kick ass boots and she'd have her own personal superhero. Okay, he could lose the tights, but the cape and boots…kinky.

"Argh geez," she groaned before flopping her head onto the table. She was acting like a teenager going on a first date. She snorted. *It was a bit late for that, usually you had dinner then sex.*

Their relationship had done a one-hundred-and-eighty-degree turn. Just a couple of months ago he had been going to force an old marriage contract on her and now… She bolted upright. The contract.

She had forgotten all about it. "And the bet!" She groaned again. Of all the things to forget about? And to make things worse, she was the one who had asked him to make love to her. "Crap!" she whined out loud.

Man, oh man, was she screwed. Her sudden panic came to a halt, running the previous night over in her head.

Nope, she was still okay. The contract was about marriage and their bet was about love. And unless sometime during the night in the heat of passion she had screamed out that she loved him, nothing had changed. She stared into space, remembering the way Will had made love to her. Nope, no screaming, just a whole lot of heavy moaning. So she was good.

"Whoa." She breathed a sigh of relief that shaped into something different. The sudden awareness was so overwhelming that her heart pounded in nervous reaction to it. The feeling was embedded deep in her chest, doing its best to overpower her every time she thought about Will. She had had a few twinges last night, but had been preoccupied. Today it was more noticeable and stronger, much stronger. She tried to ignore it, but it fought harder to spread and it only compounded when she thought about Will.

She bit her lip. Could she be reading too much into it? She didn't have the best track record when it came to love. She couldn't finish that train of thought. She had to use her mind when it came to men, not her heart. She was the only one who could control her life. A bet about love and a marriage contract would not decide her fate. She would.

* * * *

Thanks to her boss sending her a steady flow of work, the four hours quickly whittled away. Meghan was just sending off new edits to Toronto when a new email arrived. She opened it without paying attention to the sender as she began packing up her belongings.

Her jaw dropped as soon as she saw the picture on the screen. Stunned, she sat staring at the images. "What. The. Fuck?" she whispered to herself.

Her small, cosy apartment had been torn apart. Chairs tipped over, the legs to her coffee table snapped off, the glass shattered on her pictures, TV smashed. And that was just her living room. The pictures of her kitchen and spare room were just as bad, but her bedroom was the worst, everything, including her clothes and brand new mattress had been ripped to shreds. Scrolling through the pictures, she saw a frame that used to hold her favourite picture of her with her family. It was purposely snapped in two and left on the only pillow still intact so she wouldn't miss it.

Rob. "That stupid...mother...son of a... Argh, what a Dickhead!" She finally had the wits about her to snap out an insult. Wasn't it bad enough that he had stolen her meagre savings? Apparently not. This was what she got for doing the right thing, everything she owned destroyed. She continued to scroll down. "Oh goodie, there's more." And there in full colour was a picture of her running through the village.

Scroll. Her working in the library.

Scroll. She gasped. Will pinning her to the table in the library kissing her stomach. She searched the library for Grace but thankfully couldn't find her. She covered her mouth to keep the sobs quiet.

She read the message that accompanied the email.

'Didn't take long for you to open your legs for that Scot, and here I thought you were a cock-tease. I hoped to take you for a ride when I was visiting but that black bitch following you around is a very good watchdog. Which is lucky for you or I would have got a taste of the new Meg while you were in the shower.'

She gasped. Rob had been in Duncan's house.

'If I was smart, I would have just walked into your Grandpa's house while you were sleeping and fucked you

like that Scot did, bet you would have like that now, eh? Or maybe I can persuade him to join us, him in your mouth and me in your a –'

That was it, she couldn't read any more. Her face cracked. She was so humiliated. She couldn't believe he had said that, she never knew he could be so twisted.

Rob ended the taunting in the same words he had used previously, '*Come home, Meg*'.

This couldn't go on any longer. Rob wouldn't just go away. She needed to call Ryan. He'd know what to do.

Argh! She hated the idea of Ryan solving her problems, not that he couldn't handle it, she had complete faith in him. But the thought of Ryan getting hurt because of her mistakes scared her to death. Her protective instinct would always try to shield him. It didn't matter that he was a grown man and a police officer. It was a habit she had got into long ago and she just couldn't help it.

Meghan placed her hand to her chest as she felt it start to tighten. She took deep even breaths while her stomach turned. She thought of Will's large arms holding her, his warm breath on her face, and she calmed a bit. Maybe she should talk to him about Rob, actually he was the best person to talk to about this. He could probably think of one or two—or a hundred—ways to stop Rob, courtesy of the Royal Navy.

Except then he would know how she had made a fool out of herself, and he was the one person who wouldn't understand. Will was strong, a soldier, he would never find himself in this type of situation. What would he think of her if he knew? She didn't want to know the answer. She was safer talking to Ryan.

Chapter Forty-Two

"Ah, shit. Sorry, Meg." Meghan waited as Ryan sighed into his phone. "I was hoping to get my hands on him before he emailed you."

Meghan had just finished ranting about what Rob had done to her apartment. "When did you find out?"

She heard the hesitation before he answered, "Couple of days ago."

"Why didn't you tell me! Jesus, Ryan."

"I didn't want to upset you. And I was hoping to get you set up with some stuff before you found out."

How could she be mad at him for trying to protect her? "Don't bother. I'll figure something out." She sighed. "At least we know he isn't over here anymore."

"Guess not," Ryan agreed. "Did he sign the email?"

"Really, Ryan? Come on!"

"I have to ask. Meg." He suddenly became a cop.

"You want a guy who is clearly out of his freakin' mind to sign off an incriminating email by saying 'This crime was committed by Robert Cummings of 666, I'm Fucked in the Head Lane, Toronto, Ontario'?"

She chuckled when he laughed on the other end. "That would make my job easier."

"No, Officer Kennedy, he didn't sign it." She sighed, leaning back in Duncan's office chair. "But it was from him."

"What about the email address he used?"

"I couldn't make anything out of it, just a bunch of numbers. They change each time." She reeled off the recent group of numbers to him.

"Each time? How many has he sent?"

"A few. I'll send them to you."

"Hmm. This could be a phone number. Do you recognise it? Maybe one he used while you were together?"

"No, not that I remember." She gently rubbed her middle when her stomach began to turn again. "I wish I'd never opened it."

"Why did you?"

"I was in a rush to get back to have dinner with…" She paused, not knowing if she should tell Ryan about Will.

"With who? Duncan?"

"Yeah. Duncan. So I didn't look at who sent it."

"Did he send you pics of everything?"

"And then some," she mumbled, thinking about the last picture of Will making love to her in the library.

"What does that mean?" Shit. *I might as well tell him.* It would be less of a shock if he found out about it from her first, instead of from the pictures.

"Meg?" Ryan pushed.

She took a deep breath. "There are some pictures of me here in Little Glen…"

"That son of a bitch!"

"Ryan, there's more. He took a picture of me and…" Oh God, she couldn't say it.

"Of you and who?" He asked quietly. "It's okay, Meg. It's just me."

Her face crumbled from the embarrassment. She sniffed into the phone.

"Aww, Meg," Ryan whispered. "Don't cry. You don't have to tell me if you don't want too."

She sniffed again. "You'll just freak when you see it, though."

"No. I won't. Now stop crying and tell me."

She continued, "It's me and this guy I've been kind of, sorta seeing. We were...you know..."

"I get it." He sighed. "What's his name?"

"Will MacKenzie. He's friends with..."

"Duncan," Ryan finished. "I know who he is."

"You do?"

"I haven't met the guy or anything. Duncan told Scott and me all about him the last time we were all there. And he talks about him quite a bit on the phone. He's ex-Navy, right?"

"Yes, he is. I didn't know that you knew about him?" She honestly hadn't expected that.

He ignored her. "You like this guy?"

"I'm not sure..." *Like*. No way. It went far beyond that innocent description. But she wasn't even ready to admit that to Will, let alone her brother.

"Jesus, relax, Meg. Enjoy it while it lasts, you know how short life can be."

She took a deep breath. "I'll try. Thanks for being so cool."

"No worries."

"So, why do you think Dickhead trashed my apartment?"

"Looking for something is my guess."

'*Or someone.*' Jody's warning rang in her ears.

Meghan hesitated, then said, "I think I should come home."

"No!" Ryan said firmly. "That is exactly what he wants. For some reason he either *didn't want to* or *couldn't* get to you in Little Glen. And now that we know he is back in Toronto, I want you to stay right where you are. I'll handle it."

"I can't let you solve my problems, Ryan. What if something was to happen to you?" She swallowed hard.

"Nothing is going to happen to me." His voice hardened as the cop in him rose to the surface. "Meg, I'm a cop, the po-po, five-O! It's what I do."

"I know, Ryan, it's just—"

"God damn it, Meg," he snapped. "Stay put. Got that?"

Meghan's mouth dropped open as she held the receiver to her ear. Ryan had never spoken in that way to her before. He normally had an even temper and didn't get angry that often. "Okay," she agreed. There was silence on the other end. "I'm sorry about all this. I hope it won't inflict on your case load?"

"Don't worry about it. Forward me the emails as soon as you can. I'll need to have a look at them."

"Okay. What about the text messages I got?"

"What are you talking about?"

"The day I left, I got a couple of text messages before I boarded the plane. Now that I think about it they might have been from Rob."

"What did they say?"

"It was like he was describing me walking through the terminal, he even mentioned my clothes. But the last text said *'I'll be waiting for you'*. I remember that because it freaked me out a little. I can't get any bars here, so I don't know when I can send them."

"Okay." He sighed loudly into the phone, "Send them as soon as you can."

"Okay." Meghan wanted to say more but could tell he was agitated.

"Gotta go," he mumbled. "Love you, Megs." And without her getting a chance to return the affections, he was gone.

That was when everything over the past couple of months suddenly came crashing in on her. Still sitting in Duncan's leather chair, she wove her arms over her stomach and began to cry.

She missed her brother, missed her parents and friends. She hated that Rob was making everyone's life miserable. Was angry that he had destroyed her apartment and everything she had worked so hard for. Was freaked out that she had almost tried to kill herself. And to top everything off, she might be falling for a man who wanted to force an eight-hundred-year-old marriage contract on her and bet her she would fall in love with him.

It was too much. She couldn't handle this and not have some type of reaction. She was surprised it had taken this long. She sat back, the tears leaving warm wet trails down her cheeks. This was Ryan's fault. She sniffed. If he hadn't said that he loved her she would never have begun to cry. Well, not this hard anyway.

Suddenly the door flew open and Duncan came hurrying in.

"Oh no. Has it become too much, lass?" He circled his arm around her shoulders.

"Yes." She sniffed again.

"I'll get Will." He reached for the phone.

"What?" No, she didn't want him seeing her like this. "No, no, don't call him. Don't worry him about my problems."

"No. You need him. He's the only one who can help you."

She would admit that her stomach seemed to settle down when he was near, but there was no way he could help her with this. "Please, Duncan. Don't."

But it was too late. He was already dialling Will's number. He mumbled while he waited for Will to pick up. "I would never have given Will that bloody contract if I knew it would cause ye so much pain."

She blinked. "What...?"

"Boy!" Duncan barked into the phone. "Get over here now." Duncan was silent, then he barked again, "Yes, that. Now move it." He slammed down the phone. "He's on his way, lass," Duncan soothed.

She pushed his arms away. "What do you mean the contract causes me pain?"

* * * *

Will made it to Duncan's in record time, every muscle in his body was coiled tight. Damn, Meghan must be in real pain, he had never heard Duncan sound that flustered before. He marched into Duncan's and straight into Meghan's line of fire.

"You." She pointed a finger at him, stomping out of Duncan's office. "You knew about this." She pushed at his chest with both hands. "And you didn't tell me?"

"Tell you what?" He grabbed both of her arms when she tried to push him back again. He held tight when she tried pulling away. "What the hell is going on? I thought you were sick?" He met Duncan's troubled expression over the top of her head. "She doesn't look sick."

"I'm not sick. I'm fucking pissed off is what I am."

Will focused on her blazing green eyes. That was the first time he had ever heard Meghan use that type of language before. Releasing her, Will looked from Meghan to Duncan. "What happened here?"

"I was worried. You understand," Duncan began. "When I saw her bent over, crying I just assumed it was the—"

"The spell," Meghan snapped out, then accused, "You knew about it and didn't tell me. How could you do that?"

He ignored the question. "Why were you crying?"

"Wha..." She stepped back. "That has nothing to do with this."

"Yes, it does. It started this mess. So let's get that cleared up first, then you can yell at me about the spell."

"I-I called Ryan. He said something... I cried. It's not a big deal. How long have you known about the spell?"

Will frowned. "I've known about it for about for five or six weeks. What did he say to you?"

"That he loves me," she began, then in a huff crossed her arms. "Did you know about it before or after Duncan showed you the contract and we made our bet?"

"After. I don't understand why that would make you cry?"

She shook her head. "What...I... He just...never says that, it caught me off guard and made me miss him, that's all." Tears suddenly glistened. "Stop trying to confuse me. Why didn't you tell me about this binding spell?"

He sighed, running a hand through his hair. "I don't know, I was more concerned with the effects it had on you. Wait, you believe in this spell?"

"I wasn't sure at first. But then I remembered we're in the Highlands. Crazy shit has been going on here forever. But that's not the point." She poked him in the chest. "You should have told me." Her voice was getting a little high.

"Calm down. My intention was for us to sit down with Duncan so he could tell you about it, especially after what happened yesterday at the ruins."

Her lips trembled. "Well, you can stop worrying about that, Duncan told me everything, so you can just go." She turned and climbed up the stairs.

"Meghan, we need to sit and talk about this." He moved to follow her but stopped at the bottom when she faced him.

"We aren't talking about anything...ever again," she snapped, and once again began up the steps. "I hate you."

Before all the words were out of her mouth, she crumbled in pain. Will cleared the distance and scooped her up, continuing up stairs.

Duncan trailed behind, asking hesitantly, when Will reached her room, "Is there anything I can do?"

"No," Will threw over his shoulder before kicking her door shut.

Once in her room she struggled in his arms. "Put me down."

"No."

Her struggling became more and more insistent. If she kept this up he would end up dropping her on her head. "Hold still."

"No. I won't. Not until you put me down. I hate you."

He sighed as her body knotted in pain once again and she moaned.

He sat on the edge of her bed and cradled her close to his chest. He brushed his lips against the side of her head. "Every time you say you hate me, that will happen. If you say you don't like me, the nausea will cause you pain and discomfort. If you try to avoid me or if you are away from me for an extended period you will feel sick."

"No. No." She shook her head. "That's not true." She gagged.

"Yes Meghan. You've noticed that you feel better with me. You even asked me why." He squeezed her tighter when he heard her sniff. "I'm sorry I didn't tell you about it, that would have been the right thing to do, but would you have believed me? Christ, I didn't believe it at first. But it just happens to be real and so are the effects it has on us."

"But, you don't get sick?"

"No, but I do get very agitated, almost angry, when I'm not with you. I snap and sometimes yell for no reason. I feel wound so tight that I could blow apart at any second, and the feeling doesn't stop until I'm with you again."

"But I... The contract and the bet. Everything began at once. I don't know if I believe you."

"That's fine," he conceded. "But I'm telling you the truth when I say I didn't know anything about the spell until a week after I drove you back from Perth. I went to Duncan to ask why you were sick whenever I was away from you. That was when he told me."

She pulled at his shirt and he helped her to sit up.

"I don't want this." She grabbed her middle and took a deep breath.

He pressed his lips in her hair. "I know." He knew the reason why. Her history with her ex. "You can't keep fighting it. It's hurting you."

"So? It doesn't hurt you? Why worry about it?"

He wrapped his arms around her, anger causing his chest and shoulders to flex. "What hurts you, hurts me. Understand?" he bit out in a harsh whisper. "You need to stop."

"So you can win. No."

The fucking bet. All of this because she was scared of falling in love with him. He wished he had enough regret to admit the bet had caused more trouble than it was worth, but he wouldn't. "Fine, suit yourself."

"Let me go." She sighed in defeat.

Let her go? Never. He would never let her go. But he did release her.

She didn't look at him when she pushed to her feet, and she ignored him when he pulled back the covers on her bed. She crawled under the sheets and allowed him to tuck them around her. "How do you feel?"

He was surprised when she answered, "Dull."

"Want me to stay?"

Her nod surprised him even more. He circled the bed and sat in the wingback chair and watched as she snapped off the light.

Chapter Forty-Three

Leaning against the dark wood bar in The Black Ale, Will slowly took a sip of his pint. Eight days had passed since Meghan had spoken to him, eight days of hell. He was miserable, there was no denying it. The only time he'd felt better was when he'd sat in her room at night the few times Duncan had called him and had asked him to come over. Each time, he had been able to hear Meghan in the background asking him not to call. He had gone anyway — she was all that mattered.

"Will, you're back." Hamish came out of the kitchen and smiled. "How was it?" Hamish asked, referring to his latest job.

"All right."

Hamish nodded then a serious frown wrinkled his brow. "Can I have a word?" He nodded towards the end of the bar, away from the other customers.

Will followed and bent his head low when Hamish gestured to him. "Anything wrong?"

"I wasn't sure, not at first. Meghan is a beautiful woman and I've seen people stare at her before, but

with Robert a little while ago and now these two men.
I don't know."

"Out with it Hamish. I'm not in the mood for
riddles. What men?"

"Robert was first, he was here about a month ago,
maybe longer. He said he was looking to buy some
property. But after the first few times, I realised it
wasn't my pub that was drawing him here, but
Meghan."

"What did he look like?" Will asked.

"Tanned bloke, little shorter than you, not quite your
build. Brown hair and grey eyes. Wore expensive
sunglasses and sharp designer togs."

"His name? Robert what?"

"He didn't say."

Will raised an eyebrow into a high arch. "And he
went by Robert, not Rob?"

"He said his name was Robert. So that's what I
called him."

"Did he say where he was from?" The muscles in his
back and shoulders tightened.

"No, he didn't. I thought he might be American but
changed my mind after I spoke with him a few times."

"Why?"

"He sounded a little like your Meghan."

That was not what Will wanted to hear. Had
Meghan's ex come to Little Glen?

"You mentioned other men. When were they here?"

"Oh, they've been here for at least four days now.
And always the same time Meghan goes to the library.
They sit in the booth by the window and watch until
she leaves and then they leave. I don't know where
they go." He took a breath. "It was too much of a
coincidence, and I didn't like the way they were
looking at her. So I had Mary take Lucy over to

Meghan. I told Mary to make up some lie about not feeling up to taking care of Lucy and I also spoke with Grace about allowing Lucy into the library as well. We've been trying to keep an eye on her without worrying her."

"What do they look like?" Will asked, trying to contain his anger.

"One is tall, blond hair, dark eyes. The other is on the shorter side, bald head and dark beard. He's a mean bastard, that one."

His entire body tensed and he clenched his hands into tight fists.

"You know who they are?"

"I know them." Boy did he. He had spent a good ten minutes beating the two to a bloody pulp. He had been so angry that they had thought they were allowed to touch Meghan that Donnie had actually pulled him back so he hadn't killed them. And now here they were, and Meghan was their target again.

Her ex had been here, now the two of the three men from the club. Jesus. He squeezed the muscles in his jaw.

Hamish frowned at him seriously. "Was it good that I told you? I'd hate to start something over nothing."

"You haven't started anything. I'm glad you told me."

"Good. I didn't like the way those last two were looking at your Meghan."

The way they were looking at her! Fuck. That was the least of his problems.

* * * *

Once back home, he called Duncan. He filled him in on the same information that Hamish had given him.

Of course Duncan was worried, he was too, but as long as she stayed in the house and had Lucy with her he thought she should be okay. Although that was hardly enough. "Call me once she's gone to bed. I'll come and watch the house. See if I can spot them."

"Do you think they're out there watching the house?"

"I hope so."

While he waited to hear back from Duncan, he called the local authorities in Letham and filled them in on the suspicious men in Little Glen. He would need their presence reported. That way, should he or Duncan call, they would already be on file and the locals would double-time it over there.

Will received Duncan's call a couple of hours later. He left the house two minutes afterwards. He took one of the paths that circled around the outside of Little Glen and crossing the trail that lead to Letham Loch, he then doubled back towards Duncan's. If he was going to spy on Duncan's house he would do it from this path. It came out only feet from the front gate and the trees and bushes were so thick, it was hard to see through it in the day, let alone at night.

Coming up slowly to the opening of the trail he instantly spotted a dark figure standing just inside the tree line. He was a little on the short side and Will knew it was the guy with the dark beard and bald head. Stepping off the trail and into the trees, Will could see the man was nervous. He was restless, shifting from foot to foot, and he constantly turned his head, looking up and down the lane.

Will approached the man silently but when he was less than a foot away the guy turned to flick his cigarette butt into the woods, spotting him. Already in motion, Will didn't give him a chance to call out and was on him a second later. He grabbed the back of the man's neck, and using his greater size and weight, slammed his fist into his face. When the blow didn't cause enough damage for his satisfaction, Will gave him two more quick jabs and the bastard stumbled back, falling hard onto the ground. Once, on his back, he struggled to get to his feet. Will, without a sound, loomed over him, grabbing the bastard by his jacket collar, he then lifted him up and slammed his fist back into the centre of his face one final time. And that was 'night-night' for baldy.

Will stepped over the body and moved to the opening of the trail. He scanned the front of Duncan's house. He could see nothing but dark shadows until one of those shadows moved next to the front door. Moving fast, Will crossed the lane and was through the front gate seconds later, his boots scuffing along the way. The blond turned, and though he was shocked to see Will moving towards him, he was prepared for the blow Will delivered.

"What you doin' here?" the bastard gritted out between clenched teeth. "Followin' me? Police, are yah?"

Will slowly shook his head.

"Then" — the silly bastard pulled a short locking blade from behind his back — "fuck off." He lunged forward.

The blade shot straight towards him, but Will stepped to the side easily avoiding it and grabbed the man's arm, pushing it up and away. Then he quickly dropped to one knee and drove his fist hard into the bastard's crotch. The loud groans became even more strained when Will pushed up, lifting the man off his feet only to drive him down onto his back. Once the wind was knocked from his opponent Will easily twisted his elbow with enough force to snap the cartilage, and between the cries of pain, bent his wrist back and pulled the knife from his grasp.

"You fight dirty," The man groaned. "You prick." Then curled onto his side and moaned as Will allowed his arm to drop to the ground.

"Me." Will snorted, folding the blade in half and shoving it inside his thigh pocket. "You're the one with the knife."

As the bastard rolled on the around in pain, the door flew open. "What the... Will?" Duncan gasped.

Will forced the blond onto his back, then motioned to Duncan. "Come here." The older man came forward without question. "Put your foot right here." He pointed to the man's neck.

Duncan followed the order. "This is the man that wants to hurt Meghan?" he asked quietly.

"Yes." Will stood and was about to turn away when he heard a strained gurgling sound. He chuckled. "Easy, Duncan." Will turned away. "Don't press too hard, or you'll kill him."

The older man stuttered, "R-right...of course..." Then, startled, he asked, "Where you goin'?"

Will pointed to the opening of the trail. "There's another one over here."

"There is?"

* * * *

Will was back a minute later carrying the bald guy over his shoulder and dropped him like a bag of trash onto Duncan's front walk next to his friend. "Is he dead?" Duncan demanded.

"No." Will scowled. "'Course not. Go call the locals in Letham. Tell them these men two men tried to break into your house."

"Right." Duncan went to enter the house.

"Wait." He had been controlling his anger from the moment he had seen baldy, but now that things were over and the police could be called, he should be feeling better. He wasn't. Something wasn't right, he felt agitated, his shoulders and the back of his neck were still tight almost to the point of pain. It was a feeling he had experienced a lot lately. "Where's Lucy?"

"Upstairs with Meghan," Duncan informed him with a sudden frown.

"Then why isn't she barking?"

Anxious, he marched past Duncan. "Watch them." Then took the stairs two at a time and stopped outside Meghan's door. He lightly scratched the wood hoping it would stir Lucy into coming to the door. Nothing. Next he whistled lightly. Still nothing. Finally with his heart pounding, he opened the door to an empty room.

Chapter Forty-Four

Lifting her head to the dark sky, Meghan could just make out the twinkling of a few stars. The cool night did nothing to help her upset stomach or the pain in her heart that seemed to grow larger every day. With her breath coming in fast choppy bursts, she slowed to a walk and, with her hands on her hips, walked in small circles as she worked to control her breathing.

Nothing seemed to help. Running didn't help, work didn't help, plus she found it a struggle just trying to concentrate. Sleeping and eating were non-existent. Even spending time with Lucy didn't help. The only time she had felt better was when Duncan had called Will over, and for a few hours she had been at peace. Well, her body had been, her heart however had still been broken. She still couldn't believe that he had kept something as important as a spell from her.

A binding spell. *Holy crap!* She wasn't kidding when she'd said weird shit went on in the Highlands. She wasn't sure if all the stories she had heard were true but she now knew that at least one fairy tale was. Fairy tale. When she thought about the spell, confusion set in and the same questions filled her head. Were the feelings she'd been having for Will even hers? Or just a by-product of this so-called binding spell?

She placed a hand on her forehead. No. Duncan had said the spell only forced them together. The rest was up to them. If that was the case and Duncan was telling her the truth, then that meant she was falling for Will all on her own. She couldn't blame anything or anybody but herself for the mistake she seemed to be making...again.

Damn it. She was repeating the past. When would her body and heart realise it? She squatted and leant back against the wall of the old keep when the waves of queasiness rolled in her stomach. Closing her eyes, she pulled Will's face from her mind. She had come to realise that there was only one way to control her nausea and it was to replay the same scene in her head of when they'd spent the night together and of the third time he had made love to her.

She loved the way that he'd held her. His tender smile had caused her heart to melt. She loved the heat of his lips when he'd nibbled on her chin, and the weight of his body on hers as she'd wrapped her legs around his hips. Even now, the memory of him moving slow and deep while he'd gently pinned her to his bed helped settle her stomach. But it also caused such a pain in her heart that the waves started all over again. She missed him, wanted him with her, needed him in her life. She groaned into her hands, knowing full well that the only way this would stop was if she went to him. Which was what she wanted more than anything—but that scared her too.

She stood quickly and marched around the ruins. God, she was so confused. Will was a completely different man from Rob. Rob was a sleazy peeping-Tom loser, who worried about nothing but himself and kept sending her gross emails. Will cared for her, worried about her and other people in his life. In other words, the complete opposite of Rob.

Meghan came to a stop on the far side on the ruins. The same stop where she had almost thrown herself down into the dark forest below. She peered over the side of the hill where she knew the ancient steps were hidden by the moss.

Lucy instinctively came to her side and gave a low whimper. Meghan rested her hand on the dog's head reassuringly as she stared down into the black hole. "Don't worry. I won't do that again."

A low growl suddenly rumbled through the dog. Meghan jumped as an unexpected fear ran through her. Someone was there in the shadows at the top of the hill. Lucy's growl became deeper, more insistent.

Blinking, she watched as Will stepped out of the shadows. "Get th' hell away from those steps."

The moon cast a pale light on him, but it was clear to see that he was covered from head to toe in black. He looked big, lethal, she could feel the strength radiating from him. The sickening waves disappeared, leaving her stomach to be filled with excitement and need. Her head spun as she took him in. He was the most handsome man she had ever seen. His large frame was graceful as he moved slowly towards her, his gaze fixed onto her face as he closed the gap. He stopped within arm's reach and glared down at her, his face dark and laced with anger. "What are you doin' here?" he bit out, his accent rough.

She blinked again, shocked by his tone. The last few times he had spoken to her he had been gentle and very patient, even when she'd said she had hated him. "I-I didn't feel well and thought—"

"Thought what? That you should come to th' place where you almost killed yourself?"

"No. I wasn't thinking that. I just needed to get out, get away."

He opened his mouth but stopped and exhaled. "Please come away from those stairs. I hate the idea of you being that close to them."

She stepped past him and walked to the top of the hill before he stopped her.

"Meghan?"

Her heart sang. No one said her name like that. It made her shiver just hearing him say it.

He turned her. "Why are you up here? Right now? You never run at night." There was a pause as he looked her up and down. "And why are you wearin' your pyjamas?"

She tugged at the blue flannel pants before shrugging. "I told you, I needed to get out. To try and figure…" His glare hardened. "Stuff out."

"You mean try to figure this out?" He waved a finger between them.

"Yes."

"Did it help?"

Did it? She thought about that for a second and the answer was suddenly clear. She wanted to be with Will—she knew that without the help of the binding spell—but she was just so worried that she would be seen as vulnerable again that she was finding it hard to stop fighting it.

"I think so…" Her shoulders dropped a little. "I'm just—" She never got a chance to finish.

"I don't want to hear it. I want you to admit that you want me. Just like I want you. You need me. Just like I need you. Nothing else matters to me but you." He sighed, running a hand through his hair.

Her heart jumped and fluttered and sang all at the same time. His words, though spoken in anger and frustration, were the most romantic words anyone had ever said to her. She closed the gap, feeling tears well up. "Can I finish now?"

He exhaled a long slow breath.

"Thank you. I was going say I feel confused about all of this. I hate—" He visibly stiffened. "Wait." She placed a hand on his chest and finished, "I hate that I have no control over any of this. And it scares the crap out of me. But I want you." She bit her lip and frowned. "That scares me too. So much so that I have an urge to run away."

In the blink of an eye, she found herself wrapped securely in Will's arms. "But you're not runnin' away."

"No," she admitted, mumbling into his chest. "You're not letting me."

Chuckling, he raised her head with the crook of his finger. "Stop fighting. Everything will work out as it should."

Oh how she loved his deep voice. It was so sensual. And that magnetic come-hither wink, it called to her without him saying a single word. She licked her lips, already tasting his warm mouth.

Hearing Will's low curse, Meghan suddenly found his mouth covering hers. She caught her breath. The kiss was hot and demanding and she moaned when his tongue moved smoothly between her lips, fervently stroking hers. Next, he nibbled on her lips, then kissed her cheeks and chin, only to move back to her mouth. Relieved and a little giddy, Meghan slid her arms around his neck and pulled him closer, deepening the kiss by gently sucking on his tongue. She received a growl for her effort and he tightened his hold on her.

The passionate kiss went on and on until Meghan felt her knees start to give out but Will lifted her up against his chest and held her tight. Once out of breath, Will lowered her back to the ground and stared down at her for a few moments, before he clasped her hand and began dragging her behind him.

Breathless she asked, "Where are we going?"

Without turning he answered, "Where it's safe."

She couldn't help but look around. They were safe. Weren't they? Her gaze trailed over his wide shoulders picking out the definition of his muscles through his shirt. "And where would that be?"

"My bed."

"Oh." She tried not to giggle but it escaped anyway. "I'll be safer in your bed, will I?"

He smirked as he looked back over his shoulder. "You will be. Just as long as you do' nae tease me."

"From what I remember, I'm not the one who likes to tease."

His wicked laugh sent a shiver up her arms and down her legs. He stopped, then pulled her to his chest, his warm hands lifting her face to meet his. "I need you in my bed, where I can spend the night making love to you. I want you to fall asleep beside me, so in the middle of the night, I can wake you up and make love to you again."

Her heart slammed in her chest when he lowered his head, his lips mere inches from hers. Then without blinking, he swung her to his side and continued to pull her down the hill.

* * * *

They reached the bottom faster than Meghan would have thought possible and all of a sudden she was standing in Will's front hall as he locked the heavy wood door behind her. She bent down to take off her shoes, but he stopped her. "There's no time."

"You're very impatient tonight."

He tugged her up the stairs behind him. "Aye."

She giggled despite herself. "I think I like it."

Once in Will's bedroom, he dragged her straight to the bathroom and left her standing by the sink. He walked over to the shower stall, opened the clear glass door and turned on the water. While he tested the temperature of the water, she caught his gaze and held it. The flare in his eyes was downright sinful, it was also dark and held a hint of dominance. Her body jumped to life, her breasts suddenly throbbed, a hot flow pooled between her thighs. She was achy and tingling everywhere and all Will had done was look at her. She caught a breath when he turned, his shoulders flexed as he crossed the small room. When she saw the muscles in his jaw pull tight, she gave into her urge and stroked the sharp angle of his chin.

"You said bed."

"I changed my mind."

Will wanted her so much, he felt borderline explosive. A forceful need pushed at him to throw her on the tile floor and take her hard and fast, claiming what was rightfully his. His need to possess her swirled with the rage he felt. She could have easily been taken away from him, and he had only just found her, she had just come into his life. He squeezed his jaw again. He wanted to go back over to Duncan's and break the blond's other arm too. Though he wasn't sure that would be enough.

Fuck. What would have happened if she had left when those two bastards had arrived or if they had caught sight of her on her run and had followed? Fuck. He tried not to think about it but the protector in him couldn't help imagining the horrible things they could have done to her.

The fear of losing someone he loved was new. It was compounded because that fear centred around Meghan. The one emotion he'd never experienced, because nothing and no one had ever triggered it, until now. The thought of losing her was stronger, more overwhelming than the normal aggressive thrill that raced through him when he risked his life. Nothing compared to it, not the worst of fire fights or the most hostile of Wet Jumps. Nothing. The need to lock her to him permanently was very strong. He didn't know if he could wait patiently for her to realise that she loved him. It would be better for both of them if he forced her, but would her hate be worth it?

He reached for her sweatshirt, gently pulled it over her head and dropped it on the floor. Her T-shirt followed suit, landing next to her sweatshirt. Kneeling, he grabbed an ankle and pulled her running shoes off, followed by her socks. He smiled when he saw her purple polished toenails. Moving his gaze up her blue plaid pyjama bottoms, he stopped on her slender waist, not chancing a look into that beautiful face. He was close to losing it, if he locked onto those hooded blue beauties, he'd be fucked.

He gripped her waistband instead and slowly pulled the material down her legs. Once they were off, he slid his hands up her calves to her smooth thighs as he stood, stopping on her firm bottom. He kneaded the plump flesh, loved how each smooth globe fitted perfectly into his hands. Her breathing increased and he watched, entranced by the way her breasts became flushed and swollen with each ragged breath. She moaned when he squeezed her tighter. He finally gave in, and when he looked into her heavy eyes, he marvelled at the desire he saw. He loved the sight of her parted pink lips, and the flush on her cheeks. "Like that, do you?" he asked, teasing the crease of her behind.

She thrust her hips forward, pleading, "Will." She reached for the back of his neck, scraped her nails into his hair. "I need..." she began, then breathed out softly, "You." Her lips parted as she kissed him, teasing his lips with her warm tongue. All it took was that gentle touch and the heat sparked between them.

As the small bathroom filled with steam, Will tugged off Meghan's white cotton panties, and without breaking contact with her mouth he lifted her onto the bathroom counter. Her thighs parted as he pushed between them. Their loving was aggressive and passionate, neither one could get enough of the other. The need to feel Meghan's skin against his own brought out a craving that bordered on animalistic. She pulled at his shirt and tugged it over his head then began undoing his pants while he undid her bra. He cupped a breast, pinching the hard pink nipple, smiling against her mouth when she moaned, pushing farther into his palm. He gripped her neck, and forcing her head back, he kissed the pounding pulse hidden under her smooth skin, while he slid the back of two fingers through her folds. She was so hot and incredibly wet. He loved feeling the way her stomach muscles clenched as he rubbed her swollen core and how she sucked in a breath when his knuckles circled her clit.

Pulling his hips closer, her whimper sounded more of a plea.

He licked the back of his knuckles, her spicy taste pulling forth a groan. "No' yet," he mumbled against her mouth. Then squatting between her thighs, he tasted her damp centre. He kissed her, teased her, tasted her in long slow strokes, until he drove his tongue deep. She cried out, pulling at his hair, hips bucking. "Will, you're teasing again."

Chuckling softly, he stood and allowed her to tug his pants down over his hips. His cock sprang free as though searching for her. Then not being able to torment her any further, he hauled her forward, grabbed his cock and roughly plunged into her. Her tight body pulled him in eagerly, welcoming him. His groan was immediate and mingled with hers. In a hurried pace he began to pump into her, then lowering his head, he took control of her mouth.

Meghan's head fell back as Will kissed her neck—everything a hazy steam of erotic sensation. She could taste herself on his lips. It mixed with his sweet breath. His grip on her hips was tight to the point of discomfort, and his kiss was urgent, with a desperate edge, like he was afraid she would leave. His need was so great she could feel it seep into her skin and mix with her own. They seemed...he seemed almost out of control. Almost.

Wrapping her arms around his neck she groaned as he gently nibbled at her bottom lip, willing her to open her mouth again. The demanding urgency of his kiss took her breath away as his tongue swirled around hers. Pulling back, she blinked, his features were dark and ominous. His raw desire laced with tenderness and love. Placing both hands on the sides of his face, she stared up into his dark, intensely handsome face and became...lost.

The one thing that should never have happened, did. She got lost in Will. Her heart squeezed at the new realisation, her lips trembled and she fought like a demon to keep the tears away.

He slowed his pace as if he sensed her new turmoil. "Meghan?" he whispered softly.

Her heart squeezed again at hearing the tender way he said her name. "I'm...I'm okay." She traced her thumbs along his cheeks and pulled him forwards. "Please don't stop." Then she prayed silently to herself. *Never stop.*

Without a word, his mouth was on hers, kissing the fear away, his hands soothing her trembling skin. She had known it would happen sooner or later, she had just hoped she would have been better prepared. Like standing up, with her clothes on and level-headed. Not naked and vulnerable and certainly not with her ass half in a sink.

Rather than think about her scary new feelings, she focused on Will moving between her legs, his body surrounding her protectively. She raised her leg a little higher and Will tucked his arm under her knee, lifting it onto his biceps. She cried out when he drove into her again, it was deeper, more intense, he filled every inch of her. Her eyes began to drift shut, the overpowering sensations washing over her.

"No." The order was harsh. "Look at me. I want you to look at me when I make you come."

She nodded helplessly and kept her eyes locked with his. Will quickened the pace pumping harder, faster, as the familiar pulsing threatened to shatter her into pieces. It was the most intimate she had ever been with a man and she was glad it was with Will.

His hot breath brushed her face and neck, and as she held tight to him, the pulsing heat surrounded her, bringing every nerve to life. She cried out. The feeling was so overwhelming she couldn't stop herself. Will's eyes darkened as she stared into them. A savage smile tugged at his lips as he moved in her. He covered her mouth, kissing her hard, tangled his tongue with hers. She loved what he did to her, how he made her feel, she was so filled with love and passion that she kissed him with as much urgency as he kissed her. He mumbled something against her lips. His body tightened and his hands bruised her hips as he jerked her forward. He came hard, deep, filling her with his body and soul and maybe just a little bit of…love.

* * * *

Will pulled Meghan into his arms and rested his head on top of hers as the warm spray of the shower covered their bodies. She smelt like the lavender soap he had slowly washed her with. Rubbing the soft-smelling scent onto her flushed body had been very sensual, he wished he had done it before now. But the need to soothe her body and mind had never been this great. He had been rough with her, too rough, it should never have happened.

Though he would never change what had happened between them. The look she had given him as she'd cupped his face had been sobering. She had realised her feelings for him. He was sure of it. The scared but startled expression on her face, the way she'd touched him, the sudden trembling, only confirmed his suspicions. He had wanted so much to kiss her fears away, tell her she wasn't alone, that he was right there with her feeling the same way. But Meghan wasn't the type of woman that liked to be pushed, she needed time to get used to the idea on her own or she might revert back to fighting him again.

He ran his hands over her hips as he soothed her skin. "Did I hurt you?"

"No." She paused and rubbed her cheek against his chest. "It was pretty intense though."

His arms tightened around her. "Very intense."

She drew in a deep breath, which pressed her breasts into his chest. The air seemed to get caught in her throat and she began to stumbled on her words. "Will...I..."

He rubbed his chin on her head, and taking pity on her, supplied, "Missed me?"

"Yeah." She sighed, annoyed with herself. "I missed you."

What a coward she was. Yet how could she tell him what she was really feeling when she had only just realised it herself? And what would happen if he found out that she...that she was in... Geez! She couldn't even think about it without it scaring her. What would he do if he found out though? There was still a marriage contract and bet hanging over her head. She sighed again.

"Is something bothering—"

"I don't hate you," she blurted out, wrapping her arms tighter around him. "This whole spell thing scares me. I'm not...I mean I don't feel...in control."

He lifted her face. "It's not the spell."

She shook her head. There had to be something causing this need for him, she felt so far out of control when she was with him, it had to be the spell. "But I'm not normally like this."

"It's not the spell," he said again. "This is us. This is how we react to each other. If the contract or spell didn't exist, this still would have happened. It just might have taken longer."

She frowned, confessing, "It's still scary."

He exhaled a long breath. "I know." He gently kissed her forehead. "Time to get out?"

"No, I like it in here." She ran her hands over his chest, down his arms and grasped his hands, stroking her fingers over his skin. Frowning, she lifted his hand, turning it over and saw the scratches and small bruises on his knuckles. It was strange that she hadn't noticed them before now. Then again, he was very good at distracting her.

He caught her attention. "You do?"

"Mmm," she purred. "I like looking at you...naked." She released his hands and trailed her fingers down his stomach.

"You've seen me naked before."

"I haven't had a good look." She couldn't help but tease him, "You always make me close my eyes and moan in ecstasy."

He chuckled. "Are you complaining?"

"No." She kissed his wet skin, traced small circles on his hips. "But I would like my turn to make you moan." She flicked the tip of her tongue over his nipple.

"Go on then." He shot her a dark look. "Do your best."

Meghan did do her best and Will did moan. He moaned when she kissed her way down his chest and stomach. Moaned when she squeezed his cock and sucked it into her mouth. Moaned when her tongue swirled around the aching tip and he moaned, clenching his fists in her hair while he came in her mouth.

Chapter Forty-Five

"I'll only be gone for four days." Will had forced her to straddle his lap as he had sat on the leather couch in his office. "Promise me you'll call if it gets bad."

He had been getting ready to leave. He had a job in Barcelona he needed to be at. "I'll be okay." She had shrugged, patting his chest.

Will had cupped her cheeks and lightly kissed her mouth. "Please call me."

"Okay." She had to at least give him that. She had refused to stay in his house and had refused his offer at buying a ticket for her to go with him.

"I'm serious about the ticket." He had pulled her close, had kissed the top of her cheek. "Wouldn't you like to come to Barcelona with me?"

Boy would she, but it was too soon. She was still getting use to the idea of being in… "I can't, I have to get those edits in." Lying was way easier right then. "Besides, if I go there I want to be able to tour around and see the sights." She shrugged.

He'd studied her before relenting, "Okay." He'd checked at his watch. "I still have some time before I have to leave." The glint in his eye had been sexy and mischievous, and she had melted into him, willing to give him anything he had wanted and taking everything she had needed.

She remembered the last time they'd made love on his couch. She'd ridden him slowly, the heat a steady flow between them, it hadn't been until the euphoric spasms had ravaged her body that the heat between them sparked to life. The sensation had been so physically powerful, but she had never even had a chance to cry out because Will had been there swinging her to the side of the couch, and never breaking contact, had pinned her down and driven into her. Her legs had locked around his waist, her arms around his neck, and his big arms had wrapped her...in a safe cocoon.

God, it had been wonderful and tender and full of...? Well, maybe not that, but it sure had felt that way. So much so, that she had almost said yes to that ticket. Almost. But she hadn't. And now she sat in the library, alone, staring at her laptop, missing him. "The jerk!" she mumbled in a pout.

How could she have let this happen? Damn it! She had been putting up a hell of a fight even with the stomach issues, but now...after the night at the ruins...then in his bathroom... She flopped her head onto her arm remembering the way they had lain in his big bed. They had made love and talked and made love some more. He had answered all of her questions about his family and why he'd joined the navy. She in turn, had told him what it had been like growing up in Ontario's cottage country and told him about her parents and how Ryan was a traffic cop in Toronto and how Scott had been an amazing football player.

"He used to play on the high school team with my friend Troy."

"I don't think I like that smile. Are you referring to Pizza parlour Troy?"

"Why yes I am," she'd teased lightly.

He'd pinched her bum.

"Ouch! It was nothing like that, we were…are friends. Scott's death hit us both hard. I lost a brother and he lost his best friend. That's all."

"So, he's no' an ex-boyfriend?"

"Troy! No way, just friends. Besides I hardly see him. He plays for a professional team in the States."

He had studied her for a few seconds, and at the time, she'd got the feeling there had been something else he had wanted to ask her, something that had to do with Rob, especially after that boyfriend remark, but he'd changed the topic.

Then and even now, she had a feeling he knew more about Rob than she wanted him to. He never did bring up that night in Edinburgh except to apologise for his behaviour. And when he'd told her that the blond from the club had tracked her down to Little Glen, he'd never so much as pushed the issue. He'd simply told her what had happened, and had asked her to not run at night anymore. Not one peep about Rob.

She had got freaked out when Will had told her about the blond and his friend showing up in Little Glen. There had been no doubt in her mind that Rob was behind their visit, but he was back in Toronto, he'd trashed her apartment for God's sake. She wouldn't have been surprised to learn that it was a lie and that Rob was still here in Scotland. Maybe even in Little Glen, lurking in the shadows, spying on her like a little rat. She didn't know what to believe anymore, it seemed like everyone was either lying to her or hiding something from her, including Duncan. She had been told by the police that Duncan had been the one to catch the men breaking into the house and had single-handedly stopped them. Ha! What a load of crap that was. Especially since she remembered seeing bruises and cuts on Will's knuckles.

Guess she wasn't the only one with secrets.

Her stomach rolled when she thought of Will. As sad as it was, she missed him and his bruised knuckles and everything else about him. But she missed her family and friends too. She was so screwed and trapped. What would happen when Ryan finally gave her the okay to go home?

How could she go now that she realised how deep her feelings were for Will? Yet how could she stay? The thought of not seeing her family and friends tore her in two. If she left, Will would be gone from her life, but if she stayed she was leaving everything she knew, everything she was, behind. She had already made two 'Pros and Cons' lists and for every reason to go, there was only one reason for her to stay — Will.

Then the questions flooded her head. What would happen if she stayed, where would it take them? What about their bet? What about the contract? Would he use it? *Blah. Blah. Blah. Man!* She hated all these damn questions and she hated that she didn't know the answers. And why was she worrying about this now anyway? It wasn't like Will had said he loved her — and there was no way she would say it. He would win the bet.

Rubbing her hand over her face, she sighed. Why did love have to be so hard? Why couldn't it be simple? You loved a person and they loved you back. Did there have to be so many whys and what-ifs? Maybe if she hadn't met Rob she wouldn't be so cautious. But if she hadn't met Rob she probably wouldn't be here now, and she might not have met Will.

She leaned her head back and massaged her shoulders. God, she needed a drink. Her stomach heaved. Okay, she needed a peppermint tea.

Glancing at the files on her laptop, she huffed. "Forget it!" She saved her work and closed the files for later. She was never going to get anything done this way, she needed a break and that drink—or rather tea—was sounding better and better, and going to The Black Ale would be the perfect distraction from life.

She stopped eyeing her laptop, then decided, "Emails first, then tea."

After logging into her mail box, she scanned a few new emails. The first was from her mum, it was one of those emails that you had to pass along to as many friends as possible or you would have bad luck.

"Too late!" Delete.

Next was a note from Jess complaining about her job, then going into graphic detail how the new resident Doctor had the best butt she had ever seen and gave him a nine point five out of ten. Attached to her long-winded description were a few pictures of Jack playing soccer.

Save photos.

Reply—*'Give the next David Beckham a big hug for me. And pictures of that nine point five butt would have been nice too!*

Love Meg.'

Send.

She was just about to log off when a new message arrived. She frowned when she saw the odd combination of numbers.

Rob, again? Geez, talk about dedication. Staring at the screen she took a deep decisive breath and opened it.

The new message from Rob wasn't his normal 'Come Home, Meg'. There was no writing at all, just a video. She clicked on it and watched as a camera came into focus on…Jessica.

"Oh my God!" Her heart pounded in her chest as she watched the video. The camera shook and tilted to the side before straightening and zooming in on Jessica sleeping in her bed. Her beautiful dark hair was braided back from her face and she had one leg thrown above the covers. She didn't budge when her cat jumped across the bed away from the camera. It pulled back and she heard a man whisper, "If you think that is good wait for it." She recognised Jessica's upstairs hall and silently prayed that he would stay away from the second door on the left. She cried out when she saw a hand reach out and turn the knob. "No. No. Get away from him." Fear had her gripping her laptop so hard she heard the outer shell crack. And then there was Jack. Sweet precious Jack, in his bed wearing his hockey pyjamas, his arm wrapped around a stuffed teddy.

A sign appeared in front of camera, blocking Jack from her view. *'I'm done fucking around,'* it said. *'Come home and make sure you bring your cell.'*

That was it, the video ended. She had no idea if they were alive or dead or hurt. Tears slid down her cheeks as she hit the forward button. This was her fault. She sniffed. All her fault. With shaky hands she addressed the email to Ryan and typed —

'I'm on my way. No arguments! Meg'
Send.

Chapter Forty-Six

"She's gone!" Duncan announced, pushing past him. Will sighed and closed the heavy wooden door.

So he was right. He'd been agitated more than normal these last few days. Sure, being away from Meghan was the cause. But they had talked, several times in fact. He'd wanted to know she was handling his absence okay, but he'd needed to hear her voice too, it had helped calm him when he had been away from her. When he'd spoke with her she'd assured him she had been handling the bouts of nausea just fine and he hadn't got any suspicious vibes from their conversation that would have indicated she had been going to run. He clenched his jaw. *So, why had she?*

"Hello, Duncan."

"Don't take this so lightly. I tried gettin' a hold of you before you got back. So you could stop 'er." His thick accent was rougher than normal.

"Come into the office, I'll get you a drink." He didn't wait for the older man and walked into his office, heading straight for a decanter of Scotch. He had just got back, literally. He hadn't even taken off his jacket.

He could feel his shoulders and neck begin to tense. There could be a valid reason for why she'd left. *For her sake, there'd better be.*

He poured three glasses of Scotch and handed one to Duncan. He was about to ask what had happen when Gavin strolled into the room.

"I must be getting old. I keep hearing all that loud music from our last job, like a steady pounding in my ears." Gavin stopped at the door to Will's office and looked back and forth between Duncan and himself. "Okay, what've I just walked in on?" Gavin asked crossing to Duncan. "All right, Duncan?" he greeted the older man and held out his hand.

"No, I'm not bloody well all right," Duncan said as he shook Gavin's hand forcefully then threw it away. Gavin smirked, accepting the glass of Scotch Will held out for him.

Will leaned on the edge of his desk and sipped the amber liquor. He was already agitated, and his anger was growing too. He was having a hard time trying not to ram his fist through the wall. Downing the remains of his Scotch, he placed the glass on his desk and walked to the large window, keeping his back to Duncan. Staring up at the old ruins, he quietly encouraged Duncan, "Go ahead."

"You're taking Meghan's leaving very lightly. Maybe I was wrong to come here."

Will laughed. The old man really had no idea how much Meghan meant to him, or how angry he was that she had left him.

"Ah, Duncan," Gavin stepped in. "I think you should just tell us what happened."

"You're right, I'm just worried about her. I tried to reach you 'fore you came all the way back. You could have left from Edinburgh."

"From the beginning," Will ordered, turning. "Please, Duncan."

Duncan quickly complied. "She came home from the library two days ago, very pale and nervous. I thought she might have had another attack."

"But she hadn't?" Will was relieved by that thought and hoped the rest would be as easy.

"No, thank goodness. But I could tell something was very wrong. She was scared. When I asked her what was wrong she just shook her head and said she had to go."

"To Toronto?" Will clarified.

"Yes. She threw a few clothes into a bag, checked to see if her cell phone was charged, grabbed her purse and computer an' told me to take her to the airport."

"Two days ago?" Will asked.

"Yes."

He nodded, thinking back to two days ago. It made sense. The level of his patience had dropped and his agitation had increased almost to the point of anger. So, not only was the binding spell highly sensitive, but it became stronger over greater distances.

"Did you ask her why the sudden rush to go home?" Gavin inquired casually.

"'Course I did!" snapped Duncan. "She's my granddaughter. I told you, I'm worried about her. Something's not right and the only answer I got was that she had to go home to take care of a 'little problem'."

He could only guess who she'd meant by a 'little problem'. But he never guessed at things this important, and Meghan was very important. "Have you talked with Ryan? Maybe he knows what's going on?"

"I cannae get a hold of him yet."

"Ryan?" Gavin asked.

"Younger brother. Police Officer Kennedy," Will answered, keeping his gaze on Duncan as the older man paced nervously around the room.

"That's a bonus." Gavin sat on his leather sofa.

The three men were quiet for a few moments, only Duncan's steps broke through the silence.

"Maybe it's no' as bad as you think Duncan. Maybe she—" Gavin began.

"No." Duncan stopped. "Something is wrong, I can feel it. The look on her face...she was frightened."

Will felt it too. He felt it deep in his gut and with each beat of his heart. Meghan was in trouble, he didn't know what kind, but he was sure it had something to do with Rob and with the blond and his friend making a trip to Little Glen. He barked out an order, "Duncan, call Ryan again, now. Use my phone."

Duncan followed the order and sighed heavily when Ryan picked up. After a quick conversation he handed the phone over to Will.

"Does this have to do with Rob?" Will demanded.

Ryan paused, then spoke quietly into the phone, "This isn't the best time. I'm still looking into a few things." Will heard Meghan's voice in the background. His entire body tensed and his pulse quickened. He hated that she was so far away from him.

"How is she?" he asked quietly.

"Safe..." A pause. "Megs, you okay?" He could hear the confusion in the kid's voice. Will knew right away that Meghan's stomach was acting up. Jesus, this separation must be killing her.

"Peppermint tea helps. But she may need something stronger, give her a Gravol. I'm on my way."

Another pause. "Okay," Ryan said coolly into the phone.

"Good. I'll call you before I board. Make sure you are alone, I have a few questions for you."

He hung up the phone. Damn it! Why hadn't she told him about Rob? What was she hiding? He should have pressed her in Edinburgh, and after the blond had been arrested here in Little Glen, but he hadn't because he had seen how edgy she had got and had decided to wait. Damn it, he should never have second-guessed himself. His decision to wait for her was the worst possible thing he could have done.

"Shit!" Will muttered. Shifting his gaze to Gavin, he raised a questioning eyebrow.

Gavin stood. "Why not? I'll get our bags" He continued to mumble as he left the room. "Good thing I didn't unpack."

"You're going to Toronto?"

"I don't really have a choice, do I?" Will asked Duncan as he reached for his keys.

"What does that mean?" Duncan snapped.

"It means, that if I have to follow Meghan half way around the world to help her, then that's what I'll do."

Visibly relieved, Duncan exhaled. "What can I do?"

"Give me Ryan's cell." Will handed him a pad and pen. "And ah...take care of Lucy for me?"

* * * *

"Do I need to ask if you're serious about Meg?" Ryan's voice had dropped low, the question laced with a hidden warning.

Will felt his arms flex and he found himself squeezing the phone in his hand. He knew the kid was only protecting his sister. He liked him even more for that. "I wouldn't be coming if I wasn't."

There was a short pause on the other end, then a sigh. "I hope so, because she's worth it."

Will ended his call with Ryan as he and Gavin waited for their plane to depart. "Well?" Gavin asked before taking a sip of his coffee. "That sounded interesting."

"He wants to know if I'm serious about Meghan."

"He doesn't know about the contract?"

Will shook his head.

"That's reasonable." Gavin nodded. "What'd he tell you about this bloke Rob?"

"Rob Cummings. Apparently, Rob is up to his nuts in debt and in order to keep up his high-class lifestyle, he borrowed money."

"From who?"

"Well, according to Ryan the Cummings and Alexsandrovs are business partners."

"So?"

"The Alexsandrovs are a well-known crime family."

"Can't be too well-known. I've never heard of them."

Will ignored the comment. "It sounds as though they have their fingers into everything thanks to the new matriarch, Emily Alexsandrov. They do very well thanks to Emily and her business dealings, but she apparently has a taste for her father's old-school teachings too."

Gavin scowled. "A smart and nasty crime lady? That can nae be good." Then a flash sparked in his golden eyes. "Unless it's in bed." He smirked, staring off into space. "Now that would be hot."

Will paused, then chuckled. "Jesus, you need to get some." He directed their conversation back to the topic at hand. "Okay. If you were in it deep and needed lots of cash fast, and your father did business with a wealthy crime family. Who would you ask for a loan?"

"If she's hot, I would go to her too."

"I bet she's the one who loaned Rob the money but now she wants it back."

"But why push so hard to get it back? If their families are business partners, she could just take a larger cut of their business earnings to cover his loan." Gavin raised his coffee to his mouth, then stopped. "This is personal. She's vexed over something."

Will sat back. "I agree. If you think about it, it's almost like she's deliberately forcing him to..." Will suddenly stopped, his thoughts shifting. He quickly dialled his London office. "Hugh." Will caught Gavin's stare. "I need you to locate someone for me."

Chapter Forty-Seven

"Huh!" Gavin slid on his dark sunglasses. "I thought it would be colder here."

"What do you mean?" Will gazed up at the bright sky.

"You know"—he peeled off his jacket—"people walking about in snowshoes, wearing parkas, snow mobiles instead of cars."

Will moved to his side and laughed. "We're not in the bloody Arctic, besides, we're too far south. Now those prairie provinces"—Will took off his coat—"bloody freezing out there."

"You train out there?"

"Few times."

"Huh!" The brothers stood side by side taking in the warm November day. Crossing his arms, Gavin grinned, watching an attractive blonde saunter past. "Meghan's brother said he would meet us?"

"Mmm." Will scanned the people coming and going, trying to recognise anyone who might be Ryan. He noticed a guy leaning against a cement pillar, but couldn't see his face. Shit! The only thing he had to go on was an old photo Duncan had shown him before they'd left, which would have been helpful if Ryan was still sixteen.

It was a good thing that he had spoken to Ryan on the phone, at least he knew what he sounded like. The kid had filled him in on everything he'd needed to know and then some. Including the emails with pictures of her apartment destroyed, the threat against Jessica and her son Jack and the photos taken of him and Meghan at the library.

Gavin turned, a grin still on his face. "Want me to find us a place to stay?"

Will never got a chance to answer.

"Don't bother." Ryan pushed off the pillar and sauntered over to them.

Will smiled, he couldn't help it. Ryan stood a good foot away studying them. Meghan's younger brother wasn't quite what he had imagined after seeing the old pictures — Will had been expecting a small, fragile young man, but what stood before him was the complete opposite. Ryan was about his height, with a well-defined athletic frame, brown hair that hung low down the back of his neck, a neat chinstrap beard and turquoise eyes. Meghan's eyes.

He reached out his hand and introduced himself. "Will."

"I know who you are. And you're Gavin." Ryan nodded as he shook Gavin's hand.

"Duncan told you about us," Gavin guessed.

"He talks about Will and he's mentioned you once or twice." Ryan studied Will for a second. "You both served time in the Navy."

Will nodded, impressed by the kid's foresight.

"You didn't really think I would let you help without knowing who you are, did you?"

"No, I didn't" — Will paused — "officer."

A deep chuckle came from Ryan and traces of Duncan could be seen in the kid when he smiled.

"Come on, my snowmobile's over here." Ryan smirked at Gavin.

"What?" Gavin tried to act innocent. "Everybody knows how cold it can get here."

Ryan laughed again as he stopped by a black, low-profile Japanese import, with dark windows and street performance tyres. "Don't bother trying to find a hotel." Ryan opened the trunk and let them throw their bags in. "You can stay with me at my apartment." He stepped around to the driver's side door, then looked from the car to Will then Gavin and back to the car. "Jesus, it's going to be a tight fit."

Before long the three men were speeding...literally, down the highway. Will braced himself against the seat as Ryan expertly weaved in and out of traffic.

"So, this is your car?" Will asked. He had never been in a car that was used for street racing. "Tight fit all right. Shit, I thought you were referring to your apartment." The car was so damn small he was surprised that the three of them had fit in it.

"I was." Ryan grinned. "This is my car right now, but once I've closed my case, it will go back to the police garage, get an overhaul and then used for another case."

"This is a police car?" Gavin said from the back seat.

"Not in the normal sense of the word. It's been jacked up to race if needed and a few extra toys have been added."

"Extras? Like what?" Gavin asked sarcastically. "More cup-holders?"

Ryan chuckled. "That would be a waste of space. It has hidden microphones and cameras."

Will studied Ryan as he manoeuvred the car through the busy streets. "That's a little excessive for, Traffic?"

"I'm not Traffic."

"I gathered as much."

"Gang unit." Ryan continued to focus on the road. "Meghan doesn't know, and I don't want her to know."

Gavin's whistle could be heard from the back seat. "I think I'd take Bin Laden and his lot, at least they're predictable. You know right off where you stand."

Will noticed Ryan's tight smile, before he turned to face him. The boyish features were gone and the serious expression had transformed his face into that of a man who had forced himself to experience the illegal and dangerous side of society. Will recognised the look. He'd seen it many times, on the faces of his teammates he'd served with, and in his own mirror.

Will nodded. "If she finds out it won't be from us."

Ryan nodded.

"Where is she?" Will asked, changing the subject.

"Over at Jess's house right now. I called her cell before I picked you up. Thought you might ask."

"How is she?"

"There's something wrong with her." Ryan shook his head. "She says she's fine, but I know her…she's not herself."

"Did you get her the Gravol?" Will asked

"She won't take it. She's scared to sleep I think. Cause of that video."

"This Rob is a sick fuck," Gavin mumbled. "Well, now we know why she left in a hurry. Pretty solid reason." Gavin bumped the back of Will's seat.

"Mmm." It was a very solid reason, but if she had just trusted him enough to come to him, this might not have been happening.

"Damn right it's solid. She loves Jess and Jack. She's trying to protect them," Ryan said.

Great! Will tried to relax his tight muscles as the Toronto landscape flew past. This mess had been building for a while and he had done nothing, he had only been concerned about scaring Meghan away if he dug too deep into her past. Once again he regretted not following his instinct. Now, because of his being cautious and her skittishness, Meghan, and Jessica and her son Jack could get hurt or worse. What a fucking mess.

Will's cell rang. Checking the number, he answered it. "Hugh."

"Got that meeting set up for you."

"When?" He pulled a pen and a mini-field log from his jacket then scribbled down the time and address. He said goodbye and ended the call.

"When?" Gavin asked leaning over his shoulder.

"13:00."

"What's at 13:00?" Ryan asked, pulling to a stop in front of a seven-storey reddish-brown brick building.

"This is her apartment?" Will asked, staring up at the building.

"Yes. What's at 13:00?"

"I'm meeting with Emily Alexsandrov," he announced, opening the door.

Ryan jumped out of his side and followed him to the back of the car.

"Do you have a death wish I should know about? "

Will ignored the question and stared at Ryan as he grabbed the back of his neck. "Do you have any idea who those people are?"

"I know enough."

"I doubt it." Ryan pulled a white piece of paper from his back pocket and unfolded it. "Here."

Will took the paper and scanned the list of names. "These are the women he stole from?"

Ryan nodded. "Look at the sixth one down. Notice the last name?"

"Mila Alexsandrov." Will nodded.

"Bet you didn't know that?" Ryan crossed his arms. "Mila is Emily's cousin, apparently they grew up together."

Gavin stepped next to Will and whistled. "She reported him, then."

"Yah! But when we tried to get her to testify she backed out." Ryan locked eyes with Will. "Makes you wonder if her family knows about this."

"If that was our sister," Gavin began. "If that was Sarah, I would hunt that prick down."

Will nodded in complete agreement. "Her family might not know she reported him to the police, but you can bet that they know what happened to her."

"Now," Will pointed to the boot. "Open it, I want my bag."

"Why?" Ryan scowled.

"Because I'm staying here."

They were standing in the centre of Meghan's living room minutes later. The place was in a complete disarray, and gave the appearance that someone was in the process of moving into it. There were boxes piled up in one corner and at least five extra large garbage bags in another. The sparse furniture was set up as a makeshift seating area.

"Shit." Gavin walked around. "That prick did a real number here. How'd she take it?" He looked to Will, but it was Ryan who answered.

"She was pissed off at first, then just accepted it." Ryan crossed his arms. "That bothered me."

"Why?" Will turned waiting to hear Ryan's answer.

"Because it felt like she was giving up. Meghan has never given up on anything. She's too damn stubborn."

Didn't he know it. But he loved that about her and there was no way in hell he would allow her to give up.

The damage continued into every room, except for Meghan's bedroom. The room was completely empty except for one garbage bag. "What's that?" Will pointed.

"That's what's left of her clothes."

His anger had been simmering since he'd walked into her apartment but he was furious now. He completely understood why she was so damn scared to fall in love with him. That fuck had literally taken everything from her and Will wasn't referring to her belongings. Her confidence, her self-worth, her faith in others, and her heart. Everything Meghan was had been stomped on. He squeezed his hands into fists, wishing it was Rob's neck, and surveyed the room. This would stop now. Meghan couldn't live like this anymore.

Gavin stood next him, his dark scowl mirroring his own. "I call dibs."

"On what?"

"On holding that prick down while Will beats the shit out of him."

Ryan smirked. "No deal. She's my sister."

Chapter Forty-Eight

Casually leaning against a large maple, Rob watched Meghan wave to Jack as he ran to the school doors.

From the moment Ivan had suggested taking pictures of Jack in the hopes that it would scare Meghan into flying home, Rob had known Ivan was on to something. It was his suggestion to break into Jessica's house and video them as they slept. It was wrong and he knew it, yet in a disturbed way he had taken delight in the act. But none of that mattered, he had to get that list. His dad couldn't afford to lose any more fingers. He had, however, got a great sense of satisfaction when Meghan had arrived home the next day.

Now he would be able to get her alone. That was the nice thing about a big city, nobody gave a rat's ass who you were and everyone kept to themselves.

A light laugh trailed across the field. Meghan was talking into her cell as she entered Jessica's house. He hated the flannel pants she wore. They made her look fat and sloppy, but he knew there was a sexy ass hidden underneath. His body ached, he grew hard just thinking about tearing those pants off her, seeing her shocked expression, seeing her naked body. He shifted uncomfortably. It was strange this love-hate feeling that she stirred in him. He'd had the same reaction as he'd watched her around that shithole of a village. The need to devour her—mind and body. It was as if there were two halves battling inside him. One was a dark craving—he needed to have her solely for himself, wanted to feel her shock and fear. The other wanted to feel her delicate kiss and touch, needed her body wrapped around his.

At the time he hadn't understood why. She had testified against him in court, had helped her cop brother put him in jail, and yet the urge was there, burning in him.

The answer hit him on his way back home. She was back to being the hellion she'd been when they'd first met. She'd had an allure then, her crazy sense of humour, her fiery temper, her passion. He needed to break her…again.

He rubbed the sudden bulge in his jeans. *Patience,* he thought to himself. He would see her soon enough.

Meghan huddled under her jacket as she watched Jack make his way across the school yard. He turned to wave once again and she waved back, then blew him a kiss. She was going to miss him, he'd been her little shadow from the second Ryan had dropped her off three days ago. Of course, she'd encouraged it after Rob's video. Jesus, she had a hard time saying goodnight to them and she was staying in the same house.

She casually looked around the school yard and park. It was a beautiful fall day and though there had been a light dusting of snow on the ground when she had woken, the sun had melted it away, exposing the wide assortment of colourful leaves. She scanned the area. That feeling of someone watching her was back again. And just like the other times she didn't see anything weird or out of the ordinary. She was probably overreacting. Yet she couldn't shake the feeling.

Rob. It had to be him, who or what else could it be? She still couldn't believe that Rob would do this. Sending her emails and trashing her apartment was one thing, because she was the only one affected. Threatening Jess and Jack was something else entirely. It had pushed Meghan to her limits. But Rob knew how much she cared for them, that she would do anything for them. He knew because she had told him. Another mistake she had made. Damn her big mouth.

Meghan was jarred out of her thoughts when her cell phone rang. Pulling it from her pocket, she checked the number and frowned, not recognising it, and hesitated before answering.

"Hello."

Silence.

"Hello!" she said louder.

"Meg."

"Hey, Jody." The words rushed out, and she realised that she had been expecting Rob to be on the other end.

"You okay?" Background noise was drowning him out.

Ignoring his question, she asked, "Where are you?"

"What?" Jody yelled.

"Where are you?" she shouted into her cell.

"New York. Just on my way to a breakfast meeting."

"Ah! Is that the excuse you use the next morning now?" Meghan teased.

Jody laughed. "No, but that might come in handy." He laughed. "Okay, listen up, smart ass. I've been talking with Jess and we want to take you out tomorrow night to celebrate your return. Have a few drinks, maybe some food—assuming it won't get in the way of the drinking. What do you say?"

"I don't know…" The final bell went off.

"What was that? Where are you?"

"I just walked Jack to school."

There was a pause on the other end. "How can you walk Jack to school? Jess' house backs onto the school yard."

She watched as the last of the kids ran into the school. "I walked him to the path."

"That's five feet from their back door. Jesus, Meg, they'll be okay. Ryan hooked them up with a great security system."

She turned and walked into Jess' mud room, which was more like ten feet from the path, but still. "I know, I know. I just can't help it. Especially with Jack. He's just so little."

"Boy! Jess is right. You need to get out."

She had no desire to go out to a loud dance club. She had lost her taste for it after the last time. "I don't know." She kicked off her boots and walked into the kitchen.

"Look you don't have to worry about Jack because Jess is getting her parents to babysit and I'm sure if you beg, Ryan will make sure an extra cop car will join the one that's there now. Jack will be fine and Jess will be with us. So everybody's safe. No need to worry."

She poured herself another cup of coffee. "I just don't feel up to it."

"How the hell do you know how you'll be feeling on Friday? That's twenty-four hours away. And 'no' is not an option, I'll be there to pick you two up at eight."

"Fine. But no dance clubs."

Jody laughed. "Chicken shit!"

"Absolutely."

He laughed again, then added, "Then don't wear something that would cause a fight."

She groaned in her head. Man, Will would've loved to hear that. She placed a hand on her stomach. The nausea had finally calmed since she'd first arrived, but it still liked to remind her that it was still there, especially when she thought of Will, which seemed to be all the time. "That won't be a problem, I've learnt my lesson."

"Sure you have. See you tomorrow. Don't forget— eight o'clock."

"I won't. Hey!"

"Yah?"

"Was he cute?"

"You bet. Wanna hear all the nasty little details?"

"No thanks, perv. Later."

Meghan laughed. How did he do it? Whenever she felt down, that man was able to bring her back up again. She didn't care how he did it, she was just grateful that he did. A smile lingered on her face—a Friday night out. Maybe it was just what she needed, it might help her forget about the rollercoaster ride she was calling her life at that moment and she always had a good time with her friends—they would help her forget her problems...for a while at least.

* * * *

"That went easier that I thought it would," Ryan mumbled.

"Well?" Will pressed.

"Well," Ryan sighed. "It looks like Jody can talk her into anything."

"Good." Will nodded and threw the last bag of trash from Meghan's apartment into the giant garbage bin.

"No, that's not good," Ryan croaked. "You have met Jody right?"

Will brushed off his hands. "Oh, I've met him."

"So I guess this makes Meghan bait?" Ryan leaned against his car.

Will studied the kid. His body tight and his hand curled into fists.

"Yes." Will kept his tone even, he didn't want to upset Ryan, but he wasn't going to lie to him either. "She became bait by coming back alone, and seeing how she has done that, it's our job to make sure she is safe and that this 'little problem' of hers comes to an end. I don't like this any more than you do, but it's the only way to finish this."

"I don't like it," Ryan said as he stood, reaching for the car door. "But you guys are the professionals, or so Duncan tells me. He also said I should trust you to keep Meg safe. I hope he's not wrong."

Will answered both questions with extreme clarity, he didn't want any misunderstandings. "Duncan is right, and I will keep her safe."

Chapter Forty-Nine

Will eyed the security guard, making note of his height and build as the man patted him down. Then another guard stepped forward and proceeded to scan him with a metal detector. He had been expecting to go through some sort of security at the top of the Alexsandrov Group building, although he hadn't been expecting it to be this thorough. He was impressed and now he was also curious.

He was escorted into a large office promptly at 13:00. The room and its furnishings were all white, except for the occasional splash of red. The wall of windows opened onto a rooftop terrace, offering a spectacular view of Lake Ontario. He took the seat he was offered and scanned the office while he waited.

The room was nice, too cold for his liking, but orderly. The glass desk held a phone, a small writing pad and pen. It would seem Ms Alexsandrov was a private person as well, and liked to work elsewhere rather than in front of others. He studied the opposite wall and frowned. There was something odd about it. The white panels covering the wall, the spacing looked wrong. All of a sudden, a section to the wall swung inwards and out stepped Emily Alexsandrov with two very large assistants.

She walked directly towards him and held out her hand. "Mr MacKenzie, how nice it is to meet you."

He took her hand gently, afraid to squeeze too hard, she was so slim.

She gave him a sideways glance. "I have a feeling our conversation may take a while. Can I offer you a coffee or tea perhaps?" She indicated a seat and sat down across from him on an identical chair.

He inclined his head. "Please. Coffee, one cream."

She addressed one assistant with a smile. "Stefan, if you would be so kind." After the 'assistant' had left, she politely introduced the other. "William..." She stopped. "May I call you William?"

"Please." He smirked.

"William, this is my friend Ivan. He also has an interest in Robert."

Will studied the man, instantly recognising another soldier. He was at least six foot tall with wide shoulders and beefy arms, and there was a quiet confidence that hung in the air around him. There was no question that this man had had combat training. The question was, who had trained him? Will nodded and received a nod back.

"Please, Ivan, come and sit." She patted the seat next to her.

Ivan did as she had asked and turned protectively towards her. There was obviously something more between Emily and her assistant. "Royal Marines?" Ivan asked.

Keeping his expression passive, Will relaxed against the back of the leather chair and crossed his arms. He wasn't surprised that Emily and her 'assistant' knew that he had been in the Marines. Now if they knew he was ex-SBS, then he would be surprised.

"I hope you don't mind," Emily begun. "I'm not in the habit of accepting meetings with random strangers. But when your assistant Hugh mentioned that you wanted to speak to me about Robert Cummings and his interest in Meghan Kennedy, I had Ivan do a background check on you."

"I figured you would." Will never took his eyes off Emily, as her young secretary carried in a tray and placed it on the glass coffee table in front of him. He nodded his thanks and waited until Stefan had escorted the young woman out. "I of course" — he took a sip of the hot brew — "did the same."

"Of course." Emily inclined her head. "Now what can I do for you?"

"Maybe you can straighten out a few things for me. You seem to be going to quite a bit of trouble where Rob is concerned. Is this the normal practice of a successful businesswoman or are you allowing personal feelings to cloud your judgement?"

Emily simply blinked.

"I'll take that as a yes." He placed his cup on the table. "I find it difficult to believe that Rob was able to come up with this elaborate plan to draw Meghan home. Unless of course" — he paused, shifting his glare to Ivan — "he had help and there was an alternative agenda in mind." Emily gave him a blank stare, but he pushed forward, "But I can nae help feeling like this is personal. He was, after all, stealing from a smart, independent and successful businesswoman. A woman similar to you and your cousin…" He pulled the information Ryan had given him from his pocket and read the name, "Mila. I understand you two are very close." When she still didn't react he shrugged.

"Or I could be wrong and this is a simple case of jealousy. Women scorned do have nasty tempers."

"I have no interest in Rob sexually and I never will," she snapped out.

Ivan put his hand on her thigh. She took a breath as the muscle in her cheek twitched.

"Watch what you say to her." Ivan levelled his stare.

Now it was Emily's turn to soothe. She placed her hand on Ivan's tattooed arm.

"First, let me begin by saying that Ivan and myself do not condone the manner in which Rob used to lure Meghan home. Second, I am personally aware of the methods Rob has used to collect the money he owes me, as is Ivan. In fact, that is how we met. As I said, we both share a personal interest in Rob and it has nothing to do with money."

"Revenge." Will nodded his understanding, then, leaning forward onto his knees, made himself perfectly clear. "My personal interest is Meghan. I don' nae give a damn about the money he owes you or your shared interests. She is the only innocent party in all of this and I want it stopped. Which is why I'm here. I have a proposition that will satisfy everyone involved, including the police."

* * * *

An hour later Will walked out of the Alexsandrov Group building and joined Gavin and Ryan who'd waited at the car. He filled them in on what had transpired in the meeting.

"Are you out of your fucking mind?" Ryan slammed the driver side door.

"You did what?" Gavin's laugh flooded the interior of the car. "That's brilliant." Gavin patted his shoulder.

"No!" Ryan started the engine. "I can't let you do that, I'm a cop for Christ's sake!"

"The deal's done, you don't have a choice."

"You're asking me to look the other way, I can't do that. Not with him."

"You can't look the other way with Rob, yet you allow me to use Meghan as bait?" Will snapped out.

Ryan curled his hands around the stirring wheel, it was clear he didn't like hearing the truth.

"This has dragged on too bloody long. Christ, I had a chance to end this in Edinburgh but I backed off and I shouldn't have," Will revealed. "This ends tomorrow night and when Ivan's done with him, he will be begging for you to arrest him."

* * * *

"Good evening, Robert."

Shit. Rob rolled onto his side, facing away from the woman, who had decided to share his bed for the night.

Emily. How in the hell did she always know where he was? "How did you get this number?"

"I always keep tabs on my investments. And you are an investment, are you not?"

He wanted to say no, but the reality of it was that, he was an investment, so he bit his tongue.

"No response? Mmm! You must not be having a good time with the escort I picked out for you. Jennifer is her name, I believe. Let me know if the night continues in this way, I will make certain she doesn't receive a tip."

Rob rolled onto his back and stared at the blonde. She was lying on her side, sheets draped over her thin hips, very large, fake breasts waiting for his attention. He covered up the receiver and in a harsh whisper ordered, "Get the fuck out!"

Jennifer giggled. "She said you would say that. But I'm being paid to stay, so...no."

"I've paid her for her services for the night and into tomorrow. It is her job to keep you busy and out of trouble tonight and then deliver you to me, tomorrow afternoon at four."

He pinched the bridge of his nose. He was so fucking tired of this bitch running his life. The sooner this was over, the better. "Why?" he bit out.

"Oh my!" she cooed into his ear. "Have we forgot our manners?"

"Just tell me, why do you want to see me at four tomorrow?"

"After we have an early dinner with your father, Ivan is going to take you to a local pub called O'Malley's. You have heard of O'Malley's, have you not?"

"Yeah, I know it." It was blocks from Meghan's apartment.

"I have learnt that Ms Kennedy will be there tomorrow night with some of her friends. While you visit with Meghan, Stefan and will I keep your father company. A sort of guarantee, if you like, to make sure you retrieve that bank account number, and therefore settle your debt with me."

"How do you know all of this?"

"I told you, Robert, I take care of my investments. Now enjoy Jennifer, I've been told she is quite extraordinary in bed."

Chapter Fifty

"Well, just like old times, eh?" Jody asked.

"What old times? We've never been here before." Meghan looked around the pub—if you could call it that. O'Malley's Pub was a few short blocks from her apartment. The owner might be named O'Malley, but this place was definitely not a pub. Her perception of pubs had certainly changed after spending time at The Black Ale, and she was almost certain Hamish would have a fit if he ever stepped into this bad imitation.

"Who cares if we came here or not? Wave at the cuties by the bar!" Jessica sang, holding out two sweet-looking drinks. "They bought these."

Meghan turned back to the bar and smiled at the very cute, very young men who were nodding their approval.

"Cute, huh?"

"I guess." Meghan placed her hand on her stomach. "I can't drink that."

"What?" Jess huffed, then saw where her hand was. "Still upset, hey?"

"Yah. I'll just have a ginger ale."

They navigated the packed room to where Jody was waiting for them at a tall table with matching chairs. They were wedged into the oddest spot, between the outside patio door and the bathrooms. Meghan didn't really mind, they were away from the crowd of people by the bar.

"I don't suppose mine is on the way?" Jody called over the loud music.

"Nope! You're on your own, sweet cheeks."

"See the attitude that I've had to put up with while you were away." Jody huffed. Then looking at her hand on her middle. "What's the matter? Stomach?"

Meghan gave him a quick nod. "Can you get me a ginger ale?"

Jody nodded and turned to leave when Jess called out, "Great choice on the table, by the way. Close to the washrooms, how nice!" Jess gave her a teasing wink. Meghan smiled back knowing Jody would retaliate.

"Best I could do, sweet cheeks!" Jody said, laughing, then went to the bar.

"Were you serious?" Jess asked, placing her drinks on the table.

"About what?"

"The cuties?"

"You mean the kids who bought those drinks, yes." Meghan pointed to the matching drinks sitting in front of her. "Are you seriously going to drink both of those?"

Jess downed a mouthful, then answered, "Yup!" Her shoulders moved to the music.

"You're lovin' this? Aren't you?"

Jess' dark brown pony tail swung back and forth, her amber eyes twinkling. "Yeah! I haven't been out since before you left."

Meghan shot Jody an accusing look as he joined them. "Don't," he warned. "I tried to drag her out, but she wouldn't go." Jody placed a drink in front of her.

Meghan sat up straight, her shoulders becoming stiff. "That's not ginger ale."

"Nope, this is your ginger ale, that" — Jody pointed to the crantini — "is from an admirer." Jody winked at her.

Meghan just sat there staring at the red drink. She hated crantinis, they reminded her of all the times Rob would order her one when they went out. She always hated when he did that...

Whoa, shit! She took a deep breath and slowly let it out, forcing her body to relax. Now wasn't the time to panic, she wasn't alone, Jess and Jody were with her and they were in a public place.

Meghan gazed around the pub — searching but not seeing. He was here, watching her. She could feel it in her bones. Her heart pounded and nervous butterflies mixed with her nauseous stomach. Now was not the time to panic, she needed to calm down and she needed to call Ryan.

"Meghan?" Jody touched her arm gaining her attention.

Meghan forced a smile, as she pulled her cell phone from her purse.

"You okay?"

She forced a grin. "I think I'll call Ryan and see if he wants to join us." The faceplate lit up as she dialled Ryan.

It rang three times before Ryan answered, "Hey, Megs. What's going on?"

She could just barely hear him. Lord, it was loud in there. She covered her other ear hoping to block the rising noise level. Still no good.

"Hang on, Rye." She held the phone against her chest. "I'm going to take this outside." She pointed towards the patio door.

Once outside, she shivered and crossed one arm under her breasts, trying to trap her body heat. Why had she decided to wear a short-sleeved top? "Sorry, Rye."

"Where are you?"

"Jody and Jess have taken me out to O'Malley's p-pub." She began to shiver, although she didn't know if it was from the cold or the fact that she was actually scared.

"O'Malley's, really? Having a good time?" he asked. Meghan heard the doubt in his question.

"Not r-really." She could hear a song about dark places coming from Ryan's phone. The very same song that was playing behind her, inside the pub. That was weird. "Where are you?"

"On my way home." Then he asked, "Is that why you called me? To tell me you're not having fun?"

"No. I called to tell you Rob's here."

Silence.

"Rye? Did you hear me? He's here, he sent me a drink." She huffed. "L-like I would drink that. It's probably laced with arsenic. God, what a Dickhead!"

His tone was very calm when he asked, "You're sure he's in there?"

"Yes, I'm s-sure."

"Where are you this very second?"

"I just t-told you," she began, getting flustered. "I'm at O'Malley's."

"No," he said sharply. "Where are you standing inside the pub, Meg?"

"I'm n-not inside. I'm on the patio, next to the d-door that leads inside to the bar."

"Outside!" he repeated for some reason. Then he snapped out an order, "Stay put. Okay! I'm coming. Don't leave." He hung up before she could agree.

After sliding her cell into her back pocket, she rested her head on the wall behind her. Ryan was coming, thank God. Maybe this mess could get cleaned up tonight. Ryan would come, arrest Rob, and she could get on with her life. Simple. She shivered again then turned, reached for the door but it opened on its own and Rob stepped out.

Maybe not so simple after all, Meghan thought, staring into Rob's grey eyes. He followed her retreating steps and backed her against the wall. His face was inches from her own, looming over her like some dark animal. His lips curled into a savage smile. Her pulse started to race and she slowly swallowed a lump of fear.

"Didn't like the drink?"

"I never have." Meghan fought to keep her words from stuttering. She couldn't allow her fear to show, he'd already seen too much. "Excuse me." She tried to walk around him but he blocked her path.

"No!" He grabbed her by the waist. "You're not going back to your friends. We are going to leave here together —"

"I'm not going anywhere with you," Meghan snapped out. She pushed away from him and tried for the door again. Rob's hand closed tightly around her arm, yanking her back to the wall, his body pinning her still.

His mouth brushed her ear. "Don't make a scene, let's take care of a little business and then I'm gone." He forced a thigh between her legs. "Or maybe not?"

The desire she saw on his face made her stomach turn. Where were Jody and Jess?

"I can see you've turned back into a hellion you once were. I have to admit, I like you better this way. Breaking you was a big mistake."

She tried to turn her head away as he stroked her cheek but the wall stopped her.

He chuckled. "Much better."

"What business, Rob?" She glared up at him.

He grinned at her. "Business then pleasure?"

"No pleasure. What do you want?" she asked again, desperate to conceal her shivering. She could never allow him to have any control over her, never again.

"Your cell. I want it." He moved his knee back and forth between her legs, his breath cooled in the night air before it touched her cheek.

"Why?"

"I stored an account number in it when we were together. I need that number."

"What are you talking about?"

"Give me the cell, Meg." He bit out the order as he glared at her. "I won't think twice about taking it."

"No."

His nostrils flared as he hissed low, then looking her over, he sneered and ran his hand over her hip to her behind, squeezing. "Ah! Here it is. Snuggled up against my favourite part of you." He pulled the phone free and cupped her behind, harder this time. She turned when she thought she heard a low growl come from the dark shadow of the patio.

"I've been waiting a long time for this. I wasn't happy you left and took it with you and it pissed me off even more that I had to fly to that shithole and still didn't get it. But that's done, you came home." He waved the phone in front of her face. "With the account number I stored in your phone, I can settle a few debts."

"What the hell are you talking about? What account?"

"I loaded my private bank account number on your cell when we were together, thinking it would be safer with you. After all, your brother is a cop, who in their right mind would mess with you."

"You did?"

"Yes, I did."

"Wait, how is that even possible? There is no way I would have missed a bank account number stored in my own phone."

"Well, you must have." Chuckling, he searched her phone until he found what he needed. "Because here it is, hidden in plain sight." He held the phone up for her to see.

"Oh God," she breathed out, shocked that she could have missed that. "My contact list. You hid it in my contacts."

He chuckled. "Pretty clever if I do say so myself. Enter in a last name and just an initial for the first name, and use the account number as the phone number. I had to doctor it of course. I added a company name that you would recognise so it looked legit. I didn't want you deleting it after all my hard work." He wiggled his eyebrows then slid her phone into his coat pocket.

"It has the money you stole from all those women?" She wasn't sure why she asked the question when she already knew the answer. Maybe she needed to hear the truth.

"Yes it does."

"I can't believe you stole from all those women, from me." She shook her head feeling like an even bigger fool. "How many deposits did you make into that account?"

"More than what I was charged with," he revealed.

"Uck! You make me sick."

He moved his hands to her waist, holding her still when she tried to move. "Why? I never stole from you. I tried," He revealed. "But I couldn't seem to do it. Selena was the one who took your money. Not me."

"Who's Selena?"

"The blonde you caught me with. That was Selena. I would call her when I needed an excuse to break it off with one of my ladies, and what better way than finding your lover in bed with another? Some would yell and scream and a few even cried." He gave her a mock frown. "So sweet. But" — he sighed — "I was taking a long time finishing with you and Selena became jealous. You see, all the other women I was with were much older than you, work-oriented, no husband, no kids, just large bank accounts. You were the first woman who was a real threat to Selena, so she took it upon herself to set up the little scene you walked in on."

Meghan stared, her eyes becoming unfocused as she listened. She had been set up right from the very beginning. He had never been in love with her, never wanted anything but her money. "I was a job?" she whispered. A hollow, worthless feeling stirred in her chest.

She saw it then, pity. She hated that. She hated him.

"At first. You were so feisty —"

Meghan listened, her hands clenching into fists.

"I liked that about you, and thought it would be just another easy job, but then you fell in love with me. I never understood why, and then I began to feel guilty about taking your money. That's never happened to me before, you were the only one. Then you caught me with Selena, and a few days later your brother arrested me and Selena took off with your money."

She must be going crazy. Did she actually hear that? "You felt guilty?" she bit out. "What about the other women's lives you destroyed, what about them? Do you feel guilty about them?"

"No, I don't." He paused. "Though, had I known you would have been the one to have me arrested, I wouldn't have been so nice to you."

"Nice to me?" Meghan shouted pushing him back. "You treated me like trash."

"Yes, I did, and you took it too, didn't you," he taunted.

"I thought I was in love with you. You…you…douchebag!"

Rob laughed, stepping closer. He reached for her cheek and smirked when she jerked her head away. He quickly reached out and grabbed her by the waist and pulled her forwards. "You know, I've found that I've been missing you since you left. I thought it was because I needed your cell, but I realised as time went on that I missed you, and the way I could bend you any way I wanted. Watching you walk around that shithole of a village wasn't fun, until I saw you fucking that Scot in the library. You've turned back into a bad girl and I like bad girls."

"You can't bend me!" She struggled to get her arms free. "I'm not that person anymore."

"No, you're not," he whispered in her ear. "That's what's turning me on."

"You're twisted." She brought up her knee to his crotch but he backed away avoiding the blow. He let her go. She stepped to the side of the door and reached for the handle.

He laughed at her. "No, just horny for a feisty redhead. The sex was good, Meg, you have to admit that."

She stopped and let her hand drop to her side and turned to face him. "Honestly? No! It wasn't good. I have recently been gifted with good sex, and believe me, sex with you was not good, actually I'm not sure what it was, but it was definitely *not* good. Now get away from me!"

A dark scowl covered Rob's face as he stepped towards her. Before she could understand what was happening there was another deep growl and Will appeared, slamming his full body weight into Rob and knocking him against the wall.

Ryan was close on his heels and reached for her. "You okay?" he asked, pulling her away from the two men.

The only thing she could do was nod. She was so surprised to see Will...here...in front of her. Her body shivered with delight for once, instead of from the cold. She watched him yank Rob up by his coat and hammer his fist into the centre of his face. One, two. Rob fought hard trying to block the punches, then to free himself. In order to keep him still Will hammered him with another two jabs in quick succession, one to the stomach, another to the face.

It took little time to subdue Rob. He was now pinned against the wall, Will's big fists holding onto to his coat keeping him upright, as slow stream of blood dripped from his nose. The scene before her was very satisfying. But the reality of the situation slapped her in the ass and her stomach sank. What was Will doing there, fighting a battle she wanted him to know nothing about? Stepping next to him, she asked quietly, "What are you doing here?"

"I've come to help you with your 'little problem'."

Groaning inwardly, Meghan wished she hadn't said anything to Duncan.

"I was handling it."

"Oh you were, were you?" He was so calm that it unnerved her. "Was him touching you part of it? And look at your arm. His grip was tight enough to leave a bruise."

"What?" She looked down at her arm, a red welt was visible and getting darker by the second. "Ah, it's not as bad as it—"

"It's bad enough." His voice was deadly quiet. "And if it wasn't for your brother holding me back so he could get the evidence he needed, I would have come over and put this bastard's goddamn head through the wall. You"—he pulled Rob away from the wall by his coat only to slam him back against it—"shouldn't have touched her."

Oh God! Meghan froze, her chest becoming painfully tight. "You heard us talking?" Will had heard Rob saying all those things to her.

"Yes. And now that he has your cell, Rob needs to be set straight on a few things."

"W-what things?"

He slowly turned to face her. "Why do ye think I'm here, Meghan?"

"I don't...what do you mean?"

"What do I mean?" Will repeated coolly. "I don't give a shit about your cell phone or the bank account he has stored in it, that's Ryan's problem. What I do care about is you. And even though you told him to go away, I want Rob to understand what you are trying to tell him. Spell it out if you have to!"

With the blood draining away from her face, Meghan stepped towards Rob. "For months you have made my life miserable. Threatening me, threatening Jess and little Jack, spying on me. You stole from me and God only knows how many other women just so you could fix your problems. I hate you. I hate everything about you. Now go away and stay away."

Turning to Will, she asked, "Is that what you wanted, are you happy?"

"No, not yet. He needs to hear one more thing from you, for him to understand you don' nae belong to him."

"W-what?" Her hands started to shake and her heart beat nervously. Oh no, he couldn't mean that? Her stomach heaved right at that moment. Will caught her grimace, saw her hand grip her middle. She wasn't ready for that. It was too soon to say it. Wasn't it?

"You know what," he pushed. "Say it, Meghan."

Her lips twitched as tears caught in her lashes. She couldn't do it, not here, in this sorry excuse for a pub.

Her chest constricted and breathing was becoming a difficult chore. Turning, she saw Jody and Jess standing next to Ryan. She silently pleaded with them for help but was denied. Jess did give her an encouraging nod and Gavin gave her a wink... Wait a second!

Gavin was here! Sweet Jesus, everybody was here...watching. She couldn't do it, she was too scared. Her stomach turned. Admitting that she loved Will was admitting she had a weakness. Wasn't it? Her stomach flipped again, painfully this time and she fought the urge to moan out loud. She didn't want to need someone. She bent over and tried not to throw up.

"Meghan." Will drew her attention. "It will stop. Just say the words, love."

"That's not fair. There are too many..."

"Say it," he pushed. "It's the truth, isn't it? I've known for a while and thought I could wait until you were ready. But circumstances have changed—you need to say it now."

Tears spilled, sliding down her cheeks. Then she saw the look on his face. It was full of concern and frustration and...love. Her heart skipped a beat. And for the first time since meeting Will, she stopped fighting. "I love you."

An uncertain frown transformed his hard face. "Is it that bad, loving me?"

"No. But, it scares me...this feeling." She placed her hand over her heart. "I told you before I have no control over it."

"I don't want you to have control over it." The smile, so tender, dropped from his face when he turned his attention back to Rob. "Is that clear enough for you? Keep away from Meghan. She's mine, not yours. She will marry me and become the mother of my children. And when you finally get out of prison, I'll know. If you come lookin' for her, I'll know. Now"—he gave Rob a shake—"you better pay close attention." Will's voice dropped low whisper and Meghan had to lean closer to hear him. "If I find out that you haven't listened to my warning"—his voice had taken on a hard deadly tone—"I'll come back here and finish what Ivan starts. Got that?"

Rob looked confused as Will dropped his hands, setting him free. He paused for the briefest of seconds, then bolted around the corner and down the alley.

Ryan went after him but Will stopped him. "Don't worry, he'll be yours tomorrow." He stepped into the alley and pointed to the black sedan. Meghan followed and watched as Rob dove into the waiting car and a huge beast of a man returned Will's wave.

"Who the hell is that?" Ryan demanded.

"That is an ex-US Ranger. His older sister was one of Rob's victims. He wants a little payback."

"Whose car was that?"

"Emily Alexsandrov's. You were right, Emily had found out that Rob had stolen from Mila and had begun making his life hell back when he was in prison. She has agreed to return the money back to the proper owners in exchange for a little alone time with Rob."

"And you're so certain they will bring him in?"

"Rangers do not back out of their word. Of course he could possibly be limping—or worse—but he will be there."

Ryan ran a hand through his dark hair. "Fuck, I hope so."

Chapter Fifty-One

Puzzled, Meghan looked back and forth between Will and Ryan. She turned to face Jess and Jody and Gavin. Something was going on here. She stepped back onto the patio and leaned against the wall. She watched as Jess stepped forward with a strange blush on her face. Meghan frowned as the two cuties from the bar joined Ryan and began talking in low whispers. Her jaw dropped and she gasped.

"Wait just a goddamn minute." She pointed to Jess. "I've seen that look, that's guilt." Pushing away from the wall, she pushed between the two cuties and poked Ryan in the chest. "And these two are cops, aren't they?"

Ryan smirked. "Yup."

"You used me as bait!"

"Now don't get pissy."

"You did!" Her voice was unusually high. "I can't believe you did that. And you got Jess and Jody to help!" She looked back to Jess, who was looking everywhere but at her. Throwing her arms into the air, Meghan shouted, appalled, "You've got to be kidding me. And I suppose you knew as well?" She shifted her glare to Jody. "After all, it was your suggestion to come here."

"Sure did! Thought it was a great plan right from the beginning." Jody nodded, then happily informed her, "It should have happened sooner."

"Plan! Whose plan was it?" She turned back to Ryan.

"Unfortunately, I can't take the credit."

Meghan watched as Ryan shifted his eyes over her shoulder. Meghan sighed and turned to face Will.

"You did this? You planned all of this?" she snapped out.

"It needed to be dealt with."

"That's it?" she asked. "You made a fool of... And I said it... And now you've..." Her heart dropped into her stomach. "Won," she whispered to herself.

He had won the bet. He had planned this whole thing like it was some kind of military operation. He had solved her 'little problem' and had got her to confess her true feelings for him, all in less than ten minutes.

He had got exactly what he had wanted from the beginning—her failure—and she had handed it over without even thinking about it. She had lost their bet, and a bet was a bet, if she backed out, he would use the contract to force her. She had no idea if he could even use the contract it was so ancient, but if there was a remote chance it was legal, then she knew he wouldn't hesitate to use it. After all, he had said 'she will be my wife' as if it were a guarantee. She clenched her fists. She wanted to scream, he had played her so easily and she had fallen right into it. Just like with Rob.

She turned from Will, Ryan and her traitorous friends and marched into the pub. She never broke stride as she grabbed her coat and purse and pushed her way through the thick crowd and out of the front doors.

Will followed her through the bar and out onto the street. He stood behind her as she fought with her coat and he followed her down the street as she mumbled about bets, and contracts and stupid spells. Then he heard her sniff and grab at her middle. That was enough. He stepped beside her. Her eyes were puffy, her nose red and her complexion was pale with a green tinge. She was beautiful.

"Oh God!" She flapped her arms dramatically and sniffed. "You've won, okay. You've won." She swiped at her damp cheeks. "And I'm in no mood to hear you gloat, so just leave me alone."

"I'm not going to gloat and I can't leave you alone."

She exhaled a long breath. "Why? Because of a stupid spell?"

He reached for her hand. "No! I *want* to be with you."

"What?"

He didn't repeat himself as he pulled her down the street.

She blinked, startled. "Where are we going?"

"To your apartment."

She frowned. "No, there's no…" She stopped herself before she told him that she had no furniture. That Rob had destroyed everything she'd owned.

He led her into the elevator and stood beside her, quietly staring at the metal doors. Her heart jumped and her pulse sped up when the elevator stopped and the doors opened. They were on her floor. She didn't need to look at the numbers to confirm it. How did he know where she lived?

His hand surrounded hers and he led her down the hall to her apartment. He pulled a set of keys from his pocket and opened the door, pulling her inside behind him.

Meghan watched dumbfounded as Will hung her keys on the hook by the door.

"How did you know this was my apartment?"

"Ryan brought me here when I first came."

"Ryan brought you here—" She stopped and walked into the living room when she thought she saw...was that furniture? She was speechless. The room was filled with furniture. A couch, a chair, a new coffee table and a brand new flat-screen TV.

"Yes. When we first arrived."

"When you first arrived?" Meghan travelled around the room in shock.

"Yes." His tone was light. "He brought Gavin and me here first. I wanted to see what damage your 'little problem' had done."

"I know what he is." She placed her purse onto the new couch and turned to face him.

"Was," he corrected.

Meghan blinked, confused. "What?"

"Rob *was* your little problem."

"That's what I...wait! I don't care what Ryan has done here, he shouldn't have brought you here. He had no right." She gritted her teeth.

"Actually he had no choice. If he hadn't brought me here, I would have come on my own."

"Why?" She opened her arms wide. "So you could see first-hand what a mess my life is?"

Will moved quickly to stand in front of her. "Your life is no' a mess." His tone was quiet as he glared down at her. "And if it was, I would fix it for ye. That's how this love thing goes." He waved his finger between them. "I help ye, you help me. We don't hide things from each other and we don't lie tae one another."

'Love thing'. She blinked up at him—she hadn't been expecting to hear that. She was all set to condemn him for judging her and then he had to say 'love thing'...damn it! She turned away, his words echoing in her ears as she scanned the room. 'Your life is not a mess, and if it was, I would fix it.'

"Oh boy!" She exhaled a shaky breath. "You did this." She pointed to the new furniture.

He ignored her question. "Why didn't you tell me about Rob?"

"Because it's none of your business. That's why. Have I asked you about the women you've been with before me?"

"That's no' the point." His accent became thick with frustration. "And where you're concerned, it is my business." He ran a hand down his face. "Ye could have been in real danger, Meghan. He could have hurt ye, or yer friends, or family. We could have sorted this out long ago if you had trusted me."

"I didn't say that I didn't trust you."

"Then why did ye hide the problems you had while you were with him?" he challenged.

Meghan gaped, a chill running through her. She couldn't tell him the truth. What would he think of her then? "I didn't hide anything."

"You remember Edinburgh? When those men tried tae drag ye out of the club? You never answered my questions that night—"

"You know what"—she held up her hands cutting him off—"forget it. It's over and done, he's gone." She turned away from him reaching for her purse with the intent of heading to the front door. She didn't want to talk about it, Will would never understand.

"No." Will's arms encircled her waist, stopping her before she could leave. He wanted to pull her in his arms and hold her. Forget about all the torment she had put him through. But as strong as his need was to hold her, his need for protecting her was greater, and the sooner Meghan told him what had her so spooked, the sooner he could fix it. He turned her to face him and gently forced her back against the door.

"Talk to me," he pleaded. "What are you so scared to tell me? Your face" — he lightly touched her cheek — "is so pale."

She turned away, but it was too late, he saw the tears. "Meghan, don't do that."

She sniffed once and it was once too many. He tugged her away from the door and wrapped his arms around her. "Ah love, what could possibly be that bad?"

"What's so bad?" She pulled in a choppy breath, pushing away. "I'm weak, that's what."

"What?" He followed her as she backed into the room.

"I didn't tell you about Rob because I was afraid you would ask questions, and you'd find out that I'm not a strong person. That I'm..." she choked out, "that I'm weak."

"You are not weak." He bit out each word because he wanted her to know he didn't believe the lie she told herself.

"Yes I am." Tears streamed down her face. "I let him treat me that way because I thought..." She hiccupped.

"You thought you were in love with him." Will continued closing the distance between them.

Her lips trembled before she pressed them into a straight line.

"And you thought he would love you in return if you let him treat you badly?"

She nodded one final time before looking down at her hands.

"That doesn't mean you're weak." He lifted her face to his and wiped away her tears with his thumbs. "It means you want love in your life, and you're willing to sacrifice to get it. Does that sound like a weak person to you?"

"No." She sniffed again. "Not when you put it that way."

"And you're not like that now are you? You've learnt from your mistakes, haven't you?" He never gave her a chance to answer. "You have or I wouldn't be standing here telling you so. And even if you hadn't, it wouldn't have made a difference. I would've still come after you."

Meghan stared up at his handsome face, the brown in his eyes swirling darkly as he continued to speak. "Meghan, I fell in love with you. I'm not concerned with your past, it's just part of what makes you so appealing to me and without it you wouldn't be the person you are today. And I might not be here looking at your beautiful face, or touching your soft skin, or telling you how much I love you."

She felt more tears gather in her lashes, as she lightly scolded him, "You could have mentioned that earlier, you know."

"Yes, I could have. But I was a little busy trying to get you to love me." Pausing, he cupped her face in his hands. "Say it, Meghan." His mouth brushed hers.

"I love you," she whispered and that was all Will needed. He pulled her into his arms and his hot mouth came down on hers. She instantly parted her lips, allowing him entry, and she sighed dreamily when he sensually curled his tongue around hers.

She wrapped her arms around his neck, trying to deepen their kiss.

The reality of the situation hit. *Will loved her! The man must be completely out of his mind! Did he realise what he was getting himself into?*

Pulling back, Meghan frowned up at him. "Will, I can be..." She nervously played with the hair at the back of his neck. "I'm not perfect."

Laughing, he openly agreed, "No you're not. But I wouldn't have you any other way." He shook his head. "You have no idea what you do to me, do you? I'm amazed at how you make me feel. One minute you're so stubborn it drives me crazy and the next I want to throw you on my bed and act out all my dirty thoughts about you."

"I didn't know you had dirty thoughts about me." Her cheeks heated.

"Too many to count." He laughed, touching his forehead to hers. "Meghan, I love you. I'm surprised you didn't realise it sooner. I love your passion, your stubbornness, the way your hair curls when you get sweaty from your runs, and the way your eyes turn blue when I kiss you." He tilted her face up to his. "And to be clear, the bet and the contract, Christ, even the binding spell, none of them have anything to do with this love I have for you. I'm not going to deny that they helped me or you get to this point, but they are not making me feel this way. I just know in my soul that I love you. It just took all those things to make me see it."

Meghan sighed, shaking her head. "You never gave up."

"I told you I wouldn't." Will pulled back, a serious expression on his face. "It was never my intention to use the contract, you know, I'm not sure if it's even legal, but we did bet and we shook on it. A bet is a bet and I won. I plan to hold you to your end of the agreement. I want to marry you, I want you in my life, but I can wait until you're ready. Assuming it won't take too long."

Meghan stared up in surprise. "Really?"

He nodded. "Love has made me a patient man."

Meghan's heart almost seized up on her. What a fool she had been. This incredible man loved her, he wanted her. Her! For his wife, and he was willing to wait for her. Why was she waiting? Why wasn't she jumping at this unbelievable chance? Scared? Yeah, terrified. But it was a good terrified.

She put her hand to her stomach when she felt the nervous excitement swirl around. No rolling, no heaving, no urge to spew her dinner, just love and excitement. "Incredible!" It was over. The spell had faded away, just like Duncan had said it would. She shook her head, then stared up at him.

"Meghan?" She heard the familiar concern.

"No, it's not what you're thinking. I feel…" She smiled. "I feel good."

He understood her meaning. "Then it did its job." He studied her. "You love me, I love you. But I'm still waiting for an answer."

"I want to be with you too." She kissed his chin. "And I would love to marry you. Just not yet. Can't we live in sin for a bit first? Then you can make an honest woman out of me."

He gave her a hard look. "I'm not going anywhere, I won't cheat on you or lie to you or steal from you. We'll have arguments, we're not perfect, but you will never have to worry about me not loving you." He gave her waist a squeeze. "You don't have to be afraid. Understand?"

She pressed her lips together to keep them from trembling as she listened to his declaration. She nodded, tears forming.

"Still want to live in sin?"

"Please," she admitted with a nod. "Just for a little while?."

He sighed, giving in. "Then let's do this properly. Will you, Meghan Kennedy, live in sin with me and then marry me in say…six months?"

"Yes." She giggled as he sighed in relief. "But there's one other thing."

"Only one?" he teased as he began backing her down the hall towards her bedroom.

"That patience you mentioned, you better hang on to it a little longer. If you think I'm stubborn, wait until you meet my dad."

"I'm not worried." He turned her as they reached her bedroom door.

"What's going on?" She covered her mouth when she looked through the open door.

Her room. It was her room, not as she had seen it days before, empty with dust and broken pieces of glass and wood, but as she left it months before, beautiful and cosy. "How did you? When? How…"

"I asked Ryan and Jess to help and Jody did too, of course. Ryan and Jody thought you might want something different, but when Jess told me how long it took you to decorate it, I thought you might want it back that way you had it. Well, almost back anyways." He walked past her and stood next to the bed. "Was I right?"

Meghan flung herself into his chest, wrapping her arms around his neck. "Yes, you were right. Thank you," she mumbled into the side of his neck.

He held her tight, rubbing his hand down her back, kissed her head. "It was my pleasure." He pushed her back and pointed to the centre of her bed where a black box sat with a pink silk ribbon tied around it. "But don't think this was all for you. Making love to you on the ground and on a table and on a sink was mind-blowing, but I much prefer you on a bed. Gives us more room and therefore more options." He gave her an evil grin.

Meghan walked to the bed and reached for the box. As she lifted the lid Will wrapped his arms around her and pressed his large body into her back.

She stopped and concentrated on his heat, shifted her hips when she felt his hard arousal against her behind. "Options? You mean like which side to the bed to sleep on?" she teased, angling her head so that he could kiss her neck. He gently nipped at her ear as she pulled open the delicate tissue paper. She giggled as she lifted a matching red leather bra and thong from the box.

"Ah, love," he moaned, lowering her to the bed. "Who said anything about sleeping?"

Epilogue

"No?"

"No, I won't have you living with my daughter without being married."

"Dad!" Meghan huffed. "We are getting married. Just not right away."

"I won't allow it," Gordon Kennedy said firmly.

"It's not your decision," Will reminded Meghan's father.

"Gordon, you can'nae stop Meghan from living her life and you can'nae stop her from loving Will. Any more than you can stop Will from loving Meghan," Anne said, giving her husband a knowing look. She looked to Meghan then at him. "So, you read the contract. Both of you?"

Will nodded as Meghan answered, "Yes."

"Will's right, it's not your decision now." Anne stood up and went to her daughter, then cupped her face. "You're in love. I can see it on your face when you look at him."

Meghan nodded, the sweetest smile curling her lips.

Anne stood. "That won't last long" — she waved her hand at them — "soon you'll be rolling your eyes as much as I do."

Will laughed out loud. "Now I know where you get your smart mouth from."

"Anne!" Gordon snapped. "Did you forget why we left Scotland after Meghan was born? We wanted her to find love on her own, not have her forced into it."

Will slowly looked over his shoulder at Meghan who was sitting next to him. "You're Scottish?"

"Mmm," she said casually. "But I consider myself Canadian. I have lived my whole life here."

"But you were born in Scotland?" he pushed.

"Oh yeah, in Edinburgh. Right, Mum?" She was so bloody casual about it.

"That's right," Anne agreed cheerfully. "St Andrews' Hospital."

Stunned Will blinked. He had been born in that very same hospital. He shook his head. "Why didn't you tell me?"

She blinked innocently at him. "You never asked."

Will chuckled. "This is going to happen a lot, isn't it?"

Meghan gave him a mischievous pout. "Probably."

So that explained the strained relationship between Duncan and Gordon. Duncan wanted the contract fulfilled and Gordon didn't want Meghan forced into a marriage.

"Does Meghan's being Scottish change your mind?" Gordon asked hopefully.

"Gordon Kennedy!" Anne scolded.

Resting his elbows on his knees, Will felt a hand run up his thigh and curl around his arm. Meghan snuggled closer as Anne tried to reason with her husband, "I bet they wouldn't even notice if we left the room." Her breath was a warm whisper against his ear.

"Where would you like to go?" Will whispered back.

"Some place where we could elope and then lie on the beach together."

"Only lie on the beach?" he asked, threading his fingers with hers.

"No daughter of mine will be eloping," Gordon's loud order cut in. "I will be at my daughter's wedding, and I will give her to you. Is that clear?"

Will looked back to Gordon who was staring down at them. Their private conversation apparently hadn't been so private. Meghan turned her face into his shoulder and giggled uncontrollably. Will frowned at the sudden change, but decided not to question it.

"Yes, sir."

Gordon nodded.

"Finally!" Meghan sighed dramatically and stood. "That took forever. Can we eat now? I'm starving."

Will quickly stood and clasped her hand. "What the hell is going on?"

Meghan rolled her eyes. "Don't ask me."

Gordon laughed. "You didn't think I would just hand her over to you, did you boy?" he asked as he slapped Will on the shoulder. "It's my right as her father to make you work for her, and believe me, Meghan is a lot of work. You'll need the practice."

"Hey!" Meghan pointed at her father. "Watch it, you old fossil."

Gordon laughed harder. "Let me tell you about us Kennedys. We are very stubborn, nothing will ever be easy when we're involved. We'll throw you a surprise here and there, so you'd better learn to adapt. But most importantly," Gordon continued as they followed Meghan and her mother into the kitchen, "you will never get bored as long as we are around to keep things interesting."

Will smiled. "I'm looking forward to it."

About the Author

Nancy's addiction for a good trash novel began in her late-teens when her grandmother gave her a bag of Harlequin Romance books. She was hooked and spent the next few years lurking in the dark corners of used bookstores searching for her next fix. Until, one marriage and two kids later, her own ideas had her jumping up at 3 am (much to her husband's annoyance) and typing them into her laptop. Beside her husband and children, Nancy has three passions, rearranging furniture, buying bed linens and, of course, writing. Nancy lives in Eastern Ontario with her family and two over sized lap dogs.

Nancy Adams loves to hear from readers. You can find her contact information, website details and author profile page at http://www.total-e-bound.com.

Total-E-Bound Publishing

www.total-e-bound.com

Take a look at our exciting range of literagasmic™
erotic romance titles and discover pure quality
at Total-E-Bound.